"Gripping and on ta...          ...i-
mum impact. Steve Urszenyi's debut thriller never lets
up from the first page to the last. Read it today!"
— Jack Carr, *New York Times* bestselling
author of *The Terminal List*

"A stunning debut heralding an extraordinary new character and series. Alex Martel is a kick-ass special agent
in an action-packed, on-the-edge-of-your-seat espionage thriller with a jaw-dropping finish. Steve Urszenyi
writes with an insider's expertise about things that
keep our intelligence services awake at night!"
— Robert Dugoni, *New York Times*
bestselling author of the Charles
Jenkins espionage series

"A crackerjack debut novel! A compelling plot and
richly drawn characters pull readers in from the very
first paragraph and keep the pages flying by. Looking
forward to more of Alexandra Martel. Well done!"
— Marc Cameron, *New York Times* bestselling
author of *Tom Clancy: Shadow of the Dragon*

"Steve Urszenyi's powerful debut starts fast and finishes
faster. Full of high-octane thrills and intricate details
that bristle with authenticity, *Perfect Shot* is the must-
read first glimpse into what is certain to be a long
and successful series of brilliant Alex Martel novels."
— Mark Greaney, #1 *New York Times*
bestselling author of *Burner*, a Gray Man novel

"A smart and engaging protagonist, plenty of action in
exotic places, and a plotline that would make Tom
Clancy think twice."          — *The Globe and Mail*

# PERFECT
# SHOT

**A THRILLER**

# STEVE URSZENYI

St. Martin's Paperbacks

This is a work of fiction. All of the characters, organizations, and events portrayed in this novel are either products of the author's imagination or are used fictitiously.

Published in the United States by St. Martin's Paperbacks, an imprint of St. Martin's Publishing Group.

PERFECT SHOT

For information, address St. Martin's Publishing Group, 120 Broadway, New York, NY 10271.

www.stmartins.com

Library of Congress Catalog Card Number: 2023016825

ISBN: 978-1-250-87912-7

Our books may be purchased in bulk for promotional, educational, or business use. Please contact your local bookseller or the Macmillan Corporate and Premium Sales Department at 1-800-221-7945, ext. 5442, or by email at MacmillanSpecialMarkets@macmillan.com.

Printed in the United States of America

Minotaur hardcover edition published 2023
St. Martin's Paperbacks edition / October 2024

10  9  8  7  6  5  4  3  2  1

For Lynne,
My muse, my first reader, editor, and critic.
I love you with all my heart.

For Michael and Meghan,
My constant source of pride and wonder.
I couldn't love you more than I do.

# CHAPTER 1

The figure lying on the ground wasn't shivering, but she wasn't far off. The cold had seeped through her outer layers, chilling her as she lay motionless on a mound of dirt and damp moss. Though the rain had stopped at dawn, the sun's warming rays hadn't yet reached her.

Water dripped from leaves, producing a quiet, up-tempo beat tapped out on the forest floor around her. She inched her way forward through the underbrush to adjust her sightlines. Like an apparition, her body blended in with her surroundings, her ghillie suit and face camo breaking up the lines and patterns that could give her away.

Special Agent Alexandra Martel was, quite literally, hiding in plain sight.

A voice in her earbuds broke through the silence.

"All units stand by." It was the soothing baritone voice of Chief Inspector Nils Van Dijk of the Dutch National Police Corps.

Seven minutes earlier, a midsize cargo van pulled into a secluded area off a runway at the airfield, accompanied by two dark sedans on either side. Men piled out—seven in total—and gathered around the vehicles. All of them were armed. She ranged the closest at 260 meters. Like three of the men with him, he carried a semiauto carbine slung over his shoulder in the low-ready position as if preparing to engage his shadow.

The chief inspector's voice came through her in-ear headset again.

"Sierra One, report."

Alex had settled into her overwatch position shortly after dawn. It was now approaching ten. Peering through her rifle scope, she came up two clicks, settling the crosshairs over center mass of the man closest to her. Then she laid the weight of her shooting hand on the stock of her rifle, chambered in .308 Winchester, and rested her finger outside the trigger guard, lightly in contact with the cold metal. The rifle was braced by a bipod in front and a sand sock below the buttstock.

"Sierra One—Special Agent Martel—do you copy?"

She keyed the push-to-talk pad clipped to the MOLLE straps of her vest with her support hand. "Targets acquired. Seven subjects in all."

Her muscles were relaxed, allowing her skeletal frame to support her weight, averting the fatigue that could induce a tremor. She pulled the rifle butt into the pocket of her shoulder and welded her cheek to the gun, just as she had done a thousand times before, in preparation for what might happen next.

The man she sighted in was leaning against the front of the van, a cigarette nestled between two fingers. A pistol was visible in his waistband, a cell phone in his other hand. He looked gaunt and unkempt, with messy blond hair standing straight up and a week's worth of stubble, but it was clear to Alex that he was in command. That earned *Spike* the honor of being designated her primary target. He looked down at his phone and answered a call. While he listened, he took a drag off his cigarette, nodded, then clicked off and shouted something to the group of men gathered nearby. She couldn't hear the exchange but assumed it meant the rendezvous was about to go down.

Van Dijk's voice came over the radio again. "Second target package approaching."

Just as he had outlined to her and the team in the predawn briefing.

\* \* \*

DUTCH NATIONAL POLICE HEADQUARTERS,
THE HAGUE, 0400 HOURS

Chief Inspector Nils Van Dijk led the briefing in front of twenty officers gathered to prosecute the mission. While uncommon for a high-ranking officer to lead such an operation, this was an unusual situation, and Van Dijk a highly proficient commander. He was a senior officer with real-world tactical and military experience.

As Alex scanned the room filled with her colleagues, she noticed a man standing in the corner off to her left. He wore his wavy chestnut-brown hair a little longer than she preferred and wasn't particularly handsome. But dressed in the somewhat clichéd unofficial uniform of paramilitaries everywhere—khaki 5.11 Stryke pants, an untucked black polo shirt, and a pair of black-and-gray Salomon mid-height tactical boots—he communicated an air of confidence that made him attractive anyway. He carried no visible sidearm, which made her suspect he was from British or American intelligence with a military special operations background. If anyone introduced him as an advisor, she reckoned, it was a done deal—spook for sure. In fact, no one introduced him at all, which only confirmed for her his intelligence-community pedigree.

Chief Inspector Van Dijk began the briefing. He

advised that the arrests they were about to execute were part of a more extensive investigation. Then he continued with a formal review of the situation and mission.

"Our targets are two groups conducting their criminal enterprise on Dutch soil," he began. "And the commodity they are exchanging is special nuclear material."

Alex sat up in her chair. "Fissile material? As in nuclear-bomb-making material?"

"Correct," replied the chief inspector. Someone else whistled. "Twenty kilograms of weapons-grade plutonium and highly enriched uranium. Enough to construct several bomb cores." He nodded toward Alex. "Interpol caught wind of the pending sale to a jihadi group called the Islamic Levant Front and notified Dutch intelligence that they were looking to transact their business here in the Netherlands."

The room turned toward Alex. She was an FBI special agent on loan to Interpol and Interpol's liaison to the Dutch National Police for this mission.

"Don't look at me," she said. "First I'm hearing of it."

Van Dijk nodded toward the mystery man in the corner. "Western intelligence services have also been monitoring chatter about a bomb."

"Do we have any sense of a target?"

"Your guess is as good as mine, Special Agent. But since world leaders will be in Paris for the Peace Summit in only a matter of days, security agencies are understandably on edge. The priority of our mission is the recovery of the nuclear material. We cannot afford to have this package go missing."

"Can we track it if it does?" she asked.

"The Americans flew a Nuclear Emergency Support Team out of Joint Base Andrews in Maryland into Volkel Air Base here yesterday. NEST is on alert and will be nearby. Lady and gentlemen, you are authorized to use lethal force to prevent these special nuclear materials from going missing." He paused to make sure everyone was listening. "Let me repeat that: the SNM must be recovered at any cost. This mission has been dubbed Operation Valiant Angel, and the interagency team assembled in this room is Task Force Angel. Special Agent Martel has call sign Sierra One and will be on overwatch. I will maintain incident command from the TOC, but she is the tactical lead once the targets are in play. Watch your fields of fire. Maintain trigger and muzzle discipline. We don't know what the transport vessels for the nuclear material will be, and the last thing we need is a stray bullet or distraction device creating a major radioactive spill."

Alex met the gaze of the man in the corner. His eyes were focused and calm, but she could see their stillness belied a troubling disquiet within.

# CHAPTER 2

TERLET AIRFIELD, NORTH OF ARNHEM,
THE NETHERLANDS

Task Force Angel had deployed, and Alex, like its guardian angel, was on overwatch.

Her headset came alive with Van Dijk's voice from the tactical operations center—the TOC. "All units, status check."

"Alpha team ready." Alpha consisted of three two-person strike teams, waiting together in the back of a black up-armored van hidden in the forest four hundred meters south of her position.

"Bravo team ready." Bravo was a duplicate of Alpha team. They sat in an identical van inside a hangar that housed gliders six hundred meters to her north.

"Charlie en route." Charlie element, made up of eight surveillants in four cars, were shadowing the target vehicles to the rendezvous point.

"RIT team ready." Six operators from the Koninklijke Marechaussee—the KMar—made up the rapid intervention team. They belonged to KMar's Special Security Missions Brigade, known as BSB, and were loaded up and waiting on a Bell Huey helicopter at Deelen Air Base, three kilometers southwest of Alex's position. The RIT team was there to provide airborne support to cover the ground units if the mission went sideways during the arrest phase.

Alex depressed the push-to-talk pad at her shoulder. "Sierra One ready."

She closed her eyes and took a deep breath to clear her mind.

*In, out, rest, two, three.*

When she opened them again, the focus of her variable-power scope was still crisp, its illuminated tactical milling reticle on target. With her next draw of breath, she flicked her rifle's safety into the fire position and waited.

Van Dijk and other senior officers were in the TOC, set up near the KMar unit. His voice spoke through everyone's earbuds.

"When Sierra One confirms the cargo is present, we execute. Wait for her signal."

"On me," Alex said.

A moment later, two black vans and a dark sedan appeared over a rise five hundred meters in front of her and lined up facing the first group of vehicles. A ten-meter gulf of open tarmac separated them. Six dark-skinned males dismounted.

Thirteen targets to track, plus the nuke material.

"Both groups are heavily armed," she said. "I have eyes on carbines, SMGs, and handguns."

She watched through her scope as one of the newcomers walked into the no-man's-land dividing the two groups. The man she had christened Spike walked toward him and stopped ten feet away. Both were careful with their gestures, making no moves that might alarm the other side as they spoke. They kept their hands at their sides, plainly visible.

Spike turned to his men. One of them moved to the rear of the cargo van and opened the doors. Another man joined him, and together they lifted a large trunk-like box to the ground.

"Subjects have removed a Pelican case from the rear of one of the vehicles."

"Is it the cargo we're looking for?"

"Unclear. Stand by." *It would be nice if the case were covered in radiation warning stickers.* "All units hold."

One of the men wheeled the case out to the two in the middle. Both sides faced off across the ad hoc demilitarized zone. Despite their measured movements, neither was shy about presenting their weapons for the others to see. This had all the hallmarks of a mushrooming shit show.

Two of the new arrivals entered the DMZ. One held what Alex recognized as a radiation survey meter, used to detect and differentiate types of radioactive materials. Still, its presence was only presumptive evidence of the existence of the fissile material.

The wheeled case was opened, and the man with the survey meter stepped forward, scanning its contents. Five seconds later, he nodded and stepped back, and the lid was closed.

Alex depressed the PTT pad at her shoulder. "Attention, all units. Cargo confirmed. Execute, execute, execute!"

At her command, Alpha and Bravo teams launched from their respective positions. Both vans converged at high speed on the two groups standing in the middle of the disused runway. As soon as the targets grasped what was happening, they started shooting. Some of their rifles had been converted to full auto, but the shooters' muzzle and trigger control were poor, spraying bullets indiscriminately. The tactical teams had anticipated the gunfire and began to dismount behind the protective ballistic shields they carried, but they were met with a heavier barrage than expected with few opportunities for solid cover.

*Shit!*

"Shots fired! Shots fired!" came the urgent radio call from the Alpha team leader.

Alex kept her scope fixed on Spike and drew in a breath as he swept his weapon from side to side.

*Focus on the reticle,* she recited to herself like a mantra.

She exhaled and squeezed the trigger steadily until the firing pin drove forward into the primer, propelling the bullet almost three football fields downrange. It caught the man at the base of his throat, and he crumpled to the ground like a heavy sack, his finger still clamped down on the trigger, his rifle continuing to empty its magazine. One of the bullets struck a confederate in the head, killing him instantly.

Her team needed the helo and they needed it now. Alex spoke calmly through her bone mic. "RIT team, deploy."

"RIT team en route," came the response from the BSB team leader.

She retracted the bolt of her rifle and ejected the spent casing, then pushed it forward, locking another round into the chamber. She aimed the rifle to the right and lined up a figure moving fast, zigzagging as he fired at one of the arrest teams as they dismounted their van. With another squeeze of the trigger, she released a round that found its mark in the man's pelvis. He dropped but kept firing, pain and panic written on his face as he continued shooting wildly. She worked the rifle bolt and fired another shot, catching him in the temple. The gun fell out of his hands as the contents of his skull sprayed across the tarmac.

"Charlie, where are you?" Van Dijk's voice was calm.

"All Charlie units arriving on scene with Alpha and Bravo."

Alex caught sight of four vehicles approaching fast from her right. Eight operators from Charlie dismounted and fanned out to flank the group.

Two of the bogeys grabbed the black case and ran back to the van under cover fire laid down by three others. Alex took out one of the shooters first, choosing not to shoot at the men lifting the case of nuclear material into the vehicle.

As she chambered another round, she heard the unmistakable sound of a Huey on fast approach. One of the men on the ground took aim at the helicopter, and she put a round into his chest for his troubles.

She keyed her mic. "They're loading the case back into the van."

"Do not let them get away with that cargo!" ordered Van Dijk.

She looked to her right and saw members of Bravo team holding multiple tangos at gunpoint while cuffing them on the ground. Two officers from Alpha were running toward the men with the case but quickly came under fire. Alex targeted one of the shooters and felled him instantly.

The KMar operators fast-roped out of the helicopter just as the van's rear doors were closed. They immediately came under fire and took cover in a shallow ditch that ran alongside the old runway before reengaging. Alex shot at and missed the man scrambling into the passenger seat of the van. She quickly swapped out her magazine with a fresh ten-round mag and jumped up off the ground. Slinging her rifle over her shoulder, she drew her Glock from her thigh rig and broke into a run coming out of the trees, effortlessly shedding her ghillie suit on the fly.

"Bring the bird to the west tree line!" she called into her radio.

The machine banked slightly, its nose dipping almost to the ground as it turned to line up with her, kicking up a cloud of dust and forest debris. She was in an all-out sprint as the van full of radioactive material raced in the opposite direction. The man in the passenger seat held an AK-47 out the window and fired a few bursts in her direction.

"Fuck!" she shouted as bullets struck the pavement nearby, peppering her with chips of asphalt. She dove and rolled, her rifle jettisoning from her shoulder into the tall grass. She felt a sting in her calf and came up in a shooter's crouch, but she was too far away from the fleeing van to lay down effective fire with her Glock. As the gunfight continued, she holstered her pistol, retrieved her rifle, and ran for the Huey. The pilot turned the aircraft sideways for her to hot-load aboard through the open starboard door. Tires screeched behind her, and she expected to be plowed down by a car. She drew her Glock and spun in the direction of the sound, leveling her sights at a man running toward her.

"Don't shoot!"

She recognized him as the quiet one—the one she presumed was a spook—from the morning briefing.

"What the hell?" she shouted over the roar of the helicopter.

"I'm with you," he yelled as he ran past her and jumped aboard the hovering machine.

"Like hell you are! Who are you?"

"Quick! Get in!"

She looked at his outstretched hand, then back over her shoulder at the van with the radioactive payload disappearing into the distance. She unslung her rifle and handed it to him, jumping onto the skid of the helo. Before she was even through the door, he was shouting to the pilot to go after the van. She scrambled into a seat and buckled up, leaving the sliding door clipped wide open.

"Here," he said, handing back her rifle. Her new companion strapped in beside her.

She wiped grass and dirt off the front of her scope and quickly inspected it for signs of damage.

"You're bleeding," he shouted over the noise of the rotors.

"What?"

He pointed to her leg. She touched her calf at a tear in the heavy fabric. It was warm and sticky, and her hand came away coated in blood.

"Just a flesh wound," she yelled back, grinning. She wiped her hand on her pants.

"Caleb," he said, holding out his hand, still staring at her leg.

"Alex." She fist-bumped his palm with her bloody hand.

*Who is this guy?*

He pointed up. She reached for the green noise-attenuating headset with a coiled cord that hung above her seat. It fit comfortably over her earbuds, allowing her to continue monitoring the comms chatter from below as the helicopter rose above the trees.

The Alpha team leader had taken over coordinating the movement of ground assets and the situation was being contained. Ambulances and other resources were being summoned to the airfield. From the TOC, Van Dijk advised that NEST was being scrambled to the airfield to stage. Then he radioed Alex.

"Sierra One, what's your location?" Van Dijk asked.

"I'm in the Huey going after the van."

"Alex, don't lose that cargo!"

# CHAPTER 3

Alex double-pressed the shoulder PTT button of her mic to acknowledge the chief inspector's message. All she could think of was Yoda's famous entreaty:

*Do. Or do not. There is no try.*

The Huey banked east and gained a few hundred feet of elevation. She addressed the pilot through her headset's boom microphone: "Find that van and bring us in low."

The pilot nodded and dropped back down, leveling off just above the top of the forest canopy. They spotted the van speeding along a narrow service road beside the airfield and watched as it almost T-boned a fuel truck exiting a hangar.

"Jesus!"

"That was close," said Caleb, his voice clear in her headset.

"Can we block them?" she asked the pilot.

The pilot dropped onto them fast, but as he maneuvered the helicopter around to the front, the van's passenger leaned out and started shooting. Bullets punched through the floor of the Huey and into the wall behind them. The pilot pulled back on the cyclic and collective controls, instantly backing off and putting three hundred feet of sky between the shooter and his helo.

"Any ideas?" Caleb asked.

"You don't happen to have a grenade launcher, do you?"

"Not today."

"We could follow them and lead the cavalry wherever they stop," she said.

"Not an option," said the pilot.

"Why not?"

He pointed to the center of the Huey's instrument panel, where several components were lit up and flashing red. "That one's a master caution alarm. Transmission oil pressure's dropping. See that hole in the wall behind you?"

Alex turned to look.

"One of those bullets must have hit the transmission fluid line."

"How much time do we have?"

"I need to set down now."

"Not an option. Do you know what's in that van?"

"Yes, ma'am. I'll give you five minutes, or however long we can stay aloft."

"Great."

"But when we run out of fluid and the transmission fails, the blades will lock up—and we'll drop like a rock," he added.

*Great.*

She watched as the van drove off the road, busting through a gate. Then it plowed through the bushes and up onto the A50 motorway southbound toward the city of Arnhem.

"Can you take out the driver from here?" asked Caleb.

Traffic on the motorway was heavy, with commuters moving along at the speed limit.

"If I take out the driver or otherwise make that van

crash at highway speed, we'll have a major radiological disaster on our hands."

"What about disabling the engine?"

"Maybe, but that'll expose us to direct fire. If we're taken out, that cargo's gone forever."

"What other option do we have?"

As she was considering his question, she saw the flashing lights of a police car coming north on the four-lane divided highway about a kilometer ahead.

"What's he doing?"

The car stopped beside the center guardrail, and an officer clambered out.

"No, no, no!" she shouted. "What the hell's he doing?"

The officer vaulted the guardrail and scrambled across the grassy median, popping up in the southbound lanes. Drawing his sidearm, he took up a shooting stance as the van sped toward him.

She keyed her mic. "Chief Inspector!"

"Go."

"Call off the local police. We have Dirty Harry on the A50 about to engage the van."

"What? Calling now."

"Have them keep all police away. Tell them the van is full of explosives or whatever you have to, but keep them back!"

They were about twenty meters behind the van at an altitude of seventy-five feet. As the van approached the officer, he began firing.

"Move, you idiot!" Alex shouted. "Get off the road!"

They watched helplessly as the van veered toward the cop doing 120 kilometers an hour. It struck him and sent the man hurtling high into the air and back over the guardrail, where his lifeless body came to rest in the tall grass.

"Jesus!" said Caleb.

"Officer down," Alex called quietly into her radio.

There was silence for a moment, then Van Dijk's deep voice cut in. "Copy. I'll send EMS."

She double-pressed her mic, though she knew paramedics wouldn't be able to do anything for him.

The van straightened back out in its lane, then veered toward an off-ramp.

"Special Agent," said the pilot to Alex. "We have to land. Transmission oil pressure is critically low."

"Sergeant, you will not land this helicopter until we stop that van." She could hear the warning alarms sounding but she wasn't about to let the van disappear into the city. "Keep this bird airborne until we get those assholes!"

"Yes, ma'am."

The helicopter lurched as he pushed the cyclic forward and throttled up, and the alarms screamed louder.

*　*　*

Alex clipped into a harness secured to the Huey's airframe and unbuckled her seatbelt. She swung her legs around and dropped her butt to the floor, placing her feet on the skids outside the helo.

"What are you doing?" asked Caleb.

"Getting ready."

The van raced down a series of narrow streets as it entered the city of Arnhem. Lunch-hour traffic was heavy, and the driver bobbed and weaved around cars, apparently oblivious to the danger posed by his cargo. He seemed to be trying to outmaneuver the helo between the buildings, but the KMar pilot did a masterful job of keeping them on top of the van, despite the alarms ringing from the cockpit.

"I'm going to take a shot if I have one," she said. "Not sure how much more time we have."

She wound her forearm through the front of the Vickers two-point sling, which helped secure the rifle and lessened the odds of her dropping it to the ground below on the bumpy flight. Peering through her rifle-scope, she dialed back the magnification to one more suited to a close-range engagement. The helicopter continued to shudder as the pilot kept up with the van. At this point, her best shot would be to take out the driver if she got the chance. Trying to disable the vehicle had the lowest probability of success. Even if it resulted in a loss of control of the vehicle, killing the driver was the better tactical option. Now that it was traveling on city streets, she hoped a slower-speed collision would be less likely to compromise the containment of the nuclear materials inside their cases.

She took aim and lined him up in her reticle, but each time she was about to pull the trigger, the pilot corrected to avoid a building or to stabilize the unsteady bird, taking her off-target. In a crowded urban environment, a miss could prove catastrophic; the risk of collateral damage here in town—that is, shooting an innocent bystander—was considerably higher than it had been on the highway.

"Sorry, ma'am," the pilot said as the helo swerved again.

There was no point berating him—he was doing all he could to keep the helicopter in the air, let alone steady. She sighted in the van's driver again. He was driving recklessly, weaving around traffic, aiming for pedestrians, forcing them to jump out of his way. She wanted to end this pursuit. *Now.*

The Huey leveled out. She started to squeeze the trigger. Suddenly, the bird dipped and lurched, and she lost her footing on the skid. Her butt slipped out the door, bounced on the skid, and sailed on past. She just managed to hook her right elbow around the skid as the harness strap locked up. She was dangling seventy-five feet off the ground over the city. Her feet swung wildly as the pilot fought to regain control of the swaying helicopter.

"Alex! Hold on!" called Caleb.

She tried to pull herself onto the skid, but no joy. She tried to throw a leg over it, but again, the helo proved too unsteady as it flung her around beneath. At least her rifle remained hooked around her arm. She shuffled it to a more secure position higher on her shoulder.

The helicopter bobbed and lurched as Caleb appeared in the doorway.

"Take my arm," he said, reaching out.

"You're not buckled in!" she shouted, fighting to get her words out against the rotor downwash jamming gusts of air down her throat.

"Grab my arm!"

She hooked her left arm over the skid and let go with her right to snatch his hand. On her first attempt, she missed and swung wildly in the air, her one leg coming up and booting the underside of the Huey. Her harness was still attached by the monkey tail, but she had no idea what its anchor weight rating was. A bigger, chunkier piece of webbing would have offered greater reassurance.

"Try again!" he shouted over the noise of the helicopter and the wind.

She wasn't keen on the idea of letting go of the skid again. *Maybe we can land this way.* Her eyes met and held his. His gaze was intense, focused, confident.

"Alex, I'll bring you in. I swear it."

She let go with her right arm, again clinging to the skid with only her left. She swung it toward his outstretched hand. He matched its trajectory and caught hold, locking his hand around her wrist. He pulled. The helicopter dipped and bobbed again, but Caleb held fast, the strain of it written on his face. She pulled up as well, then swung her left leg onto the skid. Once she found a foothold, she pushed up and twisted around, driving her butt into the helicopter, landing on the floor, her back knocking against the bench seat.

"Welcome aboard," Caleb said.

She shortened the length of the harness webbing, repositioned herself in the door, then slipped the rifle off her shoulder, taking aim through the scope without missing a beat.

The van was turning onto a curving road headed south. She could see that, just ahead, the road was going to run past a park.

"I'm going to try to take him there," she said to the pilot. "Next to the park."

He acknowledged and throttled up to bring them alongside the van on the driver's side. Alex focused on her sight picture. But as they reached the park, she saw that the roadway alongside was lined with thirty-foot-tall trees.

*Damn urban green spaces!* "Take us a little higher. I need a steeper angle over those trees."

The pilot did as requested, increasing Alex's distance and angle on her target but offering an unobstructed shot. She squeezed the trigger just as the helo shuddered.

*BOOM!*

"You get him?" asked Caleb.

As the pilot smoothed out, Alex could see the van skidding left then right, but it regained control after a few seconds.

"Well?"

"I don't think so," she said as she chambered another round.

The van came out of the canopy of trees. The road approached a roundabout that encircled the Airborne monument commemorating the Battle of Arnhem in

1944. Alex could see the Nederrijn River just beyond. It looked like the van was going to stay on the circle and head back into the busy part of the city.

"If they go back into the city, we're screwed," she told the pilot. "But I can take him at that bridge."

The pilot understood and dropped lower, and like a cowboy on a cutting horse, he used his Huey to block the van's path, forcing the driver to veer right and take the exit off the roundabout that led to the John Frost Bridge.

"Nice move!" she said.

"This isn't my first rodeo, ma'am," he said with a Dutch accent.

The pilot throttled up so he could position the helicopter ahead of the van at a forty-five-degree angle. Alex sighted in the driver once more and was about to squeeze off another shot when the helicopter lurched left, buzzers and bells ringing from the cockpit. Her foot slipped off the skid again, but this time she managed to recover. She struggled to get back into position as the helo gyrated through the air.

"It's now or never, ma'am." The pilot's tone was calm but assertive. "Transmission fluid pressure is low and temperature is critically high. I can't keep us up here any longer. I have to set this bird down now."

"Just one more minute!"

He battled the controls and steadied the helo, but they were about a hundred meters off their target now, having drifted away from the infamous bridge and out over the river.

The van sped along the first span of the bridge. Alex tracked her target, leading it slightly in the reticle, struggling to compensate for the movement of the helo.

*It's now or never.*

She exhaled and squeezed the trigger.

*BOOM!*

A split second later, the driver's head exploded, and the vehicle lurched to the right, striking the barrier that separated the roadway from the sidewalk and bicycle path. The van became airborne and spun around, its momentum carrying it end over end through the air. She watched as it cartwheeled through the spars of the bridge span, over the railing, and off the bridge, falling twenty meters until it slammed into the surface of the river below before sinking into the dark abyss.

# CHAPTER 4

ARNHEM, THE NETHERLANDS

Alex and Caleb stood at the water's edge, upwind of the crippled Huey. It sat on the north bank of the Nederrijn River on an interlocking brick pathway, smoke creeping from the engine's exhaust nozzle and air intake vents.

Together, they jogged toward the point where the van had entered the water a few minutes earlier. The Nederrijn—or Lower Rhine—was slow and wide, meandering its way through Arnhem. Midway across the river, about sixty meters from shore, an oily patch formed around air bubbles breaking the surface. Hopefully, the van would be easy to recover.

"Do you think the passenger survived?" Alex asked.

Caleb shook his head.

"Would have been nice to question him."

He shrugged.

But the van and its human occupants weren't her biggest concern.

The local police arrived and cordoned off the area as curious onlookers gathered for a closer look. Fire engines surrounded the Huey. The KMar pilot was speaking to the fire brigade commander as his men charged hoses around them with water and foam.

Two police rigid-hulled inflatable boats with blue lights flashing converged from downriver, taking up their posts well outside the boundary defined by the oily layer on the surface. The marine unit officers placed buoys in the water to delineate a perimeter. Brandishing semiautomatic rifles, they enforced a no-go zone to keep other boaters from wandering too close.

Alex worried about the van's cargo and whether hazmat divers would be able to find the cases in the murky depths of the river. Water was an excellent insulator against the movement of ionizing radiation; still, if the containment structures had ruptured or otherwise been compromised, they would be dealing with an environmental disaster downstream as the plutonium and uranium settled into the muddy bottom and entered the ecosystem and food chain. Cleaning up the radioactive contamination would be complex and costly.

"You had no choice," Caleb said, breaking into her thoughts.

"What?"

"You did what you had to do."

"It's still a cluster—"

"You prevented the nuclear material from going missing."

"We'll see," she said, gazing out at the activity on the water.

"Could have been worse."

"Not comforting."

A blue-and-silver Bell 412 twin-engine helicopter approached from the north, coming in low overhead. It banked to the east, then briefly hovered thirty feet above the oily patch before arcing over the bridge and beginning a grid pattern. Chief Inspector Van Dijk had directed the NEST crew to Alex's location. Onboard, she imagined the Nuclear Emergency Support Team would be bringing all its radiation-sensing technology to bear, and as she watched, she wondered what its equipment was telling them.

She was classified by the FBI as a weapons of mass destruction and CBRNE interdiction specialist, but that didn't make her a chemical, biological, radiological, nuclear, or explosive ordnance engineer. Her expertise was with guns and tactical operations. Her job was to locate and secure the threats. She relied on other team members with proper training to keep her and the rest of her team safe from the *stuff*; that being any rad, nuke, explosive, chem, or bioagent. She maintained a working knowledge of detection, identification, and decontamination procedures, but otherwise, her job was to leave the *stuff* alone and allow the glowworms—her subject matter expert teammates—to mitigate the hazardous material threats.

She turned to her companion. "Are you finally going to tell me who you are?"

"Name's Caleb."

"Smartass." She turned and walked away from the river, back toward the crippled Huey. He followed her to the road.

A marked police car with its warning lights activated pulled alongside them. Chief Inspector Van Dijk stepped out of the passenger side. Passersby gawked at her as they walked past. She wanted to ask them what they were staring at, but then Van Dijk tapped his cheek with three fingers, and she understood. She was still covered in face camo. She had shed her forested ghillie suit when she ran from the woods, but the rest of her was still kitted out like a soldier in olive-drab-green BDUs. Not at all the expected appearance of someone in the center of Arnhem during the lunch hour.

The trunk of the police car popped open, and Van

Dijk pointed to her rifle. She cleared it, then secured it in a case inside the trunk.

"NEST picked up a signature in the water. They're sending in divers," he told her. "Let's head back to the MICC to debrief."

"I'd rather stay for the recovery."

"You've done your job, Alex. Members from KMar will assist in securing the scene and the materials if they can be found. Besides, your boss wants to speak to you."

"Bressard?" she asked, referring to her Interpol chief at the National Central Bureau for The Hague.

"Your *other* boss."

"Oh." *Washington. That was fast.*

Here she was, an FBI special agent on secondment to Interpol, where she was regarded as a superb operator among some of the finest in the world. But secondment or not, she was an FBI special agent first. She had discharged her firearm and people had died. In the eyes of the US Department of Justice, even bad guys were people. She had, from time to time, reluctantly conceded the point. The Office of Professional Responsibility would have questions for her, and she hoped they wouldn't pull her stateside to answer them. She wanted to see this investigation through while the trail was still fresh.

\* \* \*

A KMar officer had dropped off an INEOS Grenadier SUV at the riverfront for their use. Caleb drove the blacked-out, unmarked vehicle along the N224 out of Arnhem, taking them back to The Hague for the debrief.

He glanced over at Alex riding shotgun, who was occupying herself by playing with the radio as they drove along the smooth blacktop highway, seemingly incapable of tuning in a station. She was alluring, even with her face covered in camo paint. Her golden-brown hair was long and lustrous, tied back in a ponytail. Her cheekbones were high, lending an elegance to the profile of her face that gave her a timeless beauty. The hue of her green-blue eyes shifted with her mood. She was fit and lean and had run with and hefted her heavy rifle with ease. He admired how she had taken control of the chaos around her, fearlessly survived a tumble off the skids of the helo even as it bobbed and sputtered, and had turned a near-disastrous end to the operation into mission success with a final, fatal, extraordinary shot.

He looked at her again, still fumbling with the channel selector on the Grenadier's infotainment system. Sure, she was a formidable operator, but she sucked at working the radio.

He had memorized her service jacket, including the *eyes-only* sections that most high-ranking commanders and officials would never see. He had access to things they did not and was fascinated by her career in the profession of arms, including her time with Intelligence Support Activity. ISA was arguably the nation's most elite—and secretive—Special Missions Unit.

Alex had applied herself expertly to the military trades, from special operations combat medic to unwitting sniper and decorated war hero, to her service as one of her nation's elite shadow warriors at the tip of the spear with ISA and its various spectral sections. Her time with ISA had seen her operate covertly behind enemy lines in Russia and Syria, in both instances on the trail of violations of the Chemical Weapons Convention.

If he could recruit her to CIA's newest team—the team he commanded—it would bolster his standing within the Agency. Not that he had eyes on what would be called the *C-suites* in the corporate world: CEO, CFO, COO. He had no interest in being the *D* or the *double D* at CIA, the director or deputy director. But he had been greenlit to develop a unique team of operators within the Special Activities Center. The Advance Counterterrorism and Counterproliferation Team was a small, boutique squad, free to act globally and deploy its operators as he saw fit, with a hefty budget to support his command.

As the branch chief of ACCT, Caleb reported directly to CIA's deputy director, bypassing the section chief and other mid- and senior-level executives who, in his experience, all too often functioned more as gatekeepers and moneylenders than mission facilitators. For her part, Deputy Director Kadeisha Thomas expected transparency (to her), plausible deniability (for her), and results that would impress JSOC and, when appropriate, POTUS.

ACCT's objectives were the early detection, intervention, and mitigation of WMD threats to the United States from abroad. The strategy was simple: nothing lands in the homeland. This meant his team was to undertake every effort to interdict weapons of mass destruction that could possibly end up being deployed on American soil or against American citizens or interests abroad. That responsibility came with Title 50 authority for covert and direct action, straight from the president.

In Caleb's view, Alex was the right one for the job. As a former operator with the ultra-secret ISA and in her current assigned role as a counterproliferation specialist and FBI legat—their legal attaché to the US Embassy in the Netherlands—Alex would add depth to the team and help solidify its standing in the intelligence community. Her presence would also silence some of ACCT's early detractors, who felt it was yet another male-dominated, door-kicking, knuckle-dragging team lacking accountability.

In short, Alex had skills he could use. And she carried a certain cachet in the corridors of power as a female Silver Star and Purple Heart recipient with numerous other ribbons, medals, and decorations, plus a proven track record with the type of no-nonsense mission profiles that would make future operations with ACCT easier to sell. Sure, she had baggage, but she had been adjudicated sane and whole again; or, at least, so said several teams of shrinks with various federal agencies, including her last evaluation by the Federal Bureau of Investigation.

His undertaking in the Netherlands was simple and broke down this way: assist with securing the plutonium and highly enriched uranium. Identify the source, as well as the group aiming to acquire the special nuclear material. Determine the group's intent and purpose and end the threat. And finally, bring Special Agent Alexandra Martel into the CIA fold. These were the outcomes the DD expected of him on this mission.

No more, no less.

He could succeed in recruiting her if he remained mindful that she wasn't an asset for him to *handle*. She was an elite operator with a lust for action, so the focus had to appeal to her hunger, not for personal acclaim, but for justice and fair retribution. Special Agent Martel was one of those rare animals who still believed in duty and honor above all and worked diligently in service of both. His successful enlistment of Alex into ACCT needed to be mindful of those points. It would be more seduction than recruitment.

He dug into his breast pocket and pulled out his phone.

"Here, plug this in," he said.

She took it and connected it via a patch cable into

the Grenadier's USB port. Caleb toggled through the playlists that popped up on the large infotainment display on the dash.

"Try this," he said.

"The Sound of Silence"—the version by Disturbed, not Simon & Garfunkel—played from the speakers, its gentle piano intro acquiescing to David Draiman's lush voice.

He stole glances at her as she settled into her seat and closed her eyes. She rested her size-seven tactical boots against the dash, a smile of contentment tracing lightly on her lipstick-free lips, her head leaned back into the seatback. She played air piano as Draiman's voice shifted from black velvet to coarse gravel, the song's tempo increasing in ferocity.

Caleb felt an involuntary stirring of his baser instincts, but he suppressed his body's reaction, focusing his attention instead on the road ahead.

The drive to The Hague would take just over an hour. They had traveled for ten minutes along the scenic N224 expressway before he pulled into a Shell station.

"Why are we stopping?" asked Alex.

"They left us with less than a quarter tank. You want anything?" he asked, pointing to the convenience store attached to the station.

"I'm good."

He walked around to the passenger side to pump fuel.

A minute later, Alex hopped out of the vehicle.

"On second thought . . . ," she said, ambling to the store. "Want anything?"

Caleb was hanging up the fuel nozzle when she strode back holding two chocolate bars, two bottles of Gatorade, and a bag under her arm.

"Bounty or Mars?" she asked, holding them up as he walked around to the driver's side.

"Surprise me."

She tossed the Bounty to him over the Grenadier's roof. Then she hopped in and removed a package of baby wipes from the bag. Caleb watched as she flipped down the sun visor to use the mirror, wiping away the green, brown, and black paint from her face.

"What?" she asked.

"I prefer my women all camoed up."

"Lucky for you, I'm not *your woman*."

*Not yet,* he thought.

Two minutes later, he took the cloverleaf interchange, and they merged onto the A12 motorway westbound. The highway bisected the Netherlands, running from The Hague on the North Sea coast to the west to the German border in the east, crossing three Dutch provinces: South Holland, Utrecht, and Gelderland. Along much of the way, the thoroughfare was bordered by forests thick and green, fenced off from the highway for the mutual protection of motorists and wildlife. But presently, fields of tulips spread out from the road as far as the eye could see along flat farmland. The sight was surreal, bright yellows and reds popping in one field while the next held more pastel shades of pink and purple.

It was the first time Caleb had passed these fields in daylight, and he was captivated by the vibrant colors laid out before him. They were not unlike the poppy fields outside Jalalabad in eastern Afghanistan that shared the same growing season as these tulips. Rifle in hand, he had walked through many of those fields and set many more ablaze.

Alex had her eyes closed again. Her knees were bent, and her now bare feet rested against the dash, her toes tucked under the grab bar of the off-road vehicle.

"Hey," he called gently.

"What?" she said with a start. "We there already?"

He nodded his head toward the view out the passenger-side window. "Beautiful, isn't it?"

She turned to peer out the window. "I've been here three years now, and seeing this still blows my mind," she said. "It reminds me of Afghanistan."

He smiled.

# CHAPTER 5

Alex's phone rang as they neared the edge of the city on the A12 motorway. A picture of a smiling Martin Bressard holding a young grandson in a soccer jersey flashed onscreen.

"You going to let that keep ringing, or . . . ," said Caleb.

"Hi, Chief," she answered, bringing the handset up to her ear.

"Alexandra, how are you?" Chief Bressard's voice dripped with empathy.

"Good. We're about twenty minutes away."

"I didn't ask *where* you were; I asked *how*."

She switched the handset to her other ear. "I'm fine."

She knew what he was asking. This morning she had dispatched several men to their graves. *Five, six, more?* She did the math—by her hand: five at the airfield, two in the van. There was a pause on the other end, as if Bressard were contemplating his next remark. She decided to fill the void before he could.

"Honestly, Chief, I'm good. We'll be at the MICC for the debrief soon. You'll have my after-action report on your desk tonight."

"The debrief is postponed. It's already getting late. Go home, Alexandra. Go for a run. Or do a few laps in

the pool. Take the motorcycle for a spin. You can write
up your report in the morning."

"It's midafternoon," she replied. "What about the
Bureau?"

Van Dijk had already informed her the FBI wanted
to talk. No doubt someone in the Bureau's Office
of Professional Responsibility was anxious to get a
full accounting of the incident as soon as she could
give it.

"We still have teams of investigators in the field,"
he said. "Your masters in Washington can wait. I told
them you are otherwise engaged."

"They bought that?"

"I didn't give them a choice. Just like I'm not giving
you one, Alexandra. Take the night off."

Somehow, the chief had bought her more time. This
was his way of looking out for her. She appreciated it,
even if she didn't say so.

"Oh-eight-hundred in the MICC," he said before
clicking off.

She gazed out the window. The motorway slithered
under the A4 that headed north and south above them.
High banks of grassy slopes bounded them, reaching
up toward a convoluted series of impossibly high ramps
filled with afternoon traffic. They approached an overhead sign announcing they were two kilometers from
Den Haag Centrum, the central business district of The
Hague.

"What was that all about?" asked Caleb.

"Debrief's been postponed till morning," she said.

She saw the follow-up question in his eyes, but his
mouth stayed shut. *Good man,* she thought. She preferred her men strong and silent.

"Take the two lanes to the left," she directed.

Caleb peered over his shoulder, signaled, and changed
lanes. "Where we going?"

"Head straight for the beach. *We* aren't going anywhere. *You* are dropping me off at my apartment."

"And me?"

"Once you drop me off, you're on your own. You can do whatever the hell you like."

# CHAPTER 6

POLICE HEADQUARTERS, THE HAGUE,
THE NETHERLANDS, 0745 HOURS

The Major Incident Command Center—pronounced *mick*—was the equivalent of an FBI tactical operations center found in any of the larger field offices back in the United States. From this room, the incident commander could exercise centralized command and control over any operation. It was housed within Dutch National Police headquarters in the center of The Hague.

Once past the security screening area, Alex headed up the elevator. She waved her prox card at the reader outside the door and walked in. It was an ample, well-equipped space with a giant ultra-high-definition television monitor mounted flush against the front wall and a computer at every seat.

Flowering floor plants lined the walls in a style Alex dubbed utilitarian plus. The look was in keeping with the aesthetically pleasing architectural flair of the new government buildings scattered around the Netherlands to which Alex was growing accustomed. The thing about the Dutch, she'd observed over the years, was that—besides being above average in height—they could mix the practical with the beautiful to create a pleasing yet functional aesthetic. It complemented their forthright mannerisms by adding an element of artistry to what she felt was an otherwise lackluster cultural sensibility.

Caleb had arrived before her and was engaged in conversation with Chief Inspector Van Dijk, who summoned her over with a wave. She made herself a dark roast coffee with the Nespresso machine on the table along the wall and walked over.

"Morning, sir."

"Chief Bressard should be along shortly," he said. "Everyone else is here. We'll begin the debrief when Martin arrives."

Caleb held a steaming mug in his hand. She was envious of its sheer volume as she examined her paltry demitasse. If she leaned in over it, would it be just coffee that she smelled? There was an edge to him she couldn't quite get a handle on. He seemed always switched on and alert yet presented a calm and casual façade.

*Those are the ones to watch out for.*

The quiet warrior was a dangerous breed. In battle, they reveled in the chaos and conjured violence as a means to an end. Even the most skilled adversaries feared them because they were notoriously effective and lethal, expert in the art of combat, and fearless in its execution. Comrades-in-arms fed off their confidence and bestial demeanor. The warrior with a peaceful exterior became a force multiplier during any armed conflict.

Was Caleb like that? Were his spots the same as the ones she wore?

At five minutes before eight, Interpol chief Martin Bressard entered the MICC and strode toward them. Wavy-haired and lightly bearded, the chief was a dapper fifty-something Belgian wearing a tailored navy suit and bright orange tie.

"Oh, good, you're here. We can begin," said Van

Dijk as the chief approached. "Take your seats," he announced to the room.

"Alexandra," Bressard whispered, nudging her out of her spell. "We have to talk after the debrief. Something's come up."

"Sure, Chief." She took a sip of coffee and sat at the conference table, wondering what was going on. Usually the king of calm himself, Bressard's tone concerned her.

Van Dijk began his briefing. "Most of you have already seen the media coverage of yesterday's events." Heads around the table nodded. "We managed to keep the press underinformed regarding the contents of the van, suggesting it contained a volatile cargo that was recovered by emergency crews."

"Fake news!" someone shouted, followed by the sound of laughter around the room.

"Indeed," continued the chief inspector. "They were quite eager to believe our cover story about a turf war between rival gangs and a stolen shipment of heroin. This, though," he pointed to the big-screen TV that came to life on the wall behind him, "was a little harder to explain. So, we added a narrative about explosives and cloaked the whole affair in a veil of national security."

A shaky video began to play. It started with a woman's voice narrating in German as the camera panned from a vantage point on the bridge to three young people laughing and looking out toward the river. Tourists. Over the sound of traffic, Alex could hear a helicopter approaching, and the videographer swung her camera phone toward it.

The room full of cops watched as the entire incident at the bridge played out on the giant television. The news segment ran with the frozen image of Alex's camoed-up face pinned to the corner of the frame.

"Oh, Jesus," she groaned, sinking into her chair.

"Hey, Rambo!" someone shouted.

She buried her face in her hands as the cops around her drank in the intense action.

There was a momentary hush as the news story ended with the van hurtling over the side of the bridge and the screen went black. To a man, everyone stood and applauded, except Caleb, who leaned back in his chair, studying her from across the room. Alex reluctantly acknowledged their appreciation with a slight wave.

Their adulation wasn't necessary—she did what she did because that was her job. She enjoyed the challenge and the rush of the moment. When chaos erupted around her, her focus narrowed to take in the threat and the immediate environment. She enjoyed sending bullets downrange to meet the bad guys. There was no moral dilemma, only the clarity of the moment. She was the problem solver, the one who halted the threat. The satisfaction that gave her was her dark secret, and she accepted it.

Caleb's eyes met hers as if he saw her truth. She held his gaze for a moment before turning toward the chief inspector at the front of the room.

"Okay, settle down," called Van Dijk above the din. "Settle down, gentlemen. Take your seats."

"Wow, Alex," said a KMar operator. "That was one bad-ass—" His eyes found the chief inspector's locked on him and he reeled it in. "I mean, that was an incredible shot, ma'am."

Caleb was smiling, seemingly bewildered by her humility.

Van Dijk smiled, too, like a proud uncle. "I think we can all appreciate the skill demonstrated by Special Agent Martel in ending this incident, as well as her actions at the airfield. That was truly a remarkable display of marksmanship."

"Thank you, sir," she said, rising from her chair.

"The team did an outstanding job yesterday. Especially—" She looked around the room for the helicopter pilot. "Especially our KMar fly-boy, who exhibited exceptional skill and professionalism in keeping that bird aloft. So, thanks again for your acknowledgment, sir, but everyone here was amazing." She applauded the men around her and retook her seat.

Van Dijk let the applause die down. "Alright, now that our little love-in is over, let's get back on track." Glancing down at his notepad, he summarized the events. "You will find all this information in the summary document before you, but in total, there were thirteen bogeys. Eight are dead," he said somberly. "The remaining five are in custody, and warrants have been issued for several others. Among the sellers, six Eastern European men are dead, including the driver of the van and his co-conspirator. Two of the would-be buyers are also dead. We're still trying to confirm their nationalities, along with the remaining participants, but as suspected, among them are members of the Islamic Levant Front."

"A veritable UN of bad guys," someone said.

"Indeed. Meanwhile, other agencies are coordinating with us through Interpol to determine what the plot and target might have been and whether we have disrupted it completely. It would be good to know what else we should be focusing on. For now, though, the word from our law enforcement and intelligence partners is that the shipment of nuclear materials was recovered from the bottom of the river and rendered safe. So, job well done, everyone."

Alex's eyes were on Caleb as he sat back in his chair, playing with a kubotan, deep in thought. The five-and-a-half-inch-long metallic keychain held no keys, just a short bead chain running through an eyelet at one end with what appeared to be a deformed slug strung on it.

The instrument of attitude adjustment, as it was affectionately known, had a faded and chipped gunmetal-blue matte finish. He was absent-mindedly rapping it against the knuckles of his left hand as if to test whether he could still feel each blow. He looked over at her, like he had sensed her watching, and tucked the weapon back into his pocket, expressionless.

The briefing continued without offering much additional information or context to explain why an Islamist group was trying to buy one of the world's hottest illicit commodities. So far, any motive, target, plot, or additional players remained unknown. While unconfirmed reports outlined possible threats to several US cities, with New York at the top of everybody's hit list, no one had yet verified the information. If Van Dijk or Bressard knew, they weren't saying.

"Alright," said Van Dijk with finality, "that is all. I want all section leaders' after-action reports by this afternoon. Dismissed."

She looked over at Caleb again.

*They* might not know, but she was getting an inkling that *he* might.

# CHAPTER 7

Darkness wasn't the same as *empty* or *undetected*. Krysten knew this, and if she had considered the distinction as she had been trained, things might have turned out better.

She tapped a code into the keypad outside the door, and the magnetic lock clicked open. It wasn't her code, but given the circumstances, it was better to access the office using one belonging to somebody else. And the leering security guard's was as good as anyone's. Let him try to explain how someone was able to steal it so easily.

The only light in the room came off the green fire exit sign glowing over the door, offering just enough illumination for her to get her bearings. The windowless office had four workstations. At the back was a locked, air-conditioned server room that housed the network drives and the company's proprietary secrets. The company itself was a front for other activities. Those were the files she was after. The only computers with direct access to the servers were the four in here, tethered by an Ethernet cable to the computers inside the locked room itself.

She powered up one of the desktop systems, flinching

when it emitted a short, sharp beep. She listened for any sound in the hallway that might indicate she had been compromised, then slid into the chair when the computer finished booting. Taking a folded sticky note from her pocket, she entered the password scrawled on it. It had taken her a few days, but she had managed to get these, too, from one of the men who worked in this section. He was careless enough to post his log-in credentials beside his workstation and had been vulnerable to the charms of a beautiful woman, mistakenly interpreting her hand on his shoulder as something more lecherous than larcenous.

Getting past the home screen was one thing, but the folders Krysten was after resided on a confidential vault drive with yet another log-in. Lucky for her, the man was also a coffee aficionado. So when she reappeared the following morning at his desk bearing a cup of Jamaica Blue Mountain coffee, a plunging V-neck blouse, and a smile, she'd been able to capture his keystrokes on a Bluetooth-connected phone app.

After a failed first attempt, she again mistyped the alphanumeric string, and a red warning box flashed:

**ACCESS DENIED. ONE ATTEMPT LEFT.**

Her heart jackhammered against her rib cage as she pulled her phone from her pocket and turned on the camera light to better see the keyboard. Never a strong touch-typist, she entered each number and letter slowly so as not to make any more mistakes. Finally, she held her breath and hit *enter* after the eleventh character, and the network directory file structure appeared on the screen.

Her ears perked up at a sound outside the door. Afraid to breathe, she sat motionless, enveloped in the glow of the computer monitor, peering through the darkness in the direction of the door as if, at any moment, it might burst wide open. Hearing nothing more, she went back to her task, plugging one end of a cable into her phone and the other into the high-speed data port on the computer's front panel. She navigated to the folder she was looking for on the network drive and began downloading the files to her phone, straight into an app that ran a scripted routine. The app then hid the encrypted data within the bits and bytes of two preselected photographs.

*Come on, c'mon!*

Another sound in the hallway. This time it wasn't her imagination. She opened her ProtonMail email app and entered a name into the *to* field of a message she had drafted beforehand. She quickly attached the two photos, then proofread the prewritten note she hoped her old friend would understand just as the door erupted and two burly men rushed through.

She leaped backward as they rushed her, one seizing her by the shoulders. Her phone clattered to the floor in the struggle, still tethered to the workstation, its screen aglow under the desk. She broke free, punching and kicking at her assailants with practiced moves that found their mark. She struck one squarely on the bridge of the nose with the heel of her hand. He cried out in pain, then quickly channeled his discomfort into violence. He threw a punch aimed at her face, but she dodged it, and it caught her instead on the collarbone. She reeled backward over a chair but then leaped up and lunged at him despite her pain, keenly aware that her life was in peril. The second man maneuvered behind her and pinned her arms. The first man joined him, and together they overpowered her, one on either side.

"We are terribly disappointed in you, *tovarish*," he said in brawny, Russian-tainted Queen's English.

*Sergei?* His words both surprised and burned her. *Tovarish.* Comrade.

She struggled to escape their clutches, yanking her arms from their grasp and tearing herself free. As she circled back into a fighting stance, something hard cracked into her skull above her ear and she crashed to the floor, her vision alight with bursting fireworks and flashing lights. In her struggle to remain conscious, she saw her phone glowing under the desk, barely within reach. She hoped the scripted routine had finished downloading and encrypting everything she needed. She brought a finger down on the *send* button as a steel-toed boot connected with her cheekbone.

The phone made a glorious *swoosh* sound just as her world went dark.

# CHAPTER 8

Major General Pavel Tikhonov sat at a grand mahogany desk in a cavernous office inside the Russian Ministry of Defense building at nineteen Znamenka Ulitsa, Moscow. It had been his desk for more than thirty years, but even in the new Russia, what was *his* indeed wasn't. It belonged to *Matushka Rossiya*. And these days, what belonged to Mother Russia and her children invariably found its way into the pockets of President Sergachev and his confederacy of oligarchs who plundered the country's wealth for their own enrichment.

Above the general, a pendulous chandelier dangled at the end of a black chain twelve feet below the ceiling, its ring of low-wattage incandescent bulbs offering up more heat than light on this uncharacteristically steamy morning. The general stared at the glowing ember at the end of a Cohiba Esplendido, nestled on the side of a platter-size crystal ashtray. A wisp of smoke rose from the cigar and floated to the ceiling. He seized the cigar, rose from his chair, and stepped toward the window, feeling only a meager suggestion of cool air on his face as he pushed back a lock of gray hair.

To the southeast, the Bolshoy Kamenny Bridge ferried commuters over the Moskva River from which the

Russian capital gained its name. The murky river flowed east, past the glorious Kremlin less than a kilometer downstream, before joining the Oka River a hundred kilometers southeast of Moscow. The Oka then poured into the Volga River that terminated at the Caspian Sea, but not before coursing past the general's hometown of Volgograd perched on the great river's western shore.

Tikhonov was born when the city still called itself Stalingrad and not long after the battle for which it received the title of Hero City. Its citizens had resisted the onslaught of the advancing German Wehrmacht forces during the Great Patriotic War—a victory gained at the cost of over one and a half million lives. But it was Stalingrad no more, despite its citizens' wishes, as the politburo under Premier Nikita Khrushchev had carried out a campaign to de-Stalinize the motherland and rid the country of any cult of personality. So, despite the sacrifices of Tikhonov's family and the pleading of the people of the city, the central government of the formerly great Union of Soviet Socialist Republics stripped them of the eponymous link to their heroic achievement and in 1961 renamed the city Volgograd.

Now it was he who would reshape Russia's destiny and thrust the motherland into its rightful role of geopolitical supremacy over a world crippled by impotent alliances. His Directorate 13, a direct-action element of the country's foreign military intelligence agency, the GRU, was leading the charge to restore Russia's global superiority. The agency had in recent times taken a backseat to Russia's Foreign Intelligence Service, the SVR, and her Federal Security Service, the FSB.

But no more. Directorate 13 would change that.

Tikhonov moved to a side table next to the window and poured himself two fingers of Rémy Martin XO. He gently swirled the cognac as he raised it to his nose, breathing in the smooth notes of vanilla, citrus, and ground cinnamon. Before he could take a sip, there was a knock at his office door.

"*Zakhodi!*" he called. *Come in!*

Tikhonov's assistant escorted an officer in. The man stopped at the threshold and proffered a crisp salute. The general met him halfway across the floor.

"*Dobroye utro, Generál-mayór,*" said the man. *Good morning, Major General.*

"*Privet,* Viktor." *Hello.* "So good to see you again," he said, switching to English. General Tikhonov gave his visitor a warm embrace, kissing him on both cheeks.

Standing six-two, Colonel Viktor Gerasimov cut a dashing figure in his Army uniform. It was adorned with a chestful of military honors and decorations, including a gold star suspended beneath a tricolored ribbon, the Hero of the Russian Federation medal, pinned to his uniform by President Dmitry Sergachev personally.

Blond-haired, blue-eyed, and densely muscled, Gerasimov was a graduate of the Military Diplomatic Academy, better known as the GRU Conservatory, in Moscow. A veteran of the 14th Spetsnaz Brigade, he had survived countless military campaigns and battles, most alongside his Special Forces unit in Chechnya and other former Soviet republics. His covert assignments had included tours in Crimea and the Donetsk region to help soften Ukrainian defenses and civil resolve ahead of the insertion of Russian forces. He had served in Syria and many other locales as well.

Like any Tier One operator, Gerasimov carried himself with an air of confidence. Some might even say arrogance. Though barely older than Tikhonov's desk, the colonel was the general's right-hand man. Where Tikhonov was *objectives,* Gerasimov was *strategy* and *tactics.* He was the brilliant architect behind every operation devised by his boss and carried out by Directorate 13, the elite clandestine operations cell formed out of GRU Unit 29155 that was headed by General Tikhonov. Tikhonov officially reported to the Chief of the General Staff of the Russian Armed Forces. Unofficially, President Sergachev himself sanctioned all of Directorate 13's missions.

Except this one.

"Welcome home, Viktor!" said the general. "I trust your travels were fruitful?"

"Thank you, Comrade General. It was a most successful journey."

Tikhonov indicated toward a leather sofa against the wall.

"Please, sit." He walked over to the side table and picked up the decanter of cognac. "Rémy?" he asked. He saw Colonel Gerasimov hesitate. "Or would you prefer bourbon?"

Gerasimov smiled.

"Indeed," the general said. "Ice?"

Gerasimov waved off the suggestion, and the general poured him two fingers, neat, into a crystal tumbler like his own. He carried it to the sofa and handed it to Gerasimov, who raised it to his nose.

"Old Forester?"

"Yes, my friend. You have an excellent nose. To your health!"

"Cheers," Gerasimov replied before taking a gulp of his drink.

The general took a more modest sip of his Rémy, then lowered himself into an antique leather wingback chair next to the sofa and studied his young colleague.

"The results from the mission so far have been excellent," he said. "Perhaps a few more casualties than we had expected, but still, the outcome has been most impressive."

"Men like those come cheaply," said Gerasimov of

the debacle in the Netherlands. "A little greed mixed with the right ideology makes for motivated associates—*friendly pirates,* I believe I once heard you call them."

"Yes, but I prefer Stalin's expression—*useful idiots.* But results are what matters. And one cannot deny the results in Holland. The authorities will be tripping over themselves for days, if not weeks, trying to solve the puzzle we set out in phase one of the operation at Arnhem. Meanwhile, we move ever forward."

"Agreed," said Gerasimov. "The art of magic lies in misdirection. Our little endeavor should leave Western intelligence baffled and chasing their tails." He downed the rest of his bourbon. "They will believe the threat has been neutralized while again laying the blame on our poor persecuted Arab friends. That will leave us free to focus on phase two."

"Which you are still planning to oversee personally, yes?"

"Absolutely, General. I have a team in Turkey executing the second phase as we speak. I will join them within twenty-four hours. Then I will meet you at the Paris Peace Summit at the Sorbonne to ensure preparations are in place before launching the third and final phase of the mission."

"But you will, of course, leave Paris before—"

"Yes, of course, General. You and I will be gone long before the operation concludes."

"Good," Tikhonov said, satisfied with the chronology. "And what of the complication you are overseeing in London?"

"Resolved."

"Any problems?"

Gerasimov dismissed the thought. "Barely an inconvenience."

The general pursed his lips pensively. "And her

friend, the Interpol agent with whom she was corre
sponding?"

Gerasimov nodded his head. "The American woman
FBI Special Agent Alexandra Martel. No problem. She
is under surveillance. In the meantime, I am returning to
London to wrap up the matter. Then, as I said, on to Tur
key as planned, to ensure our operation runs smoothly
there."

"Excellent," said the general. "I am a simple man,
Viktor. I do not like complications."

# CHAPTER 9

## THE HAGUE, THE NETHERLANDS

Alex shot the last few drops of cold coffee and stood to follow Caleb out of the briefing.

"Hey, wait up," she said, catching him at the door.

"You coming, Shooter?" he said.

"Where?" she asked as he strode to the bank of elevators. "And don't call me that."

"Why not? It fits."

"Not the point."

"Alexandra, can I have a word?" It was Bressard, on her heels.

"Ah, sure," she said, stopping to speak with her boss. She glanced back over her shoulder at Caleb disappearing into an elevator.

"See ya, Shooter," he called, saluting her as the doors closed.

"What's going on, Chief? You said something's up."

"Have you checked your email today?"

"I don't think I have any. My phone's been quiet all day."

Several officers filed past them, some of them giving her high-fives.

"That's the point, Alexandra. Information Technology detected unusual activity on the server and passed it to the cybercrimes unit. Your account was one of the targets."

"Target of what?" She pulled out her phone and scrolled through her email. "Nothing since yesterday morning."

"Isn't that unusual?"

"Very."

"Okay, call IT. Let them sort you out. They'll probably ask you to change your password or something." She stared at him. "What?" he asked.

"This coming from the man who keeps his passwords on a Post-it Note on the bottom of a flower vase on his desk."

"You're not supposed to know that," he said sheepishly, dimples on full display. "Point is, it was not *my* account that was compromised, Alexandra. Call IT and get your account sorted out."

"*Touché.*"

"Also, complete your use-of-force report for the FBI. They're crawling all over me. And Inspector Van Dijk and I need your after-action report."

"Right, Chief."

"And watch out for what's his name," he said, tipping his head toward the elevators. "I don't know what to make of him."

"Caleb? I haven't figured out his angle yet either."

"Well, when you do, let me in on the secret."

\* \* \*

INTERPOL'S NATIONAL CENTRAL BUREAU,
THE HAGUE, THE NETHERLANDS

Alex sat in the middle of the bullpen in her nineteenth-floor office in The Hague's Willemspark district. Today she was one of only a handful of special agents at their desks at Interpol's National Central Bureau in the

Netherlands. Her mobile phone lay in front of her. With a mixture of awe and terror, she watched as an information systems security analyst working from Interpol headquarters in Lyon, France, navigated through its contents remotely like some digital poltergeist floating through the Apple ether.

"Your phone is clean now, but someone hacked your corporate email," he reported over the speaker of her landline.

"Thanks, Jonathan. Random infection or targeted?" she asked. If Interpol's servers were breached, she wondered if it was a global issue or if somebody was explicitly looking for something from her.

"Can't tell," said the disembodied voice. Before being scooped up by Interpol, Jonathan Burgess had been a twenty-something computer wizard working for Canada's national cryptologic and foreign signals intelligence agency, the Communications Security Establishment. "Yours wasn't the only account hacked, but you're the only one with a top secret security clearance."

Alex didn't much believe in coincidences. If Interpol's exquisite and considerable network security had been penetrated and her email hacked, then it stood to reason that someone had explicitly targeted her. Everything else was a red herring.

"Okay, that should do it," he said. She watched as the phone went dark and then rebooted, the bitten-apple logo glowing iridescent on the screen. "I'm out of your phone now," he reported.

"How would I know?"

"You wouldn't. I sent you a link to reset your network and email passwords. If anything else goes wrong, power it off and back on again—"

"That's helpful."

"—and call us back. Your email should restore over

the next few minutes, but it looks like some messages might have been permanently wiped or redirected. We're still working on that. I've set up a spider to backtrack any intrusions into your phone. If we're lucky and we find anything, we'll let you know, and we'll flag anything problematic."

"Like Nigerian-prince oil schemes?"

"Like stolen classified documents."

"Oh, like that. Okay, thanks, Jonathan."

She hung up and noticed a voicemail notification flash on her mobile.

*That's odd. Someone must have called while my phone was restarting.*

Bressard breezed past her desk, and she detected the faint smell of cigarettes on his otherwise immaculate suit.

"I thought you quit," she called as he stepped into his glass-walled corner office.

"I did," he replied, swinging the door closed.

She punched a button and dialed into her voicemail.

"Hi, Alex." The voice on the recording bore a thick Scottish accent. "You don't know me. My name is Cara. I guess you know Krysten. Well, sure, you must. I found your name and phone number written on the back of a wee photo in her apartment in London. It looks like it was taken a few years ago, I would say. You're both standing in front of the Eiffel Tower. I don't know if she has any family or if you know who I should call. Look, something's happened to Krysten. Could you please ring me back on this number? Right, sorry to be a bother. Hope to hear from you. Bye-eee, bye, bye."

*Krysten.*

She played the message again.

They had met at the annual International Security Symposium attached to the Paris Peace Summit. The conference had been held at the newly expanded

Sorbonne University International Conference Center, located in the heart of the Latin Quarter in the fifth arrondissement of Paris. Alex was still with ISA at the time. In a sea of testosterone, the two women had buoyed each other with their unlikely circumstances. Both were at the pinnacle of their respective roles in their country's national security apparatus. Each had carved out an unparalleled reputation in the profession of arms. In a field of a thousand individuals at the summit, Alex and Krysten comprised an exclusive sorority of two.

Krysten was a former member of Britain's elite Special Reconnaissance Regiment. Its specialty was conducting surveillance operations focused mainly on counterterrorism activities. The regiment was a virtual copy of Intelligence Support Activity. And, like Alex, Krysten was a veteran of numerous covert missions in Afghanistan and other regions ravaged by war. Her current domain—or at least what it had been when they were together in Paris—was agent recruitment for MI5, the United Kingdom's internal Security Service. She had spent considerable time abroad eliciting intel on plots against the homeland. Last Alex had heard, Krysten was working at Thames House—the headquarters of MI5—running agents and mentoring younger intelligence officers.

Alex scrolled through photos in her album of favorites on her phone and found the one Cara was talking about. There was Krysten, hair billowing in the breeze, Alex's cheek pressed against hers. She zoomed in on the image and was pulled back into the joy of that moment.

# CHAPTER 10

Alex and Krysten came to the edge of the Jardins du Trocadéro in Paris's sixteenth arrondissement, Krysten still clutching the bottle of Sancerre they had been sharing on their walk along the banks of the Seine. The gardens, created for the International Exposition in 1937, were spectacular.

Standing next to the fountains with their backs to the river, the women hammed it up cheek to cheek for a selfie on Krysten's phone as the evening breeze danced around them, entangling their hair like kite ribbons in the wind. Their laughter made the shot almost impossible. The Eiffel Tower gyrated in frame behind them on the opposite bank of the Seine, the sky beyond streaked with hues of pink and orange as sunset fell around them. Ten attempts at a selfie later, one succeeded.

They checked the photo. Their laughter said it all—life was good, and friendship between them came easy. They were two formidable young women with the world by the tail.

"I still can't believe I'm here," marveled

Krysten, her accent a hybrid of London English and something Alex couldn't quite place. She looked across to the left bank of the river at the iconic symbol of the City of Light. "And can you believe we're looking at the Eiffel Tower? It's magical," she said, topping up their clear plastic cups with wine.

This was Alex's first visit to Paris as well, a city she had always dreamed of seeing in person. She had listened to and fed off the stories her mother would tell of her visits and exploits here as a young woman before her father had entered the picture.

Looking around, she spied couples strolling through the gardens, posing before magnificent fountains. Artists painted and sketched on easels. Down the hill from where the two women stood, the Seine was a living organism. Tour boats cruised upriver past Notre-Dame Cathedral and back again. Restaurant boats floated nearby, pumping out music, the smell of their French and international cuisine filling the air.

Krysten was right. It *was* magical.

The evening continued with the two women singing eighties rock anthems on a rickshaw ride, the final drops of Sancerre teasing their lips as the flirty cyclist guide called out the sights for them along the way.

"You ladies want to go to a party tonight?" he asked enthusiastically.

"Sure! You know where there's a good one?" Krysten asked, although Alex could tell she was leading him on, or so she hoped.

"Oui, mademoiselle. There is a party starting at midnight in the catacombs, down in one of the underground vaults known only to *les catas*—the cataphiles."

"Cataphiles?" asked Alex. "You're making that up."

"No, mademoiselle. *Les catas* are real. You have heard of the catacombs of Paris, yes? The underground network of tunnels and vaults that contain the neatly stacked bones of six million dead Parisians?"

"Of course we have," lied Krysten.

"Well, only a bit of the tunnels—one and a half kilometers—is open to the public. But hundreds of kilometers of the ancient quarries and ossuaries exist and are forbidden to go in. The catacombs reach everywhere in Paris."

"And they hold parties down there at night?"

"Yes, the people known as *les catas* are addicts of the catacombs."

"Drug addicts in the catacombs?" asked Krysten.

He laughed. "Not drug addicts, catacombs addicts—those who love and explore the catacombs, which is not legal. They know where all the sealed-off entrances are; the places where no one is permitted to go. They host the best parties imaginable."

Urban myth or reality, Alex wasn't sure.

"Sounds enchanting."

"So, you will go?" he asked.

"No, but we'll keep it in mind for next time."

The young man had been disappointed when they rejected his invitation and disembarked at Place Charles de Gaulle, the road that encircled the Arc de Triomphe. The two women opted instead to stroll arm in arm along the Champs-Élysées on the warm spring night.

Soon they found themselves sipping Aperol spritzes on the patio of Le Deauville, next to the famous luxury macaron bakeshop, Ladurée. A little spearmint-green-colored box was open between them.

"It's so enchanting!" said Krysten, all sparkly-eyed and staring up at the sign above the shop. "I always wanted to come here," she said, biting into a strawberry-candy macaron and moaning as the airy, sweet meringue-like confection melted on her tongue.

Ferraris, Lamborghinis, and McLarens lined the avenue, their testosterone-fueled drivers strutting like peacocks past the patio now and then, vying for the ladies' attention, utterly oblivious to how little they impressed these uber-accomplished women.

"Should we tell them about the party in the catacombs?" joked Krysten.

The conversation between them turned inescapably to men. Krysten spoke of a string of lovers, none serious enough to warrant the effort of monogamy. But Alex's heart was already possessed by her Delta Force fiancé, Kyle, who was currently on deployment. She knew it would be days before she heard from him again, but imagined what it would be like if he were here with her. He'd appreciate the beauty of Paris, too, though maybe not the spritzes.

Music blared from one of the supercars. "Come on," said Krysten. She rose out of her chair and grabbed Alex's hand, pulling her up between the tables. "Let's dance!"

The two women danced and drank the night away, then strolled back to their hotel for a nightcap before drifting off to sleep in Krysten's room. Not surprisingly, they were late for the plenary session the following morning.

\* \* \*

Paris seemed like a lifetime ago, and even though work had taken her back there several times, none of those subsequent trips had been with either Kyle or Krysten. The City of Light was beautiful, but she hoped that one day it would be magical again, too.

Alex checked her phone's recent call log and tapped to return the missed call.

"Hello?" came a Scottish-accented voice on the other end.

"Cara?"

"Yes, hi, it's me. Thanks for ringing me back."

"You said something happened to Krysten. What's going on?"

"Alexandra, I don't know how close you were to Krysten—"

*Were,* thought Alex. "What's happened, Cara?"

"I'm so sorry to be the one to tell you this, but . . ." There was hesitation, as if she were searching for the right words.

"Cara, just tell me."

"Look, I'm so sorry, but Krysten is dead."

She took in the words. Death was shocking to most people but, ordinarily, not to her. She had delivered the news, or delivered the means, many times. She wore her own scars—both inside and out—from the times she had cheated death while others around her had not. Enemies had died. Fellow soldiers had died. Her husband had died. Her mother had died. Everyone but her, it seemed, had *died*.

"How did it happen?"

"A drunk driver killed her. Or at least that's what the police are saying."

"But you don't believe them?"

"They said she was walking home. But the police found her car in the car park at her work."

Alex wondered if Cara knew Krysten was with the United Kingdom's domestic counterintelligence and security agency, MI5. "Where did she work?" she asked, probing.

"She was with a tech company here in London."

That answered that. Cara didn't know Krysten was with MI5. "Maybe she had car trouble."

"It was dark. If she needed a ride, she would have called me. Or a taxi. We live in the same building. She wouldn't have walked along a dark road alone. Look, I don't know what else to do. I thought you were her friend and might be able to help. Your voicemail greeting said you're with Interpol. Isn't that the police agency? Are you an investigator?"

"I am."

"Can you help me or do you know anybody else I can call?"

Alex did not and said so. She and Krysten had been close briefly. They'd kept in touch for a few years, exchanging cards at Christmas, that sort of thing. And they sent text messages and emails occasionally to check in, talking about work or men they had met. Nothing of substance. Certainly nothing about Krysten's family. But even that banter had faded away, as casual friendships do. Theirs was like any long-distance relationship, and she understood better than most what they could be like.

"I'm sorry. We were friends," she said feebly. "But we've been out of touch for a long time."

"I don't know what else to do." Her voice was shaky

through the sniffles. "I'm sorry to have bothered you."
*Click.*

*What the . . . ?* Cara had hung up on her. She stared
at her phone for a moment, trying to decide whether to
call her back.

Before she could make up her mind, Bressard was
standing beside her desk.

"I need your after-action report by this afternoon.
Something wrong with your phone?"

"What?"

"You're staring at it like it just insulted you."

"No, it's fine. Actually, it's not. I just had a strange
phone call." Bressard's eyebrow went up. "A friend from
my past just died."

"That's terrible," he said. "I'm sorry, Alexandra."

"It's weird. The story sounds a little hinky."

"How so?"

"Krysten was an intelligence officer with MI5, but
something about what this friend of hers is telling me
sounds off."

"What are you planning to do?" he asked guardedly.

"Nothing, I guess."

Bressard gave her a skeptical look as if he didn't believe she was capable of doing nothing. Ever.

"No, really, I think it's fine. The woman who called
me will probably find someone else to notify. She must
have had family somewhere. And I'm sure MI5 will step
in anyway."

"Okay," he said, turning to walk away. "After-action
report."

"Yes, Chief."

As she placed her phone down on the desk, it rang.
She picked up.

"Sorry for hanging up on you," Cara said. "Look, I
feel quite lost here."

"I'm an investigator, I ask questions. It's what we do."

"I know. Krysten and I were friends. That she died is bad enough, but something about all this doesn't add up." She paused, and Alex picked up the question that hung in the air.

It's not that Alex didn't *want* to help; she simply didn't know what she could do. Besides, surely the local authorities and MI5 were fielding resources to look into anything that might be amiss.

"I'm in the middle of a big case, Cara. I might not be able to get away—"

"It's no bother. I'll find someone else. But I thought the two of you might have been closer."

"That's not fair—"

"Fair?" Cara interrupted. "Bollocks to *fair*. Like you said, you're an investigator. Can't you . . . investigate?"

"Listen, Cara . . ." She trailed off, collecting her thoughts. She recalled the image of her and Krysten in happier times against the backdrop of the Eiffel Tower in one of the world's greatest cities. "Give me some time," she said. "I'll get back to you soon."

"Right," Cara said. "I don't believe you." *Click.*

Cara had hung up on her . . . again. A few minutes later, Alex stood outside Bressard's corner office. His back faced her through the glass walls as he spoke on a video call. The image of Secretary General Clicquot, the head of Interpol, loomed large from a monitor on the wall in front of him.

"Madame Clicquot, I will have a full report for you within twenty-four hours," she heard Bressard say.

"See that you do, Chief Inspector," she replied, a distinct Parisian accent punctuating her speech. "And try to have Special Agent Martel refrain from killing anyone else for a few days, could you? Interpol is not an FBI SWAT team. We are here to *support* the police of member countries, not to run their operations for them with American-style cowboy shenanigans."

"Yes, Madam Secretary."

Alex watched Bressard bob his head up and down in response. The video screen went blank as Madame Clicquot hung up. He looked up from his desk and noticed her hovering outside his office.

He rose from his chair and opened the door, an unlit cigarette dangling from his lips, then stepped aside to let her pass. He moved behind his desk and sat, twisting the cigarette.

"You going to light that?"

He tucked it away into the top drawer.

"I gather you heard the secretary general's comments?" he asked.

"I did. I'll see what I can do."

"Not funny, Alexandra. Look, I know what transpired in Arnhem wasn't your fault—"

"Not my fault? Chief, it's not like I had a choice."

"That's not what I meant. Frankly, I want to put you in for a commendation. You acted boldly and decisively, you saved the lives of many of your colleagues, and you kept the nuclear material from disappearing into the hands of who knows who."

"I don't need a medal for doing my job."

"Good, because I couldn't do it even if I wanted to. Don't worry about the secretary general," he said, swiping his hand dismissively toward the video monitor. "She's a senior administrator in a very political organization. She has bigger fish to fry."

"Great pep talk, boss."

"She'll cool down. Now, what can I do for you?"

"I need some time off."

"Oh? I'm not sure I like where this is going."

"I need a couple of days in London to help this woman, Cara, wrap things up regarding my friend Krysten's death."

"And exactly what am I to tell Van Dijk?" he asked. "He still needs your after-action report."

"Tell him I'll finish it as soon as I can."

She didn't mention she'd be doing a little digging of her own.

# CHAPTER 11

The last-minute decision to fly to London didn't give Alex much time. She raced to her apartment, changed into something casual and versatile, and grabbed her go-bag, a cedar-green Osprey backpack. Then she called an Uber for the forty-minute ride to Amsterdam Airport Schiphol, where the gate agent hurried her onto the jetway. She was the last to board the KLM Cityhopper flight.

The twin-engine Embraer 190 landed at London City Airport an hour and eleven minutes later. Alex descended the staircase from the plane and made her way into the terminal through passport control, then outside to the row of black taxis waiting for fares.

"Where to, luv?" The driver spoke with a heavy cockney accent, full-on East End of London.

She tossed her pack into the hackney cab and hopped in. "The Grind on Old Street," she said, recalling Cara's text.

"Right. The Shoreditch Grind."

As they drove along, Alex checked her phone. She had seven new emails in her Interpol inbox, but nothing suspicious or even remotely interesting. She couldn't figure out why anyone would hack her phone specifically.

*What were they after?*

She texted Chief Bressard to let him know she had arrived.

MB: How's London?
AM: Gray and chilly
MB: I need your after-action report ASAP.
AM: I know. On it, boss

The road ahead curved seemingly forever as they entered a tunnel. After a minute and a half, they were still in it, going thirty miles an hour.

*Are we ever coming out again?*

"Where are we?" she asked her driver.

"Limehouse Link Tunnel, luv."

After another minute and a sweeping *S* curve later, they reemerged into daylight. The cabby was glancing behind them in the mirror, his eyes flicking back and forth.

"Something wrong?"

"No, everything's brilliant."

They made a right on Butcher Row at St. James Garden. Coming out of the turn, his eyes flicked back to his rearview.

"Don't bullshit me—" Both the point-of-sale terminal and the license card behind the driver's seat listed his name. "—Gareth. What do you see back there?"

"I think I've seen too many James Bond movies," he said. "Either that or someone is following you."

She raised her phone and turned on the camera, switching to selfie mode to see over her shoulder what he saw in his mirror.

"How long has that Beemer been behind us?" she asked, spotting the black BMW sedan in their lane two cars back, peeking out around the car immediately behind them. She noted the M5-series badge on the blacked-out grille.

"Since we left the airport. And he has a friend."

That's when she saw the second BMW, a black X5 SUV. It trailed the sedan by two car lengths and stuck to the inside lane.

"You in some trouble, luv?"

"Depends who you ask."

"Want me to try to shake 'em?"

Alex watched the Beemers on her phone while he turned the taxi left at the White Swan onto Commercial Road. The tail followed, which wasn't a complete surprise since the natural flow of traffic at midday was to turn toward the center of London, not away from it.

"Miss, should I lose 'em?" he asked again.

"Not yet. Let's see what they do."

The road narrowed with cars parked along both curbs. Gareth passed a red double-decker bus that had stopped to pick up passengers. It pulled out behind them as they passed, and for a few seconds it formed a barrier between them and their tail. But the sedan darted out and around it during a gap in oncoming traffic.

*Amateurs.* That move eliminated any chance of coincidence and confirmed her cabby's assumption.

*What's the game here?* She had been in these situations before as both tailer and tailee. Counterterrorism was her specific arena, and both surveillance and countersurveillance tradecraft had been drilled into her at ISA and the FBI. For now, her options were limited. They were driving through Whitechapel along a busy road. Unlike in the movies, it wasn't probable that her driver could outmaneuver two tail vehicles in close quarters through narrow streets and heavy traffic without killing someone—her included.

Suddenly, the taxi banged a right across oncoming traffic as a double-decker bus approached. The cabby

hit the gas and accelerated up Cavell Street past a Holi-
day Inn.

*So much for the wait-and-see approach.*

"Hold on!" he said.

As the cab straightened out, Alex reached for the
grab handle and did as she was told.

"You know that any chance they didn't know we
were on to them is ruined now, right?" she said.

"Ah, blimey, that ship has sailed, luv."

Another block east, and he put the front-engine, rear-
wheel-drive taxi into a Tokyo drift around a left-hand
turn onto Varden Street, the X5 having replaced the sedan on their tail. He deftly avoided other cars, passing
in the oncoming lane of traffic whenever it was clear.

"I'm going to get you near Old Street, and you can
hoof it from there. Or would you prefer I drop you at
Scotland Yard for your safety?"

New Scotland Yard was one of several names for
the London Metropolitan Police Service and their headquarters building. She wasn't prepared quite yet to deal
with the local constabulary, not having a clue what was
going on.

"No, the Grind," she said.

"Thought you'd say that."

He hung a quick right through a residential block.
The X5 had fallen back, and the M5 Competition was
nowhere to be seen. As they approached the next intersection, the sedan suddenly reappeared, bearing down
on them at high speed from the right. Gareth hit the
brakes and swerved at the last minute, the sedan missing them by inches and continuing past.

"Shit!" said Alex.

"*Shite!*" said Gareth. He dodged into an alleyway,
avoiding pedestrians and garbage bins, then plunged
back out onto Commercial Street near the Old Spitalfields Market. "Take my number down, miss. I'm going

to drop you up here. You might stand a better chance of losing them on foot."

"What's your number?" she asked as he rounded a corner into another graffiti-lined alley. She watched over her shoulder as the X5 missed the turn they had taken and continued north on the road behind them. She caught a glimpse of a brunette woman in the front passenger seat as it sailed past.

"It's there on my license. Call me if you need a lift. I'll come get you anytime."

She took a picture, then another, trying to steady her phone. "Are you sure? Could be risky."

"Bollocks," he said. "I did two tours in Afghanistan, luv. This here's just a little shits and giggles is all!"

She thumbed through her billfold for a banknote. "We may have met then," she said with a glint in her eye.

He gave her an approving smile over his shoulder. "I knew you were different the second you got into my cab. I recognize the look."

"What look is that, Gareth?"

"Your eyes, miss."

"My eyes?"

"Yes, miss. I'd know a combat veteran anywhere. Man or woman, we're all the same. Your eyes are sharp and focused, always ready for something." She let him carry on. "I can tell you've seen real action, miss. You're alert, like a jungle cat, if you don't mind my saying. You have the eyes of a warrior, miss, not just an everyday soldier."

*Warrior eyes. Apropos.*

"Thank you. You're not wrong. I'm sorry, but I didn't have time to get any pound notes," she said, fishing out a couple of blue twenty-euro notes.

"Forget it. It's on the house."

"Baloney. Here." She dropped the bills onto the front

seat next to him. "Consider it a thank-you gesture from a fellow warrior."

"Well, if you insist. The Mrs. *does* like Chunnel trips to France." He scooped the notes into a shirt pocket and brought the taxi to a stop in the alley behind a row of Indian restaurants. "Go through that door," he said, pointing ahead on the left. "Stroll right through the building to the market on the other side. Walk along to your right, then follow the side streets up to Old Street. That's where you'll find the Shoreditch Grind."

She swung her door open and stepped out. "This was fun," she said, sincerely.

She dug her holstered Glock out of her backpack and threaded it onto her belt under her coat as Gareth watched. No need for a press check. She lived by the motto *A gun with an empty chamber is nothing more than a clumsy hammer.*

"Nice *chunk*," he said. He peeled away down the alley as she dodged into the greasy kitchen. It filled her senses with dishes that smelled of cardamom and curry.

Confused voices raised around her, and she smiled back at the cooks who no doubt wondered what this woman was doing in their kitchen. Steam rose off a chicken tikka masala being plated—it was one of her favorite dishes. She inhaled deeply, and the fragrances carried her back to another place and time. She reached the front door and emerged into an outdoor bazaar half a block from the Spitalfields Market. The stalls were wooden, some covered with burlap for shade. They were filled with produce in one section and household goods in another. The area was packed with shoppers, and she paused on the step of the restaurant's entrance to reconnoiter the area. She saw families shopping, mothers with children moving up and down the aisles, bartering for fruit and vegetables. Nearby, a young girl carried a basket of oranges. As Alex gazed at her their eyes met, and Alex was transported back in time to a small town northeast of Baghdad years ago.

\*\*\*

### JALAWLA, DIYALA PROVINCE, IRAQ

The howl of an incoming 82mm mortar round tore through the air. Alex's overwatch position shook from the explosion immediately below her rooftop perch. She buried her face in her arm as shrapnel and dirt fell around them.

"Alex, we have to move!" her spotter shouted, low-crawling toward her.

Before the torrent of debris had even ceased raining down on them, she raised her M24 sniper rifle again to sight in her next target 220 meters away. She wiped grit from her face and blinked through fresh blood that stung her eyes.

She was here with an ISA team supporting intel operations and had teamed up with a squadron of Delta Force operators for this mission. It should have been simple, but Daesh fighters had streamed into the market that the Tier One element was working to clear.

"Two tangos, west side," she called calmly into her radio headset.

"I see them." Sergeant First Class Kyle Ward's voice came across crystal clear through her earbuds.

She watched through her scope as he turned to his right to engage the enemy. The muted pops from his carbine arrived at her ears in slightly under a second, making it seem like she was watching an out-of-sync video. A medic pinned down by gunfire was tending to a fallen squad member nearby.

The howl of another mortar split the air, and the shell exploded on the rooftop of the building behind them.

"Alex!" her spotter called. "They've got us dialed in. We have to bug out. Now!"

She aimed down a wide dirt avenue, focusing on the man shooting at the squad medic. The shooter broke cover, turning toward the wounded operator lying on the ground. She dropped him with a round to the chest, racked the bolt on her rifle, and prepared for a follow-up shot. But none was needed.

Just then, another tango emerged from the south end of the market stalls and moved toward the squad leader.

*Focus on the reticle,* she recited to herself.

Alex sighted him in and squeezed off a round, then sent a second for good measure. The man fell, his AK spraying bullets into the air as villagers hid beneath the stalls.

She continued to gaze through her scope, ready to engage more tangos. Twenty meters behind the fallen gunman stood a young girl, twelve or thirteen years old. She wore a loosely fitted red scarf around her head that accentuated her impossibly green eyes. Alex hadn't noticed her there before the shot. She had been blocked from view by the charging insurgent but was now in plain sight as he fell out of the way. Alex saw blood spread over the front of her pale-blue dress. One of her bullets had gone clean through her target and caught the little girl in the upper chest.

The girl dropped to her knees, then fell to the

ground. Alex watched through her scope as the girl's breathing became shallow, then stopped. Her eyes met Alex's across the distance as she took her last breath, the oranges she'd been carrying glowing brightly in the midday sun, rolling away in the dirt.

"Cease fire! Alex, cease fire!" called Sergeant First Class Ward.

But Alex had already stopped shooting.

# CHAPTER 12

Sergeant First Class Kyle Ward's voice in her head echoed through her soul, even here in the present, burning her chest until she raised a fist to rub away the painful memory. She became aware of someone jostling her from behind.

"I said, excuse me, miss. You're blocking the door. Would you mind getting out of the way, please?" A young woman carrying takeout lunches in a canvas bag stood behind her, trying to exit the shop.

"What?" The intrusive memory had left her breathless, her heart racing. She had broken out in a cold sweat that coated her skin and raised goosebumps on her arms, despite the warm breeze floating through the market. "Sorry," she said, stepping to the side.

The memory came to her infrequently, often triggered by an innocuous smell, sound, sight—like chicken tikka masala or oranges. But when it did, it felt like she was braced against an onrushing tsunami, draining her of energy. Her visual field narrowed, and the intrusive sights, smells, and sounds left her wishing she could curl up in a ball and disappear. But that hadn't been an option on that day or any day since. Frailty wasn't a luxury she could afford, and while others had worked hard to convince her that it wasn't a weakness to suffer the effects of a mental injury, that's not how she saw it. Nor did others in the military communities she had worked in, no matter how much they publicly professed otherwise.

*A warrior who choked up from a bad memory was a liability,* or so she believed others thought. Alex was no one's PTSD poster child. The only person who had understood this about her was her late husband, Kyle. He had been the Delta Force squad leader on the mission with her that day. And years before that, he had been the one who had coached her into picking up a sniper rifle in combat for the first time. Under the circumstances, there had been no other choice.

She took a deep breath and forced the air out through pursed lips, then wiped the sweat from her forehead with the sleeve of her coat. She plunged in toward the market stalls, looking around to see if anyone was still following her. She wondered if her pursuers had dismounted and were nearby on foot.

She scanned all around but noticed no one suspicious. Moving through the market in a westerly direction, she pulled out her iPhone and searched for the Shoreditch Grind. Her navigation app said she was eighteen minutes away on foot. She figured she could easily halve that, although she had to be careful—it would be easy for whoever might be hunting her to pick out a runner over someone walking in a crowd.

She tried not to stay on any street for too long, preferring a zigzag pattern to a straight line. She kept casting her eyes around her surroundings. She stuck close to couples or groups for short bursts so that a glance from someone searching for a person walking solo might overlook her entirely.

Why was she being followed, and by whom? Was it related to the theft of the special nuclear material in the Netherlands? After all, her face had been all over the news. Or was it linked to the conversation with Cara about Krysten? She wanted to speak to Cara in person. And to do that, she had to make it to the coffee shop.

Pedestrian traffic was light. She veered right at Holywell Row, knowing it would take her off the main thoroughfare. A blue hackney cab drove past, followed by a black BMW sedan. As it went by, she turned toward a shop window. In its reflection, she counted three men in the small sedan. The man in the backseat was studying her a little too carefully.

As she turned back up the street, the BMW came to a stop. At the sound of its tires chirping, she broke into a run. Looking over her shoulder, she saw the man in the back get out to run after her. The BMW's reverse lights came on, and the car hurtled toward her. She jumped out of the way as it careened into a stack of garbage and recycling bins. She took off at a full sprint. The man from the back of the Beemer was thirty feet behind her. She checked his position and ran out into the street in front of a motorcyclist who honked and yelled obscenities as she went past. The bike ran straight into the man following her, but he pirouetted off the handlebars and kept running after her.

Ahead was a choice—hook right and follow the road around in more or less the direction from which she had come, or run straight into the eight-foot-tall steel picket fence. The gate through was closed, but she could see between the slats that there was a residential complex on the other side. Not knowing where the BMW with the other two men had gone, she made her decision.

A street sweeper and his cart rested against the fence,

which jutted upward from eighteen inches of brickwork. She ran straight at the man, apologizing as she stepped onto the low brick wall, leaped onto the top of his garbage cart, and shimmied the rest of the way over to the other side, carefully avoiding the three-pronged pickets on top of each post. When her feet touched the ground, she turned to face her pursuer, visible between the galvanized steel posts.

The man was young, tall, and fit, dressed in black jeans and a brown leather jacket. Their eyes met, and for a moment, he seemed to be contemplating whether to chase her over the spike-topped fence. He instead went for option B and drew a semiauto from under his jacket. She suddenly found herself face to face with the business end of what she was sure was a GSh-18, a striker-fired polymer-framed Russian pistol designed to shoot armor-piercing bullets.

The man assumed a tripod stance, and Alex dove behind a metal dumpster at the side of the alley as the sound of gunshots pierced the silence of her surroundings. Daylight shone through two smoking through-and-through holes in the side of the garbage dumpster.

She stared at the holes.

*Who is this guy?*

She drew her Glock but stayed crouched behind the bin. Under the circumstances, the dumpster did not provide adequate cover, but it still offered marginal concealment.

Two more high-velocity AP rounds pierced the dumpster.

*And why the hell is he shooting at me?*

One lucky shot and she'd be dead. Even if she'd been wearing a ballistic vest, unless it were outfitted with ceramic plates, the rounds he was firing would go through it like butter. Her only way out of this shooting alley was twenty feet behind her. She had to move.

She peered around the corner of the dumpster and fired three shots at her assailant. Sparks flew off the fence, and the man bolted for cover. She ran to the gap behind her and dodged around the corner onto the street as more gunshots rang out.

As far as she knew, only Russian Spetsnaz units were equipped like that. And the best of those still belonged to Russian military intelligence, the GRU.

She hid in an alcove, using the cover of the brick wall to look down the road. There was no sign of her pursuer. The BMWs were nowhere in sight either. Mark Street Gardens lay across the street from her position. It was a small park that appeared to offer both concealment and a path out of the immediate area through a gated exit on the far side. She sprinted across the street, vaulted over the fence along the sidewalk, and pressed her back up against a tree.

*But why would the GRU be chasing me through London?*

She glanced over her shoulder. Still nothing. She checked the map on her phone. As near as she could figure, her rendezvous spot was four hundred meters away. She weighed her options, which admittedly looked a little bleak at this point.

*Breathe.* This was no time for *cerebral fibrillation,* aka panic. The way to win in any physical confrontation was to stay focused and in control, which meant control over her breathing as well as her mental state. Achieving the former would lead to the latter.

*Don't hold your breath. Breathe!*

She bolted for an opening through the gate out of the park to the west. Two gunshots rang out behind her. She spun to face the shooter but couldn't get a shot away as he ran behind a group of people running toward her to escape his gunfire. She took cover behind the brick structure of the gate and reacquired her target. Tires skidded to a stop behind her, and she turned to face a man leaping from the left side of a BMW sedan. He leveled a pistol at her, but she dropped him with two shots center mass before he could fire a shot. She took aim at the driver, who was now speeding straight at her. She fired four shots through the windshield as she dove out of the way. While she was mid-flight, the M5 struck her leg before hitting the wall beside her. The driver slumped over the wheel, his lifeless eyes staring straight through her.

Her gun lay six feet away, loosed from her grasp by her impact with the car and the ground. From flat on her back, she turned her head to see her pursuer advancing, holding his GSh-18 extended, wearing a self-satisfied grin. She rolled to her left to retrieve her Glock. As she reached for it, her pursuer fired, the bullet striking the pavement between her hand and her gun. He was toying with her, like a cat with a mouse trapped between its paws.

The roll left her prone and vulnerable with her back exposed to the shooter, and she expected that at any second, she would hear the gunshots that would take her life. She flinched at the sound of two shots but felt no pain. Letting out her breath, she turned cautiously to glance over her shoulder.

The man who had been chasing her lay facedown on the ground, a pool of blood swelling around him. Another man stood over him and kicked the gun away from his hand.

"You okay, Shooter?"

Her ears were ringing from the sound of the multiple gunshots and the pounding of the blood in her head.

"Alex, are you hit?" he asked again.

She looked at the man speaking to her.

*Caleb?*

She grabbed her gun off the road and jumped to her feet. A wave of dizziness overtook her, and she dropped to a knee to keep from falling.

"Whoa, easy there." He ran over to steady her.

"Huh?" she said. Her face was stinging. She must have banged it when she hit the ground. She dragged the back of her hand under her eye and looked down at the blood.

"Are you hit?"

"What?" she asked again, feeling woozy.

"Did you get shot?" he said more slowly.

He holstered his sidearm and stooped down beside her. Gripping her by the shoulders, he examined the laceration under her right eye.

"Just a flesh wound," he said, smiling.

Then he ran his hands down her ribs and sides, looking down at them after each pass. He moved around behind her and raised her jacket and shirt.

"Hey!" she protested.

"Take it easy," he said. "I'm doing a gross-bleed check—looking for holes, checking for hemorrhaging."

Satisfied she hadn't been shot, he stood and hoisted her up by the elbows, keeping a tight grip on her. She finally regained her bearings and focused on him, then indicated toward the dead man who had been chasing her.

"I thought you weren't armed," she said, nodding to where he had tucked his SIG Sauer into the IWB holster under his shirt.

"Please, I'm a Republican."

"I didn't see you with a gun in the helicopter yesterday."

"I try not to telegraph I'm carrying. Besides, you were doing just fine without me."

*Fair point.*

"What are you doing here?" she asked.

"You're welcome," he answered.

"No, seriously. Why are you here?"

"No time to explain. We've got to get you out of here before the police show up."

"What? No, I'm staying put."

"No, Shooter, you're leaving."

"Stop calling me that. I'm not going to flee a crime scene—*my* crime scene."

She looked over her shoulder for her pack, then jogged back to the gate to get it, limping from the pain shooting through her left knee where the bumper of the BMW had struck it. She picked her backpack up off the sidewalk and swapped a fresh mag into her Glock. Then she reached in and pulled out a small package of Kleenex, which Caleb took from her. He tore it open, folded one, and held it under her eye, applying gentle pressure.

"And you won't be *fleeing.* Consider it a tactical retrograde after a defensive engagement," he said. "And I hate to be the bearer of unwelcome news, Little Miss Interpol, but this isn't *your* crime scene."

"Well, whatever you call it, I'm not running from the police. I *am* the police."

"Point of order, Mr. Speaker," he said, raising his hand to address an invisible audience. "The member opposite is, in fact, a federal law enforcement agent of the United States of America. She is not *the police.*" He emphasized that last point with air quotes. "Look, we don't have time to argue." He pointed up the side of the five-story building next to them to a CCTV camera. "We're in London. *England.* You are an FBI special agent and legat, on loan to Interpol, stationed in The Hague, in a country within the European Union. Tell me again, Special Agent Martel, by what authority are you carrying a firearm on British soil and employing lethal force to neutralize three foreign nationals?"

"Under the authority of extraterritorial jurisdiction granted to me as a US federal agent."

"Oh, bullshit. You're making that up."

"I'm not. *They* were trying to kill *me*," she protested.

"Semantics."

"And I only killed two of them. *You* killed the third one."

He took the tissue away and examined his work. "Bleeding's stopped."

"How do you know they're foreign nationals?" she asked.

"The same way you do. Who else carries a GSh-18?"

He was leading her by the elbow to the next street over. A crowd was forming around the bodies and the Beemer. "You're about three blocks from your rendezvous point. Go. I'll sort things out here and meet you."

She pulled her elbow out of his grip. *Meet me? How does he even know where I'm going?*

"Go!" he said.

As much as leaving the scene made her uncomfortable, Caleb had a point. She had been intercepted on foreign soil by—judging by their tactics and firearms—men likely connected to Russian military intelligence. And there were more of them still out there looking for her. Their motives were unclear, but their intent was not. They were trying to kill her.

*What the hell's going on? Russian agents, stolen nuclear material, Krysten—WTF? Is everything connected? Krysten was, or at least had been—back when I first met her—an intelligence officer with MI5. If she was still with them when she was killed, she must have been working undercover, judging by the story her friend told, and now she's dead.*

"Fine," she said, holstering her gun as people dodged out of the way to make a path for her. "But keep your eyes peeled for a black BMW SUV. And you've got a lot of explaining to do later."

# CHAPTER 13

### SHOREDITCH GRIND COFFEE SHOP,
### LONDON, ENGLAND

Leaving Caleb and the chaos at Mark Street Gardens behind, Alex hurried along Old Street. Her knee ached where the car's bumper had connected with it, and a small welt was forming around the laceration beneath her eye. But, otherwise, she was unhurt. And she was alive.

More than ever, it was vital for her to find out what Cara knew. How were today's events connected to the others, if at all? Alex was skilled at finding links between seemingly disjointed events, but perhaps she was trying too hard.

The Shoreditch Grind looked as if a stack of old record albums had fallen from the colorless London sky and landed at the side of the road. It sat round, squat, and black, its entrance beneath a vintage concert hall marquee professing SEX COFFEE & ROCK 'N' ROLL.

She stepped into the packed café with its exposed brick walls and pink neon sign. The aroma of coffee was strong. Halfway to the back, a woman sat alone, glancing at her phone. She was in her late twenties, pretty with a narrow face, high cheekbones, and an edginess to her hair and attire. Alex was sure it was Cara. The woman looked up, and a glint of recognition washed over her. She smiled and stood up as Alex approached.

"You're Alex," she said, her Scottish accent rich and melodic. "You look just like your photo." She flashed her phone toward her, and Alex saw the image of herself and Krysten at the Eiffel Tower. "Oh my God, what happened to your eye?"

"It's nothing. Just a little mishap along the way."

"*Little mishap?* Looks like you had a wee dustup with the Kray twins."

"Who?"

"Doesn't matter. You sure you're alright?"

Alex nodded and they sat. A server came by to take their order. She glanced at the menu and was tempted by the margarita but opted for a chai tea instead.

"You're not eating anything? I'm going to eat. I'm famished." Cara ordered a poached egg and smashed avocado on toasted sourdough bread with smoked salmon and a cup of tea.

"Okay, same," Alex told the waitress, feeling her own hunger pangs kicking in as her body shifted into post-combat rest-and-digest mode. She eyed the front door, not sure how long she might have with Cara before the police showed up.

*Never pass up an opportunity to eat or pee,* she thought. *Better refuel now, while I still have the chance.*

"How well did you know Krysten?" Alex asked once the waitress walked away.

"We weren't besties or anything," Cara said, "but our flats were in the same building, and we went out a few times to grab pizza and drinks after work or on the weekend."

"Did you work together?"

"No, but our offices were very close, in the same business park. We would sometimes find ourselves in the same pub after hours with our work chums. Then we'd stumble into a cab together or ride the Tube home."

"Where did she work?" asked Alex as the waitress dropped off their drinks.

"I thought you knew her." Almost an accusation.

"Humor me."

"Is this a test then? Part of your official police inquiry?" Cara added three packets of sugar and a splash of milk to her tea and stirred. "She was a manager for a tech accelerator company that provided venture capital and other resources to start-ups. She worked with financial data."

Alex couldn't picture the woman she knew having anything to do with computers and data. "How long had she been doing that?"

"I don't know, about a year, I think," Cara said, sipping her tea. "I've known her—knew her—for six months or so, and she was there I think for six months or so before we met, so—"

"Do you know what she did before that?"

"No, should I? Is there something you're not telling me?"

"Like I said, I ask questions."

The waitress returned with the rest of their orders. Alex dug in, slicing through the thin wall of her poached egg and releasing the intensely yellow yolk onto the layer of avocado. She took a bite, and the combination of flavors made her close her eyes. Despite how good it was, she ate fast, just in case.

"Did Krysten ever talk about her job, the people she worked with, specifics about what kind of data she handled? Anything like that?" she asked between bites.

"No, not really. I talked about my work all the time. She was more secretive. In hindsight, I should have asked her more about it, shouldn't I?"

"Secretive? Like she was hiding something?"

"No, like she didn't want to share."

"Was she seeing anyone?"

"No one in particular."

"What does that mean? Anybody stand out?"

"She saw several men. Don't get me wrong, she wasn't a floozie, but you could say she had a few suitors sniffing around. Different blokes would drop by her apartment at odd hours."

Alex made a mental note of that.

*Different blokes. Odd hours. Should I ask if any of them had a Russian accent?*

"Anything at all unusual about her behavior before . . ." She trailed off.

"Before she died? No, but it doesn't add up. Krysten was a survivor."

"What makes you say that?"

As Cara started to reply, Alex could hear sirens getting closer. It was possible they weren't coming here, but she doubted that was so. She sipped her chai tea.

"She was a very assertive woman. She had no problem putting men in their place. I once saw her flip a big hulking drunk man over her shoulder onto a table in the pub after he pinched her arse. She didn't put up with any *shite* from anybody."

*That's Krysten alright.* "Where is she now?"

Cara brought her fork to a halt in midair.

"Sorry," offered Alex. "We don't have much time."

"No, it's alright," Cara replied, scrunching up her nose. "She's in the Westminster Public Mortuary. They'll only release her to next of kin, but there isn't any, at least none that I could locate."

Alex could see blue flashing lights coming along Old Street toward the Grind. Sure enough, two gray BMW SUVs with neon yellow-and-blue checkerboard decals pulled alongside the curb in front of the coffee shop, their lightbars still activated. Yellow circular stickers in the corners of their windshields denoted them as cars assigned to SCO19, the Specialist Firearms Command of the Metropolitan Police Service.

"Cara, I will probably have to go away with those men," she said, nodding toward the door. "But I don't want you to talk to anybody else about any of this just yet."

"What's going on?" she asked.

"Remember that little incident I mentioned when I arrived? Well, it wasn't so little. And I don't know yet if it has anything to do with Krysten's death, so be careful."

Cara gave her a quizzical look but didn't press the matter.

"I'd like to see Krysten's apartment. Can we meet up later?"

Cara watched with fascination as the police officers approached the building.

"I know where she kept a spare key," she said, as four uniformed and heavily armed officers gathered outside. Another man in plain clothes approached, Caleb right on his heels. The two entered the shop, followed by one of the specialist firearms officers carrying a Heckler & Koch G36C tactical rifle. The trio walked directly to the table where Alex and Cara were seated while curious patrons and restaurant staff stared.

Alex took a last bite of her meal and a couple more sips of her chai tea.

"Special Agent Martel, I presume?" said the man, dressed in a tweed sports coat. Before she could answer, he added, "I'm Detective Inspector Kane with Scotland Yard. Please remain seated and hand me your backpack. Slowly."

She swung it toward him off the arm of the chair. Caleb stood silently beside him, his hands tucked casually into his pockets. The man took her pack and rifled through it, pulling out her Interpol identification, FBI shield, and passport.

"Hey—" she protested. Caleb signaled her to go along with it. She sat silently, waiting.

"I'm going to ask you to slowly retrieve your firearm for me and hand it over, Agent Martel."

She was about to protest but again caught a not-so-subtle signal from Caleb.

"May I stand up?" she asked. DI Kane nodded. The firearms officer looked on intently, his rifle in the patrol carry position, as she gingerly fished her Glock from its holster, ejected the magazine, then racked the slide to free a chambered round, which she snatched out of the air. She placed the magazine and the bullet on the table, then locked the slide open and handed it to DI Kane.

"Look, I really—" she began.

"I advise you to remain silent, Ms. Martel," he said, cutting her off. She would have preferred for him to call her by her proper *special agent* title. He was six-one, thin but solid looking. Forties with an experienced face. His hair was dark and wavy with a shock of gray. He handed her Glock over to the uniform, who didn't look happy about having to take a hand off his rifle to take control of the pistol. "I would like you to accompany me to Scotland Yard, please." He paused and sized her up. "It is, of course, not an actual question."

"May I speak?"

"I'd rather you didn't," he said abruptly before turning to Cara. "Who are you?"

Alex jumped in. "She's my friend. We were catching up."

"Ms. Martel—"

"*Special Agent* Martel."

"Right, Special Agent Martel, you appear to be quite skillful at shooting, but the same cannot be said about your ability to follow verbal instructions, including those that might be in your best interest. I would be most pleased if you would allow your *friend* to speak for herself."

Caleb was smiling now, entertained by the sight of her getting dressed down by the Scotland Yard police inspector.

Cara spoke up, her Edinburgh accent thick and meaty as she accentuated her words. "As Alex said, we're old friends. We were enjoying a lovely lunch together until you lot showed up." She turned to Caleb. "Mind you, you can stay for a bite anytime."

Alex gave her a disdainful look.

"What? He's cute!"

Caleb grinned.

*I'm going to puke,* thought Alex.

"Ms. Mar—" began DI Kane. She glared at him. "Special Agent Martel, please follow this officer. He'll show you to my car."

"I'll call you as soon as I'm able," she said to Cara.

Detective Inspector Kane remained inside with Cara. The SCO19 officer escorted Alex and Caleb out to an unmarked Range Rover as a black BMW X5 cruised past them on the square.

# CHAPTER 14

Colonel Viktor Gerasimov arrived at the residence via the secure entrance through the portico. Harrington House, as it was more commonly known, was the former London townhouse of the earls of Harrington on Kensington Palace Gardens, the gated avenue along the west side of Hyde Park. These days, it served as the home to the Russian ambassador and his wife. Conveniently, the unconventional nineteenth-century gothic mansion also housed the operations center for Directorate 13 of the GRU in the basement.

Gerasimov strode to the locked interior door and punched his code into the scramble pad affixed to the wall. A flashing green LED preceded a *click* that signaled the magnetic locks had released. He pulled open the door and descended the stairs into the basement, its fourteen-foot ceilings giving the room a cavernous feel and plenty of space for wires and cables to run. Computer workstations and monitors filled the room from wall to wall. At this moment, they were tapped into the central Scotland Yard surveillance system feeds, an irony not lost on the colonel, who had grown up in an authoritarian state. But it was one without the surveillance capacity and sheer volume of cameras that targeted Britons daily.

"Major Fedotov, status report," Gerasimov barked at a man at the back of the room who was standing behind a large monitoring station.

Major Vasili Fedotov was a computer coding wizard and the operations chief for the section. He spoke plainly. "Three men down, sir. The woman escaped."

Gerasimov wasn't expecting this. *How could this be?* "Their orders were to *surveil and track*. What happened?"

"Yes, sir," replied Fedotov. "The taxi driver began evasive maneuvers and our surveillants attempted to keep up. Then the Interpol agent dismounted the cab to proceed on foot."

"Our surveillants were not to engage. They were to *surveil*. Were they not able to track this woman without blowing their cover?"

"It appears not . . . sir."

"Show me," Gerasimov commanded.

Major Fedotov instructed one of the techs to transfer the live video footage from Mark Street Gardens to a bank of monitors at the front of the room. A police forensics team was on-site, and a group of CSIs was actively processing the area behind a cordon of yellow tape, where the three Russian agents' bodies were still lying in situ. The camera angles and resolution were good enough that Gerasimov could identify his dead operators.

He found the scenario unfathomable. These were three seasoned Spetsnaz operators, two of whom had only recently left their active military units to join his unit.

"The Interpol agent did this on her own?" he asked, incredulously. "How is this possible?"

Spetsnaz were no longer the elite operators they had once been. Everything in Mother Russia, it seemed, was on the decline.

"She did not act alone, Colonel," Fedotov said. "She was able to neutralize two of our operators, but just as Nikulin was going to put a bullet in her head, a man appeared from behind and shot him."

"*Appeared?* What, like a ghost?"

"No, sir."

"Show me then."

Fedotov called out more instructions to another tech. Gerasimov watched as the video played, and a series of images of the same man seen from different angles appeared on the monitors. He leaned forward and studied the high-resolution close-up of Caleb's face on one of the screens.

"Find out who this mystery man is," he said. "We cannot afford to have our operations disrupted by assassins who materialize out of thin air."

# CHAPTER 15

NEW SCOTLAND YARD, LONDON

**O**verhead banks of suspended LEDs lit the conference room inside Met Police headquarters, aka New Scotland Yard. Its glass walls made Alex feel as exposed as the bare brick in the main office. From out in the bullpen, everyone could look in, and everyone had, not sure what to make of Detective Inspector Kane's fresh catch, whom they heard had just gunned down several men.

Caleb was across the room talking to Kane and a senior uniformed officer. Then, as the trio walked to a corner office, each police officer they encountered rose from their chairs to nod deferentially to the officer, piquing Alex's curiosity. She watched with fascination as the group disappeared into a corner office along the back of the bullpen, leaving her here in the middle of it all, yet so isolated from it.

Her backpack had been returned to her, minus her phone, gun, and extra magazines. With the men secreted away elsewhere, she was left with little to do but to turn and stare out the window. So she sat alone with her can of Coke, gazing across the river at the London Eye, the giant Ferris wheel on the south bank of the River Thames. As she watched, she replayed in her mind the events of the past two days that, even by her standards, were strange days indeed.

***

Caleb heard the words but wasn't really paying attention. The Scotland Yard superintendent was droning on about illegal possession of a firearm, extrajudicial killing, American imperialism (of all things), manifest destiny, the Magna Carta, pacts between British and American intelligence services, FBI, Interpol, *blah, blah, blah*. He hit on every cliché. What Caleb didn't hear this shitbird in a navy-blue tunic say even once was, *Great job, mate! We are putting that gorgeous brunette and her Glock in for a bravery citation signed by the King of England himself for killing a bunch of Russkies up to no good on our sovereign soil!* Or anything close.

*Hypocrites. Thank God we broke free of this bullshit centuries ago.*

When Superintendent Cartwright finished speaking, Caleb responded. "Yessir. An FBI special agent shooting Russian spies—that fact now having been confirmed by your own intelligence unit—who were trying to kill her on British soil is a troubling situation."

Kane jumped in, "Let's not forget you also eradicated one, Mr. Copeland."

Caleb scowled. "Truth is, back home in the States, when someone's trying to kill you, and you kill them first, we call that self-defense. Special Agent Martel did what she was trained to do and is alive because of it." He couldn't help adding, "And then we'd pin a damn medal on her chest and promote her. These, sir, were exigent circumstances."

"*Exigent circumstances?* Twaddle. Neither you nor FBI Agent—"

"—Interpol Special Agent."

"Neither you nor Special Agent Martel, from wherever the hell she hails, should have been in possession of a firearm without prior explicit authorization from Scotland Yard while in the United Kingdom."

"True," conceded Caleb. "But since Scotland Yard is Britain's official liaison with Interpol, it would be in your best interest to say that Special Agent Martel had authorization from your office to have said firearm and, therefore, to defend herself and the subjects of the Realm by any and all means necessary against the hostility and nefarious misdeeds of agents of a foreign power."

"Quite convenient to switch allegiances between the FBI and Interpol so quickly, wouldn't you say, Mr. Copeland?"

Caleb smiled. "Opportune, I'd say."

"And, by the way, under what authority should I be discussing this matter with you? Which agency did you say you represent again?"

"I didn't say."

"It was a rhetorical question, Mr. Copeland," the superintendent snapped. "I received a telephone call from the home secretary who, in turn, had received a call from the American secretary of state requesting all due consideration for the actions of Ms. Martel." *Special Agent Martel,* thought Caleb, but he didn't correct him this time. "Now, why on earth would such high-level authorizations be sought for just a simple FBI agent? It seems there are larger and more complex issues at play of which I have not been informed. Would you care to enlighten me?"

"I am afraid I'm not at liberty to discuss the matter," Caleb replied.

"*Hmph.* I am not accustomed to being bludgeoned by the home office and kept in the dark on domestic affairs. But . . . one of you has very persuasive friends."

Caleb said nothing, his hands folded in his lap. He had no intention of sharing his CIA affiliation with anyone unless necessary. All this man needed to know was that he had influential friends and could make things happen. Besides, he enjoyed seeing this stuffed tunic squirm a little.

"Fine," the older police official conceded at last. "Scotland Yard will assert that both you and Special Agent Martel were authorized to be armed while investigating the death of a British subject on British soil—one who was killed by what we suspect was a drunk driver who fled the scene of the incident. But it's surely the thin edge of the wedge, allowing American law enforcement to carry firearms whilst in this country."

"Tell whoever you need to tell that you believe there is a nexus between Ms. Krysten Gosling's death and a joint Met Police and Interpol investigation and that you are not authorized to discuss it further. But, for the record, all three of us here know that a drunk driver didn't kill her."

Superintendent Cartwright glanced over at Kane, standing next to the window, then glowered at Caleb, his knuckles white from tightly gripping the arms of his chair. "Mr. Copeland, I'm not accustomed to being told what to do in my own country by an American."

Caleb ignored his remark. "Let's lay our cards on the table, shall we?" he said. "We also know that Krysten was working undercover for MI5."

Cartwright's face turned a deep shade of scarlet.

"Yes, Superintendent. We are aware of that fact. And please don't insult my intelligence by saying you didn't know Krysten Gosling was MI5."

"I cannot confirm or deny any such assertion," said the superintendent feebly. "But how did you become possessed of this notion?"

"Special Agent Martel had a previous professional relationship with the deceased," said Caleb. "And they were friends."

The color of Cartwright's balding pate had gone from red to mottled. He gave a slight nod to DI Kane, who said, "I can confirm the Scottish woman with whom Special Agent Martel was lunching—" he referred to his notebook "—one Ms. Cara Maveety—contacted Special Agent Martel to inform her of Ms. Gosling's death, and that they indeed had a prior relationship. Ms. Maveety herself knows nothing of Ms. Gosling's possible connection to MI5."

*Possible connection to MI5. These guys are so full of it.*

Cartwright took a few deep breaths before speaking. "Anonymity is key to the work of MI5, Britain's Security Service." He continued, "Their mission is as critical as that of MI6 or the CIA. Their mandate includes domestic terrorism, not unlike your FBI. Ms. Gosling was an excellent officer and will be sorely missed." His dark eyes bored into Caleb's.

A long pause followed before Caleb breached the silent void. "With respect, sir, Ms. Gosling's death needn't be in vain."

"I can assure you, Mr. Copeland, we have no intention of allowing her life to have been snuffed out for no reason," the superintendent said.

"Of course not. But you need to recognize that Special Agent Martel is a force of nature in her own right."

"Yes, so we are aware," said the man. "Rather a bit of a monsoon, I'd say."

Caleb continued. "Well, with that in mind, England has a rich nautical tradition, sir, so forgive the metaphor, but you don't try to hold back the wind. Instead, you think of a way to let it drive you forward, to make it work for you rather than against you." He tried to further the analogy. "You unfurl the sail and pull it in just tight enough to harness all that energy."

"Perhaps," Cartwright said. "But I don't need to like it."

# CHAPTER 16

NEW SCOTLAND YARD, LONDON

The senior officer whom Alex had seen earlier entered the glassed-in conference room ahead of Caleb and Detective Inspector Kane. His tunic was adorned with medals representing a life spent in service to Crown and country. Out of respect, she stood as he entered the room.

"Special Agent Martel, thank you for waiting," he said as if the choice had been hers all along. "My name is Superintendent Cartwright."

"Sir."

"A nasty business, this," he said.

"Yes, sir," she replied. "Which part?"

"I beg your pardon?"

A uniformed constable trailed behind the trio carrying a paper bag that, for a moment, Alex thought was a Harrods shopping bag. She eyed Alex and smiled, set the bag on the glass conference table, then exited.

"I mean, which part of this exactly is a *nasty business,* sir—the part where I landed in your country and was immediately pursued by Russian agents?" She reached into the bag and retrieved her sidearm and magazines. "Or that I had to employ lethal force to protect myself on British soil?" She retracted the slide and locked it open. She cleared her weapon, punched a full mag into the well and released the slide to chamber a round. "Or is it the death of a British intelligence officer under suspicious circumstances that's got Scotland Yard so tied up in knots?" She holstered her Glock and felt whole again.

"Ms. Martel—" said DI Kane. "We haven't officially declared those men were Russians."

She rolled her eyes as she tucked her spare mags into elasticized sleeves sewn into the lining of her jacket. Lastly, she retrieved her phone from the paper bag, about to respond, but the superintendent raised a hand to stop her.

"Ms. Martel—" he began.

"*Special Agent* Martel, sir," she corrected, cutting him off.

"Of course. Please, be seated," he said, gesturing to the chair she'd been occupying. He took the seat opposite her and continued. "Detective Inspector Kane and I have reviewed your statement and that of Mr. Copeland."

Caleb, aka Mr. Copeland, stood behind him, poker-faced. Kane moved around the table and stood behind the chair beside her.

"First of all," began Cartwright, "I should like to thank you for your cooperation with our inquiry. Any use of force, of course, is examined closely by Scotland Yard. This isn't Texas, after all, Special Agent Martel. Therefore, these kinds of events don't happen as frequently as *you* may be accustomed to." He leaned forward, resting his forearms on the table. His fingers were large and gnarled, like an old boxer's.

She nodded politely while strangling the arms of her chair.

"A few moments ago," he went on, "I spoke with Chief Inspector Bressard, your commanding officer at

Interpol. I informed him of today's incident, and he shared with me some of the details from yesterday's events in Arnhem. Curious, don't you think?"

"What's that?" she asked.

"How one individual can be responsible for taking so many lives in such a brief period of time."

She was on her feet in a flash. Caleb was too far away to have prevented her from ripping out the superintendent's larynx had she been so inclined.

The superintendent raised a hand to settle her. It didn't work, but he continued anyway. "Still, Chief Bressard indicated the shootings were justified, if not necessary. Must have been rather a nasty business over there."

Her nails stung her palms where they dug in. She was already pissed off that she had been made to wait here like a common criminal while Caleb had joined the men in a corner office for a smoke and a brandy, or whatever the hell they were doing back there, and now this. This pompous windbag was layering his words with insinuations of wrongdoing.

"Superintendent," said Caleb, "this path you're on, it's not going to be very productive. You have examined the circumstances of today's shooting. You have been given information about yesterday's as well, but that hardly equips you with any moral or legal authority to render judgment against Special Agent Martel, who acted lawfully."

She turned and stared at him. "I don't need you to defend me, Caleb," she said, but he continued, unfazed.

"Her actions were not only necessary, they were heroic, and they saved lives. Both yesterday and today."

Superintendent Cartwright glanced at Caleb, then stood and addressed Alex. "I assured Chief Bressard that Scotland Yard would assist in any way it can. DI

Kane will be your liaison. Try to stay out of trouble while you are a guest in our country, Special Agent Martel." He gave a nod to Kane and left the conference room.

Alex glared at Caleb, who stared back blankly. She turned to Kane. "What the hell was that?"

"The superintendent can be intense," he replied. "Please be seated."

She looked again at Caleb, who now sat in the chair at the head of the conference table. Reluctantly, she sat.

Kane laid a file folder open, spreading the pages out on the table. "How well did you know Ms. Gosling?" he asked.

She took a deep breath to settle herself, like she was getting ready to make a long-distance shot. "Krysten and I met several years ago," she began, "at the Paris Peace Summit. We became fast friends and spent a few days attending conference sessions by day and exploring the city by night. We kept in touch on and off for a couple of years after, but I don't think I'd heard from her in maybe a year or more."

"Well, you were correct, Special Agent Martel. Ms. Gosling—Krysten—was indeed an intelligence officer with MI5, though she shouldn't have told you that."

"Please," she said dismissively. "Why was she working undercover?"

"I'm not at liberty to discuss MI5 secrets with you. But I can tell you that in its role to protect national security, domestic radicalism and terrorism are at the top of its mandate."

"You're not really with Scotland Yard, are you, Kane?" said Alex. It was more statement than question. "You're MI5."

Kane remained expressionless, shuffling papers in the file.

"Is that true?" Caleb asked.

Silence.

Alex continued. "I can tell a spook when I see one, Caleb. Your radar is slipping. Krysten was working for you, wasn't she, Kane? You were her handler."

He stopped shuffling papers. "It's true," he said. "I, too, am with the Security Service. But Krysten didn't work for me. She was my partner."

"Why was she undercover? What was the case?"

He sat for a beat, staring at the pages in front of him. Finally, he asked, "How did you know she was working undercover?"

"Her friend, Cara, the woman I was having lunch with, told me Krysten was working as a manager at a tech accelerator company."

"That was her cover. She was surprisingly good with computers."

"So, what happened?" asked Caleb.

"We had been alerted to the existence of a transnational money-laundering operation serving state entities through a UK tech accelerator company. We inserted Krysten to determine the extent of foreign government involvement."

"What did you find?"

"After months of undercover work, she was finally gathering valuable intelligence to support MI5's suspicions."

"Such as?" asked Alex.

"She was following a money trail involving an Islamist group—"

"The ILF."

"Yes. Vast sums of money were being funneled their way," Kane said. "Krysten suspected there was a large operation in the works."

"Why didn't you notify other intelligence agencies?" asked Caleb.

"We didn't have enough information to wave the

red flag yet. She was compiling a dossier that we could share, but then Interpol caught wind of a pending exchange of nuclear materials in the Netherlands."

Caleb added, "And that went to support the theory about the ILF."

"Yes, your operation at Arnhem yesterday appeared to support Krysten's hypothesis."

It seemed to fit. Extremist groups were funded by all sorts of criminal—and often non-criminal—activities.

"What about their target?" she asked. "Did she uncover any intel on where they are planning to use the nuclear material?"

"Nothing we hadn't already been hearing, including possibly in America."

"What about the Paris Peace Summit? Most of the G20 leaders will be there in a few days."

Kane shook his head. "The conference site is already locked down. Our analysis suggests it's an unlikely target. SIS and the DGSI agree," he said, referring to Britain's MI6 and France's General Directorate for Internal Security, their counterpart to MI5.

"Surely you must suspect the Russians are behind all this?" she asked. "The events of today and yesterday and plots involving weapons of mass destruction have all the hallmarks of an operation by a particular GRU unit."

"Agreed, it does sound similar to the modus operandi of the GRU, but we don't have anything concrete linking yesterday's events with today's."

"If not them, why would any other Russians be chasing me all over London?"

"Excellent question, but we will continue to consider both the ILF and the Russians as the prime suspects in this matter."

Alex sighed. If the GRU was involved, it wouldn't be her first clash with Russia's foreign military intelligence agency and likely not her last. She had previously dealt with one of their elite operations units, Unit 29155, and a new team Interpol had begun to track called Directorate 13. Both were formidable adversaries.

Alex said, "We know the GRU recruits *young.* Russian mothers and fathers willingly give their children over to the state to send them to better schools with the promise of a better future. And the state trains them according to each student's particular aptitude."

"Sad, but true," lamented Caleb.

"Right," agreed Kane. "And these children then grow up to be operators in these various groups, including Unit 29155, whose sole purpose is to sow chaos while making Western intelligence agencies believe they are either extremely sloppy or plain inept."

Unit 29155 was routinely implicated in overseas disruptive operations, executing missions of chaos, murder, and mayhem directly for Russian president Dmitry Sergachev.

"They're like a twenty-first-century Praetorian Guard," mused Caleb.

Kane nodded his head in acknowledgment and picked up the thread. "What appears to Western intelligence as bungling is, in fact, a systematic approach to mayhem. Like the Novichok poisonings of the Skripals, right here in the UK, in Salisbury. It was inept enough for the plot and the players to be discovered and traced by open-source intelligence aggregators, yet effective enough to create chaos and confusion in intelligence circles and to spawn conspiracy theories leading blame *away* from Russia. All the while, President Sergachev is on television denouncing Russia's involvement while enjoying the havoc he has spawned. It had all of us at MI5, as well as our colleagues across the river at MI6, chasing our tails for months. All these operations are run by a three-star general from his office in the Ministry of Defense in central Moscow."

"Major General Tikhonov," offered Caleb.

Alex nodded. "And his second-in-command, Colonel Viktor Gerasimov. Interpol and the FBI have files on them both. And now they've branched out by adding an even more specialized team headed by Gerasimov."

"Directorate 13," Caleb said.

"President Sergachev is a complete megalomaniac," said Alex. "He embraces his bad-boy image and taunts the West. Meanwhile, Unit 29155 and Directorate 13 compete for his attention and favor, like spurned and jealous suitors."

Kane swiveled in his chair. "It is chilling how organically ruthless the Russians can be."

Caleb chimed in. "But the question before us is this: Is Krysten's death, the events in Arnhem, and the attempt on Alex's life linked to GRU activities?"

"There's only one way to find out," said Alex.

# CHAPTER 17

Somewhere in London, a carload of Russians was driving around, likely none too happy that Alex and Caleb had killed three of their comrades. If the tables were reversed, she'd be out for blood, so enticing them into the open shouldn't prove too difficult. Revenge was a strong motivator.

Whoever her assailants were, and for all their disastrous tactics, they had good intel. And while Jonathan Burgess—the Interpol information systems security analyst—had cleared her mobile phone, she suspected it was how the Russians were tracking her. Meaning they likely knew where she was, even now.

*But to what end?*

"You mean, use yourself as bait?" asked Kane once Alex had laid out the plan.

"Or at least a decoy," she replied. "I mean, if it were me, I'd be redrawing the whole operation. But there's no telling how foolhardy this group is, so—"

Caleb interrupted her train of thought. "Maybe we should continue this over dinner."

As soon as Caleb mentioned they should eat, she felt her own hunger sneak up on her. And it could be that a public venue like a restaurant rather than an interrogation room inside Scotland Yard headquarters might pose an irresistible opportunity for the Russians to follow up on their earlier efforts if that was what they had in mind.

Dinner, then, was the next logical step.

"I need a burner phone first," Alex said as they walked through the lobby of New Scotland Yard. "Do you have those here, Kane?"

"First of all, if we're going to be working together, you may as well call me Daniel. And of course we do. Do you think we're some backwater monarchy? Brexit hasn't left us completely hapless. There's a shop up the street and around the corner," he added. "It's on our way."

"On our way *where*?" asked Caleb.

"Why, my favorite pub, of course."


They stepped out onto a sun-drenched Victoria Embankment along the River Thames. Alex checked the time: 4:45. Her wristwatch—a Rolex Oyster Perpetual Submariner Date—was a gift she had given herself after earning her assignment as a special operations combat medic with the 75th Ranger Regiment. The timepiece was flawlessly reliable and reflected the best qualities of the woman who wore it: dependable, attractive without pretense, and a trusted and trustworthy partner. If it were true that every Rolex tells a story, this one's would be endlessly redacted.

Kane led them toward Bridge Street, and Alex marveled at the sight of the Palace of Westminster in front of them, home to the United Kingdom's Parliament. It wasn't until they reached the corner that the full scale of the 316-foot-tall Elizabeth Tower housing Big Ben came into view. This was Alex's first time seeing it in person, and its size and grandeur drew from her an un-expected gasp.

Kane pointed to a Tesco Express stand in front of the Westminster Tube station around the corner, where she stopped to buy a pay-as-you-go smartphone. "Anything but Huawei," she told the clerk. "Better yet, I'll take two." She tapped her bank card to pay, then removed the phones from their packaging as she walked to rejoin the men who had ambled up the road a half block to St. Stephen's Tavern.

She stepped inside the airy pub with its high wooden coffered ceiling and circular, medieval-looking chandelier. The smell of fried food and malted ale hung in the air around her. The building nurtured the ambiance of its nineteenth-century heritage and, in fact, looked much older. Tufted green leather banquettes under the windows ringed the main level.

An attractive woman behind the bar was pulling a pint. "Upstairs, luv," she said, smiling. She nodded toward the curving staircase leading to a dining section in the second-floor loft. "I reckon you're the pretty brunette Daniel mentioned."

"I reckon I am." Alex returned her smile and proceeded up the enclosed staircase, its walls lined with framed lithographs and front-page newspaper articles from *The Independent,* among others. She found the men in a booth and slid in next to Kane just as a server came by and offloaded a tray of pints.

"I ordered you a Tangle Foot," said Caleb.

She examined her ale—a clear, golden, effervescent liquid with a modest head. In her world, beer was like ammunition, and no one should presume to know your preference. Caleb had a way of getting under her skin like that. A reckoning was coming.

"A Badger Best Bitter for you," said the waitress,

placing an amber-colored beer in front of Kane, "and a Wicked Wyvern for the wicked wee man." She deposited a frosty glass in front of Caleb.

"She's got you pegged already," said Alex.

"I know the look," the waitress replied. "This here is a seriously good IPA," she told him. "If you don't like it, you're daft. I'll be back for your order," she added as she turned and meandered away through the tightly packed tables.

"To fallen comrades!" said Kane, raising his glass.

"To Krysten," replied Alex.

Caleb tapped his glass on the table, then silently took a long pull with the others.

Her beer was good, but she didn't tell Caleb that.

"So, Special Agent Martel, what's the plan?" asked Kane.

"First things first," she said, reaching into her backpack to retrieve the burner phones. She punched in a number.

"Bressard," came the voice on the other end.

"Chief."

"Alexandra? This is a surprise. My call display said 'Unknown Number.' Everything alright?" She could hear the genuine concern in his voice. "I heard you had another interesting afternoon. How are you?" he asked.

She filled in the blanks for him with details the superintendent from Scotland Yard hadn't provided—the possible connection with Krysten's death, the involvement of DI Kane, the ILF investigation, and her suspicion about Directorate 13's involvement. She asked him for another favor. A little bait.

"It would give me great pleasure," he replied. "Keep me posted."

She clicked off and turned to Kane.

"Okay, Daniel, your turn. Answer a question for me."

"Shoot," he replied.

"Never say that to her unless you mean it," Caleb joked.

She ignored him and continued. "Scotland Yard and MI5 are two distinct organizations, so why does the London Metropolitan Police—Scotland Yard—let you use the title *detective inspector*?"

"It's quite simple," he said, taking another swig of his beer. "I was a detective inspector with Scotland Yard before moving to MI5. So, while I'm no longer with the Met, I work alongside them on investigations with a national security nexus. The younger police officers call me Mr. Kane, but the old blokes still call me by my previous rank. Cerebral muscle memory, I suppose."

"Is Krysten's murder a joint investigation?"

"The inquiry falls squarely within the purview of Scotland Yard as a criminal matter. But given Krysten was an active intelligence officer working undercover on a matter of national security, Scotland Yard, MI5, MI6, as well as GCHQ—our signals intelligence service—have formed a task force under the home secretary."

"Did you or Krysten ever come across anything in the investigation that pointed to a connection between this ILF group and the Russians?" she asked.

The waitress appeared at their table. "Okay, Danny. What can I get you and your mates?"

Kane turned to his new colleagues. "Shall we make this simple?" he asked, looking between Caleb and Alex. They nodded. "Fish and chips then? You'll love it. Three orders, please, Angie," he said to the waitress.

"Right," she said and headed off toward the kitchen.

"Look," he continued, "the Russkies are always up

to no good, so they're constantly on our radar." He glanced around and lowered his voice so other patrons might not overhear. "Several days ago, MI6 reported that they'd heard talk of nuclear materials, plutonium and highly enriched uranium in particular, being sold and exchanged by black marketeers throughout the Eurozone—the same intel that initiated your op. But nothing solid pointed to Russian state involvement directly. Although," he continued, "that operation has now drawn plenty of resources that are all focused on finding the smugglers and identifying possible targets of radiological dispersion devices."

"Dirty bombs," she said.

"Yes, and even talk of an improvised nuclear device—a nuclear IED, if you will."

Angie returned, carrying a large tray loaded with plates.

"Alright, lady and gents, three orders of Tangle Foot Ale–battered cod with chips and peas." She deposited the hot plates before them. "Let me know when you need another round of pints," she said as she walked away.

Alex squeezed drops of lemon juice onto her fish and cut into the crispy battered cod. The flaky fish steamed as she brought the fork to her mouth. It melted on her tongue.

"Ohmigod, so good." She took a sip of cold beer to quell the heat.

"I should have warned you. Both the chips—French fries, I suppose, for you both—and the fish come straight from the deep fryer, so be careful."

"Anything else British intelligence knows about that you might not be telling us?" Alex asked. She looked at Kane and would have pointed her fork at him if it weren't loaded with peas that were already rolling off of it.

Before he could answer, his phone rang. He glanced

at the display. "I'm afraid I have to take this call. Sorry, chaps, be right back."

She watched from the loft as he descended the steps and walked out onto the patio beside the pub. As if on cue, her Interpol phone began vibrating in her pocket. She washed down another bite of fish with the cold ale before answering it.

# CHAPTER 18

"Colonel!"

Major Vasili Fedotov's voice over the intercom sounded urgent. Colonel Gerasimov put his cell phone call on hold to answer his operations chief.

"What is it?"

Gerasimov sat at his desk in the basement of the Russian ambassador's residence, discussing today's events. He and his caller were strategizing how best to manage the conversation he was yet to have with General Tikhonov, his commander in Moscow. Explaining how his team had lost three ostensibly capable operators would not be easy.

"We are tracking a call," replied Fedotov.

"And?" Gerasimov asked impatiently.

"Sir, it's Agent Martel."

"We'll speak later," he said into his cell phone, cutting short the conversation.

Moments later, Gerasimov entered the ops center and approached Fedotov's console. Seated on a couch at the back of the room were three people who hadn't been present in the ops center when he'd arrived earlier. The two men and a woman stood as Colonel Gerasimov entered. He acknowledged them with a glare.

Fedotov removed his headset and worked the control panel, activating a speaker.

—*and you haven't found out who the attackers were?* asked a male voice.

"That's Interpol chief inspector Bressard," announced Fedotov.

*Not yet,* said a female voice.

"And this?" asked Gerasimov.

"Special Agent Martel."

—*they dragged me to Scotland Yard like I was the criminal,* Alex continued. *I spent hours in an interview room being interrogated while my GRU assailants got away.*

*Alexandra, please,* intoned Bressard. *You might try to feign some diplomacy. Interpol and Scotland Yard both think it might have been Russian mobsters, not a GRU hit squad.*

*Seriously?*

Ignoring that, he went on. *None of us is sure how you fit in, though. Some are leaning toward yesterday's events at Arnhem for an explanation. And I would hardly say anybody got away.*

*What?*

*You said the Russians got away. I would hardly characterize it that way—three of them are dead.*

"So, they know about our involvement?" asked Fedotov.

"Perhaps not," answered Gerasimov.

*Scotland Yard has released you, haven't they?* asked Bressard.

*Yes, Chief.*

*Good. I want you back here in the morning.*

*I'd like to stay another day or two to help with funeral arrangements for Krysten.*

There was a pause while Chief Bressard considered her request.

*Okay, Alexandra. But just one more day. We need you back here by tomorrow night at the latest. Understood?*

*Yes, sir,* she replied.

*Now I have to go call my boss and explain how it is you managed to kill three more men.*

*Two.*

*Alexandra—*

Gerasimov stood straighter, a smile creasing his young but war-hardened face.

"Excellent, Vasili," he said, clapping the major on the shoulder. "For all their smugness, it seems they still haven't been able to identify our operators."

"But they know they are Russian," said the woman seated on the couch.

"Yes, Captain Burina, they know they were Russian, along with seventy thousand other Russian expatriates living in England," Gerasimov said.

"It will take them a while then, sir," Fedotov said. "We built them strong background histories to hide their true identities."

"Thank goodness for our comrades in our great country's criminal underworld," said Gerasimov. "They make it easy for us to hang the blame on them for *our* unsavory activities."

The woman spoke again. "Should we resume our surveillance of the Interpol agent, sir?"

He glanced over at the threesome on the comfortable couch. "Come with me," he ordered, and together the four of them walked down the hallway to his office.

Colonel Gerasimov circled behind his desk and sat, leaving them standing before him.

"I'm not sure you understand the concept of surveillance," he said. "The purpose of the exercise is to observe without being observed."

"Sir, if I may."

He wasn't surprised when the woman spoke first. Captain Tatiana Burina had long, straight, dark brown hair hanging below her shoulders. Her face was round, her complexion bronze. She was ethnically Russian, coming from the small Tatarstan region seven hundred kilometers east of Moscow.

"Please," he said, waving her forward and indicating for her two colleagues to take a seat on the sofa. "Enlighten me."

The men sat. She remained standing.

"We were in a separate car—the trailing car. We had discussed the plan in advance. We were supposed to follow and observe, to record Special Agent Martel's movements, and to discover what she knew about our mission, if anything."

"Why did you deviate from the plan?"

"Captain Nikulin. He was the team leader in the other car. When he lost sight of the taxi that Special Agent Martel was riding in, he grew impatient for fear of losing her."

"And did you share Captain Nikulin's concern?"

"No, sir."

"Good. Action and accomplishment are not synonymous, Captain. But you blew your cover anyway and joined your comrades in the pursuit."

The woman straightened up and gazed at an imaginary mark on the wall behind Gerasimov. "Once they broke cover, we felt it necessary and prudent to support them. To provide backup for them in the event something happened."

"Necessary, perhaps. But not prudent. Something *did* happen, Captain Burina. Captain Nikulin and two of your comrades were killed like stray dogs on a London street. Is this the support you envisioned giving them when you broke cover?"

"No, Colonel."

"I will not tolerate this level of incompetence in my unit." He made eye contact with each of the three in turn. "We are Directorate 13, the chosen few. Do you know what that means, Captain Burina?"

"Yes, sir. President Sergachev himself approves our missions directly."

"Correct. General Tikhonov and I personally oversaw the selection and training process that produced the most elite operators in Russian intelligence. So, yes, you and your comrades are the chosen few. But our beloved president will not be pleased with the actions of Captain Nikulin and his team.

"Because of what he did, this woman has been alerted to our presence. We have lost the tactical advantage, and it will be more difficult to learn what she knows. And, while President Sergachev is unafraid of Western saber-rattling and threats of retaliation from America that have followed similar operations, he is a proud man, unaccustomed to failure and not fond of having egg on his face."

"I don't think—" she began, but he didn't let her finish the thought.

Gerasimov slapped his desk. "I believe this is the most accurate statement you have made so far, Captain Burina," he shouted. "You did not think. None of you *think*!"

Gerasimov stood abruptly, struggling to contain his anger.

"Is this what you were all taught in your home Spetsnaz units and during your onboarding for Directorate 13? Is this the current state of Russian intelligence special operations?"

Tatiana Burina snapped to attention. "No, Colonel."

"Good," he said. "Tatiana, please tell us what you believe we should do next."

# CHAPTER 19

"Well?" Kane said, returning to the table. "What have I missed?"

Alex updated him on the conversation with her boss. She had made arrangements with Bressard when they spoke on her burner phone for him to call her on her Interpol phone to discuss innocuous details of her plans in London. She counted on the Russians listening in, but if not, she hoped they had at least been tracking her location. Even if they didn't know what her plans were, they might still be tempted to come after her again.

*But why? What did it mean?*

"Do you really think the Russians will come for you? They would be fools to make another attempt," said Kane.

"They're nothing if not persistent," Alex said.

"I'm not authorized to tell you this, but in the spirit of interagency cooperation between MI5, Interpol, and—" Kane glanced over at Caleb. Caleb took a sip of his beer. Kane continued. "In the spirit of cooperation between MI5 and Interpol, as I have already said, we are tracking chatter related to a threat to the US suggesting an upcoming 9/11 memorial event at Ground Zero in New York as the target. But the information was as wispy as clouds in the sky and just as solid. That's what Krysten was trying to uncover."

"And that's what you think got her killed?"

"Now more than ever."

"Seems plausible," said Caleb. "We'd have to agree."

"Who's *we*?" asked Alex.

"Me and the people I work for," he said, stuffing another forkful of battered fish into his mouth.

Kane continued. "I only wish I could have been there to protect her properly."

"She knew the risks, Kane," Caleb said. "You said it yourself—undercover work can be deadly."

"You're a master of understatement, Mr. Copeland." Kane took his last bite and washed it down with the bottom of his pint. "I don't think we're making much more progress here, so I believe it's time for me to push off, as they say."

Alex also drained the last of her beer. "You're not going to wait with us to see if the Russians show?" she asked.

"I'm sure they won't," he said. "But if they do turn up give me a shout if you need a cleanup team."

"Funny."

"Cheerio!"

With that, Kane was gone.

"Bit of an odd duck, isn't he?" said Caleb. "And I think he stiffed us with the check."

She shrugged her shoulders. Odd ducks were par for the course in their line of work.

"So, Shooter, what now? Do we wait?"

On Caleb, though, the jury was still out.

"Kane is right," she said. "We should probably go."

"Do you have a hotel room?"

She met his gaze with hers. He had that foggy three-beer look that men often got around her. It happened in high school, in the Army, and at every stop along the way.

"I'm good," she said, giving him her best shut-down glare.

"No, no, I didn't mean anything like that. I was just making sure you were going to be okay tonight."

"Look," she said, "let's get something straight. I don't need you to make sure I'm 'going to be okay.' My dad was an Army general. He taught me to hunt and shoot."

"I get it. I've seen you kill people. We're good."

"He gave me my first rifle when I was ten."

"Shooter, we're good—"

"He taught me to fight, to shoot, to field-dress a bear and a moose in my teens, and to be smart enough to know when to engage and when to back away from an adversary. What he didn't teach me was to be anybody's victim."

Caleb's eyes were locked on hers as she spoke, melting into them.

"I don't need a knight in shining armor to rescue me—not from tired old Scotland Yard superintendents, not from Russian spooks, not from scary old London town, not from anything or anyone."

"Except for that one who was about to put a bullet between your eyes."

"I would have done the same for you."

"You mean save my life, or put a bullet between my eyes?"

"That moment notwithstanding, I don't need any cowboys riding in to save the day. I'm not now, nor ever will be, someone's damsel in distress."

"Why, no, ma'am, I can most assuredly see that," he said in a mock Southern drawl à la Rhett Butler. "But I'll be here if you need me. And since you've invoked the notwithstanding clause, I'm going to sulk off back to my hotel now and call it a night. After a nightcap."

# CHAPTER 20

As conversations go, that one had gone south pretty quick. But Caleb liked that about Alex—she didn't take crap from anyone. He wasn't overly surprised when she'd lashed out at him. He should have expected no less.

As he stepped outside, Whitehall was awash with a constant stream of pedestrian and vehicle traffic. The façades of its Victorian buildings blended into the diminishing light as he walked to his hotel, his mind drifting back to thoughts of *her*. She was on his mind. A lot. Beyond her physical presence—tallish, long, golden-brown hair, fit, with hypnotic green-blue eyes that bored into him whenever they met his—were Alex's other qualities: grit, intellect, courage.

Across the road, black iron gates and a security detail at the entrance to Downing Street shielded the residents at Number 10—the prime minister and her family—from the unholy deeds of evil men. But those gates, and the few who kept watch there, stood little chance of thwarting the next attack without the combined efforts of those who worked in the shadows to prevent such eventualities—ghosts like him and, he hoped, Alex. That's why he needed her. She was a warrior.

Her military dossier and a battery of personality and psychological tests had revealed in her a fierce streak of self-reliance. During her time in the Army and with ISA, she had earned multiple decorations and commendations in theater before an incident in a remote village in Iraq sidelined her until military shrinks determined she was fit to redeploy. And not long after, she married a Delta Force operator, the same soldier from whom she had taken direction on the sniper rifle in Afghanistan and who was later killed in action while on an undisclosed mission.

What Alex brought to the game were the instincts of the hunter, the skills of the fighter, and the cold calculus of a pragmatic warrior. In short, she was exactly who he was looking for to advance his unit's mission in the modern threat landscape on his nascent counterproliferation team, ACCT. Her country needed her. His job was to see that she came to this conclusion herself.

He strolled down Horse Guards Avenue; the cool night air was refreshing after the crowded pub. This area of London oozed with history. Although he enjoyed mocking the Brits, the truth was that being here gave him a renewed purpose and a desire to ensure that his own homeland continued to survive and thrive as England had for more than twelve hundred years.

Soon he came to the Royal Horseguards Hotel, a colossal French chateau–style building at number 2 Whitehall Court. Its lobby was lavishly appointed, with red velvet chairs and high ceilings from which hung ornate crystal chandeliers. Caleb walked through it and down the hallway to the Equus Bar, where the red velvet theme continued. The sumptuous room was almost empty.

"Evening, Mr. Copeland." The barman wore a dark suit, accented by a white oxford shirt, a solid red tie, and a white pocket square, plainly folded. He spoke with a refined but unpretentious accent. "Your usual, sir?" he asked, depositing a leather coaster on the bar before him.

Caleb nodded. In this bar, the usual for him was a tasty concoction called the Churchill, named after Britain's former wartime prime minister, an acclaimed aficionado of fine alcoholic beverages. The eponymous drink on the menu was made with bourbon, homemade tobacco syrup, Islay malt whiskey, tobacco-infused bourbon, and bitters. Churchill's love of whiskey was the stuff of legend, but Caleb doubted his tastes ran so keenly toward the kind from Kentucky. Nevertheless, Equus's libation, created in his honor, was one Caleb had taken a liking to.

He sat comfortably in the tall swivel chair, his back to the room. A mirror behind the bottle shelves gave him a 120-degree field of view behind him. His peripheral vision could manage the rest. Only the hallway entry he had walked through was notable as a route that someone with malicious intent could use, and he had that easily covered. There was one other exit from the bar, not counting the two windows, to his immediate left.

The bartender placed his drink on the coaster before him.

"Thanks, Nigel."

Nigel nodded and moved away to restock garnishes.

The current danger, Caleb knew, was graver than he had let on. He didn't have all the pieces yet, but something big was in the offing. In the era of the Neo–Cold Wars against America's two foes, Russia and China, no threat like this had ever hit their radar.

He swirled the liquid around in his glass, the single ice cube clinking off the sides, before taking a sip. He had taken the kubotan out of his pocket and began rapping it against his knuckles. Inside his fist, the deformed 7.62mm slug that a surgeon had removed from his heart rested against his palm, attached by a beaded chain to the machined aluminum stick. And so he tapped: *lub-dub, lub-dub, lub-dub.*

He flashed back to the moment when he had scrambled over the two-tiered HESCO at his unit's outpost along the Arghandab, where the river flowed southwest past Kandahar. Their outpost was about to be overrun, and Caleb had leaped across the rock-filled barrier to retrieve the unit's injured lieutenant who had stepped outside the wire to confront an onrushing insurgent force.

As he reached the top of the HESCO, a bullet had struck him in the chest with the force of a major-league line drive—only exponentially greater—and penetrated his body armor and plate. All he could remember was tumbling face-first to the other side while someone yelled for a medic. The next thing he knew, he was at a combat support hospital in the desert being hot-loaded onto a medevac chopper bound for Kandahar in preparation for a flight to Landstuhl Regional Medical Center in Germany. There, after removing the bullet from where it had lodged in the wall of his left ventricle, the surgeon had praised him for having a heart made of stone.

*Amen, doc.*

He had also repaired his punctured lung, caused by a chunk of Caleb's rib that had instantly become shrapnel when the AK round hit his chest.

Caleb put away the kubotan and gazed deeply into his drink, pushing the ice around with a finger and reminiscing about the fog of war.

"Something for you, miss?"

At Nigel's words, Caleb raised his eyes from the bottom of his glass, stunned by the image reflected in the mirror of the person walking up behind him.

# CHAPTER 21

Captain Tatiana Burina stood in front of Colonel Gerasimov inside his office in the basement of Harrington House. Her two surveillance colleagues sat silently behind her, indistinguishable from the pair of stuffed cushions next to them on the sofa. Gerasimov had asked for her opinion.

"We must reevaluate our objectives," she said.

"Please elaborate."

She felt her heart rate surge slightly, eager to speak her mind as her commander leaned back in his chair. He perched his elbows on the armrests, his fingers interlaced before him. The colonel seemed to be in full mentor mode now, ever the patient tutor, having tucked away his earlier annoyance.

"Colonel," she began, standing at attention, her eyes locking on his. "Our primary objective has not been found out."

"How can you be so certain that our mission wasn't compromised, that it shouldn't be discontinued?" asked Gerasimov.

"Because if it were, all the resources of the British and American intelligence and security agencies would have broken radio silence to prevent what's coming. And, according to Major Fedotov, there has been no appreciable increase in chatter on our signals monitoring networks."

She spoke formally to her commander. Perhaps too formally.

"At ease, Captain," he said, obviously aware of her discomfort. "Tatiana, speak freely. This is not your former military unit."

"Yes, Colonel."

He gestured to a chair in front of his desk. She sat. "You confirmed this?"

"With Major Fedotov, yes."

Gerasimov leaned back in his chair, rocking slightly. "Go on," he said.

"Sir, if the primary mission is secure, and our comrades in Turkey are actively pursuing its success, then our most pressing objective is to ensure Agent Martel doesn't learn of it before it's done. Fedotov said he penetrated the Interpol network and intercepted an email sent by the traitor. He further confirmed that he had purged Interpol's server after its interception so that no copies of the email remained. Whatever message she was trying to send to Martel has not reached her."

Gerasimov stopped rocking. "And yet she is here, in London."

"Yes, despite not receiving the emailed signal, she found her way here to London. It leaves us to consider that either she knows something about our operation but not enough to stop it, or something about our former deep-cover agent. But perhaps neither."

"And your assessment?"

"We have had intermittent voice intercepts on her mobile phone. Fedotov said the end-to-end voice data encryption methods employed by Interpol are strong, but we were able to listen in, as well as to see where incoming calls originated, and, of course, we can track her location. Once Major Fedotov breached their security, we were able to listen to her last call with Chief Bressard at Interpol. We know she met with a woman who lived in the same building as Krysten did. I am convinced she was summoned here by that woman to discuss her death."

She paused. The colonel leaned into his elbows on the desk.

"Continue, Tatiana."

She edged forward in her chair, becoming more animated. "I believe, based on the photographs we have seen of them together and the fact that this Scottish woman lives in the same building as the traitor, that Alexandra Martel was brought here for personal reasons that had nothing to do with us."

"And? What else?"

She took a deep breath, held it a beat, then exhaled. "Captain Nikulin and his team made a critical error; in fact, a series of them. And they paid a heavy price for their incompetence."

Gerasimov looked past her, eyeing the Mute Boys on the couch. Tatiana was sure she had impressed him with her initiative and demeanor. There was no need for them to say anything when she could think and speak on their behalf and at twice their speed.

"I will instruct Major Fedotov to increase the flow of information pointing to our Islamist friends. Do you have any other recommendations, Captain Burina?" Gerasimov asked.

"We should continue to follow Agent Martel discreetly with covert surveillance and electronic means. Her phone is still supplying us with information. I do not believe our mission is compromised. We will know what she knows by the actions she takes next."

"And if she demonstrates she knows too much?" he asked.

"Then, Colonel, I will kill her myself."

# CHAPTER 22

EQUUS BAR, ROYAL HORSEGUARDS HOTEL, LONDON

She strolled in, looking every bit as though she owned the place. Caleb knew the air of self-confidence when he saw it, and Alex had it in spades. He swiveled in his chair, eyeing her as she took the seat next to his.

"I'm feeling a little Bond girl tonight," she told Nigel. "Martini, very dry."

"Of course," he said, starting to move away.

"Just a minute," she added. "Three measures of Gordon's, one of Tito's, half of Lillet Blanc. Shake until it's ice-cold. Then add one olive and a twist of lemon."

"Certainly, madam," he said, seemingly pleased with her instructions.

"My own twist on the Vesper," she added.

"Mr. Ian Fleming himself would be pleased."

Caleb was caught up in her eyes, her smile, her subtle hand movements. She had a formidable pull on him.

"How did you find me?"

"I have my sources," she said. He tried to read her expression but couldn't. "Oh, relax, I followed you. Your tradecraft needs work."

He knew better. There had never been anything wrong with his tradecraft. Either someone had told her where to find him, or *her* tradecraft was better than he thought. True, he had let his guard down on the walk back to his hotel, but after so many years of watching for people watching him, countersurveillance had become second nature. He could admit when someone had caught him unawares, and Alex had.

After a brief silence, he asked her, "Do you know where we're sitting?"

"It's just a guess, but I think we're in a bar in a swanky hotel." She leaned toward him. "Did I win a prize?"

Her eyes met his. They sparkled. The welt on her cheek made her all the more attractive. She broke contact to survey the room. She was toying with him, but he went along.

"It is also the former home and office of the first MI6 chief, Sir Mansfield Cumming."

"I did not know that," she admitted.

Nigel returned, placing a stemmed cocktail glass before her and a fresh Churchill in front of Caleb. He watched, fascinated, as she seized the thin lemon rind and deftly dabbed it around the rim of her glass. Then she gave it a gentle squeeze with her fingertips, releasing an atomized gust of lemon oil above her libation before letting the yellow peel slide to the bottom of her glass.

"Cheers," he said, raising his glass to her. She wiped her fingers on a napkin and lifted her own. "To you, Special Agent Martel."

"And to you, Caleb of CIA."

They drank.

"Tell me more," she said.

He leaned in. "This incredible five-star property was built a long time ago."

"Such vivid description. It's like I was there."

"You are. Its construction was at the center of a huge pyramid scam that left thousands of investors penniless back in the eighteen hundreds."

"My delusions of a storied history have been shattered."

"Don't despair. Since then, lords and ladies, dukes and duchesses, prime ministers and princesses, misters and mistresses have all stumbled out of this very same bar and up to its sumptuous rooms. Sometimes together."

"Scandalous."

"In fact, this was the office of the Secret Intelligence Service—MI6—during the First World War. I'm actually staying in the apartment on the eighth floor that was the former office of the equivalent of the deputy director of the day."

"Should I be impressed?"

"Yes. It's one of our safe houses."

"Now I know you're lying."

"I'm not."

"It's a good thing you're not driving anywhere."

Caleb noticed that he was starting to feel the effects of the bourbon-fueled drinks, on top of the beer he had had with dinner. But not Alex. She seemed just fine.

"No, not driving," he said. "Listen, I have a proposal."

"Oh, no." She raised a hand, like a cop guarding a crosswalk. "You better stop there. This won't end well for you."

"No, no, we already established that. I'm sober enough not to shoot myself in the foot."

"It's not your foot I'm worried about," she said, draining the rest of her martini. "What is it, then, this proposal of yours?"

"Come work for me."

An eyebrow shot upward. "You *are* drunk. Bartender, another round!"

Nigel scooped up her empty glass.

"*With* me," he corrected.

"Either way, I have a job."

"Not like the one I'm offering."

He watched as she sat silently, her eyes fixed on him in the mirror's reflection. Nigel finished straining her cocktail and added the finishing touch, a carefully drawn strip of lemon rind. He placed the libation before her, and Caleb allowed her a moment to complete her drink ritual.

"We're on the same team, Alex. We're made of the same stuff. We both pursue justice with relentless passion and vigor."

"*Vigor?*"

"Neither of us can stand to see the bad guys get away. I mean, truly evil asshole bad guys. I'm promising you justice on a grand scale." He gently pushed the back of her barstool so that it swiveled to face him. "You were once part of the big game. You're a decorated soldier. A legendary operator."

She held her cocktail in her hand, tracing the rim with her index finger.

"ISA recruited you, recognizing the warrior within you, and fed that fire in your belly. The one that made you hunger for action, for the pursuit of justice. I know you wanted to have a family and a normal life with your late husband, Kyle. It's why you eventually left ISA and joined the FBI. I get it. It brought you home to the States, and gave you a chance to have a permanent base of operations. A place to start that family. I'm so sorry Kyle was KIA before that could happen."

Her green-blue eyes turned stormy gray and misty.

He kept going. "Alex, I'm offering you a chance to work with the cream of the crop again. You won't be a Feebie special agent, won't be an FBI legat, won't be an Interpol investigator trapped between bureaucracies. You'll be a bona fide Tier One operator again, doing the kind of work you were born to do. We'll be chasing phantoms invisible to everybody but us. You can be the hidden hand of an avenging angel if you want, if that's what your country and your president request of you. Alex, I'm asking you to come home."

"Come home *where*?"

"To CIA. To my team in the Special Activities Center."

She looked at him, her face taking on a new aspect of curiosity. Or hope?

"I'm fine where I am, Caleb," she told him.

But he wasn't convinced.

"Are you?"

He looked around the lounge, at the people seated on red velvet settees and in intimate booths. The posh bar had filled in around them with the regular denizens of a civilian existence who would never know what it was like to stand behind the heavy velvet curtain that shielded the great unwashed from the machinations of the world's security apparatus.

"Sure," he continued. "You might find some of the gratification you need doing what you're doing. You might track down the guns, the chemicals, the radioactive shit, the bad guys. You might have people arrested, charged, tried, and some may even be convicted. But you'll never know the satisfaction of going after the big fish at the top, the ones who set events in motion, the untouchable asshats who write the playbooks that all the bit players follow—unless you come back into the ultra-secret paramilitary operations and covert action fold. You used to know how small the world was. It was small because you could see how all the pieces fit together. That's what I'm offering you again." He could see the wheels turning. She was thinking about it. He'd found her weak spot. "I'm just saying, whatever events are in motion are coming from so high up the ladder that you'll never see them from your lonely pit in the basement. For that, you need to be in the penthouse. And right now, I'm offering you the key to a very elite club at the top of the most exclusive, grade A building in town."

She was listening intently. The look of defeat had turned to determination. It was like dangling a shot of Basil Hayden in front of a recovering alcoholic. At one point, she even licked her lips.

But then . . . "What you don't know about me, Mr. Secret Agent Man," she began, "is that I'm happy where I am. I served in the Army. I did tours of duty in Afghanistan, Syria, Iraq, and a few other places even you might not know about."

*There's nothing in your service jacket I don't know about,* he thought.

"And I worked with the most elite of all covert intelligence units," she said. "I wear the scars I've picked up along the way with pride. I *like* being an FBI special agent. I *like* being an Interpol agent. I enjoy my overseas posting. My expertise puts me on the front lines. I do things I love to do. You saw me in action yesterday. I'm there for my team. I don't need to prove myself to anyone anywhere. Period."

Caleb looked into her eyes. The fire was lit. He knew now she was just trying to convince herself. Her passion burned deep. He was sure she was in.

\* \* \*

"No," she said emphatically.

She saw disappointment flash in his eyes. She had listened to his ardent appeal and then made a decision he didn't like. She had never been easily swayed by arguments that contradicted her own desires.

*Wishful thinking wasn't seduction.*

She finished her drink, tipped the bartender, and left Caleb behind in the bar, surrounded by hope and his unfulfilled desires, nursing a glass of sparkling mineral water. She set out on foot for her hotel a few blocks away, his arguments still rolling through her mind, unwanted but inescapable.

# CHAPTER 23

Alex blinked, then blinked again to focus her vision. The indigo-blue LEDs on the bedside clock blazed 4:35. She lay on her side, staring past the alarm clock to the faint glow outside her window. Dawn arrived with a muted palette. A siren wailed in the distance, but otherwise, the room was silent, suffused only with pale light and the stillness of her thoughts.

Beside the clock, the display on her phone flared briefly. She resisted the urge to read the new notification. She was an avowed night owl. Despite her predawn wake-up calls and zero-dark-stupid sojourns during her time in the Army and with ISA, she was not a morning person. But despite that, the quiet solitude of a new day had often afforded her the most significant opportunities for self-reflection.

She thought of Krysten: her smile, her zest for life, her beauty. She was special. Had they not been separated by the Atlantic Ocean or the English Channel or by various other barriers over the years, their friendship might have blossomed into a longer-lasting bond.

But Alex had been raised to be independent and unbound by the trappings of traditional friendships—her own nature made her so—and her father had instilled in her a martial mindset at an early age. The way of the warrior was not particularly compatible with building lasting friendships. Besides, the Army had given her all the companionship she needed, and then some.

She rolled onto her back and stared toward the ceiling; a blank canvas nearly invisible in the dark. In her mind's eye, Kyle's face hovered over her. It was stubbled and tanned, but his eyes sparkled with life and mischief, as they had the first time they met. She had been immediately smitten, though it would be months before she would see him again and acknowledge the feeling as being a bud of the emotion it was—love.

She smiled and pushed the memory aside, threw back the thick comforter, and flung her legs over the edge of the bed, her feet touching down on the plush, warm carpet. She stretched, rubbed her eyes, and reached for her phone. One new email. Unlocking her phone, she tapped an app icon, and the message loaded.

She blinked again.

It was an email from the dead. It was an email from Krysten.

The subject line was blank, but there was a note:

Alex,
I've been thinking about you lately and was reminded again of our time in Paris. That city had everything we needed, like that lovely, chilled wine we shared straight out of the icebox in my room. It was as if that bottle held the key to all our desires back then.

And speaking of the conference where we met, lucky for us we kept a close eye on Cronus and Rhea. I'm worried for their kids, though. You were always such a diplomat. Threading the needle came so easy for you!

But everyone has skeletons they'd rather keep hidden in their closet, and our secrets will be forever safe with me here on High Street.

I attached a couple of pics. We looked radiant, didn't we? I hope you remember these moments as fondly as I do. They will always remind me of you and all we stood to lose!

Well, I must sign off now. I don't know when or where, but I hope to see you again soon!

Krysten

*Was it just a coincidence that Krysten sent me this email right before her death? No, she must have known she was in trouble and hoped I could help.*

She reread the note.

Turning on a light, she walked over and popped a pod into the coffeemaker. Within moments, the room filled with the comforting aroma of fresh coffee as the hot, frothy liquid filled a ceramic mug.

*It makes no sense.* This time, she deconstructed it sentence by sentence. She supposed Paris had everything they needed, but it was an odd sentence. While they *had* shared a bottle of wine or two, none had been in her hotel room. They had enjoyed a bottle of Sancerre while sitting on the banks of the Seine right before Krysten had taken the selfie of the two of them opposite the Eiffel Tower. As for being *chilled* and *straight out of the icebox,* well, it was *cool,* but had just been purchased from a nearby restaurant.

And was a bottle of Sancerre really *the key to all our desires*?

They had mainly kept to themselves at the conference except when they were in sessions or lectures with dozens or even hundreds of others. Alex didn't remember anyone named Cronus or Rhea, let alone their kids.

There were two photographs attached to the message. The first was the picture of Alex and Krysten in Trocadéro Gardens, the Eiffel Tower looming in the background. And it was no surprise they looked radiant. Alex chalked that up to the bottle of wine that had painted a blush across their cheeks, together with the golden glow of sunset reflecting off everything in the lavish gardens around them, bathing them in a rich palette of dreamy light.

The second photo was a streetscape she didn't recognize, but as she squinted at it on her phone, it appeared it might also be from Paris: a narrow street lined with cream-colored stone façades resembling Paris's typical Haussmann-style architecture.

*Is there a hidden message here, or was Krysten just possessed of a completely different memory of Paris?*

She could forward the email to Jonathan, the information systems security analyst at Interpol headquarters, but he probably had access from his end and could get into everything she could. Sending it across the digital ether might bring it back to the attention of whoever had intercepted it in the first place.

*Who else could have intercepted my emails?*

The prime suspects, in her mind at least, were still the Russians. But Britain's Government Communications Headquarters, commonly known as GCHQ, could also have been monitoring Krysten's computer and phone activity as a measure to protect her. Perhaps *they* had intercepted her email. Since she was a member of MI5, it would be prudent for them to know what she knew and with whom she shared that knowledge. The adage *Who's watching the watcher?* sprang to mind.

She considered the question some more as she walked to the window and looked out over the pedestrian plaza in front of her hotel. The theaters ringing it remained dark, their marquees and lights dimmed overnight. She raised her window and was rewarded with the sound of rustling leaves from the trees that filled the square, their gentle susurration in the predawn breeze reminding her of her mother's home in upstate New York. The farmhouse sat on a rural property lying along the shores of Cayuga Lake, where the onshore breeze stirred the maple trees in their yard each morning, lacing her childhood memories with the sweet sound of tranquility.

*Right, call Jonathan.* She used one of her burner phones. It rang several times before going to voicemail. She hung up and dialed again. After the fourth ring, a vaguely human-sounding voice answered.

"Did I wake you?" asked Alex, knowing full well she had.

"Who is this?" came the reply.

"It's Alex."

Silence.

She tried again. "Still there?"

"Special Agent Martel?"

"Yes. I need your help, Mr. Burgess."

"Do you know what time it is? And don't call me that. That's my *grand*father's name."

She checked the clock and told him.

"It was a rhetorical question."

"I don't do subtle," she said. "Listen, I received a strange email this morning from a dead MI5 officer."

"I think you could have left out the word *strange* from part A of your sentence, and I still might have drawn my own conclusion from part B."

"You're pretty funny for a computer nerd."

"I'm also attuned to sarcasm. What do you need?"

"I think Krysten wrote the email in code."

"Who's Krysten?"

*Oh, right.*

It took a moment for Alex to clue in that she hadn't discussed the matter of Krysten with Jonathan, so she quickly brought him up to speed.

"And so why do you think her email is in code?" he asked.

She recapped for him her thought process and described the photos.

"Does any of that make sense?" she asked.

She sipped her coffee and watched Leicester Square outside her window fill with the golden glow of dawn. She gave him a moment to gather his thoughts.

"You said there were a couple of photos attached?"

"Yes."

"Do they mean anything to you?"

"Sort of, but not really."

"What does that mean?"

"One is a selfie of Krysten and me. The other is some street scene."

"But you don't recognize it?"

"Nope. Just some random buildings along what looks like an old and narrow street, maybe in Paris."

"Maybe not so random. Have you ever heard of steganography?"

"Who now?"

"Not who. *What.* It's the practice of concealing a file, message, image, or video within another file, message, image, or video. It's a form of cryptology. Specifically, with computer files, we're talking about digital steganography."

"Naturally."

"It's a process that was first used a couple thousand years ago."

"I didn't know they had computers back then."

Ignoring her, he continued. "Its first documented use was in ancient Greece. In that primitive first attempt, some guy wrote a message onto some other guy's head and sent him out as a messenger. To read the message, the recipient had to shave his head."

"So, I should shave my head?"

"Funny. The modern version of steganography uses various methods to embed coded messages into computer files. Sometimes, decrypting the message is simple. Other times, it's impossible to decipher without an encryption key."

"What should I do?"

"Are you an award-winning MIT-educated information technology forensic specialist like me?"

"No."

"Then don't touch it. I'll access it from the server and analyze it—after I've had a coffee. Then again, I could be wrong."

"How so?"

"Maybe they're just two cheesy vacation photos. I take those all the time."

# CHAPTER 24

Alex ventured along Panton Street into the early-morning bustle of pedestrians circulating through Leicester Square. The hotel concierge had pointed her toward a coffee shop less than five minutes away on Haymarket.

The rainy night had yielded to a dreary morning with low-hanging clouds and light rain. A brisk breeze blew head-on as she walked along the narrow road between the buildings. Her light jacket did little to protect her from the chill, and she made the journey in under three minutes.

She was eager to hear Jonathan's analysis of the email from Krysten, but in the meantime, her stomach was insisting on sustenance. Caffè Nero was already busy with commuters picking up their cuppa as she stepped in out of the rain. The barista suggested a cortado, a two-to-one brew of steamed milk and espresso, topped with a thin layer of microfoam. As she made it, Alex also ordered a warmed-up *pain au raisin* and an almond croissant to go.

As she added sugar to her coffee at the condiment stand, one of her three phones pinged. She pulled the two burners from her back pocket. On one was a text from Caleb.

*Odd. I didn't give him that number.*

> CC: Morning, Shooter! I have to jet. Something
> big has come up. I know what you said last
> night, but today's a new day. Are you in or are
> you out?

She stared at the screen and contemplated a response. She had been unequivocal in her answer to him last night. It was a firm *no.*

Why, then, was she so much less sure today?
She typed back.

> AM: What's going on?
> CC: No dice. If you're in, call me. If you're not,
> don't.

*So high school! You know my answer!*
She typed.

> AM: B-bye. Have a nice trip.
> CC: See you 'round, Shooter!

*Dammit!*

She snapped the lid onto her cup and, with her *pain au raisin* and almond croissant dangling in a paper bag, ran back to her hotel in a minute and a half. She wolfed down the raisin swirl on the elevator ride up, then burst into her room, pulled a burner phone from her pocket, and dialed his number.

"I knew you'd come around," he said.

"Look, I can't say your offer doesn't tempt me, but I need to know what's happening first."

"Alex, you know I can't read you in unless you join my team."

"Team? Come on," she said. "Don't give me that secret agent BS. What's going on?"

"Ordinarily, I might play along," he said. "But not on this one."

She hadn't known Caleb long, but he was sounding more somber than his usual self.

"Look," he continued, "to use the full gobbledygook, this is a waived, unacknowledged special access program tasking. You remember what that is? Full IN-SAP and OS-SAP."

She paused before replying. Only the director of national intelligence had the authority to create an intelligence special access program. And an operations and support special access program had to originate with the SecDef or higher. To breach OPSEC on such highly classified information constituted an act of treason against the United States. Knowing this, she wouldn't press him for more information.

"I'm asking you again, Shooter, but I won't ask a third time—you in or out?"

The hairs on the back of her neck were standing up, and she knew it wasn't from the room's air-conditioning. Thoughts swirled as she considered what it would be like to be back in the society of secret squirrels again. That was how she referred collectively to the eighteen or so intelligence and counterintelligence units at the federal government's disposal. She missed it, and Caleb knew it.

"Time's up, Shooter. Gotta jet! Bye!" With that, he disconnected, and the line went silent.

*Dammit! Bressard—he'll know what's going on.*

She dialed her boss.

"You're still using the burner phone?" he asked in lieu of a greeting.

"Chief, are you aware of something big unfolding?"

"Hello to you, too, Alexandra."

"Everybody seems pretty riled up about something."

"Everybody? I don't have any details, but—"

"Bullshit—"

"Stop right there, Special Agent Martel." Bressard's baritone voice could sound as soothing as a whisper or as harsh as a winter storm. It had taken on the timbre of the latter now. "What you said a moment ago is still as true now as it was when it left your lips—I am your chief, your boss. Remember that."

She was letting Caleb get under her skin. All this talk of being on the inside, of seeing what was behind the curtain. But Caleb was right. It was who she was. Who she needed to be. Damned if she'd let him see that, though.

"I'm sorry, Chief. Caleb texted me and told me something big is up."

"Why would he do that?"

"Because he . . ." She almost slipped up and told him, but she didn't want Bressard to know Caleb was courting her, trying to recruit her. "I don't know, boss. I guess he just wanted to show off in front of the cool kids."

"You being the *cool kids* in this example?"

"Something like that." Alex knew there was a good chance Bressard could see right through her. He was no fool and had never had a problem reading her. It was one of the reasons they worked so well together. And yet another reason she didn't want to leave Interpol.

"Try again," he said patiently.

"We were comparing war stories last night, and he was boasting about some of his exploits, that's all. I guess he couldn't resist one-upping me this morning." She hoped he'd buy that explanation.

After a few seconds' pause, he said, "We got word of an incident overnight. Something big. Something . . . a significant event. Every official network comms link is talking about it. Every intelligence and security agency in the western hemisphere is mobilizing resources. I haven't been read in, so I don't know a lot, other than the location."

"Well?" she said. "Where is this alleged incident?"

There was silence on the line as Bressard evidently weighed the pros and cons of sharing the information with Alex over this line.

"Chief?"

He remained silent on the other end. Sometimes, silence spoke louder than words.

She pressed again. "Boss, what's going on?"

"Alexandra, I am just another cog in the wheel. A mere civil servant. I am not privy to everything that goes on in the world."

"With respect, Chief, I don't believe that," she replied. "You're the head of Interpol's National Central Bureau for The Hague and the senior commander for all of Western Europe."

"Turkey."

"What?"

"Something I'm not privy to discuss over a mobile phone is going on in Turkey. If your friend Caleb—"

"He's not my *friend*," she protested, perhaps too much.

"Then allow me to rephrase. If Mr. Copeland has been tasked to this incident, it's big. As for Interpol, we are not directly involved at this time."

She considered this for a moment. Something big that Chief Bressard and Interpol were not directly involved in. But something with global implications. Something with military overtones. And something the chief wasn't willing or able to discuss.

*I want in.*

Caleb had been right. Having peeked behind the

curtain, knowing what was on the other side meant everything to her. The thought of being left out, of not being in the inner circle of those in the know, was in a way humiliating. If pride was her wilderness, as her late husband Kyle had been fond of saying, then she was feeling as alone right now as if she were in the wilds of the Yukon or Alaska.

*Let me in!* her insides screamed.

"You still there?" asked Bressard.

"I'm here. Chief, what would it take to get me assigned to whatever's going on?"

"That's not going to happen as long as you're with Interpol, Alexandra. It's outside our operational scope. Wrap up your visit to London, then come home. Do whatever you need to do as quickly as you can. MI5 and Scotland Yard are leading the investigation into your friend's death. We need you here on the nuclear material smuggling investigation. Which reminds me, I still need your after-action report."

She thought about what he was telling her and what her next move should be.

"Alexandra, understood?" he asked.

*Plausible deniability.*

Sometimes, silence spoke louder than words.

# CHAPTER 25

After ending her call with Chief Bressard, Alex texted Cara in the hopes of seeing Krysten's apartment, or *flat,* as she called it. Cara suggested they meet again at the Shoreditch Grind coffee shop, close to the apartment building she'd shared with Krysten in East London.

Alex walked to the Leicester Square Tube station on Charing Cross Road. Along the way, she couldn't shake the feeling she was being followed, but each time she checked, she came up dry. She headed for the Piccadilly line inside the station and descended the escalator to the subway platform deep below.

Her mission in life was simple: track down, isolate, and eliminate. She existed to help ensure the normal flow of daily life. To intervene where others could or would not. To accept the call, divine or otherwise.

Though not a pious person, Alex had embraced two things from the spiritual realm. The first was adopting St. Michael, the patron saint of warriors and police officers, as her protector. As the saying went, there were no atheists in a foxhole, and she had prayed for divine intervention on more than one occasion. So, besides her dependable Rolex Submariner, the only piece of jewelry she regularly wore was a silver St. Michael medallion on a box chain around her neck.

The second was an oft-quoted passage from the Old Testament that had stuck with her since her early days in the Army when a chaplain had cited it in a sermon she had been obliged to attend.

> Isaiah 6:8. Then I heard the voice of the Lord saying, "Whom shall I send? And who will go for us?"
> And I said, "Here I am. Send me!"

She hadn't known it at the time, but the passage would have a profound effect on her.

*Here I am. Send me!* became her mantra.

When soldiers were wounded. When an operation was deemed too dangerous. When teammates were in peril. When the enemy needed to be neutralized.

*Send me!*

She had long ago come to terms with the fulfillment she derived from ridding the world of evil people. Jailing them gave her a sense of gratification. Killing them on a field of battle left her without remorse.

She often wondered, *What does that say about me?* Perhaps to compensate, she bore a tattoo on her side in simple script: *Isaiah 6:8.*

The train arrived in under a minute. With the seats filled, she grabbed a handrail by the doors and stood among the morning commuters, glancing about. All around her were civilians, their heads buried in their phones, largely oblivious to the dangers of the world around them and the actions of those who put themselves in harm's way to protect and keep them safe.

Her thoughts drifted to Kyle and her time in Afghanistan when she had first picked up a sniper rifle. She had been her platoon's *68-Whiskey,* their combat medic. She was ordered out of her Humvee one kilometer before it reached its objective and sent up the side of a rugged mountain to care for a sniper element who had sustained injuries under fire in their overwatch position.

*Send me!*

And they had.

\* \* \*

### KORENGAL VALLEY, AFGHANISTAN

When Alex arrived at the objective, she found a dilapidated old structure—a *grape hut* in the local vernacular. It was a hardened and weathered two-room building made from mud on a tiny, rock-strewn plateau.

"Hello, fellas," she called as she stepped inside.

"Hi, doc!" said a man lying on the ground, scoping through a sniper rifle. "Welcome to our little casbah in the Valley of Death." He tapped the scope on his rifle. "You looked a little winded coming up the hill." The operator's voice was as gruff and grizzled as his beard.

Disconcerted by the notion of having been caught in his rifle's optics, she glanced around the space. Part of the roof was collapsed, and the walls were broken in several places, providing a gaping hole on the front side through which the sniper team had an unobstructed view of the terrain for miles around.

"Martel," she said by way of introduction. "Alex. Charming place."

"Renovations courtesy of the Red Army. Or the Mujahideen, maybe. Not entirely sure. What took you so long anyway?"

Ignoring his question, she turned to the other soldier in the room and noticed blood had soaked through a dressing on his forearm.

"You do that carving your rib eye last night?"

"Comedian, huh?" he said, a grin set on his chiseled face.

Despite his three-day growth of stubble, she couldn't help noticing how handsome he was.

*Those eyes,* she thought, checking for rank insignia. Seeing none, she fished for his name as she lowered her med pack to the floor.

"Kyle Ward," he said. "And that's Donovan. Call sign Asshole."

"Hey," said the other guy, his eyes still focused downrange through his scope. "It's Donny, doc."

"How'd you really do this, Kyle?"

"Bear wrestling."

"Just for that, this is going to hurt." She unwrapped the old bandage that was partially adhered to the wound. The curved laceration stretched from just below the elbow to the wrist. The edges of the wound were clean and wouldn't require debridement. She irrigated the wound with sterile saline out of her pack, then doused it liberally with antiseptic. As she continued to work, she sized the men up. She had been told they were from 1st Special Forces Operational Detachment–Delta, or simply Delta Force. Hence the absence of any unit or rank insignia.

"I didn't know The Unit was here," she said, referring to one of Delta Force's many aliases.

"We're not."

"What do you mean?"

"I mean, this is Operation Mudslide, and your unit is playing defensive end for our little covert action here in the Korengal Valley."

"Don't listen to him, doc," chimed in Donny. "We're just up here trying to win over the hearts and minds of the local populace."

Kyle laughed. "Donny's idea of winning hearts and minds is two to the chest and one to the head."

"I'm just a medic," Alex said. "No one tells me anything. Speaking of which, where is your 18-Delta?"

The Unit typically had their own Special Forces medical sergeants attached to their troop, but these guys were operating by themselves, up here without medical support.

"That action you didn't know you're supporting? Our doc's up there with the rest of the guys," answered Donny.

She finished cleaning Kyle's wound, then began applying some butterfly skin closures.

"It could use some stitches, but I know you're not going to head back to the command outpost yet."

"Got that right, doc."

She overlapped a few thick nonstick gauze pads along the length of the wound on top of the Steri-Strips, wrapping them snugly with a roller bandage. All the while, his eyes were locked onto hers.

Donny grinned. "You want me to leave? I can go for a walk if you two need to be alone."

"Fuck off, Donny," said Kyle. "Don't mind him, Alex. Everyone who knows him thinks he's a dick."

"That's right, doc. A big one."

Reaching into her pack, she pulled out a bottle of pills and tossed them to Kyle. He caught them with his good hand and gave her a blank stare.

"Antibiotics. Take one three times a day for ten days. Get it checked when you get back to the COP in the next couple of days. It's not infected yet, but infections can set in fast out here, and you wouldn't want to lose your arm."

"Then you'd only have one set of knuckles to drag on the ground," said Donny.

Kyle threw a water bottle at his partner. As it landed, a loud blast shook the building and brought chunks of the ceiling down around them. The explosion was followed by gunfire coming from the direction of Alex's platoon's convoy.

"Fuck! Contact!" shouted Donny. He rubbed grit out of his eyes and squared back up to his rifle.

Alex looked down into the valley in the direction her platoon had traveled. A thousand meters away, a thick column of black smoke and gray dust rose from the valley. Judging by the sound of the explosion, one of the vehicles in the convoy must have set off a roadside bomb. That, in turn, had triggered an ambush from over a rise ahead of them.

Kyle leaped past Alex and squatted behind a spotting scope mounted on a tripod.

"Forty-plus fighters coming over that hill," he said, calmly but with urgency.

Alex's radio squawked with reports of enemy contact from her unit. Lieutenant Sykes's Humvee—the one she had been riding in—was hit. Sykes was already calling for a quick reaction force to assist. Requests for the platoon medic were going out as well. Alex scrambled to put together her backpack, but Kyle yelled at her to drop the pack and pick up her M4.

"Cover our flank, doc. You're not going down there."

Kyle called out a target for Donny, who sent a round with the McMillan TAC-50.

BOOM!

"Hit!" called Kyle. "T-man with an RPG, high right."

"Got him," said Donny, as he ejected the spent round and fed another from the magazine into the TAC-50's chamber.

BOOM!

"Hit!"

Alex kept her head on a swivel, one eye on the action out front and one out the previously blown-open back of the building. She stepped outside and held her M4 at the ready, peering through its Trijicon ACOG scope, scanning the ridge below her to ensure their position wasn't about to be flanked by insurgents. But her mind was on her platoon up the road. They had been hit with an IED, then ambushed by fighters. Her friends were under fire. They were taking casualties. She felt utterly useless, trapped up here with a pair of Tier One operators while members of her own platoon were injured, or worse, and calling for help.

She had sworn she'd be there for them, caring for them. She had made them that promise and had made that same commitment to their wives, kids, and parents. And now, when they needed her most, she wasn't with them.

A trail of smoke arced its way toward their position.

"RPG!" she shouted. She hit the dirt as the rocket-propelled grenade filled with high explosives slammed into the partially crumbled north wall of the grape hut next to her, its warhead detonating on impact. Chunks of the building fell all around, narrowly missing her.

She rose onto a knee and set her sights on two men running in her direction from behind the cover of a boulder and heavy undergrowth forty meters away. One carried a grenade launcher. She targeted the lead man swinging his AK-47 in her direction and dropped him with a three-round burst from her M4. The second man kept coming, so she obliged him with another three-round burst of his very own. The first two bullets caught him in the upper chest. The third caught him in the lower jaw. Through her scope, she watched the spray of blood as his head snapped impossibly to the side, the lower half of his face flying away as he fell dead into the dirt.

The adrenaline that coursed through her gave her a heady thrill. As she continued to scan the terrain for more tangos, a smile raised the corners of her mouth ever so slightly. But the joy ebbed fast when she heard the shrill call from one of the operators inside the hut.

"Doc!"

# CHAPTER 26

**E**xcuse me, miss?"

Alex blinked and turned to see the young man in a London Fog coat whose face was much too close to hers. She pulled away.

"Miss?" he said again.

The jarring of the train coming to a stop in the Old Street Tube station brought her out of her trance. She found herself standing in front of the doors as they opened onto the platform and rode the wave of commuters toward the escalators.

After a twenty-minute journey from her hotel, she had arrived. Outside the London Underground station, the Old Street public square bustled with traffic. The Shoreditch Grind loomed in front of her, its marquee now proclaiming, BECAUSE WHY NOT.

She had no argument with that.

She stepped into the café and scanned the room for the Scottish woman who had initiated this whole adventure. The shop was filled with patrons, but Cara was nowhere to be seen.

She approached the barista behind the counter.

"What can I get ya?" asked the very chipper woman.

She ordered her coffee to stay and was handed a

large red-and-white cup and saucer with steam rising from the brew. It was still early, and already Alex was on her third coffee of the day. Finding a stool along the front counter, she sat staring out over the traffic that passed by the window—not a Russian surveillance team in sight. Or, at least, none that immediately jumped out at her. But that was the point. The crew she encountered yesterday had made mistakes, and it got three of them killed. Alex was sure the next team sent after her would level up.

Her mind shifted back to memories of Kyle, whose arm she had repaired in a grape hut far away and long ago on the occasion of their first meeting. As far as cocktail-party love stories went, it was a doozy.

*How'd you meet your husband, dear?*

*Well, he and his partner were shooting insurgents who were setting IEDs, but he got wounded. Then, the insurgents blew up their mud hut with an RPG. I bandaged his arm with my rifle slung around my back and fell head over heels when I looked into his eyes. Canapé, anyone?*

Being deployed overseas had been challenging, but it was what she had always wanted and where her calling in this life had been confirmed. Thinking back, she felt the same exhilaration she'd felt then as the battle had raged on.

\* \* \*

### KORENGAL VALLEY, AFGHANISTAN

"Doc!"

Sergeant First Class Kyle Ward called out from inside the grape hut. What was left of the ceiling had come down on him and Donny.

Alex scrambled over a debris pile and saw him lying on his side, his formerly good arm pinned under part of the collapsed structure. She sat down on the floor with her back braced against the wall and pushed with both legs against the piece of the building that held him trapped. It yielded just enough that he was able to pull free. When he did, she saw the obvious deformity of his forearm: his radius and ulna both broken mid-shaft, the distal part of his forearm hanging down, their broken ends threatening to punch through the skin between his elbow and his wrist. If that happened, the compound fracture would likely evolve into a badly infected wound, compromising any chance Kyle had for proper healing.

He howled as it dropped into a freakish position before he could cradle it with his bandaged arm.

"Support it with your good hand," she directed, jumping past him to check on Donny.

When she got to him, she found that a large chunk of the ceiling had fallen on him.

"What?" shouted Kyle when he saw her hesitate. "Do something!"

"I can't, Kyle." She looked over again at Donny, his brains exposed through a large avulsion of his skull, glistening red in a ray of sunlight that streaked into the hut from the west side.

"Alex, help Donny!"

"There's nothing I can do, Kyle. He's gone."

Fighting her own queasiness at the gruesome sight of a fellow soldier mortally wounded and knowing she could do nothing for him, Alex ran outside the building in the direction from which the RPG had come, keenly aware that they were still vulnerable to attack. Three more military-aged males were fifty yards out, coming up fast toward their position. Each cradled an AK. She dropped to a knee and sighted in the first, the four-times magnification of her scope bringing him much closer than he was. She let loose with a burst of fire from her M4 that took him out instantly. The other two immediately dropped prone, aiming through iron sights and sending rounds that tore up the ground in front of her. Rock chips and sand struck her face. Her ballistic goggles shielded her eyes, but she tasted the dry grit inside her mouth as it scraped against her teeth. She missed the closest fighter on her first try but got him with a follow-up volley. The other tried to bug out, but she took him down with a burst that landed between his shoulder blades, and he plunged facedown onto a rock. Even from this range, she imagined she heard the crack of his skull.

She scanned the mountain slope for more insurgents. Seeing none, she ran back into what was left of their firing position. A gray-blue cloud of smoke from the exploded RPG lingered, engulfing them in a pungent, slightly sweet odor. The sound of heavy fighting a thousand meters up the road filled her with anger. Columns of smoke rose from damaged vehicles. Her platoon was engaged in an intense battle while she was back here fighting to defend this grape hut.

"Kyle, you have to get on the gun."

He looked at her, then down at his arms. His eyes were wide with pain, adrenaline, and frustration.

"I can't," he said. "*You* have to get on the gun!"

"Me? No way. I don't have any training on a fifty-cal."

"It's the same as any other rifle. I'll spot for you."

"But—"

"No buts, Martel! Pick up that rifle and find a spot to set up. I'll talk you through."

He was right. There was no other option. Running up to her platoon was out of the question. She would have no cover except for a couple of trees and some rocks dotting the slope here and there. She'd be dead before she got within five hundred yards. She looked at the McMillan TAC-50, then back at Kyle. He glared at her from behind the spotting scope.

Balancing on the debris of the grape hut, she swung her M4 to her back and tugged on the thirty-pound sniper rifle locked in Donny's grasp. It came away, and she hauled it to a spot with less debris and set it down on its bipod, but quickly realized she didn't have enough clearance over the collapsed wall of the damaged building. She shoved her med bag under the rifle's fore-end, giving it added height.

"Feed a round," said Kyle quietly.

The rifle was nothing like her Army-issued M4. She retracted its bolt and a spent round ejected. She had fired lots of different hunting and competition rifles growing up, but this one was heavier than any she had ever used. Its action was surprisingly smooth, though. She slid the bolt forward firmly, locking a .50 BMG round into the chamber.

She placed her cheek against the stock of the rifle and felt Donny's sticky, wet blood on the side of her face. Suppressing her revulsion, she looked through the scope.

"The technical—the pickup truck on the road with the Dushka mounted on it, see it?" Kyle asked.

"I see it."

"It's out nine hundred and fifty meters. Take out the machine gunner in the back."

She watched a man strafe large-caliber rounds at her platoon with the Soviet-made DShK heavy machine gun while they dove for cover behind overturned vehicles in the wadi. She tried to keep him in the middle of her crosshairs, but his image danced around inside the scope.

"Everything's moving. I can't get a clear shot."

"Nothing's moving," Kyle said calmly. "Control your breathing, Alex."

"I can't do this, Kyle! I don't know how—"

"Sergeant, follow my orders! You are going to work that rifle. We clear?"

"Yes, Sergeant."

"Good. Pull that rifle butt tight into the pocket of your shoulder. Now, take a full breath in and let it out slowly. Focus on the reticle. Your sight picture will stabilize. There will be a natural pause when you finish exhaling. Squeeze the trigger during the pause. In, out, rest, two, three. Got it?"

"Yes," she replied, following his instructions. *Focus on the reticle.*

*In, out, rest, two, three.*

The image in her scope settled as she exhaled, the crosshairs landing over center-mass of the shooter. She squeezed the trigger.

*BOOM!*

The force of the rifle's recoil scared the hell out of her. It felt like someone had slammed her in the shoulder. The pressure wave jolted the room and kicked up a cloud of dust that briefly obscured her vision downrange. More debris fell around them from the partially collapsed ceiling.

"Miss. You're low left. Your round punched a hole in the side of the truck. See it? Try again," he said with all the patience of a parent teaching a child to tie their shoe. "Steadier this time. Slow is smooth, smooth is fast. Breathe. Get a clear sight picture. Slowly squeeze the trigger like you're closing a fist, then hold the trigger for a few beats before releasing it after the shot."

She chambered another round and pulled the butt of the rifle more snugly into her shoulder.

*Focus on the reticle.*

*In, out, rest, two, three.*

Squeeze.

*BOOM!*

She was ready for the recoil this time and didn't flinch. When the rifle steadied again, she saw the man on the machine gun crumple and fall off the back of the pickup.

"Hit!" called Kyle. "Nice shot, Alex!" He tossed a loaded five-round magazine to her. "Swap out your mag and reload," he said.

She found the magazine release, dropped out the old one, and seated the new one.

"There's two guys on an eighty-two-millimeter mortar twenty meters behind the truck."

"I see them."

"Come up three clicks. Understand what I'm saying?"

"Yes."

It was coming back to her. Her dad had taught her to hunt, and she was good at it. But when they hunted, their quarry was a quarter of this distance or even closer. She chambered another round, then adjusted her aim.

Breathe. Squeeze. *BOOM!*

"Hit! You're doing great!"

She chambered another round and took out the second guy on the mortar.

"Hit! Holy shit! Your first three kills on a TAC-50 are out at over nine hundred meters! Awesome, Alex!"

She reloaded.

# CHAPTER 27

SHOREDITCH, EAST LONDON

Alex stared out the shop window, sipping her coffee. She had no control over when a memory would surge back like the onslaught of a rogue wave. The last few days had been filled with more intrusive memories than usual, both good ones and bad. Had Krysten's death triggered a release valve in her mind, or was Caleb slipping into her subconscious in a way and a place that she thought she had walled off for good? She didn't know and felt uneasy about what that could mean.

Coming out of her daydream, she noticed a pretty woman with a narrow face and high cheekbones approaching the coffee shop. She recognized Cara immediately.

"Hi, hi!" she said as she stepped inside, greeting Alex like an old friend with a wave and a half hug.

"Hi, Cara. Do you want a coffee?"

"Lord, no. I'm wired enough already from my two cups of tea, but I thought it would be easier to meet here than to try to give you directions to Krysten's flat."

"Shall we go then?" suggested Alex, draining the coffee from her cup.

Cara led them along the sidewalk past brick-fronted low-rise buildings to a rejuvenated factory that had been given new life as an upscale complex of loft apartments. As they crossed the lobby's wide-planked wood floors, Alex noted the framed prints on the exposed brick walls depicting scenes from the Blitzkrieg. A commemorative plaque revealed that the building—or at least a former incarnation of it—had been a casualty of war on that first night of the bombing campaign that began on September 7, 1940, with the arrival of three hundred German Luftwaffe bombers over London. The impoverished East End had suffered more than its fair share of death and destruction.

She slowed her pace to look at the pictures.

"This way, Alex," Cara called.

Alex caught up, and they boarded an elevator that took them to the uppermost level. The doors opened onto a large and airy vestibule, an open staircase to the right leading three stories back down to the main floor.

Three hallways ran off the elevator lobby, a kind of central column in the middle of the old factory floor, it seemed. Cara led them down the one to the left. Skylights in the ceiling bathed them in natural light. At the end of the hallway, crime scene tape was strung across the door to what had to be Krysten's flat.

"What should we do now?" asked Cara.

Alex reached up and tore away the tape. Cara looked at her, mouth agape.

"Can you do that?"

Alex shrugged.

Cara opened the door using a key she pulled from her purse.

"My flat is one floor down," she explained. "Krysten never gave me a key, but she told me where she hid a spare, and I grabbed it right after she died."

"You have a devious mind," said Alex.

"Thank you. I think." Now it was her turn to shrug.

The bright and airy theme continued as they stepped into a narrow corridor. Large pendant bulbs hung suspended on red electrical cords strung from the high ceiling. The women walked along the wide-planked wood floors through a decorative iron gate into an open-concept kitchen/dining room/living room combination. The original exposed brickwork, soaring ceilings, Crittall windows, and steel beams gave it a vintage feel.

Simultaneously, the furnishings—a mix of modern and traditional—imparted a more contemporary tone. A bright, sky-blue seventies-era matching sofa and ottoman opposed a set of distressed leather club chairs that Alex assumed were antiques, with a wooden crate between them that served as a coffee table.

The apartment seemed to fit Krysten, but was an even more pronounced expression of the woman Alex had known, and she suddenly missed knowing her all the more. She was filled with a profound sense of loss, more than she had expected, and she put a hand to her mouth as if to keep her emotions from spilling out.

She stepped into the living room and studied the shelves along the wall. They held an eclectic selection of books. The diverse collection spoke to Krysten's curiosity and intellect. Alex remembered her as a bright woman, a shining star in the shadowy world of international security and intelligence.

*Why was Krysten killed?*

This was both the central question in the investigation being carried out by Scotland Yard and MI5, as well as being at the forefront of Alex's thoughts.

*What did she know or what had she discovered that put her in someone's crosshairs?*

Alex looked around the room. Krysten had been living well. Her cover, of course, had to mesh with her supposed station in life. As a manager with a tech accelerator firm, her lifestyle had to reflect that she was a woman of means. This place indeed said that, and then some.

She walked from room to room, getting a feel for a side of Krysten she hadn't known. Her furnishings were a mixture of high-end modern pieces and expensive, restored antiques. When she peered into the master bedroom and the guest room, it was apparent that someone had already searched them. She concluded that Scotland Yard had done a cursory examination of the premises, but the flat didn't have the feel of having been *tossed*.

Cara shadowed her like a puppy, seemingly unsure of what she should do or say.

An empty picture frame sat on another bookshelf in Krysten's bedroom.

"That's where I found the picture of the two of you in Paris," Cara offered.

Alex nodded and acknowledged the intimacy of that fact. She was surprised Krysten kept the photo on display, let alone here in her bedroom. *Was it part of her cover? Was it genuine fondness? Had I missed another chance to get close to someone?*

There were other pictures as well. One was of Krysten with an older couple who Alex presumed to be her parents.

"She said they had both passed," said Cara. "I don't know who's in the other photo."

The other photo was of a much younger Krysten with a man about the same age. They looked like a couple. Alex picked it up and removed it from its frame, inspecting the back. No names, no dates. Just another mystery.

Her work phone began vibrating in her pocket and she pulled it out. *Kane* appeared on the display.

"Where are you?" he asked when she answered.

"I'm at Krysten's apartment."

"I'll pretend I didn't hear that," he said. "I have an update."

"Go on," she said.

# CHAPTER 28

SHOREDITCH, EAST LONDON

The call from Daniel Kane was not altogether unexpected. He had cut things short the previous night at St. Stephen's Tavern, claiming he had work to attend to. And while he clearly wasn't pleased Alex was on the premises of a crime scene, he didn't order her to stand down. Not that she would have, had he done so.

"The forensic pathologist who conducted Krysten's postmortem examination reported that her death can be, how did she say it—" Alex heard pages in a notebook being flipped. "—can be attributed to a single traumatic injury, even though she suffered multiple life-threatening injuries."

"Go on."

"The cause of death was a blow to the head."

"What else did she say?"

"She said that while Krysten could have sustained these injuries by being struck by a car, the single lethal blow seems to have been inflicted by a hard object, like being kicked with a steel-toed boot. Seems there was an imprint left behind."

"Anything else?"

"The coroner said there were bruises and abrasions on her arms as if she had been manually restrained and had fought against it. There were no other life-threatening injuries and no indication that she was sexually assaulted. Both the forensic pathologist and the chief coroner agreed that these signs were consistent with a violent altercation—a fight—and not a bodily collision with a motor vehicle."

"So," she summarized, "somebody beat Krysten to death and then staged her death to look like an accident—a hit-and-run." Alex caught sight of Cara standing in the doorway. Her face blanched, and Alex thought she might fall over, but she sat on the side of the bed to steady herself.

"As clumsy as it sounds, that would be the truth of it. Alex, the coroner has ruled Krysten's death a homicide. It's now official."

Silence.

"Special Agent Martel?"

"Homicide. I heard you. Krysten was murdered."

*How did this make anything better?*

She thought she'd be relieved, but she wasn't. What she *was* was more resolved to find and punish her killers.

"Well, we suspected that, didn't we?" he replied. "But this gives our investigation more impetus to go after them, whoever they are. Alex, they were clumsy."

*Very clumsy. Or just didn't care if they appeared that way.*

"Thank you for calling and catching me up with Krysten's case. I'm going to finish up here, then I have to catch a flight home. I'm needed there."

"Right."

They said their goodbyes, and she hung up.

Alex walked around to Cara and put a hand on her shoulder. "I'm sorry," she said. "I shouldn't have been so blunt."

Some of Cara's color had returned, and she asked, "Now what do we do?"

"We keep digging," Alex said.

"What are we looking for?"

"We'll know when we find it, I guess."

She looked around Krysten's bedroom, surveying it with a critical eye this time, not as an estranged friend but like an investigator. Then she walked through the other rooms—the guest room, home office, and bathroom. Except for a section where it appeared as though a few tiles were being replaced, everything was tidy. Everything was unremarkable. Cara was at her heels the whole way.

"Maybe I could be more helpful if I knew what I should be doing," she said.

Alex entered the kitchen and opened the refrigerator door.

"Hungry?" asked Cara, who had sunk deep into the cushions of a leather chair, her knees up, the soles of her shoes resting against the edge of a wooden crate coffee table.

Ignoring her, Alex scanned the contents of the fridge. A bottle of milk. Packaged meats, cold cuts, some fruits and vegetables. A shelf load of condiments. A bottle of San Pellegrino in the door next to a bottle of wine. Four cans of Diet Coke.

Normal. Everything looked normal.

She closed the refrigerator and took a seat at the island, the quartz surface cold under her arms. She thought about Krysten's email, its mysterious message teasing her, forcing her not just to recollect the time they'd spent together in Paris but to reevaluate her own investigative skills overall. She acknowledged that she was a more highly skilled shooter than a detective, in the truest sense of the word. Shooting solutions came naturally to her— angles, arcs, trajectories, ballistics, ballistic coefficients, and terminal ballistics. These things spoke to her, and she could understand them.

Cara came over and sat next to her at the island.

"A quid for your thoughts?" she said, resting her chin down on her hand.

"I'm thinking that I need to get back to my own job. That I should leave this matter to the local authorities."

"What about Krysten?"

"I don't know what else I can do, Cara. I'm sure the police will help locate next of kin if there are any. Anyway, it's outside my scope. I've been recalled to The Hague to resume working on another critical case." Cara looked defeated. "I'm sorry. I know you wanted to hear better news."

"It's not that," she said. "I just feel so helpless. I know the police will help, but it's all such a tragedy."

Alex got up and fetched two glasses from the shelf above the sink, placing them on the island. The morning coffees had left her feeling parched.

"It *is* a tragedy."

"Maybe if I had tried to get to know her better, like a friend should, she would have told me if she was in trouble."

*Like a friend should.* The words stung.

Alex opened the fridge and retrieved the bottle of sparkling water, twisting off the cap and sniffing the bottle's contents before pouring. She filled their glasses and gulped hers down, feeling the cold, bubbly mineral water chill her mouth and throat as she drank. It felt good. Refreshing. Cold.

"What's wrong?" asked Cara, seeing Alex staring at the bottle.

# CHAPTER 29

KRYSTEN'S APARTMENT, SHOREDITCH,
EAST LONDON

Alex turned and opened the fridge, staring at the bottle of wine in the door. It was a Sancerre, a white wine from the Upper Loire Valley of France. Specifically, it was a bottle of La Vivandière, the same delicious wine she and Krysten had enjoyed along the banks of the Seine in Paris.

The email.

*Chilled wine. Icebox.*

Cara's eyes bulged. "Now you're talking. Like I always say, it's never too early for wine!"

*There were no iceboxes in either of our hotel rooms in Paris.*

Alex studied the bottle. It appeared unopened. A foil cap covered the cork.

The words from Krysten's note played in her mind.

*. . . like that chilled bottle of wine we shared straight out of the icebox.*

"What's wrong?" Cara asked.

Alex held the bottle up to the light. She could see there was liquid in the bottle. It appeared full.

She pulled Krysten's email up on her phone and read it: *It seemed as if it held the key to all our desires . . .*

She shook it. It still had the weight of a full bottle. She tipped it upside down. Everything appeared normal.

Alex held the bottle closer so she could examine it more carefully. She rotated it in her hand and, using a fingernail, started working at a corner of the label, trying to peel it away. She kept her nails clipped short, making the job all but impossible.

Cara noticed Alex's futile efforts and reached across the island, gently snatching the bottle from her grasp. "Give it here," she said in her thick brogue. She used a long, glistening, scarlet-painted nail to lift a corner. She pulled gingerly and the label slowly came away from the glass. When it was off, Alex reached out her hands.

"Good work," she said, carefully taking the bottle from Cara and setting it down on the countertop. She twisted it around in a circle. "Well, I'll be damned."

"What is it?"

Removing the label revealed a crack around the circumference of the bottle. *No, not a crack. A cut.* Someone had deliberately and meticulously cut the bottle in half, then glued it back together. She tried to pry it apart, but whatever glue had been used for the job, the bond was holding fast. She studied it closely. Whoever did this had also fitted some barrier between the top and bottom sections, locking the liquid in.

"Why would she have something like this?" Cara asked. "We should smash it open," she said, motioning like she was swinging a hammer.

"Well, *smash* wouldn't exactly be my first choice," replied Alex.

There appeared to be a compartment of some kind glued into the bottle, separating the top section from the bottom midway up. It had been hidden from view behind the label. She rummaged through shelves in the island and drawers under the counter, looking for some way of opening it. Nothing.

"What are you looking for?" asked Cara.

"A hammer." In the bottom drawer, Alex found a

stainless steel meat tenderizer. "This'll do," she said, gripping the bottle and raising the kitchen tool into the air.

"Wait! What are you doing?" asked Cara, turning to the set of drawers beside the sink. "You'll make a right mess." She fumbled around and returned with a wine key—a waiter's corkscrew. "Give me that," she said, taking the bottle from Alex. "Let's at least empty it first."

Cara deftly cut the protective foil off the top of the bottle, then removed the cork. It came out with a slight *pop*.

"Impressive," said Alex.

"I worked as a waitress for years. Do you think we can drink it?"

Alex gave her a wry look.

"Never hurts to ask."

Cara turned and poured the contents of the bottle into the sink, then stopped.

"What's the matter?" asked Alex.

"It stopped pouring."

Alex took the bottle from her and peered down through the opening at the top.

"That compartment in the middle is preventing the bottom half of the bottle from emptying."

"Let's see that." Cara snatched the bottle back from Alex and wrapped it in a tea towel. "Don't want to scratch this beautiful sink," she said.

Then, holding the bottle by the neck, she swung the steel mallet, striking it with a muted *tink!* But it didn't break. She took a mightier wind-up and, with greater force, slammed the steel hammer into the side of the bottle. The top cracked, and the bottom fell away with the towel, dropping together into the sink. Cara let out a squeal of delight.

"You did it!" Alex said.

Cara set the lower half of the bottle down on the island, and the two women sat around it.

"What is *that*?" asked Cara, pointing inside the lip of the glass.

They were both looking at a circular plastic container fused onto the perimeter of the bottle with a strip of wax.

"I think it's a petri dish," said Alex.

It was filled with a translucent substance, similar to what was adhering the dish to the inside of the bottle. With a knife from Krysten's cutlery drawer, Alex pried the Petri dish free. Opening it revealed a white substrate. Breaking even more chem-bio-rad rules, she scratched the surface with her fingernail and brought it to her nose to sniff.

"I'm pretty sure it's just a paraffin wax."

She dug in and pulled out the soft material from the dish, then began to pull it apart, searching for whatever was inside. She cleared away most of the wax, revealing a dark shape.

"It looks like a key," said Cara.

*It seemed as if it held the key to all our desires . . .*

"Let's clean it up," said Alex.

Cara pulled a length of aluminum foil off a roll from the cabinet and laid it across a grate on the gas stove.

"Great idea," said Alex, placing the remaining blob onto it.

She turned on the burner. Within seconds, the wax began to liquefy, revealing a shiny brass key. The bow, or head, was in the shape of a three-leaf clover. The blade had several distinctive cuts, some shallow, some deep. The number *407* was stamped on one side of the head.

"What kind of key is that?"

*Good question,* thought Alex, picking it up gingerly

with a paper towel from under the cupboard and wiping it clean.

*Private locker? Safe-deposit box? Backyard shed?*

She turned the key over in her hand. The opposite side of the head was stamped with the word DIEBOLD in all caps. Alex recognized the name. Diebold Safe & Lock Company was one of the most renowned in the world.

They could sit there guessing all day, but Alex was quite sure she knew someone who could give them an answer pronto.

"Do you have any coins?"

Cara gave her a quizzical look, but she reached into her pocket and fished out a silver-colored ten-pence coin. Alex laid it on the counter, lion side up, to provide a sense of scale. It was roughly the same size as an American quarter. Its diameter was about two-thirds the length of the key. Using her phone, she snapped a photo of both sides of the key, then fired the images off to Jonathan at Interpol in a text:

AM: Need to know what this is for. ASAP.

A moment later, a reply:

JB: On it

"What now?" asked Cara.

"Now we tidy up."

"I mean, about the key?"

"I'll have to wait to hear back from my colleague," said Alex.

As they cleaned up the kitchen, Alex contemplated the significance of the key. Or, more to the point, what it meant that Krysten had concealed it.

*Who was she hiding it from? What secrets did the*

*key unlock? Daniel Kane was her partner, but did he
know about the key? Or was Krysten concealing it from
him as well?*

She held the key up between her thumb and forefinger, studying it, thinking about its purpose, its meaning.
One thing was for sure—it was evidence. And for perhaps the first time in her law enforcement career, she
wasn't sure what to do about that inconvenient detail.

As they finished tidying up, Alex heard the distinctive sound of the front door opening.

# CHAPTER 30

Alex tucked the key into her pocket, put a finger to her lips to silence Cara, and waved her into a corner of the kitchen behind her. Drawing her Glock, she held it close in front of her, elbows bent, the weapon pointed toward the hallway.

The sound of leather-soled shoes striding along the wooden floor filled the now-silent apartment. A figure wearing a long, dark coat came out of the hallway and into the kitchen.

"Stop right there!" Alex commanded.

The man was startled backward. "Don't shoot!" he said, raising his hands.

"Kane?"

"Yes, it's me. Of course it's me. For goodness' sake, who else would it be? Put that thing away."

"Keep your knickers on, Danny boy. I wasn't about to shoot you." She holstered her Glock. "Why didn't you tell me on the phone that you were coming over?"

"It was an afterthought. Since I was close by, I thought, why not pop over and see how your illegal search is going? The Westminster mortuary isn't far away."

"Convenient."

She wasn't a fan of people just *popping over* under

such circumstances either. It carried with it a whiff of something not unlike the smell coming off the Thames at low tide.

"Quite," he replied.

"I thought the apartment had already been searched and was no longer considered a crime scene," she said.

"Yes, well, it was searched, but to the best of my knowledge, Scotland Yard hasn't yet released it. So, technically, you're mistaken. And you're breaking the law."

"Good thing you're here then. More official this way."

Kane wore a dark suit under a navy overcoat. Polished black oxfords completed the ensemble. He walked around the apartment, looking at the shelves, eyeing the furnishings, the coffee table. He scrutinized Alex closely, then looked at Cara, still backed into a corner of the kitchen. His arms hung limply by his side.

"Miss Maveety, so good to see you again," he said, his eyes distant. He suddenly looked sad, regretful.

"You as well, DI Kane," said Cara, stepping over to stand by Alex, almost hiding behind her.

"She certainly had a flair for interior design," he said to no one in particular. "Quite a remarkable aesthetic."

"Did Scotland Yard find anything when they searched it?" asked Alex.

"Not that I'm aware of," he replied. "They took some of her things into evidence—her phone, her purse, her computer, that sort of thing. But to my knowledge, I'm afraid they found no clues that would point us to her killers."

He walked to the shelves and studied the books more closely.

"She was a voracious reader," he said, pulling an illustrated edition of *Jane Eyre* by Charlotte Brontë from the shelf, fanning the pages as if hoping for a clue to fall out. "Anyway, what about the two of you?" His eyes searched theirs. "Any luck? Finding anything, I mean."

Cara started to speak. "We—"

"We only just started when you called," said Alex, touching Cara's hand to signal that she should stop talking. Alex knew it was time to leave. They had searched the apartment. She had the key, and she didn't want Daniel Kane to know she had it. At least, not yet. She wasn't sure why, but she had learned long ago to trust her instincts. For now, the evidence it might reveal was hers alone.

"Well, Kane, I have to return to The Hague."

"Yes, of course," he said. "You'll keep in touch, though, won't you?"

"Of course. And I hope you'll continue to keep me in the loop with regards to Krysten's murder."

"Naturally," he offered, seemingly distracted by whatever thoughts were running through his mind.

"The key to the apartment is on the coffee table. You'll lock up, won't you?" said Alex.

She tapped Cara's hand again in a manner that said, *Come with me now,* and the two of them made a beeline for the front door.

\* \* \*

"What's going on?" asked Cara once they were outside Krysten's building.

"Call it a gut instinct. Look, I really do have to leave. I don't know what Kane knows, but I want you to be careful."

"Okay, okay," said Cara. "You're kind of freaking me out, but I'm asking you to promise you'll let me know when you have any information about what happened to Krysten. I mean, it still makes no sense to me."

"I promise," said Alex, taking Cara by the hands.

"One way or another, I'll be in touch and let you know what I find out."

The women split up, Cara waving goodbye as she crossed the road. As Alex walked away, one of her burner phones buzzed in her pocket.

\* \* \*

"Here in London?" asked Alex.

"Right there."

Jonathan Burgess explained that the key Alex and Cara had discovered was a model unique to a series of safe-deposit boxes provided by Diebold Safe & Lock Company and found in only a few banks in the British capital.

"Also, the streetscape in that second photo attached to Krysten's message was taken on Threadneedle Street in London. If you zoom in, you can see a small sign sticking out above the sidewalk from the wall on the right, by the intersection. The sign has a black horse on it that's rearing up, and it's looking over its back toward its behind. That's the logo of Lloyds Bank, the largest retail bank operation in Britain," he said. "There's a retail branch at that location right in what's referred to as the High Street District, at the corner of Threadneedle and Bishopsgate." He waited for the penny to drop. "Alex, that's what her note was telling you. It *is* a coded message. *Threading the needle came so easy for you.* She's talking about Threadneedle Street. *Our secrets will be forever safe with me here on High Street.* High Street isn't an actual London street name; it references a district in London. Specifically, the business and financial district, of which Threadneedle is arguably the centerpiece."

"Good Lord," Alex said.

"I'm sure that Krysten's note is, in part at least, pointing you to a safe-deposit box inside a bank in downtown London. A safe-deposit box for which she even handed you the key."

"Can you send me an address?"

"Already texted it to you."

"Anything else, Sherlock?"

"Who are Cronus and Rhea?"

"No idea," she replied.

"Okay, I'll keep looking into it. Look, I scanned your work phone again. There was some code embedded in the OS that I wiped out, but I wiped it out before, too," he explained.

"Like a Trojan?"

"Something like that. I'd wiped it out of the operating system before, but it showed up again. Which leads me to believe we're dealing with some pretty high-level actors here."

"Like, *state* actors?"

"Probably. An Israeli tech firm called NSO Group created spyware called Pegasus a few years ago that was capable of remote zero-click surveillance of smartphones. They leased it to governments around the world to bolster counterterrorism initiatives, but some of them used it for less noble purposes. Whatever's on your phone seems like an enhanced version of that. Maybe it's an upgrade. Or it could be that someone reverse engineered the source code and created a whole new app."

"Who'd be capable of that?"

"Well, quite a few groups, actually. But because of everything else that's happening, I'd lay odds on Russian intelligence. We're at war, Alex. In cyberspace. But no one wants to talk about that."

"That fits."

"It does? Care to explain?"

"Not now," she said. "Can you guarantee my phone will stay clean?"

"I honestly can't, but I installed my own code in case it shows up again."

"Like a tripwire?"

"Exactly like that. It'll notify me the second it detects any non-native code going active on your device. And if I'm notified, you'll be notified."

"Thanks." She pulled the phone away to look at the notification that had just buzzed against her ear. "Just got your text with the bank address."

"All the same, you should assume your agency-issued comms are compromised and stick with other methods if you need to send secure messages or have private conversations."

"Copy."

"Happy hunting."

"Thanks," she said, ending the call.

The midmorning traffic in London never seemed to ebb. Cars and buses flowed in a steady stream. It was like walking beside a great river and seeing neither its beginning nor its end.

Alex contemplated her next move, which would be to persuade Chief Bressard to let her follow up on what she had learned. It would mean a trip to Lloyds Bank to see what was inside Krysten's safe-deposit box.

*Had the contents of that box gotten her killed? What other secrets had Krysten hidden there, and why?*

As she psyched herself up for her conversation with Bressard and lined up her rationale for staying in London longer, her phone began buzzing in her pocket again.

# CHAPTER 31

SHOREDITCH, EAST LONDON

I'm going to Turkey?" she repeated.

She had barely said hello to Chief Bressard before he jumped in with the news that an aircraft was on its way to pick her up at RAF Northolt, a Royal Air Force airfield west of London.

"I received a call from the secretary general herself," said Bressard. "Your FBI handlers in Washington called Madame Clicquot directly to request you fly immediately to Turkey."

"Is this related to the incident at Arnhem? Is it where Caleb was heading after I spoke to him this morning?"

"A nuclear bomb has been stolen from Incirlik Air Base in Adana."

"What? The American air base? When . . . How?"

"I wasn't given any details. It's still very compartmentalized. But my guess is that all these recent events are somehow tied together. And now, for whatever reason, people at FBI and Interpol want you on the ground in Turkey."

Her mind reeled from the idea that a nuke had been stolen.

"Alexandra," he continued, his voice dropping an octave. "For the FBI national security branch to jump over my head and go straight to the secretary general in Lyon speaks volumes about the gravity of the situation."

She considered this. It was what she had been asking for—to be brought into the inner sanctum as events were unfolding—so she couldn't quite believe her next words.

"Chief, I need a couple of hours before I leave London."

"Are you joking? You are to proceed immediately to the airfield where a jet is standing by."

"I know, I know, but hear me out."

She brought him up to speed on her discovery of the key in Krysten's apartment, the email's meaning as deciphered by Jonathan, and the connection to the nearby Lloyds Bank branch.

"Whatever it is that Krysten is pointing me toward must be germane to the incidents in Arnhem and Turkey," she said.

"But you can't be sure of that," he countered.

"No, I can't," she admitted. "But, Chief, I never ask you for anything—"

"Come again?"

"Okay, scratch that, but you have to admit I'm not often wrong with my hunches."

There was silence on his end of the call that she dared not interrupt.

"Fine," he said at last. "I'll tell them you'll be at the airport in ninety minutes."

Alex did a silent fist pump as she picked up her walking pace. Traffic continued flowing along Great Eastern as she approached the Grind at Old Street. She wasn't sure she'd be done and able to get to the airfield so quickly, but somehow, she'd make it work.

Now to get to the bank.

\* \* \*

SHOREDITCH, EAST LONDON

After the call from Bressard, Alex crossed to the south side of the square and waited. Soon, a taxi pulled along the curb, the passenger-side window rolled down.

"It's great to see you again, miss," said the cabby. "I'm dead chuffed you kept my number."

"It's been an interesting couple of days, Gareth," she replied, climbing into the backseat. "Thanks for coming to get me."

"I wouldn't have missed a chance to see you again for all the tea in China," he said. "Now, tell me all about it."

After she gave him the address for Lloyds Bank at 39 Threadneedle Street, he made a U-turn and merged with morning traffic. When she had finished recapping the highlights of yesterday's events and the foot chase, he glanced at her in his rearview mirror.

"You don't look none the worse for wear, miss, except for that nick under your eye. The news on the telly wasn't saying much, other than three people were dead. I was worried until they said they were all men that were killed. Scotland Yard isn't doing much talking, neither. We don't get many shootouts in London, so I figured it must have been you, but glad to see you're still among the living, that's for bloody sure."

"Me, too," she replied. "Turns out the folks tailing us yesterday were a determined bunch."

"I should say so. Do you know what it was all about?"

"Not really." She had already told him more than she should; she wasn't about to tell him about the missing nuke, too.

"Understood, miss. I don't have the proper security clearance anyways." He chuckled. "Well, better you than me. I left my running and gunning days behind me in Afghanistan." Despite his concern for her well-being, he wore a broad smile as he regarded her in the rearview mirror.

Now and then, Alex peered over her shoulder. She was trying to be discreet, but her attempts to detect a tail didn't go unnoticed.

"I don't blame you for being jittery. I'll let you know if we have company, miss," he said. "So far, we're running clean. I've got them caterpillar drive engines engaged."

She caught his reference to *The Hunt for Red October,* one of her favorite Tom Clancy books and movies growing up.

"Not so much jittery as not wanting the extra attention again."

"Understood."

They entered a section of London dominated by tall office towers, all of which seemed of a newer vintage. She surmised they were driving through the commercial and financial district.

*High Street.*

"There she is, luv."

Up ahead on the right, Alex saw a classical stone building, four stories tall, its entrance facing diagonally into the intersection. In the archway above a short flight of stairs hung a circular sign displaying the Lloyds Bank black horse on a white field. Once again, her senses tingled. Once again, she tapped the Glock at her hip.

Alex hopped out of the passenger side of the cab—the left side—and stood on the sidewalk in the shadow of the building behind her. Across the road, the entrance to Lloyds Bank was sunlit and welcoming. But time was ticking.

# CHAPTER 32

ADANA, TURKEY

Viktor Gerasimov caught an overnight flight from London to Belgrade via Air Serbia, then boarded a Turkish Airlines Boeing 737-800 bound for Adana, a city of two million that was one of the oldest continuously inhabited settlements in the world and whose name had remained unchanged for four millennia.

Not everything in this world was as everlasting.

Gerasimov gazed through his window and spied the six sky-scraping minarets arranged around the massive central dome of the Sabanci Merkez Mosque. It stood out against a cerulean-blue sky as if guarded by a crop of nuclear-tipped ballistic missiles. The Ottomans had built the country's second largest house of worship upon the confiscated grounds of an Armenian cemetery. It was colossal, capable of holding nearly thirty thousand true believers within its walls. Beyond the city and to the east through the dusty, humid haze, he could see the outline of Incirlik Air Base, the joint Turkish–American military installation.

By the time he deplaned, it was midmorning local time. As he exited Adana Şakirpaşa Airport, he was met curbside by a driver in a Mercedes-AMG G65 SUV, its air-conditioning blasting on high.

"Good morning, Colonel," he said in Russian, re-claiming the driver's seat after loading Gerasimov's travel bag into the rear. Sergei Malkin was a big man, as tall as Gerasimov with twenty added pounds of muscle. He bore the signs of a recent battle. His nose appeared to have been broken, and bruising ran bilaterally beneath his eyes.

The colonel replied in English. "It seems unusually humid today, Sergei."

Gerasimov hailed from a small town outside St. Petersburg that straddled the sixtieth parallel; there weren't many days from his childhood that had approached these conditions.

"Yes, sir," said the driver, switching to fluent but heavily accented English. "I'm afraid it is always this muggy."

"You arrived back here yesterday, yes?"

"Yes, sir."

"Thank you again for assisting with our London operation."

Malkin's eyes met the colonel's in the rearview mirror. "Yes, sir. It was my pleasure."

*Interesting choice of words.*

His trip to London to assist in dealing with a security matter must not have been pleasant, but Malkin had proved himself a trustworthy and loyal asset. Such loyalty must eventually be rewarded. "It doesn't appear your mission was without its challenges," he added, smiling.

"Yes, Colonel. She was a fighter."

Gerasimov pulled out his computer tablet and reviewed the secure email he'd received overnight, confirming that the complex operation to steal a nuclear bomb from the American airbase here in Adana had been a success. Months of planning and laying the groundwork to execute the mission had translated into a truly historic achievement. He would tolerate no less from his minions. Failure was not an option for those who wished to continue breathing.

His presence in Turkey so close to the campaign was risky. It could be viewed as the Russian Federation's complicity in what was to happen next. But then, he had always been a maverick, as calculating and cunning as a fox. He and General Tikhonov had painstakingly laid out the plan together in such a way as to ensure that a recently formed radical Islamic group would be blamed and would indeed take credit—as they always did—for what would ensue. In this way, the fledgling Islamic Levant Front would achieve notoriety surpassing even ISIL's wildest wet dreams.

And for their role in this ruse, their coffers would fill with American dollars stashed in accounts scattered among various friendly banks across Europe. If traced, the money trail would lead back to Iraq and Afghanistan from where it had been stolen; money redirected from bulk shipments of cash the Americans had planned to use to reward the various tribes for encouraging peace in their territories. Except the cash had been intercepted and diverted by Russian proxies. And now the Americans were gone altogether.

The payment would allow the ILF to carry their newfound momentum forward as they continued to grow and do the devil's work. Such was the arrogance and naiveté of the Americans. One does not *win* hearts and minds—one seizes control of a country with brute military force, strategic and tactical domination of essential infrastructure, and the subjugation of its people. It had taken a while, but even Russia had relearned this lesson from history.

It pleased Gerasimov to know that the events that would follow from this day on would bring a reckoning for America, which loved to insinuate itself into the business of the world as if it had the moral authority to do so. The United States of America's prideful belief in the flawed notion of its own exceptionalism would prove to be its undoing.

As for *Matushka Rossiya*—Mother Russia—its glorious leader, President Sergachev, had gone soft lately. Where once he had faced down the bluster of America's presidents, now he was too frequently willing to bend like a stalk of wheat in a hailstorm. When dealing with the insecurities of NATO and the incessant whining of the United Nations, he was more likely to back down than to assert Russia's supremacy over all others—America, China, East, West.

Russia was even poised to lose all of Ukraine. Again.

It was well known that President Sergachev favored enriching himself and his friends over continuing to strengthen the homeland. But in the fallout soon to be experienced from Gerasimov's actions, Mother Russia would be forced to step up as the world floundered in a state of upheaval. As America and her *coalition of the reluctant* would respond to the acts of a ragtag group of insurgents by prosecuting another inevitable war against Islam, Russia would seize more territories formerly surrendered in Eastern Europe and the Baltic states. Russia would no longer play the role of eunuch. Directorate 13 would undo generations of impotence on the world stage. Gerasimov and his general would come to be known as the saviors of Russia.

*Create uncertainty. Sow discord. Deny and deflect. Seize control from the chaos.*

Malkin whisked them from the airport to the Sheraton Grand Adana Hotel that sat on the banks of the Seyhan River across from the central mosque. He turned onto a palm-tree-lined boulevard and drove up the placid slope of the hotel's driveway. Gerasimov emerged from the SUV into the oppressive morning air. As he passed through the doorway into the spacious lobby of the luxury hotel, a gust of cool air washed over him. Malkin caught up with him as he stepped into one of the elevators.

"Wait, wait!" a man shouted, running toward them.

Gerasimov pressed himself against the elevator's back wall, guided there by the outstretched arm of his driver. Malkin dropped the colonel's bag and reached under his untucked shirt into his waistband. The approaching man correctly interpreted the non-verbal cues as a threat and thrust his hands into the air, the pits of his pressed white oxford shirt dark with perspiration. Between the thumb and index finger of his right hand, he pinched a small envelope.

"I have a note for the colonel," he said, the fear of impending death catching in his throat.

Malkin kept one hand at his waist, hidden from view under his shirt, while he beckoned the man forward. The man stepped forward gingerly and placed the paper into the outstretched hand of Gerasimov's driver.

"I am the hotel concierge. This was left for Colonel Gerasimov."

Gerasimov plucked the note from Malkin's hand.

"Thank you," he said to the man, who scuttled away. He tore open the flap of the envelope, and a vellum card slid into his palm. Then he grunted.

"What is it, Colonel?"

"The meeting has been moved up." He checked the time on his Vostok Airborne Troops watch. It was 11:30. The rendezvous was in thirty minutes.

\* \* \*

Viktor Gerasimov stood under a stream of water in the marble shower of the twenty-five-hundred-square-foot presidential suite, the icy spray cleansing him of sweat and fatigue from his overnight journey. He had hoped to unwind with a coffee under the umbrella on the room's private terrace while enjoying the splendid view of Merkez Park and the mosque. But unfortunately, it was not to be.

Evidently, the members of the Turkish Grand National Assembly were on edge. But rather than go to the mercurial president with their questions, they chose to seek assurances from Interior Minister Ahmet Çakir, President Karaman's closest confidant and most senior advisor. He, in turn, had requested an earlier meeting to allay their fears.

*Panic is such an unsightly response to a crisis,* thought Gerasimov.

He stepped from the shower and dried himself, pausing to admire his toned physique in the full-length mirror as he dragged the ultra-soft towel across his back and shoulders. He dropped the towel to the heated floor and strode into the master bedroom, donning boxers and a pair of khaki chinos, completing his ensemble with a white, short-sleeve linen shirt he left untucked, the top two buttons undone. He slipped on a pair of brown leather loafers and Maui Jim sunglasses, grabbed his Vostok wristwatch from the top of the dresser, then marched into the living room. His driver sat on a leather sofa watching a football match, sipping a frosty can of San Pellegrino Aranciata.

"*Poshli,*" said the colonel. *Let's go.*

Malkin took a final pull from the can, then crushed it in his grip and placed the remains on the granite countertop in the kitchenette on his way out the door. He stepped into the hallway ahead of Gerasimov and led the way to the elevators.

"It won't take us long, sir," said Malkin as he pulled the SUV onto the road.

They rounded the traffic circle on Girne Boulevard and exited onto the branch heading south on Karataş. They drove past the Hilton Hotel and the Roman stone bridge, continuing past unimpressive two-story commercial units and storefronts lining the wide route before turning off the main road. Malkin drove them eastbound until they entered a neighborhood consisting of narrow streets of mostly broken pavement that challenged the suspension of the mountain-capable SUV. These, in turn, led to smaller streets in even greater disrepair. The multi-family dwellings and apartments along the road had boarded-up windows and gated storefronts. The stink of raw sewage hung in the air.

Gerasimov looked up from his phone long enough to be disturbed by what he saw. And smelled.

"Do you know where you're going, Sergei?"

"Yes, sir. I'm following the GPS, Colonel. It is taking us to the location we were given for the meeting."

"Very well. But if we don't arrive soon, get us out of this pigsty. I haven't seen such misery since I was outside central Baku with my Spetsnaz unit. It smelled of shit and rotting fish there, too."

Malkin grinned. "*Da, Polkovnik.*" *Yes, Colonel.*

Three streets later, Malkin turned right, passing from the derelict neighborhood onto a cobblestone roadway encircling a green park with a small but ornate mosque and a stand of palm and fig trees. He pulled alongside the curb, where a Mercedes sedan was already parked in front of a row of small shops and cafés.

Gerasimov exited the vehicle and dodged pedestrians as Malkin raced ahead to the door and stepped through first, scanning for threats. Gerasimov considered that his driver would need to be promoted out of Turkey soon and offered a more permanent position in

Directorate 13, affording him a chance to further demonstrate his value to the unit.

But first, Malkin would have some key duties to perform that could test the mettle of even this battle-hardened soldier.

# CHAPTER 33

LLOYDS BANK, THREADNEEDLE STREET, LONDON

Alex stepped into the open foyer of the bank. Beyond the doors was a reception area that featured a pair of katydid-green Herman Miller modular two-seater sofas opposing each other across a Chiclet-shaped teak coffee table. A young woman sat at an information desk, typing on a keyboard. Tortoiseshell-frame glasses rested on the bridge of her nose, a silver chain looping down her cheeks and around the back of her neck.

The woman at the desk spun from her computer monitor, looking out above her glasses. "Good morning. How may I assist you?" She wore a fitted white Ted Baker dress with a vibrant floral print.

"Good morning." Forcing a smile, Alex held up her key.

"Ah, yes. Follow me," the woman said, rising from her chair. Her long, dark hair flowed nearly to her waist and danced in waves as she turned and walked toward the back of the office.

Suddenly, Alex felt underdressed. In a bank.

To her left, a row of wooden wickets with plexiglass barriers separated tellers from clients. Several offices lined the back wall and a staircase descended from the rear corner of the space. The woman led them into an office next to the staircase, where an older woman sat

behind a desk perusing a stack of documents. Her outfit was more subdued than her junior colleague's but
equally fashionable.

The younger woman explained that Alex had a key
for a safe-deposit box.

"I'd very much like to check on it," Alex said, showing the woman the key.

"Of course."

She reached beneath her desk for a ledger bound in
burgundy leather with the bank's horse logo gilded on
the cover, then held out her hand. Alex handed over the
key while the younger woman looked on. The woman
behind the desk took the brass key and consulted the numeric marking, then leafed through the book to a page
containing rows of handwritten numbers that Alex assumed was a concordance file of sorts that matched
keys to boxes and owners.

"Ah, yes. Four zero seven," she said, reading the key.
"From our Elite series." She matched the key to a row
and slid her finger across the page to a note scrawled in
the last column.

"Everything alright?" asked Alex.

"Yes, of course," she replied.

She dismissed the other woman from her office.
Turning to a cabinet behind her, she opened it and
entered a numeric code into the keypad of a small safe.
From within, she removed a ring that contained another
twenty keys identical to Alex's.

"Follow me, please," she said, rising from her chair
and handing Alex back her key. "You must be careful
with this one. I'm sure you're aware that your key, by
itself, will get anyone into the safety deposit box."

"So, the key is like a bearer bond?"

"Yes, it's exactly like that," she said. "Just as bearer
bonds are unregistered investment securities, this key is
tied to a blind account. Consequently, no records exist

to list the owner's name. So, whoever physically holds the key is the presumed owner and has unfettered access to the contents. It's just like bearer bonds."

They descended the semicircular staircase into a red-carpeted reception area outside what seemed like a golden jail cell. Behind the gilded bars was another small anteroom that led through the opening of a two-meter-wide vault door.

"It's only for show," said the woman as they passed through. "The real security is the steel door in front of us. This round vault door was part of the original building construction in 1864. It's mere ornamentation now."

She waved a magnetic prox ID card at a scanner mounted on the wall, where a red light flashed to yellow. A numeric scramble pad lit up, and the woman punched in a six-digit code. The sound of magnetic locks releasing echoed in the air, the light turned green, and the woman stepped back as the door slowly swung open toward them. As they entered the room, it gently swung closed, locking them inside.

The room was brightly illuminated by LED fixtures from above. A rectangular table sat in the center of the room, lit by a traditional banker's lamp with a green glass shade. Alex placed her backpack on the table.

The two walls lining the sides of the room held gray steel boxes in two different sizes, numbered sequentially. The woman proceeded to a middle row halfway down the right-hand-side wall to the one with the number 407 embossed on a brass plate on its face.

The woman used her key, then removed it and stepped out of the way. Alex inserted her key and paused, suddenly unsure if it would work, or if she was even doing the right thing. Thoughts of what the box might contain flooded her mind.

*What skeletons was Krysten directing me to discover? What truths will I learn from her? Or about her? And, once released, will I ever be able to put those secrets back in the box, or will they haunt me forever?*

She pushed aside her trepidation and turned the key clockwise. She was both startled and relieved when the spring-like resistance of the lock yielded as the notches and teeth of the blade lifted the pins against the cylinder springs and retracted the bolt.

\*\*\*

LLOYDS BANK, THREADNEEDLE STREET, LONDON

Tatiana drove this time, tired of her male associates' carelessness and testosterone-induced audacity. She opted for the nondescript Peugeot 208 in silver—or cumulus gray, if one read the sales brochure—instead of any of the BMW automobiles from the ample motor pool.

She'd kept well back of the hackney cab carrying FBI special agent Alexandra Martel. Tatiana maintained the tactical advantage. Major Vasili Fedotov had texted her Alex's coordinates after intercepting a signal from Alex's dormant phone. Following the taxi hadn't been as difficult as Captain Nikulin had made it out to be yesterday. When the cab pulled over and stopped along the left-hand curb, she kept watch from a safe distance as Martel walked across the road and into a bank.

"Should we follow her?" asked one of her colleagues, the large one crammed into the backseat.

"Into the bank? Of course not," she replied. "Agent Martel is not on a SpecOps mission. She won't be infil'ing via the front and exfil'ing through the rear as if this were a combat zone. We will wait here for her until she comes back outside."

He grunted in reply, possibly more disappointed he couldn't get out to stretch his legs than being denied the opportunity to tail the Interpol agent.

The two surveillants with her were both former soldiers from the Vympel Group, an FSB Spetsnaz counterterrorism unit, and they were as dumb as the plows on the farms from which they hailed. Unlike American Tier One teams, who searched for operator candidates possessing intelligence as well as battle acumen, Vympel Group often recruited men of questionable cognitive abilities possessed of raw and unfettered brawn and bravado. Tatiana had experienced this firsthand when she had served in Syria and again in the Donbas region during Russia's special military operation in Ukraine. These men had joined Directorate 13 straight from FSB's special operations center in Balashikha, a suburb just outside Moscow.

She, meanwhile, had received her education from GRU academies for the gifted, paid for by the Russian state in exchange for a lifetime of military servitude. She had expressed her concerns from time to time over the quality of candidates being welcomed into the special units. But her opinions on the matter were of little consequence. Of all Mother Russia's societal illusions, the greatest fallacy was that the viewpoints of women mattered, that they were on an equal footing with men. They didn't, and they weren't.

She tucked the little Peugeot up onto the sidewalk in front of 22 Bishopsgate. Through the building's four-story glass façade, she could see people going about their business inside the modern workspace. It was a bright and seemingly fun and attractive building in which to work, nothing like any building she had ever known in Moscow, or any other city in Russia for that matter. Despite its occasional brushes with democratization, Captain Tatiana Burina's Russia was a melancholy land filled with brooding people possessed of a tragic view of their collective past.

She put the car in park. "You can get out now," she said to the hulk in the back. "Smoke your cigarettes but don't go far."

The large man gladly exited the tight confines of the small car and, once outside, lit up. Tatiana rolled down her window and fanned the air. "Please stand downwind. And check your radio," she added.

The people in America, Britain, and the other countries of the West were well off by every measure compared to their Russian counterparts. But wealth was relative and tenuous. There was a fine line separating abundance from paucity. What was given could be taken away. It was her calling to teach them humility, which was why she was proud to have been chosen to serve on Directorate 13, at the pleasure of President Sergachev.

If Special Agent Martel interfered with or discovered their true mission, Tatiana would know it. And the American would be dealt with as any other enemy of the president of the Russian Federation.

Terminally.

# CHAPTER 34

LLOYDS BANK, THREADNEEDLE STREET, LONDON

Alex felt gentle resistance as she turned the key in the lock and a sense of relief as the bolt retracted. She pulled on the door, and it swung open on brass hinges, revealing a covered gray box the size of a shoe box that she slid out and carried to the table.

"Press that to call me once you're finished, and I'll return to lock up," said the banker, pointing to a button in the wall. With that, she excused herself and left the secure room, closing Alex in alone.

Alex could feel the weight of something inside the box. She placed it down gently in the center of the table. Pausing for a beat, she wiped her sweating palms onto the front of her pants, then lifted the lid.

A folded manila envelope sat on top of a pile of similarly folded manila envelopes. Alex removed the one on top, undid the string, and reached inside. She first pulled out a British passport, looking new and unused. She flipped it open to the bio-data page and examined the photo. It was Krysten's picture, taken recently. She ran a finger over the high-res image as if, by doing so, she could conjure up her friend's physical presence. But she couldn't, and her stomach knotted. How real she seemed. How close. How alive.

The passport identified her as Krysten Gosling,

British citizen. The information page listed her date of birth, as well as her place of birth—London. Alex flipped through the pages. All were blank. No stamps.

She reached back into the box and lifted out the next envelope. Inside was a short stack of four-by-six-inch photos, bound with a broad rubber band. She removed the elastic and slowly shuffled through them. There were pictures of landmarks and tourist destinations in London and Paris, most seemingly taken years ago, before cell phones and memory cards had supplanted cameras and film for documenting everyday life. There were newer photos, too. Krysten had likely made prints of these from cell phone shots.

*But why?*

Among the photos: an ornate house behind an iron gate on a tree-lined street; a familiar-looking building along the Thames; and a Paris Street scene, looking up toward Sorbonne University, where they had attended a symposium at the Paris Peace Summit together. Next were photos of the two of them together in Paris: the selfie in Trocadéro Gardens with the Eiffel Tower looming behind them across the Seine; a snapshot taken on the patio of Ladurée on the Avenue des Champs-Élysées; another of the two of them at the Paris Peace Summit, standing in front of one of the conference rooms inside the Sorbonne University International Conference Center.

She raised that last one closer to read what was written on the board behind Krysten. When she did, she remembered the session. The speaker had been a doctoral fellow from Harvard Kennedy School, Belfer Center for Science and International Affairs. Her presentation had been on the topic of nuclear non-proliferation and disarmament. Specifically, she'd spoken on the subject of the inherent challenges and dangers faced by nuclear-armed countries in attempting to maintain the security of their stockpiles of nuclear weapons.

Dr. Sylvia Campbell had spoken passionately on the growing global security risk posed by the ongoing illicit trade in stolen nuclear materials, as well as the omnipresent threat of nuclear terrorism and the theft of nuclear weapons.

*How ironic, given today's news.*

Dr. Campbell had insisted that it wasn't a matter of *if* but *when* a nuclear weapon would go missing, through theft or misadventure, and postulated that such a scenario would lead to a critical escalation of tensions between the existing and emerging global nuclear-armed superpowers. She further believed that such an event would cause an erosion of confidence among partners in the Western alliances of NATO, the UN, and other international organs of peace and security.

*And here we are.*

Alex quickly flipped through the rest of the photos. She paused at one showing a squad of soldiers, twelve in all, posing for a picture, just as she had done many times throughout her own military career: one row crouched in front of another. All wore green cammies, rifles cradled. Some wore ballistic helmets, while others were without cover, wearing only face camo.

She saw a face she recognized. "*Shit,*" she muttered, taking a closer look.

There were two women in the squad. The one in the front row bore a striking resemblance to Krysten, only at a much younger age. Even wearing a Kevlar skull bucket, there was no mistaking her features and her beauty. It was definitely her. Alex raised her phone, zoomed in with the camera, and took a picture. Then she opened her Photos app, selected the image, and swiped up. A thumbnail image of the same woman from among her own photo collection appeared.

*Shit, shit, shit!* Even Siri recognized Krysten.

Trouble was, the photo was of a squad of *Russian* soldiers.

Alex's throat tightened as if someone's hand had clenched around it. She glanced up at the door, feeling entombed inside the vault. The walls around her closed in, and the room grew dark.

A pair of leather wing chairs sat off in the corner. She dropped into one to center herself and think, but her thoughts were unsettling. She closed her eyes and breathed slowly, the way Kyle had taught her: in, out, rest, two, three.

*There must be a reasonable explanation. Maybe she was working on a deep-cover assignment? But who would go deep undercover inside another country's military like that?*

Despite the coolness of the temperature-controlled room, beads of sweat formed on her forehead, above her lip, and on the back of her neck. Despite her body's response, she stepped back to the table. Next in the stack was a photo of the same woman receiving a medal from a Russian general. They were standing in an open area surrounded by barracks, a boulder-strewn mountain ridge in the background. Alex was sure she recognized the Russian flag officer but was unable to recall the details.

The photo reminded her of when she had been presented with her Silver Star for valor in combat. In her case, it had involved the hasty assembly of a presentation dais in a hangar at Bagram Air Base. The aircraft-size doors had been open, revealing a spectacular view of the snow-capped peaks of the five-hundred-mile-long Hindu Kush mountain range. Behind her, a banner bearing the insignia of the 75th Ranger Regiment had luffed in the breeze as the vice president of the United States pinned the medal to her chest.

*Breathe,* she told herself. *What did I miss? Why hadn't I known?*

She studied the photo.

Alex and Krysten had connected the moment they met in Paris. Had Alex been her mark, an asset to be developed, a patsy? If so, to what end? What was the play?

Krysten had served in the British military, of that she was sure. *How was it possible for her to also have been a member of the Russian military? It wasn't. Or was it?*

She took a few deep, cleansing breaths, sat in the chair, reached into the box, and removed the next packet. From inside the envelope, she extracted another passport. This one bore the coat of arms of the Russian Federation with gold Cyrillic lettering above and below. Near the bottom of the cover, in English, were the words *Service Passport*.

She was afraid to open it.

She flipped to the information page, which bore the digitized photo and signature of the passport holder.

*Shit.*

It was Krysten. Except, not Krysten.

The name on the passport read Anna Baronova. She shared the same date of birth as Krysten. Baronova's place of birth was written in the Cyrillic alphabet, although USSR was stamped below it in the Latin alphabet. But the photo was definitely Krysten, right down to the small birthmark on her left cheek.

She took a picture of the cover and the identification pages with her phone and texted them to Jonathan with the message:

AM: Call me ASAP. 911.

A moment later, her phone rang.

"I can see your day is getting more interesting by the minute," he said when she answered.

"What's a Russian service passport used for?"

"Checking." She heard the clicking of keys on a keyboard. "According to our Interpol Wiki, a Russian service passport is issued to civil servants and their dependents assigned overseas. It's also given to members of the Russian parliament who travel abroad on official business and judges of the supreme and constitutional courts. It's like a diplomatic passport, but without the benefits of diplomatic immunity or fancy license plates or the ability to escape customs lineups and taxes at border points, stuff like that. It's also issued to military personnel deployed overseas."

"Why would Krysten have one?"

"Is that a rhetorical question?"

"No, Jonathan, I need you to find out. Why did Krysten Gosling—a woman I knew to be a former member of British Special Forces and was, up until she was murdered, an intelligence officer with the British Security Service—have a Russian service passport? And why does it appear this same woman I knew was a member of Russian Special Forces sometime before that?"

She knew the tone in her voice betrayed her frustration. It wasn't her intent to take it out on Jonathan, but he was a big boy—he could handle it. This was no time for mollycoddling people's feelings.

"Send me whatever other photos you have there," he said, "and I'll get on it. Whatever you find, shoot it and send it. I'm still trying to decode the rest of her email."

"Get back to me as soon as you can," she told him.

With increased dread, she reached into Krysten's— *Anna's*—safe-deposit box. Another manila envelope.

*This box is the gift that keeps on giving.*

The envelope held another stack of photos. These were older. Some were yellowed with time, bent, wrinkled, or otherwise damaged. Some had pinholes in them as if they had been tacked up on a bulletin board or a wall, like in a girl's bedroom or dorm room.

Some depicted a little girl playing sports at a young age or with friends in a playground. Others showed the same little girl with a couple who appeared to be in their thirties. They resembled the people from the photo she had seen in Krysten's apartment, but younger.

She examined an image of that man and woman sitting on a sofa with that same little girl, at maybe eight or nine years old, in a tiny room. It was a cramped apartment with cracked plaster walls. She had a pixie cut, and though her clothes appeared clean, they were old and worn. She was smiling at the camera. The couple had pained expressions on their faces, their eyes weary, their figures gaunt.

*Who took the picture?*

Another photo showed the same girl again, perhaps a year or two older, standing outside a school. On one side of her were her parents, happier and healthier looking, as if they had been eating well and feeding their daughter better. On the other was a military officer, his hand placed gently on her shoulder. All of them were smiling for the camera.

*Damn.*

She shuffled back through the stack of photos on the table until she found the one of Anna receiving her medal. The Russian general making the presentation was the same military officer. She looked more closely at the little girl. The resemblance between her and Anna as a young woman was uncanny. Alex imagined that if she could zoom in on the photos, she'd find a birthmark on the little girl's cheek, too.

Alex was forming a picture in her head. If this *was* her friend Krysten, the image developing was one of an impoverished family trying to make ends meet in a country where that wasn't always easy or even possible for many. Alex knew that Russia's Foreign Intelligence Service and its foreign military intelligence agency recruited children as young as eight from poor Russian families.

Could the young girl have been taken away from her family at such a tender age to be educated by the state and groomed for a life as a spy? That would explain why the family looked better off and healthier in the later photos. That would explain some of what Krysten had done. Maybe not excuse it but paint a sympathetic picture as to *why*. But Alex struggled with the fact that she hadn't known, hadn't even suspected a thing. It gnawed at her gut.

Pushing the photographs aside, she reached back into the box. There was one more envelope.

She pulled out a letter-size envelope bearing the seal of the British Security Service. The flap was only tucked in. She removed an A4-sized piece of paper and read the handwritten letter:

Alex,

If you're reading this, something terrible has happened to me.

First, I want to apologize. Right now, you're probably pretty pissed off at me and feeling betrayed. Please know that I genuinely liked you and valued our friendship. I won't bore you with the details, but suffice it to say, growing up in a poor family in Russia, there are limited choices for bettering one's circumstances. My parents chose the only option available to them to give me a good life. And then I, too, made my choice.

Most of the time, I didn't mind being an agent for the mother country, and I did get to live a better life and meet people like yourself who I truly liked. Sometimes I even pretended to forget who I really was.

I'm not writing this for your pity or your forgiveness—you will ultimately decide what to do with your memories of me. I always knew there might come a time when I would be asked to do something that went too far for me, and the cost of defying such a thing would be my life.

So, if you're reading this, such a thing has happened. I can't say what it might be but know that whatever it is, I couldn't do it, and I have likely given my life to warn you.

Krysten

It was signed and dated a year ago, as if Krysten had known this day would come. Had she known about the plans to steal a nuclear bomb, even then? Was this confirmation that the Russians were behind the theft?

Alex shot photos of everything on the table and sent them to Jonathan. She stuffed the passports and pictures into her backpack but put Krysten's handwritten note in her pocket. She placed the empty box back into the vault in the wall, turning her key before pocketing it. Then she hit the buzzer and waited for the banker to appear.

She needed to catch a plane.

# CHAPTER 35

She had been watching the door for forty minutes. For such a high-end location, the in-and-out traffic at this bank branch seemed light. Tatiana decided that people with lots of money and no spare time must perform all their banking tasks online. Why go to a bank if the bank could come to you? It was different for people back home who had lots of time and no spare money. For them, going to a bank to perform routine transactions and chat with tellers was the highlight of their weekly social calendars.

On her instructions, Tatiana's colleague Ivan Gavrikov—the large man from the backseat of the Peugeot—had taken up a position next to the seven steps leading into the bank. He stood there looking as nonchalant as a bull in the middle of Red Square, smoking cigarette number eight or nine. Andrei Morozov, the third surveillant, stood across the street from him. Together, the three formed a kill triangle that Special Agent Martel would have to enter, regardless of which direction she walked when she left the building. From there, they could follow her and decide what actions, if any, they should take. But Tatiana suspected that one way or another, this was leading to a confrontation.

The fact that Martel was here at this bank was highly

suspicious. She was in England at the Scottish woman's request to look into Krysten/Anna's death; that much they had learned from her telephone—the same phone the GRU computer wizards had tapped into when they learned of Krysten's email to her friend. So what would bring Martel to this location if not something linked to Krysten?

Martel's presence virtually confirmed Krysten had been a double agent, a traitor. Why else would she have stolen the mission plans from the computer server and emailed them to Martel? Fortunately, Colonel Gerasimov had been tipped off to Krysten's activities leading up to the theft, and Directorate 13's operations chief, Major Vasili Fedotov, had intercepted the email when it left Krysten's phone before it arrived on Interpol's servers. Who it was that had tipped the colonel off was a mystery still, even to Tatiana. And while she'd hoped the Krysten situation could have been handled differently—they had been friends, after all, once upon a time—it didn't surprise her that Sergei Malkin had been summoned to employ lethal means to manage the job. Within Directorate 13, the mission came first, irrespective of any other consideration.

Tatiana sat behind the wheel of the car, coordinating her team's movements and tactics with hand signals and messages across their encrypted portable radio net. She was sure Major Fedotov was monitoring their communications back at the operations center in the basement of Harrington House. He might even be reporting her actions to Colonel Gerasimov, who had himself flown to Turkey to carry out the next phase of their operation.

At last, the front door of the bank opened, and Martel emerged. She took the steps lightly, as if she were a young girl skipping out of school at the end of the day, appearing annoyingly cheerful.

Tatiana keyed her mic. "Be alert," she directed in Russian.

Gavrikov flicked his smoldering cigarette into the gutter and turned toward the steps Martel had just descended while Morozov paralleled her movements on the other side of the street.

As she exited the venerable old building, Martel turned left up Threadneedle Street. She walked as if the weight of the world weren't upon her shoulders. But there was no telling what she knew.

"Should we take her now?" asked Gavrikov, the bull.

"Follow her but keep a discreet distance back. Let's see if she's alone."

Tatiana watched as Martel made her way up the street. When she was fifty meters ahead, Tatiana eased the Peugeot back onto the road and turned up Threadneedle, hugging the curb so traffic would move around her.

Martel crossed the street about ten meters in front of Morozov. Half a block ahead of them was the entrance to a laneway on the right.

As Tatiana watched her semi-competent crew in action, her phone pinged with an urgent message from Vasili Fedotov. She opened the Signal app and read his brief but alarming report, then spoke into her voice-activated mic.

"Ivan, move up. Then cross the street and come back toward Andrei. Take her at the alley."

"*Da.*" Yes.

She watched as he complied. Thirty seconds later, Gavrikov's, Morozov's, and Martel's paths were about to intersect.

# CHAPTER 36

She noticed the two men the moment she exited the bank. One was standing to the right of the staircase as she descended. He immediately discarded his half-smoked cigarette, telegraphing his intentions even before he began to move up the street behind her. The other man stood directly across the street, trying *not* to look at her, which confirmed he was doing just that. His journey along the road started the instant she turned up Threadneedle.

A four-year-old could have spotted these two buffoons.

She scanned the route ahead. The road was a tall canyon of eighteenth- and nineteenth-century stone buildings. Other than some light traffic, it was clear of immediate threats. She was at a disadvantage, not familiar with the layout of the area. Not ideal. She couldn't see any obvious escape routes. No side streets nor a conspicuous, sizable public building like a shopping mall to dodge into. Still, a short distance ahead on the other side of the road, a gated entrance to what seemed like a laneway, or perhaps a courtyard, looked promising. It might contain multiple exit points. Or none.

She aimed for the alley as a primary means to break out of her surveillants' visual field. She'd be there in under a minute. Maybe she would lose them before needing to confront them. Either way, she was perturbed; she had no time for drama.

She crossed the street and the big man behind her picked up his pace, keeping to his side of the road. The more diminutive fellow was now a short distance behind her. She slowed her pace to force the men to adjust theirs.

*Thirty seconds.*

Whoever they were, whatever they had planned would be more challenging to accomplish if she kept her movements less predictable. And since altering her destination wasn't in the cards, playing with the game's timing was.

Twenty seconds and she'd hook right, into the laneway.

The big one, the man who had been smoking outside the bank, had soared ahead, then crossed over and doubled back toward her. The other one hadn't slowed to match her speed but seemed content to gain on her. It appeared, then, that their plan was the same as hers. The laneway would prove to be the intersecting point of their engagement. She knew it, and they knew it.

Alex was sure they were Russians, but the question remained—what did they want? It seemed her phone was compromised again. Using it had been a careless mistake on her part. She had let her emotions throw her off her game inside the bank vault, and this looming confrontation was, therefore, of her own making.

Had they listened in on her call with Chief Bressard outside Krysten's apartment? Or her call with Jonathan from inside the bank? Had they intercepted the photos she had sent to Interpol? Or were they merely tracking her phone's location? Of course, it was also possible that her surveillants had utilized the low-tech option and simply followed her from Shoreditch and Krysten's apartment. And, having seen her go into the bank, now they were wondering what she had been doing there. If that were the case, she thought wryly, she would have to talk to Gareth, her cab driver, about stepping up his countersurveillance techniques.

She hooked right, passing through the black wrought-iron gates of Adam's Court. Making the turn, she came face to face with a woman holding a pistol. A Russian-made Makarov, to be precise.

"Hello, Special Agent Martel," said the woman, more than a trace of an accent bleeding through. "Keep your hands where I can see them. Please don't make me shoot you by reaching for your pistol."

Alex recognized the woman from the second car that had pursued her yesterday. Her male counterparts kept her boxed in from behind. The big one snatched her pack off her shoulder.

"Hey, bozo," Alex said. "Your mother not teach you any manners? You do have a mother, don't you?"

He swatted the back of her head. Alex wasn't fond of men who hit women. Reflexively, her fist closed, and she started to wheel around.

"Uh-uh," said the woman, raising her gun. Alex could see the hammer was cocked, allowing her a quick and accurate first shot if needed. "Maybe someday, but not today." Then, to her colleague, she added something that even to someone who didn't speak Russian sounded like a chastisement.

"My Russian is a little rusty," Alex said, tucking her hair behind her ears. "What did you say?"

Gavrikov rummaged through her backpack while the woman draped a fleece sweater over her arm to hide the gun. She barked an order to the other man, and he reached under the back of Alex's shirt.

"Don't get any ideas, Alexandra," he said, removing her Glock from its holster.

"I'll need a receipt for that," she replied.

The woman smirked but held her gaze and her Makarov steady. Gavrikov took her gun from the other man and put it into the backpack, then rummaged through its contents, pulling out the thick manila envelope and handing it to the woman.

"Do you mind?" asked Alex. "Do you know how much trouble I went through to get that?"

"Perhaps in due time. Walk this way," said the woman.

The four of them walked casually into a covered passage between adjoining buildings and out the other side into a square lined with ornamental trees and shrubs between narrow pathways. It reminded Alex of the unofficial smoking quadrangle behind her high school.

The quad was surrounded by old low-rise buildings; again, not unlike her high school. A man and a woman strolled through in different directions, their faces buried in their smartphones, paying their foursome no heed.

The woman stopped and turned as they approached a fountain, tucking her Makarov away at the small of her back. The men stopped short behind Alex.

"Don't do anything stupid, Alexandra," she said. "My colleagues can shoot better than me and have more of a taste for it."

"I never doubted it for a minute. Sorry, I didn't catch your name."

"It does not matter. I am thinking we will not become friends."

"Don't be so sure. This could be the first of many pleasant encounters."

"Or the last of one."

The men behind Alex chuckled.

"In that case, you might as well humor me."

The woman shot her an appraising glance and a

tight smile. It wasn't that Alex was desperate to become friends. On the contrary, she took it very personally whenever someone aimed a gun at her, especially one with the hammer cocked. But when she found herself free again from these Russians, whom she was now sure were members of Directorate 13, it would be handy to begin her search for them with a name or alias.

"Tatiana," she said, opening the manila envelope. "I am disappointed my colleague chose to share these things with you instead of giving them to me. You must have been close, yes?"

"*Nyet,*" replied Alex, all but exhausting her Russian vocabulary. "But she apparently thought me a better friend than I was."

"It's a pity we don't realize such things until it's too late."

"*Da,*" agreed Alex, realizing her knowledge of working Russian was quite extensive after all.

"So now you know your friend was a spy, a traitor. This is something else you and I have in common. Please, follow me."

Alex got the impression this wasn't a request and followed Tatiana through the courtyard. At the south end, they entered another building, walking across a terrazzo floor toward a set of large wooden doors. There were more people here, some in business attire, others casually dressed, but she opted not to create a disturbance in the hopes of avoiding collateral damage.

"Your preparation is admirable," said Alex.

It wasn't a lie. Tatiana had done some fine location scouting.

"Thank goodness for Google," she replied. "I found myself with spare time while you were inside the bank. London has excellent cell phone coverage. And, of course, it helps to have a good data plan."

"Naturally."

They exited the building through an archway to a car waiting along the curb, facing the wrong direction, which in London seemed utterly normal. The bigger of the two men opened the rear door for her.

"Get in," Tatiana said.

Getting into a car under these circumstances was never a good idea, but Morozov kidney-punched her for encouragement when she hesitated.

*Umph!* "You're going to regret that, little man," she said.

"Get in," repeated Tatiana.

Alex slipped into the backseat of the small car. Gavrikov walked around to the other side and got in, pulling his own Makarov and pointing it at her.

"Don't do anything stupid," he said.

Tatiana climbed into the driver's seat on the right-hand side of the Peugeot while the little man with the little hands rode shotgun. She took the passports out of the envelope and placed them on the dash.

"Anna was one of our best officers," she said. "Like me, she was educated in special programs from an early age. But she had a gift for languages and a musical ear that helped her absorb not just the dialect, but the accents; something most of us will never be able to master."

"And what were you good at?"

"You should hope you don't find out."

Alex watched her rummage through the photos, pausing at one of Krysten on a set of monkey bars in a playground.

"Did you know she was good at sports? Her father was an intellectual—literature, I think—but her mother was a great gymnast who won Olympic bronze and silver medals in Los Angeles. Or maybe Seoul? But circumstances changed for them when the university dismissed her father. Her mother held a low-wage job at the telephone company that couldn't pay the bills when inflation shot through the roof when Anna was very young. When we were all very young. For a while, we attended the same academy, but she was a grade above me. Everyone liked her. She was sweet but very tough. I looked up to her."

"And then you killed her."

"I did no such thing, Alexandra," she said. "But I proudly would have if I had been given the task. She betrayed her country and president. Did she tell you why she grew a conscience? I'm curious what caused her to abandon her principles."

She was shuffling through the photos, pausing now and then to examine one more closely.

"We didn't talk about it, I'm afraid," Alex said. "But I have a good idea. Krysten left us a lot of good intel that's now in the hands of Interpol, including photographs of everything you're holding there in your hands."

Tatiana studied Alex in the rearview mirror.

"We know what you know, Agent Martel. And what we don't, we will find out soon enough."

Alex didn't like the sound of that.

"Unlock your phone and hand it over, please."

"Sorry, not going to happen. I have a lot of private photos I'm too shy to share."

"Take her phone," Tatiana commanded Gavrikov.

As he reached for her, the roar of a revving engine caught her ears. Then the startled look on Tatiana's face made Alex duck down and cover her head.

The force of the collision threw her sideways onto the big man beside her. The small car went airborne, its flight halted by the side of the building they had just stepped out of. Upon impact with the wall, she was hurled back to the right side of the car, glass windows exploding all around her. Dazed, she seized the moment of disorientation to begin pummeling her seatmate with her fists and elbows. Gavrikov tried to block her blows, but a few connected before he reached out and grabbed her by the throat, his large hand almost entirely encircling her neck. As she fought to breathe, she cocked her arm back, then drove the heel of her palm upward with all the force she could muster, connecting on the point of his chin. The crunching sound made as his teeth smashed together was sickening. His eyes rolled back, and it was lights out.

Morozov in the front seat had taken the brunt of the collision on his left side and was unconscious or dead, dangling out the window at the waist. Tatiana was shaken but managed to swing around with her pistol. Alex deflected her aim, and the gun went off, the sound deafening within the confines of the car, the bullet piercing the thin metal skin of the roof. She punched the Makarov out of her hand before she could take another shot. It flew out the window and skittered across the sidewalk. Tatiana shouldered the door repeatedly, trying to force it open. Finally, it gave way, and she tumbled out onto the sidewalk, blood running down her face from a scalp laceration earned during her impact with the side window.

Alex tried to shoulder her way out through the rear door as well, but it remained jammed. Tatiana picked the Makarov up off the ground and aimed it at her. She squeezed the trigger, but nothing happened. The previous round's empty cartridge case was caught partway out of the ejection port. Tatiana noticed as well and racked the slide to clear the stovepipe malfunction. She reached into the front of the car and grabbed the manila envelope that had fallen to the floor, keeping the gun trained on Alex the whole time.

"It was good to meet you, Alexandra. I suppose we now know that this was the last of one pleasant encounter. Say hello to Anna for me when you see her."

Alex saw her backpack on the passenger-side floor. She could sit there and be gunned down in cold blood by this crazy woman, or she could keep fighting. She dove for the pack to retrieve her Glock, but it was snagged in the twisted metal of the damaged car, and she was unable to tug it free. As she struggled with it, she heard another gunshot. She whirled around to see a man wrestling with Tatiana on the ground, fighting for control of her weapon.

In the distance, she could hear the hi-low siren tones of police vehicles fast approaching.

Tatiana and the man were still rolling on the pavement. Finally, she heard a grunt and saw the man roll off her after taking a knee to the gonads. She instantly recognized him.

"Gareth!" she shouted.

Tatiana stood, hovering over him, and kicked him in the face. By now, a loud crowd had gathered but were silenced when she picked her Makarov off the ground and waved it at them, daring them to come closer. The sirens were almost on them as she swung the pistol from the crowd back to Gareth, lying on his back. He raised his hands in surrender as Tatiana lined up the gun's iron sights with his head, her icy stare fixed on him.

"No!" shouted Alex, still trying to bash the door open with her shoulder. "Shoot me, you crazy Russian bitch!" she spat in full fury.

Tatiana's face, already painted a glossy crimson on one side by the streaming blood, now turned scarlet with rage as she swung the pistol at her and took aim. Alex's heart pounded in her throat as the black hole of the barrel's aperture loomed twenty sizes larger in her mind's eye. She stared into Tatiana's cold steel eyes, bracing for the flash of burning cordite and the impact of the bullet that would end her life. But the shot never came.

Tatiana lowered the gun and smiled at her.

"*Yeshche uvidimsya*, Alexandra," she said, fleeing into the crowd.

*See you again.*

# CHAPTER 37

The three-way intersection in front of Lloyds Bank was located within the one-square-mile territory and ceremonial county of the City of London, an urban enclave within the metropolis of Greater London. Within minutes, its police force had the area locked down tight. Emergency vehicles and flashing blue lights flooded the intersection. By any standard, it was a circus.

Traffic was diverted and every vehicle except the iconic red double-decker buses was shunted elsewhere. Three units from London Ambulance Service were still on scene. The man Alex had fought with, Gavrikov, had been medically cleared by LAS paramedics and was being escorted in handcuffs to a waiting police van. Morozov, the front-seat passenger in the Peugeot, had been worked on furiously by another team of paramedics and then transported in critical condition to the Royal London Hospital, the capital's leading trauma center, under police escort.

Gareth was lying on a stretcher raised into a semi-sitting position in the back of another ambulance. His head was wrapped in a bandage that covered the laceration made by Tatiana's boot. A paramedic leaned over him, assessing his vitals.

"What the hell were you thinking, Gareth?" Alex asked.

A shit-eating grin lit up his face.

"That was more fun than being back in the 'Stan, Alex!" he said, excitement lighting up his wide eyes, his pupils still dilated from the rush of adrenaline. "I saw them blokes hanging around after you went into the bank, but your phone went to voicemail when I called. I even texted you—twice!—but you must not have gotten it."

She checked her phone. Sure enough, she had a missed call and two text messages from him.

The paramedic leaned toward the back of the ambulance to pull the doors closed. "We need to get your friend to the hospital," she said.

Alex nodded. Judging by Gareth's smile, he would survive his ordeal, but she was filled with pangs of guilt for having involved him in an altercation with the Russians that had almost ended with him eating a bullet meant for her.

She reached in and touched his leg. "Thanks. You've saved my life at least twice now."

"Aw, only an arse would keep score, and I'm not that. You saved mine back there, too, Alex. She would have shot me in the face if you hadn't pulled her attention away."

"I have a way of getting under people's skin like that."

"I'm glad you do. But if you ever see her again, shoot first."

She saluted him, then stepped back to let the medic close the door.

"Special Agent Martel," came a voice from behind her. "I was hoping you could have refrained from killing any more Russians while you were still in London."

She turned and came face to face with Daniel Kane. "I see now that may have been a whimsical notion on my part. Care to tell me what incited this confrontation?"

"It seems our Russian friends don't like people looking into their affairs," she answered.

His eyes bored into hers.

"You would tell me if you've unearthed any additional evidence, wouldn't you?"

"That was our agreement, Kane."

Agreement or not, Alex wanted more time to process today's events and wasn't in a sharing mood.

The police were packing up to leave the scene. Only a small contingent remained to support the crime scene investigators, who were busy taking measurements and doing whatever it was CSI types did.

She checked her watch. Bressard had ordered her to Turkey to investigate the stolen nuke. It was what she had practically begged him for.

"I'd love to stay and chat, Kane, but I've got a plane to catch," she said.

"Right." He summoned a sergeant over. "As soon as you've finished giving this officer your statement, you're free to go."

# CHAPTER 38

ADANA, TURKEY

Gerasimov stepped inside the coffee shop and delicatessen, led by his bodyguard. Sergei Malkin was an efficient, soft-spoken man not prone to idle conversation, but when he planted a scowl on his face and puffed out his formidable chest, few stood in his path. He was the perfect close-protection specialist—a Rottweiler standing sentinel in the yard, daring anyone to push open the gate.

The fragrance of lamb and veal roasting on hand-forged flat metal skewers, the fat dripping, popping, and sizzling onto red-hot coals below, intermingled with the sweet smell of Turkish pastry. Fresh-baked *börek* made with *yufka*—Turkish phyllo pastry—and filled with cheese and herbs and savory meats sat on rectangular platters behind a glass barrier. Pots of coffee were brewing on a side counter where a grinder whirred away, reducing the darkly roasted arabica beans to an ultrafine powder.

Malkin cleared the way through a small crowd until the pair met an equal hulk of a man blocking the entrance to a back room, its contents obscured by beaded curtains. There was a brief pause before he opened a gap in the beads with his hand. Malkin stuck his head into the room, then turned and waved Gerasimov inside.

The room was a square, twenty feet by twenty feet. Opaque rectangular windows high up the walls let in light through the back and side. Tables filled the space but remained empty except for one, where a nervous-looking man sat alone at a table for four. Another man stood alert in the corner beside a gray steel door that led to an alley behind the shop.

Interior Minister Ahmet Çakir rose to his feet as Gerasimov entered. He rubbed the sweat from his palms onto his pant legs and stuck out a hand as the Russian colonel approached. The Turkish official wore a navy-blue bespoke suit over a white shirt, a scarlet silk tie complementing the ensemble. The look was accented by an Audemars Piguet Royal Oak in a hammered eighteen-carat pink gold case, the expensive timepiece glittering from beneath his French-cuffed shirt sleeve.

This was a man who treasured fine things. Gerasimov wondered how he wasn't melting in the heat.

"Colonel, so good to see you again," said the minister.

Gerasimov shook his hand firmly and took the chair opposite. His bespoke suit and fancy watch and shoes couldn't hide how ugly he was. The minister had the face of a bulldog, along with unkempt gray hair and mustache, thick, bushy eyebrows, and lush nasal hairs.

"It's been far too long, Minister Çakir." In truth, he'd sooner the weasel was a decomposing corpse in the desert. But, for now, he at least continued to be somewhat useful.

"My friend, welcome to this traditional Turkish *kahvehanes,* owned by my wife's brother." He held up his hands, gesturing around the coffee house. The Turkish minister of the interior could be as insincere as any politician, but he couldn't hide his authentic pride in this family venture, a fact that endeared him at a rudimentary level to Gerasimov. At the same time, Çakir exposed his discomfort and anxious demeanor with little tells, like his flitting eyes and restless, trembling hands. His erratic gray hair clung to his scalp in waves, and his jowls swayed as he spoke, like those of an aging mastiff. "Thank you for meeting with me."

"Of course! But call me Viktor. There is no need for rank or titles between us. We have known each other a long time." This was true. The interior minister had held a cabinet post for almost a decade. The two men had often discussed matters of consequence to their respective countries, such as the sale of missile defense systems and the going rate for securing votes in the Grand National Assembly of Turkey. "There is no need for such formality, my friend."

"In that case, Viktor, call me Ahmet."

Gerasimov looked at the Turk standing within earshot by the door.

"He can be trusted, Colonel," Çakir said, as if reading his thoughts. "My men are paid handsomely for their discretion."

"Of course," replied Gerasimov, signaling to Malkin that he should keep an eye on him. "But, as they say, *two can keep a secret if one of them is dead.*"

Ahmet waved at his man, signaling he should take a few more steps out of earshot.

"Distressing news about the power failure last night," Gerasimov said. "I understand it lasted hours."

"Yes," replied Minister Çakir, as a man in a flat cap entered the room bearing a tray. "It was most inconvenient. Very costly for our city as well."

Çakir stopped talking and allowed the man to deposit the tray onto the table. He offloaded a small carafe of chilled water with two glasses, then set out two *kahve finjanı*—traditional Turkish ceramic demitasse cups—in front of them, into which he poured a foamy concoction from a *cezve,* a small, long-handled copper pot.

Çakir indicated toward the coffee as the man poured.

"I hope you won't mind, but I took the liberty of asking my brother-in-law to prepare it *orta şekerli,* which means moderately sweet," he said, pointing to their cups.

The two *kahve finjanı* each had a creamy head on top, much like an Irish stout. Çakir's brother-in-law said something in Turkish before bowing his head to his guests and walking away. A boy of eleven or twelve years brought a tray of pastries to their table, then left.

"Please," said Çakir. "Enjoy a piece of *börek* while the coffee grounds settle."

Gerasimov reached forward and plucked a piece of the warm phyllo pastry from the platter. As he lifted it, strands of straw-colored cheese formed, dangled, and fell back to the tray.

"General Tikhonov and I are terribly sorry for the inconvenience to the city of Adana. Compensation will be forthcoming, of course," Gerasimov said, stuffing the two-inch-square pastry into his mouth. It melted like butter on his tongue.

"Excellent, yes?" asked Çakir, watching him eat.

He nodded. Between chews, while licking his fingers, he added, "Though, I might add that the rather unfortunate timing of the blackout assisted our mission greatly."

Çakir smiled. "Yes, well, the Americans aren't quite as pleased with the outcome as you and General Tikhonov." His eyes held Gerasimov's. "There have been consequences already as a result of last night's events."

"Of course. Heads will roll on the American military base, I'm sure of it."

"It's not just that, Colonel. My government was advised by your team that there were only to be some harmless acts of vandalism. Mischief, as you had described it. A way to harass the Americans and keep them on their toes. President Karaman was most agitated by these newer and more—" he searched for the right word "—consequential developments. He and I received word quite late from Turkish intelligence that an American nuclear bomb would be stolen. It was a shocking revelation that we were too late to stop. This incident represents an unprecedented breach of Turkish sovereignty that has infuriated my government and the Americans."

"Come now, Ahmet, what did you expect? Did you think we were going to merely wrap American airplanes with toilet paper in a childish prank?" Gerasimov waved a hand dismissively as Çakir started to speak. "But for our oversight, wherein we may have inadvertently misled you regarding our true intentions, your country will receive additional S-400 Triumf missile defense systems, along with upgrades to the ones we installed only a few short years ago. We have also already provided you with the construction, operation, and security for your Akkuyu Nuclear Power Plant in Mersin Province. Where would you be without the Russian Federation's friendship and ingenuity, Minister? How many times has your government had to kill such aspirational plans before we got involved? How many, my friend?"

"Six," the minister said sheepishly.

"Exactly, six. So, you see? Russia is your number one strategic ally. This was the agreement, Ahmet."

"It was *not* the agreement," said the minister, through gritted teeth, his fists clenched.

Malkin stepped forward, as did the Turkish freight train standing at the door.

Gerasimov raised his hand to bring down the level of testosterone one could almost smell within the small room. He spoke in a calm tone, as if to a small child.

"I might have underrepresented what was going to happen at the American airbase, Ahmet. If so, I apologize profusely. Perhaps we can offer additional inducements to you and your president?"

Çakir looked at him expectantly, hungrily, as if Salome's seventh veil were about to fall away.

"I understand you are still having problems with the Kurdistan Workers' Party, the PKK?"

Çakir nodded slowly. "The Kurds remain a threat to the peace and security of Turkey."

"We Russians know something about such things. Our country is familiar with managing extremist groups at home, and indeed throughout the former republics—Georgia, Chechnya, Azerbaijan, where, of course, we share mutual interests."

Again, Çakir nodded. "The PKK has stepped up their attacks in the southeast region of my country. It is a challenge containing their activity and influence."

"Remember, my good friend, power is conveyed through bullets, not ballots. We have a special group capable of dealing with this. Consider them an advisory team composed of elite Spetsnaz soldiers. They will help train Turkish troops on how to eliminate the Kurdish problem once and for all. They will work with your armed forces directly if your defense minister allows it. Another tactical alliance between our two great nations."

A pensive nod.

"And, of course, you will find a significant cash bonus has been deposited into your offshore account. A finder's fee, as it were, for your loyalty and hard work at helping solidify our two nations' growing friendship." He leaned in, speaking softly. "And to help cover your expenses, naturally," he added, looking over at the Turkish bodyguard by the door.

Çakir leaned back in his chair. "Our two countries continue to have mutual interests after all," he said, a tight smile coming to his lips.

"Indeed." Gerasimov picked up his coffee cup and took a sip, the strong, sweet brew adding the perfect counterpoint to the salty and savory pastry. "Not the least of which is to see Turkey more independent while strategically aligning with your new friends, the Russian Federation."

The Turk smiled.

"Excellent! I am most pleased we have come to an understanding."

"Me as well, Colonel. But we must still deal with the fallout from last night's adventures."

The young boy reentered the room. The beaded curtains rustled as he passed through them, like the sound of sleet falling onto the frozen streets of Gerasimov's childhood. The boy walked with all the calm and confidence of a well-loved child, depositing a tray of glistening pastries onto the Formica tabletop. The gridded pastries shimmered golden brown in the light streaming in through the window, a rich nectar oozing from each piece of the decadent dessert.

*Baklava,* thought Gerasimov, filled with anticipation.

Çakir noticed his shift in demeanor.

"*Teşekkür ederim,*" he said to the boy. The boy returned a vulnerable smile, pivoted, and ran from the room.

The same man who had filled their *cezve* earlier returned with a steaming copper pot, refilling their cups with the strong brew.

Çakir lowered his voice. "This incident last night will bring the Americans down on our throats with tremendous force, like a hammer dropping."

Gerasimov waved his hand as if swatting away a fly. "The Americans will sputter and run around beating their chests, but their alliances will work against them. The European doves will say that American nukes in Turkey are too dangerous a relic to leave in place. After last night, the global peacenik community will demand that the rest of the bombs be removed, serving both our purposes. We have achieved many goals here today, my friend. You should be proud of your accomplishments. We are playing chess now, thinking many moves ahead of the Americans. And as you know, Russians are the masters of this game."

Çakir bent forward and used a clean fork to lift a square of baklava from the tray, placing it on the plate before Gerasimov. "Of course, Viktor."

"President Sergachev will also demand that the remaining American nuclear bombs at the base be removed. He will argue, along with some of our friends on the United Nations Security Council, that they present a destabilizing influence in the region and that the risk has grown unacceptable and disproportionate to any strategic value they hold for Turkey or the United States, as evidenced by the theft of the warhead. This unprecedented new danger of a rogue nuke in the hands of some unfriendly party will put everyone on high alert. Meanwhile, Russia, of course, will support you in the international community. The presence of these munitions within Turkey presents an untenable situation and a clear and present danger to peace in the region."

"And what of the missing bomb, Colonel? The United States is going to be quite—how shall I say—*distressed* about the disappearance of one of their primary thermonuclear gravity bombs. How should Turkey manage this diplomatic crisis?"

"A jihadi militant group will claim responsibility for the theft. It will not fall upon the shoulders of any

Turkish citizen. The Americans will be cited for their
incompetence pertaining to security of their nuclear
weapons. Russia will come forward and offer assistance
in securing Turkish territory and in hunting down the
missing warhead. The Americans will vociferously and
strenuously object, at which point your president will
yield and accept their assistance in the very grave matter of finding the missing bomb."

Çakir studied Gerasimov's face. "And what is to
actually become of it?"

Gerasimov smiled. "That, my dear friend, is not
your concern."

# CHAPTER 39

RAF NORTHOLT, SOUTH RUISLIP, LONDON

RAF Northolt lay in northwest London, six miles north of Heathrow. A security guard checked Alex in at the guard post and directed the Uber driver to wait at the traffic circle next to the Supermarine Spitfire. The once-working version of the World War II–era hero of the Battle of Britain sat perched atop a pedestal in front of a three-story administration building.

A black Range Rover sat along the curb, and as her driver tucked his red Vauxhall Corsa in behind it, a young airman emerged. Alex climbed out of the car and approached him, her pack slung over her shoulder.

"Flight Lieutenant Stevenson, ma'am. Your plane is fueled and waiting. I'm to take you airside."

She hopped into the shotgun seat of the Range Rover, the flight lieutenant climbing in behind the wheel.

"Is this airbase still used much?" she asked.

"Yes, ma'am," he said. "Both the Royal Squadron and the Queen's Colour Squadron are based here. It's where the king and other members of the royal family fly in and out from."

Stevenson took the roundabout onto a service road that eventually ran southward along the airfield.

Another minute down the road and they came to an apron, where small commuter jets sat outside a hangar, but Stevenson drove past them all. Alex's jaw dropped as the next plane came into view. A Gulfstream G550, or, in US Air Force parlance, a C-37B, sat on the tarmac. The plane was decked out in the same blue and white livery as Air Force One, right down to the big, bold lettering above the row of windows as its larger, presidential sibling—UNITED STATES OF AMERICA. Having worked abroad for the past couple of years, it was a sight to behold. The engine nacelles were affixed with the Air Force roundel graphic, the National Star Insignia, sending a tingle up her spine.

"*Holy crap,*" she whispered.

"The American VIP jets usually land at Stansted Airport in Essex, ma'am. That's where they brought this one in from."

"Are there any other passengers on board?"

"None coming, ma'am. You must be special," he said. "They brought her in just for you."

He pulled the Range Rover alongside the plane's airstairs on the port side, aft of the cockpit. As she exited the vehicle, a flight attendant appeared at the top of the stairs. The woman wore a navy-blue vest and pantsuit with a sky-blue oxford shirt.

"Special Agent Martel?" she asked.

"That's me."

"I'm Staff Sergeant Davis, ma'am." Davis was a brown-skinned woman with a soft Southern accent.

"Nice plane," said Alex. "I usually fly coach."

"No coach here, Special Agent. Welcome aboard. Can I take your bag?"

Alex declined. "I'll keep it with me, thanks."

She climbed the stairs into the cabin, divided into three salons. She moved to the coziest one and plunked herself down into a plush leather seat. Davis followed her.

"We'll be taking off shortly. Once we're at cruising altitude, I'll be serving beverages, and shortly after, lunch. But before that, can I get you anything? A glass of wine, soft drink, sparkling water?"

"Call me Alex."

"Imani, ma'am," she said.

She was thirsty from the morning's tumult. She hadn't had a drink since leaving Krysten's apartment.

"Maybe just a Coke?"

Imani smiled and disappeared into the forward section of the airplane, returning moments later with a glass full of ice and a can of Coke, droplets of condensation running down the sides.

"Buckle up, Alex. We're about to take off."

\* \* \*

The view out the window as they climbed to cruising altitude was dizzying. Sunlight flooded the cabin, and the sky had turned cloudless, revealing a rare unobstructed view of the Channel Islands standing out against deep azure waters.

A short while later, Imani emerged from somewhere ahead of the salon bearing a food tray she placed in front of Alex. Grilled salmon with a butter, garlic, lemon, and dill sauce adorned her plate. Alex was suddenly aware how hungry she was.

As she ate, her thoughts nagged at her:

*Why had Krysten sent the email in the first place? Why had she laid the clues for the discovery of her safe-deposit box at my feet? Why not just tell her partner, the MI5 officer, Daniel Kane? Why out herself as a Russian spy to me? What benefit was there in my finding out, versus Kane? Or maybe Kane already knew—but if he did, why hadn't he reported it? Could it be that Krysten's coming out was her way of making amends?*

A message from Jonathan popped up on her phone.

JB: Once you're on the plane, log in on the secure connection to access a briefing from Chief Bressard.

AM: 10–4

# CHAPTER 40

The aircraft was registered to an Australian company but leased back to a CIA shell corporation to service flights like this one out of Olsztyn-Mazury Airport in Szymany, Poland. The Agency had learned long ago that aviation buffs and members of the news media liked to track the comings and goings of government aircraft. This often led to uncomfortable questions back home—questions that politicians, as a rule, preferred not to be compelled to answer. Hence, Caleb had gone out of his way to catch this flight and cover his tracks.

Previously bearing tail number N379P, the Gulfstream GV—pronounced *G-five*—had been owned by another CIA shell company, Premier Executive Transport Services. It had enjoyed a notorious past transporting suspected terrorists to undisclosed locations for extraordinary rendition or to CIA black sites. None of this was purely legal, of course, but it wasn't as if prison camps were being built adjacent to battlefields across the caliphate to house captured holy warriors.

Because of its flight log history, and despite the many dummy flights used to mask its actual missions, the international media had christened the jet with its wartime moniker, the Guantánamo Bay Express. Caleb didn't much care what the critics thought about the work performed by the US's security and intelligence apparatus. He wasn't distracted by trivialities like civilian outrage over the presumed mistreatment or extralegal transport of prisoners and enemy combatants. One might say he was possessed of a firmly held and diametrically opposed viewpoint to theirs.

He gazed out the window down to the rolling countryside miles below and reflected on his career—the highs, the lows, and the never-ending uncertainties that accompanied a life of working in the shadows, stalking evil. He bore the scars, both visible and unseen, of many years of service. When the quiet moments came, as they did ever so infrequently, they were brimming with self-recrimination and guilt. He was constantly assessing whether his efforts had been enough, second-guessing moves he had made and things he had done. Or hadn't done. It was reason enough to never stand still.

He mulled that over as his eyes grew heavy and sleep came blessedly to quiet his inner demons. When he opened them again, they were in Turkish airspace and flying over the Bosphorus Strait that separated Europe and Eastern Thrace from Asia and the Anatolian Peninsula. Istanbul and her seventeen million inhabitants lay below him. A complicated city, it embodied a fusion of East and West, where Islam abutted Christianity, and the millennia-old conflict between the two endured, like a pot of broth on simmer.

It was afternoon when the Gulfstream GV landed at Şakirpaşa Airport in Adana, Turkey. Caleb checked his watch, a Breitling Avenger GMT Night Mission, and adjusted it to local time. Typically, they would have flown directly to the airbase. Today, though, the

civilian-registered fixed-wing GV had been denied
clearance to land by the Turkish military authorities
who controlled that part of the base following what was
described locally as a security breach at Incirlik.

Caleb knocked on the doorframe twice for good luck
as he deplaned, as was his habit after every flight. He
was met at the bottom of the airstairs by an airman
first class who shuttled him out to a military hangar
next to the passenger terminal. There they boarded a
US Army UH-60 Black Hawk helicopter belonging to
the 5th Battalion, 101st Combat Aviation Brigade, and
were flown out to a rear sector of the United States 39th
Air Base Wing at Incirlik—the section of the base controlled by the Americans, not the Turkish Air Force.

He surveyed the sprawling airfield as he dismounted
the Black Hawk outside a hangar next to the control
tower. A pair of armed sentries stood at the entryway to
each of the hardened aircraft bunkers as far as the eye
could see. Two A-10 Thunderbolt II aircraft—better
known as the Warthog and Caleb's favorite aircraft as
a former ground-pounder—were taking off, one trailing less than half a football field behind the other. He
watched as they took to the skies. The sound of those
twin-engine jets was unmistakable. And to anyone who
had ever been saved by an incoming Warthog strafing
enemy positions, there was no sweeter sound than the
*brrrrrt!* of its 30mm Gatling gun laying down the
sound of freedom at 3,900 rounds a minute.

High above the base, two F-22 Raptor fighter jets
circled the 3,320-acre airbase.

"FPCON Delta."

"Say again?" said Caleb, turning around in search
of the voice behind him.

"The airmen on guard duty. The flyovers. Incirlik
is at Force Protection Condition Delta. The base is on a
security lockdown. I don't know who you are, but no one

se—not base personnel and surely not the locals—are
etting on or off right now."

"Lucky for me, I'm neither."

"Guess so. I'm Major Douglas, 39th Air Base Wing
ecurity Forces squadron commander. Welcome to the
ick, NATO's southern flank."

Major Douglas was a tall, squared-away airman in
is late thirties. He wore a dark blue beret with a Secu-
ty Forces flash inscribed with *Defensor Fortis,* mean-
g *defenders of the force.* A Velcro flash stitched with
F on it was also affixed to the upper arm of his battle
niform. He had an M4 rifle slung across his chest and
SIG Sauer M18 on his hip to complete the package.

"Copeland," Caleb said, shaking the major's hand
while noting the hardware. "I come in peace."

The major didn't smile. "This way."

Caleb swung his Bullet Ruck over his shoulder and
yed the two airmen standing behind Douglas, also
porting the SF patch and blue berets.

"They're with me," said the major, tracking Caleb's
onfusion. "Don't confuse the SF patch with a Special
orces tab," he offered. "It's not. It stands, obviously
nough, for Security Forces. But if anyone messes with
ese two, you'd think they were part of JSOC."

The two airmen smiled at the remark and the ref-
rence to Joint Special Operations Command, which
versaw all Special Missions Unit activities.

Caleb nodded. *Nice to see an officer boost his troops.*

"Think of them as MPs," he said, indicating toward
n idling Humvee. "Our job is base security and force
rotection. The big stuff is handled by the US Air
orce Office of Special Investigations—AFOSI or OSI
or short. Get in. I'll take you to base HQ in the Wing
uilding."

Caleb looked up to the sky at what appeared to be
atrolling aircraft. "What's with all that?" he asked.

"They're enforcing an extended no-fly zone ove the base and generally asserting air supremacy, i case anyone is watching. Force protection conditio is one of many alerts used in the military. Think o DEFCON—defense readiness condition. You've hear of that, I'm sure."

Caleb climbed into the Humvee. "Sure," he said. H had, of course, along with everyone else on the planet

"Our FPCON Delta alert only affects this base, bu the fallout—pardon the pun—could move the defens alert needle to a more global DEFCON level. Maybe a high as DEFCON 2, depending on what happens next."

*What happens next.*

He mulled it over. Only the Cuban Missile Crisi and Operation Desert Storm at the beginning of th Gulf War, version 1.0, had put the country at DEFCON 2. The September 11 attacks had moved the needle o American defense readiness to DEFCON 3, and only fo a few days.

*What happens next* wasn't exactly something he wanted to think too much about until he had more in formation on *what happened last night*. He was eage to meet the base's command staff and get a sitrep so he could update his deputy director.

From his seat in the front of the Humvee, Caleb scanned the multitude of aircraft parked outside hard ened shelters or grouped on the tarmac. Fighter jets bombers, helicopters, and other strategic aircraft sa at the ready, like aluminum-skinned steeds tied to a hitching post, waiting to be mounted and taken into battle. Major Douglas dodged and weaved past them pulling up to a pale yellow, two-story structure. The ai wing commander's office was on the second floor.

Douglas brought the Humvee to a stop under the portico with a 39th Air Base Wing sign affixed. Old Glory fluttered in a breeze out front.

"Leave your ruck in the truck," he said. "We won't be here for long."

After passing through a security checkpoint, they entered a central atrium. The ground-floor offices appeared deserted. Other than the sentries, there was no one else in sight.

"Doesn't seem very busy for an admin building," said Caleb, taking the steps two at a time to keep up with the major.

"Shit's got a little hot around here since last night," said Douglas. "All base activity is suspended. Titans are restricted to quarters unless they have an official tasking."

"*Titans?*"

"Base personnel at Incirlik are known as Titans."

They reached the top of the stairs and walked down a wide hallway with offices every few feet. Midway down, Douglas stopped outside a door and placed his hand on the knob.

"Titan 1 is a good man, but you might find him a little abrasive today."

"*Titan 1?*"

Douglas nodded. "Colonel Greeley," he said, turning the shiny knob. "Base commander."

The door opened into an anteroom with two doors leading off it. The door to their right had the colonel's name stenciled on the opaque window. To their left, a closed conference room door barred entry. A desk faced them, where an airman was studying the screen of his computer. He stood as the men entered.

The major addressed the airman. "Lieutenant, this is Mr. Copeland, fresh from stateside. Is the colonel ready for us?"

Inside the conference room, Caleb could hear agitated voices engaged in spirited conversation, but he couldn't make out what was being said.

"Let me check, sir," said the airman, lifting the handset of a desk phone.

The voices fell silent as someone answered the phone.

"Yes, sir," replied the lieutenant into the phone. "Knock before you enter, Major," he told Douglas.

Major Douglas did as instructed. A booming voice beckoned them in.

# CHAPTER 41

Caleb filed into the conference room behind Major Douglas. As they entered, he scanned the faces of the two officers present. It was often those brief moments of first contact that revealed the most about a person's intentions: What they knew. What they were hiding. Whether they were prepared to kill or die to keep their secrets.

Caleb himself had survived many a lopsided meeting by bearing in mind the timeless wisdom espoused by the warrior monk, General James "Mad Dog" Mattis. The retired United States Marine Corps four-star general had once been quoted as advising his Marines in Iraq, *Be polite, be professional, but have a plan to kill everybody you meet.*

*Sound advice. Probably won't go that far today.*

"Sir," said Major Douglas, addressing an officer standing at the head of a long table. "This is Mr. Copeland." He turned to Caleb. "Our base commander, Colonel Greeley."

"Copeland," he said. "I spoke to Deputy Director Thomas. You'll have my team's full cooperation." Kadeisha Thomas was Caleb's boss at CIA, and the person who had tasked him with recruiting Alex. "Anything the Titans can do to assist, we will," he added. "Whatever you need. Major Douglas here will give you whatever access or cooperation you and your partner will require."

"My what?"

"I was told—" He was cut off by the ringing of a phone. He grabbed the handset. "Yes? Send him in." Hanging up, he added, "Good timing. He's here."

*He who?*

Caleb turned to the door, confused, as it swung open.

There are moments that the mind processes in slow motion. This was one of those. First, he noticed the shoes and the stride. Neither was unusual in and of themselves. Then came the pants and the backpack slung over a shoulder. Then he registered the face and its self-assured smile. Then the hair, restrained in a ponytail.

"You must be Special Agent Martel," said Colonel Greeley, meeting the newcomer halfway across the room.

"Yes, sir."

"I'm sorry if I look surprised," he said. "When I was told *Alex Martel,* I made an unfortunate assumption. Please excuse my error." He led her over to the conference table, where another officer waited.

Alex smiled at Caleb as she floated past. "Happens all the time, sir," she replied.

Caleb hoped his jaw wasn't agape. *How did she get here?*

"Copeland," said the colonel. "You going to join us?"

*Sure, why not? Not like this is my operation or anything.*

Caleb strode over to the group.

"This is Colonel Sheila Mendez," Greeley said, indicating an officer dressed in OCP fatigues. "Colonel Mendez is my vice commander at the 39th Air Base Wing."

"We're glad to have you both here," Colonel Mendez said.

Greeley introduced Alex and Major Douglas, then continued. "I don't know what you all are going to add to what's been put in place," he said, "but I've been assured you'll be a force multiplier. So, you're welcome at Incirlik."

"Thank you, Colonel," Caleb said.

"Our job," said Alex, "is to track down the bomb and retrieve it—no more, no less."

*Since when?* thought Caleb.

"I don't envy your mission," said Greeley. "I can't stress enough, as I'm sure you all know, that the incident overnight is of the gravest concern to the interests and security of the United States of America. The president, of course, is fully briefed on the latest sitstat. And I'm in constant contact with the SecDef as well."

"And what *is* the current situation status, sir?" asked Alex.

With a wave of his hand, he indicated they all should take a seat. The colonel claimed the head of the table. Caleb sat to Greeley's left, and Alex took the seat opposite Caleb.

"Here it is, Special Agent Martel," he began. "I just got off a secure teleconference. The sixth fleet is moving two carrier strike groups into the Med. Both the *Dwight D. Eisenhower* and the *George H. W. Bush* have been mobilized and are steaming east as we speak. The fifth fleet is moving the *Nimitz* and *Theodore Roosevelt* into the Persian Gulf. Between them, that's thirty thousand personnel, give or take, along with about two hundred aircraft and a shitload of other boats. Add to that another five thousand US Marines in two Marine expeditionary units. Plus, JSOC is sending a Delta Force nuclear squad, whatever the hell that is, from Fort Bragg—"

"That would be their H-Squadron, sir," offered Alex. "They're a Special Forces explosive ordnance disposal team for nukes. But you didn't hear that from me."

"Well, then, I think it should be quite clear, folks, we're in a pretty big shit storm, if you don't mind me saying."

"Colonel," Caleb said. "Would you mind filling us in on the actual incident?"

He had taken the kubotan out of his pocket and was tapping it against his knuckles. He glanced across at Alex, who was giving him that patented look of hers, a blend of concern, curiosity, and something else. *Admiration maybe? Nah.* He put the kubotan back in his pocket and straightened up but then absent-mindedly rubbed at the rib with the missing chunk, feeling the notch along its top edge.

Colonel Greeley turned to his vice commander. "Sheila, why don't you get us started."

"Of course, Colonel. I'll get right to it," she said, leaning forward. "We have a missing nuclear weapon."

\* \* \*

Hearing the words *missing nuclear weapon* spoken aloud was more than a little jarring.

Alex had read the incident report on a secure connection to Interpol on the flight to Incirlik. She'd familiarized herself with details of the missing nuke, a B61 Mod 12 thermonuclear gravity bomb. She had called Bressard over secure comms to discuss whether this incident could be somehow connected to her case involving the special nuclear material being exchanged at Arnhem. Inconclusive, analysts had decided. But a nuclear weapon going missing wasn't something that happened every day, let alone so close to another similarly themed event.

She had also asked whether the events at Arnhem

could have been a distraction meant to draw attention away from those about to unfold in Turkey. Again, *unclear* had been the response from her chief, but it was being considered as a possible motive. She thought back to the Terlet Airfield outside Arnhem. Two groups of men intent on exchanging special nuclear material for cash.

*What was the purpose of the exchange?*

For the sellers, greed. The simple exchange of an in-demand commodity for cash. But what about the buyers of the plutonium and highly enriched uranium? Surely they couldn't have hoped to make a fully functional nuke. Even these days, that would be a heady dream. Too many variables. Too great a chance of discovery. It wasn't as if there were a plethora of nuclear engineers or subject matter experts out there looking to help John Q. Public make a homemade improvised nuclear device. So what was the plan?

And what tied these two seemingly distinct events together? On the one hand was a well-funded fledgling jihadi group, the ILF, trying to take possession of the nuclear material. On the other was a missing nuke.

*Could the ILF have pulled off an operation this sophisticated?* Alex didn't think so. *If not, then who?*

Everything kept pointing back to the Russians. They *were* capable of such a complicated intel- and resource-dependent plan.

"Colonel Mendez," she said. "You've used the term *missing* both here and in your report. Could you please tell us exactly what happened?"

Mendez glanced at Titan 1, who nodded.

"Incirlik Air Base houses several different units, including the team that manages, maintains, and secures the nuclear weapons. The weapons on this base form part of America's nuclear triad."

"For the sake of clarity, what exactly is that?" asked Alex.

"The nuclear triad is a force structure comprised of land-launched nuclear missiles, nuclear-missile-armed submarines, and strategic aircraft with nuclear bombs and missiles."

"And within that nuclear triad, what is Incirlik's role?" she asked.

"Strategic bombers, Special Agent Martel. The nuclear armaments on base are a component of NATO's nuclear sharing and deterrent program, dating back to the Cold War." She stood and walked around the table to an easel at the side of the room, next to an urn of coffee and a tray of pastries.

"Here at Incirlik," she continued, "we hold fifty-six B61 bombs. They are not guided missiles or anything quite so advanced. The B61 is simply a gravity bomb meant to be dropped from various aircraft."

She flipped the chart on the easel from an overview page of the airbase to a series of diagrams. "There are thirteen variations of the B61—mod zero through mod twelve. We keep four versions on base. The mod twelve is the newest variant. Of that model, we have—" She corrected herself. "We *had*—eight. A B61–twelve was stolen overnight." She straightened and adjusted her cammies. "I'm afraid we have an *empty quiver* situation."

One needn't be an expert in weapons of mass destruction to understand the implications of an actual stolen thermonuclear bomb.

"I thought a missing nuke was called a *broken arrow*."

Alex regretted her interjection the moment it left her lips.

*Who cares what it's called? We have a missing thermonuclear bomb!*

Mendez smiled graciously, like a patient professor. "The term *broken arrow* can refer to a missing nuke if it goes missing in transit. It also refers to an accidental or unexplained nuclear detonation, among other things. *Empty quiver* refers to the seizure, theft, or loss of a functioning nuclear weapon."

Caleb jumped in. "Can you tell us more about this missing nuke?"

"Absolutely," said Mendez. "The B61 bombs are the primary thermonuclear weapon in the United States' arsenal. All the variants are low- to intermediate-yield strategic and tactical nuclear weapons; *yield* being the term meaning *energy released in the detonation of an explosive weapon,* which is representative of its destructive power in this context, but you already knew that, I'm sure."

Alex did, but she appreciated the colonel's explanation anyway. *Always good to make sure everyone is starting on the same page.*

"Just what is the destructive capability of the B61?" she asked.

"Different models have different yields. Some are fixed-yield, some are variable."

"*Dial-a-yield,*" said Caleb.

"Yes, colloquially, they're often called *dial-a-yield* or *D-A-Y* bombs because the explosive power is user-selectable at the time of arming."

"How quaint," said Alex.

"So, the yields vary," continued Colonel Mendez. "For comparison, the atomic bomb dropped on Hiroshima had an explosive yield of roughly fifteen kilotons of TNT. The lowest yield of the B61 is only zero-point-three kilotons. That's one-fiftieth as powerful as Little Boy, the Hiroshima bomb."

Alex did the decimal conversion in her head. "But that's still the equivalent of three hundred tons of TNT. That's a huge explosion, not to mention the radioactive fallout. Especially if it goes off in a major city."

"Like New York," said Caleb. "You said the yield of the mod twelve is user-selectable. What's the highest yield?"

There was a pause before Mendez replied. "Fifty kilotons," she said matter-of-factly. "Over three times as powerful as Little Boy."

*Lord help us.*

"Commander Mendez," Colonel Greeley chimed in. "Why don't you and Major Douglas take our guests over to the weapons maintenance building for a closer look."

"Yes, sir," she replied.

Her stomach rumbling, Alex grabbed a cherry Danish off the side table on their way out.

# CHAPTER 42

Alex and Caleb followed Major Douglas to the waiting Humvee. Titan 2 rode shotgun. Alex hadn't sat in a Humvee since her last deployment, and she was gripped by a sense of nostalgia; not that she missed being shot at.

She noted an M24 rifle with a Leupold scope racked behind her seat.

"You a sniper, Major?"

"Air Force–qualified counter-sniper," he answered. "But I wouldn't try putting a round downrange these days, not since I took command of base security. I leave that to my young run-and-gun tech sergeants. One of my guys commandeered this patrol vehicle from another squad member. It's her rifle. She was on the range with it yesterday."

"Nice weapon system."

"I heard a rumor about you," he said. "Word is you're a crack shot."

"I hold my own." She'd been down this road before. Her Army and ISA service record opened doors. Still, sometimes it got in the way, as people tended to focus on her legendary achievements and not on her overall capabilities and skill set.

"You're too modest."

She turned to look out the window, never comfortable being the center of attention. She flashed back to the airfield in Arnhem, the ensuing helicopter chase, and a long-ago moment frozen in time with the painful memory of a young girl's impossibly green eyes.

The interior of the Humvee was oppressively hot. Major Douglas rolled down his window and everyone else followed suit. Ahead of them, the sun crashed through the windshield on its way toward the horizon, but there was still plenty of daylight left before it would set after eight P.M. local time. Alex took a bite of her cherry Danish, wiping ultra-sweet filling from her lips with a napkin. She caught Caleb looking at her.

"You were telling us about the yield of the B61," she said to Mendez.

"I was," she replied. "There are four settings on the mod twelve. Those settings are point-three kilotons, one point five, ten, and fifty."

"So, at its highest setting," said Alex, "you said the yield is more than three times the size of the bomb dropped on Hiroshima?"

"Yes, ma'am," replied the colonel.

Caleb whistled.

"But it gets worse," added Colonel Mendez.

"I can't wait," he said.

"The mod twelve incorporates an earth-penetrating warhead capable of taking out a facility like the Russian Continuity of Government compound built beneath a thousand feet of granite in the northern Urals. That complex is not unlike our own Cheyenne Mountain or Raven Rock facilities. An underground detonation," the colonel continued, "while reducing the overall fallout potential, actually increases the relative yield."

"By how much?" asked Alex.

"By a factor of twenty. So, at the mod twelve's

maximum yield of fifty kilotons, an underground detonation would have the equivalent above-ground yield of roughly one megaton."

"That would be huge," said Caleb.

"Cataclysmic," answered Colonel Mendez. "The damage a blast like that would cause is unfathomable. But this is all sounding very fatalistic. There is some good news here, too."

"How's that exactly, Colonel?" Caleb asked.

"The stolen bomb is a gravity bomb," she replied. "It's meant to be dropped from an aircraft, not to be randomly set off by malign actors, or anyone else for that matter, without proper authorization. And that part is almost impossible to achieve."

"You're not missing any aircraft, are you, Colonel?" Alex asked.

"Not last we checked," said Mendez. "Officially speaking, there are no capable American delivery aircraft on the base. Fifty-six B61 nuclear bombs, but no American aircraft capable of delivering the payload. *Officially*. And a nuclear bomb without a delivery device is just a bullet without a gun."

*Well, almost.*

"So why keep them here?" Caleb asked.

"It's the paradox of Incirlik. If we remove them from the airbase, we would be signaling the end of the Turkish–American alliance at the very moment the Russians are sidling up next to them. Keeping them here, though, perpetuates a nuclear security vulnerability we should have eliminated years ago."

"Amen," said Major Douglas.

"The bombs are here just as much to appease our allies as to meet America's strategic objectives."

"You said *officially*," said Alex.

"Yes," replied the colonel.

"To me, that implies there's more to it."

Mendez hesitated but then answered, "*Unofficially,* I can tell you we have several F-15E Strike Eagles that are compatible with the B61–twelve. Those aircraft can walk the talk."

Major Douglas drove along the airfield's perimeter road. Alex noted the omnipresent double chain-link fence topped with thick coils of razor wire on both the external perimeter fencing to their left and the area to their right. They were on US Air Force property, distinctly fenced off from the city around them, their borderlands buffered by fields of fig and date trees, and intrusion detection systems with multilingual signs that read NO TRESPASSING. USE OF DEADLY FORCE AUTHORIZED.

Everywhere, they were reminded of the additional layer of security around the Titan base.

"Any theories on who took the bomb, Colonel? Or how?" Caleb asked.

"The theft of the B61 could well have been a Turkish scheme to force the US out of Turkey," she said. "Air Force OSI is on that, as is Major Douglas's team. Someone on our side facilitated the crime, that's for sure."

"It's not like an army drove tanks through the gates and demanded we hand over a nuke," added Major Douglas. "Somebody literally drove it off the base in the middle of the night."

"Any idea how they managed that, Major?" asked Alex. The report from Interpol had said as much, but without speculation as to how the feat was accomplished. "I mean, it's pretty hard to fathom."

He shook his head. "Not yet, but my job is to find out how this happened and who's responsible," he said. "I'm working on that, and I'm confident that between my Security Forces team and the US Air Force Office of Special Investigations, we'll find out who did it. But tracking the bomb down and retrieving it, now that's a different matter, and quite frankly, that's your problem."

The Humvee passed another double fence line with cameras on posts and pressure plates in the roadway. A big sign next to the road read ENTERING NATO ZONE. Alex could see several roads laid out in a circuitous fashion surrounded by even more fencing around a series of aircraft shelters.

"We'll be at the weapons maintenance building in a minute," said Mendez. "Get ready to meet your nation's mighty nuclear arsenal."

Alex's stomach lurched and it wasn't the Danish. It suddenly occurred to her that she wasn't particularly enthused about coming face-to-face with her nation's tools of global annihilation.

# CHAPTER 43

Major Douglas parked the Humvee under a covered entry in front of a loading bay big enough to house a couple of semitrailers. Alex was relieved to step out into a cool, light breeze blowing in from the south.

"Glad you're parking in the shade," she said.

"I'm just getting us out of the line of sight of satellites—Russian, Chinese, Google. Everyone has an eye in the sky watching what goes on around here. If I didn't, you'd find yourself on the front page of the *New York Times* or *Washington Post* by morning."

Colonel Mendez looked at her phone.

"Major Douglas," she said. "Will you join me inside? Copeland, Martel, you'll have to excuse us a moment. Titan 1 needs us on a conference call with the SecDef."

"Mind if we join you?" asked Alex.

"No can do, Special Agent," Mendez replied.

The two airmen disappeared into the squat building, leaving Alex and Caleb alone next to the Humvee.

"Nice try," said Caleb. "So, how exactly did you manage to finagle your way on to my case anyway?"

"*Your* case?"

"Last I checked you were running around London trying to evade Russians."

"You're behind the news cycle then, *partner*. Keep up."

"Oh? Enlighten me."

Alex told Caleb about her visit to Krysten's apartment and the discovery of the safe-deposit-box key, her conversation with Jonathan about the decoding of Krysten's email, the phone call with Kane, and the visit to Lloyds Bank. She described the contents of the box—the passports, the photos, the note—and told him about her encounter with Tatiana and her goons.

When she finished, a look of shock washed over his face. She expected him to say something along the lines of *Thank God you survived that ordeal,* but instead, he asked, "So, your friend was a Russian spy?"

Alex didn't much like his tone, but it was the truth.

"Guess so," she answered feebly.

"How did you not see this coming, Alex?"

"What are you talking about? How could I have known?"

"It's literally your job to know!" he snapped.

"Go to hell, Caleb. I attended a conference with her a few years back. We went to lectures and drank wine, and from that, I'm to deduce she's a Russian mole?"

"You're to question the intentions of everyone around you—especially the ones that materialize out of thin air, like a woman at an international security conference for intelligence personnel."

"Or spooks who stand in the corner of briefing rooms and jump onto helicopters uninvited?"

"Well, yeah. Your problem, Special Agent Martel, is that you're too proud to admit you could ever make a mistake. It's fine if it's me you're trying to convince that you didn't do anything wrong, but it's a whole other problem if you're deluding yourself."

"Fuck you, Caleb! You read my service jacket, and from that you think you know me?"

"You're not that hard to figure out, Alex."

Alex glared at Caleb, her trigger finger twitching. *In, out, rest, two, three.*

Just then, Mendez reappeared from inside the building and called them in, leading them past two armed sentries. A hallway led them to a brightly lit room of slate-gray walls. A mechanic's chain hoist with a big metal hook hovered over a pair of empty metal racks. It was the same setup her dad used to pull motors out of vintage cars and boats in the garage behind his country house at the lake. What she wouldn't give right now to be sitting with him on his dock, shooting the breeze over a cold beer.

"Everything okay?" she whispered to Alex. "It's none of my business, but it looked like you were about to kill him."

"The thought crossed my mind," Alex mumbled. "Partner stuff."

"I get that," Mendez said. Then, loud enough for all to hear, she said, "This is where the B61 was being held before being taken."

Alex walked around the room, taking it all in. It looked like any other maintenance bay in any other mechanical workshop. Across the room behind a partition, another rack held two long gray objects. She froze in her tracks.

"Are those—?"

"Yes," Colonel Mendez replied. "Two B61 Mod 12s. Identical to the one that's missing."

A chill ran down her spine. The devices were each eleven-and-a-bit-feet long and maybe a foot and change in diameter. The nose cone was painted black. The tail assembly was bright orange and held four fins.

"Frightening, isn't it?" asked Mendez. "The innocuousness of it all. It's what first struck me when I arrived here to take up the role of Titan 2. The unspeakable power of those munitions you're standing beside should be jarring. But it isn't. You get used to it."

"It's terrifying."

"In about five minutes, after I describe how it works and all the safety systems in play, that feeling will fade."

Alex wasn't convinced.

Mendez smiled. "You were in the Army—a combat medic and then a sniper." Alex stared at her. "I got a briefing package," she said by way of explanation.

Alex nodded.

"I understand you held the world record for the longest kill shot. Is that right?"

Alex felt a little uneasy. "Yes, ma'am. For a while, I did."

"I can appreciate the attention to detail and the self-discipline that a sniper must have to be *that* good—to be world-record good. Because, as you know, no matter how humble you are, not everyone can be that good."

"But that's just a rifle, Colonel. A sniper only takes one life at a time."

"It's a microcosm of what we do here. Ultimately, to do what you do requires the same understanding and discipline that I need to do what I might be asked to do—to order planes into the skies carrying those little eight-hundred-and-fifty-five-pound babies strapped on."

A moment later, Caleb appeared from behind the partition with Major Douglas.

"Whoa," he said. "Are those—"

"Yes," Colonel Mendez said. "One of these would have been next to impossible to steal when stored inside its Weapons Storage and Security System vault within the protective aircraft shelters around the airbase."

"Then why aren't these in a vault?" asked Alex.

"Like the stolen bomb, these are here to be shipped

back to the Pantex facility in Amarillo for an upgrade to the guided-tail assembly kit and an onboard software upgrade."

"Are bombs disabled before being shipped to the States?"

"Not entirely. In fact, the only time their robust security systems are vulnerable is when they are being readied to go to the plant in Texas."

"What do you mean?"

"The B61 has a circuit that can be triggered remotely, which will fry its onboard power and initiation systems in the event of a broken arrow or empty quiver scenario."

"Like this one," said Caleb.

"Yes."

"Except . . . ?"

"We disable that feature prior to transport."

"But why disable a system that would disable the bomb at the exact moment it's most vulnerable to tampering?" Alex asked.

"Process," she said. "Because it's no longer under the care and control of personnel on the base, I suppose."

"So the bomb is otherwise still functional?" asked Caleb.

"As far as we know."

"And it can't be disabled remotely anymore?" asked Alex.

"No, there's only one way to cripple that bomb now."

"And that is . . . ?"

"Damage the unit in such a way as to initiate its self-destruct mechanism."

Despite their quarrel, Alex and Caleb stared at each other in disbelief. The bomb was a functional nuke seemingly without a feasible means to render it safe.

"Come on, I'll open one up and show you."

As they stepped over to the pair of B61s, Alex asked, "Could whoever stole the bomb mount it onto another aircraft and deliver it to a target of *their* choosing, Colonel?"

"Theoretically, maybe. But to do that, they would have to bypass the onboard security systems and then mimic the communications link between the aircraft delivering the weapon and the weapon itself. So, practically speaking, it's impossible."

"Completely impossible?"

"There's only one kind of *impossible,* Alex."

"How does this security system work?"

Colonel Mendez waved them over.

Alex wasn't so sure she wanted to stand any closer.

"Don't worry, it won't bite." Mendez squatted beside the bomb's fuselage. Along the side was a hinged access panel secured with small screws. "Hand me a Torx driver," she said to Major Douglas.

He rummaged around on a workbench and grabbed a ratcheting screwdriver from a tool chest, then handed it to Mendez. She removed a row of screws and lifted the curved lid on its hinge.

Alex worked up the nerve to approach. They crouched around Titan 2, staring into the void behind the hinged door where a control panel measuring ten inches by four inches came into view featuring a series of buttons, knobs, and displays.

"This is one component of the B61's Aircraft Monitoring and Control System interface," said Mendez. "Inside this compartment, we have access to two essential elements of the system—the variable yield setting and the PAL."

"What's a PAL?" asked Alex.

"Permissive action link, the security and arming system." She reached in and woke the digital system up with her touch.

Alex reflexively took a step backward when the system's green LEDs lit up and beeped.

"Don't worry, we're miles away from a triggering sequence," Mendez said. "It's a highly sophisticated, all-digital, and heavily encrypted system."

Alex thought about her phone being hijacked and wasn't comforted by the *all-digital and heavily encrypted* reassurance.

"Plus, there's an onboard anti-tampering system that would purposely mis-detonate the warhead," Mendez continued, "destroying it without causing an actual nuclear explosion. This is the self-destruct mechanism I mentioned a moment ago."

"*Mis-detonate* sounds a lot like the word *explode* to me," said Caleb.

"One of the effects of the anti-tamper system *is* to cause a small explosion equal to four or five pounds of TNT, roughly the yield of a pipe bomb. It's a shaped charge intended to deform the plutonium core of the warhead, rendering it useless."

"Wouldn't that cause a radioactive spill of the fission materials?" asked Alex.

"No, or at least it shouldn't." She pointed to a series of roller switches on the panel inside the bomb that resembled the dials on a bicycle lock. "This cryptographic security lock consists of a twelve-digit alphanumeric string controlled with these twelve dials, and the list of those with knowledge of the code is extremely short."

"Do you know the code, Colonel?"

"There are only two people on the base with *access* to the code, but neither should *know* it."

"Would that be you and Colonel Greeley?"

She nodded. "Just like the launch codes on a nuclear submarine or in the president's nuclear football, the two-man rule applies. The code can only be accessed by unlocking the safe where the codes are stored using two separate keys. And before you ask, yes, I am wearing one of the required keys," she said, tapping her OCP uniform.

Alex leaned in closer to the panel. "What are those other dials?"

There were two additional rotary knobs to the right of the twelve-digit window. One was gray, the other black. Caleb leaned in, too, and she could feel his breath on her cheek. She resisted the urge to shove him away.

Mendez pointed to the gray one. "This one controls the yield," she said. Alex noted the numbers around the dial, just as Mendez had stated earlier, indicating the settings that portended the deaths of a few thousand troops on a battlefield or potentially millions in a major city. "And the black one next to it sets the environment sensing device, an advanced accelerometer that allows the bomb to determine its position relative to when it should detonate."

"Pretty clever design spec," said Caleb.

Colonel Mendez was clearly familiar with the workings of the weapons in her care and custody.

"It is clever," she said, moving to the tail end of the bomb. Alex and Caleb followed. She pointed to the brightly painted orange rear section. "It's three to four times more accurate than its predecessors. These fins help stabilize it during descent to provide for more accurate targeting after the pilot or weapon systems officer—the *wizzo*—inputs the final coordinates in flight."

"Wait," said Alex. "There's a remote communications capability?"

"Yes, as I hinted at earlier," the colonel replied. "The wizzo plugs any corrected coordinates into the nav interface before releasing the weapon. Then the comms system works over a series of encrypted ultra-low frequency channels during delivery."

Alex was stunned by this bit of news. *If my phone can be hacked . . .*

Major Douglas, head of Incirlik Air Base Security Forces squadron, chimed in. "Which leads us to the next problem."

# CHAPTER 44

Let me get this straight," said Alex, summarizing their conversation as impassively as she could. "One of the safety features of this bomb is a system—you called it a weak link system—that can be triggered remotely to fry the electrical circuits and kill all the power to the bomb, rendering it useless."

"Affirmative," said Major Douglas.

"So, although that entire system was deactivated as a fail-safe in preparation for the bomb going stateside, when technicians tried to reactivate that feature in the missing weapon, the system wouldn't respond. Correct?"

"Affirmative again."

"So, if the Air Force can't get in, does that mean that someone—or something—is blocking the attempt?"

"We don't know," said Colonel Mendez. "It's possible the system was already triggered, and we aren't able to establish a connection precisely because the weapon's fail-safe system has kicked in and already self-destructed."

"Or," said Alex, trying to contain her growing concern, "we have a fully functioning thermonuclear bomb out there under someone else's control."

"It is possible," Mendez conceded.

The startling revelation altered the mission profile. *Their* mission. Based on her briefing notes, she had been under the impression that the missing nuke was more of a public relations nightmare; that it was improbable it could be used for anything but scrap metal, and that the primary hazard it presented was to the hapless thieves who might try to disassemble it.

But if the knowledge that someone could deploy the nuke, or sell it to someone else who could, was to be made public, the ensuing panic could have drastic repercussions. The revelation would likely derail trilateral nuclear arms–reduction talks scheduled for the Paris Peace Summit between the United States, Russia, and China—maybe even permanently scuttle them.

The current administration in Washington would also take a massive political hit from both sides, the hawks and the doves. While there had been previous *adverse incidents* and even losses of US nuclear weapons, none had ever been stolen.

To acknowledge one was stolen and not be able to guarantee it had been rendered safe was another matter entirely. And what if whoever had taken it could find a way to actually detonate it? This was the doomsday scenario long feared by politicians and often foretold by opponents of America's nuclear weapons program.

"Colonel, this changes the complexion of the situation exponentially," Alex said. "We really need to get a move on to locate your missing nuke."

"Then we better pull chocks and go to my office to finish this briefing."

\*\*\*

### INCIRLIK AIR BASE, ADANA, TURKEY

Colonel Mendez's office was across the hall from Colonel Greeley's inside the admin building where they had met earlier. Mendez, Douglas, Caleb, and Alex sat at a small conference table reviewing the sitstat.

"I liaised with the CIA station in Ankara," reported Caleb. "Our analysts reviewed hours of satellite imagery, but in the end, they weren't able to determine where the nuke was taken."

"Whoever took the bomb or helped in the undertaking must have known the system was disabled," said Alex.

Mendez looked over to her Security Forces squadron commander.

"That's quite likely," replied Major Douglas.

A big-screen TV was mounted on the wall next to the colonel's conference table. Titan 2 tapped on a keyboard and the screen came to life.

"Your people sent me this satellite footage," she said to Caleb.

Night-vision video imagery showed the area around the base at a medium-steep angle. The base's ten-thousand-foot runway was visible in the center of the frame, prominently illuminated on the screen. The image flickered, and each time it did, the resolution increased until the moving picture panned and zoomed onto a truck from the base traveling along the same service road they had been on earlier.

The colonel explained, "It's a normal occurrence for trucks to arrive and depart the base at night. Base operations are a twenty-four-seven undertaking—food services, logistics, aircraft maintenance. These things happen around the clock. The B61 maintenance shed is normally a single-purpose facility. But our F-15s have also been undergoing retrofitting of their own, so traffic in and out of the maintenance yard was to be expected."

The image zoomed in on a semitrailer pulling away from the maintenance building.

"This, then," she continued, "captures activity that

was not altogether unexpected. The operator of this truck and the company it's affiliated with are longtime Turkish contractors to the Air Force. They are now also a central part of the Office of Special Investigations' inquiry."

Alex nodded. Satellite imagery was a regular part of her own day-to-day process, but it always felt surreal watching footage of an event as it happened some sixteen hours ago.

The monochrome video feed captured the truck pulling out of the NATO section of Incirlik Air Base, traveling along the service road, pausing for inspection at the gate, then merging into local traffic before pulling onto a highway.

"So, as you can see, a suitable-sized semitrailer *was* detected in the approximate time window that the bomb went missing, leaving the base before traveling east along the highway out of Adana," Mendez said.

The moving truck filled most of the frame. It was smaller than a traditional North American eighteen-wheeler but clearly large enough to accommodate an eleven-foot-long thermonuclear bomb.

"That's a promising lead," said Alex.

"It might have been," replied Major Douglas. They continued to watch the truck driving toward the heat signature of what appeared to be a populous area. "But the truck fell off the imagery shortly after this sequence, in a city called Ceyhan, forty-five kilometers east of the base. Ceyhan is a main transportation hub in the region for Middle Eastern, Central Asian, and Russian oil and natural gas."

The screen went blank, except for a time signature of T01:47:32Z, or 4:47 A.M. local time.

Caleb, silent until now, chimed in. "So, we have a nuclear weapon traveling east along a highway toward the Turkish border with Syria, a geopolitical Chernobyl of a country if ever there was one, and along the way passing through an area that Russians and other groups have easy access to for legitimate commercial transport purposes." He raised his voice uncharacteristically. "Or, just as easily, they could have doubled back and gone in any direction. That bomb could literally be anywhere in the world by now."

Alex interrupted. "Caleb—"

But he ignored her. "Maybe it just floated down the Suez Canal and landed in, oh, I don't know, Somalia." He was animated as he stared wide-eyed at the vice commander, waiting for an impossible response.

"Your sarcasm isn't helpful," Mendez said.

"Sarcasm? This isn't sarcasm, Colonel. It's amazement, incredulity, mockery—"

"Mr. Copeland," said Colonel Mendez, "I understand why you and the CIA are upset—"

"Colonel Mendez, me and Central Intelligence aren't *upset*," he said. "The director of national intelligence, the deputy director of CIA, the president of the United States, and a whole bunch of other folks aren't *upset*. They're absolutely and implacably perturbed and confounded that there is possibly a completely usable thermonuclear weapon in the hands of terrorists whose plan is to blow up a city in the homeland, just for the fun of it."

"The safeguards should—"

"Stop!" Caleb threw his hands in the air. "Please, you have already conceded that the bomb's safeguards might be compromised, so don't tell me what the safeguards should or shouldn't be able to do."

Mendez and Douglas were struck silent.

Alex jumped in. "Colonel, we've gathered enough information. Please let Colonel Greeley know we're grateful for being shown the weapons maintenance building. We'll link up with AFOSI and coordinate with them further, but please pass any other developments on through my office at Interpol or through CIA." She stood and punched Caleb in the shoulder. "We need to get moving."

The colonel stood and smoothed her military fatigues. "Where are you going?"

"Are you a hockey fan, ma'am?"

"*Ice* hockey?"

*Is there any other kind?*

"As Walter Gretzky taught his son Wayne: Skate to where the puck is going, not to where it's been. So, ma'am, in a manner of speaking, and please excuse the lofty comparison, we're like the Great One—we're going after the puck."

# CHAPTER 45

PORT OF MERSIN, ADANA PROVINCE, TURKEY

Colonel Viktor Gerasimov strode with authority toward the small group of men gathered inside the fish processing warehouse.

The Port of Mersin on the northeastern coast of the Mediterranean Sea was the second largest seaport in Turkey. Because of its remote location, combined with the magnitude of the port's operations, concealing their illicit activities from Turkish authorities had proven simple. Privacy wasn't just a question of discretion but economics. When money was no object, prudence and circumspection could almost always be assured.

Across the harbor, immense cranes loaded forty-foot sea cans onto giant container ships destined for ports all over the globe. The air was damp, the skies gray and leaden, as they frequently were along the coast, giving the operation a modicum of concealment from overhead spy satellites run by the Americans and other NATO allies. The sea beyond the factory docks was dingy green with high, rolling waves. If he were a seaman, its appearance would seem an ominous portent. But Gerasimov was a soldier, not a sailor, and so he put the sea and its troubles behind him as he walked into the center of the room.

Six men huddled around a table, awaiting his

arrival. A large boning knife sat at its center, blood and guts residue still moist on its surface, even though the Russian-owned company had dismissed the plant's workers for the day to allow this meeting to take place.

"Well, what news?" he asked.

One of the men stepped forward, handing him a computer tablet. "It is ready, Colonel."

Gerasimov seized it from his grasp as Sergei came up beside him. He tapped the screen, and it came to life. A graphical interface popped up, instantly displaying an illustration of the B61-12 and controls for the nuclear weapon they had separated from the Americans. Beside them, the bomb sat on a wheeled rack next to the processing table.

"Is it live?" he asked, pointing to the tablet.

"It is, Commander," replied the man.

Gerasimov tapped some more on the tablet's display, and the nuke emitted a series of beeps. The bomb's control panel was open, and a green LED display glowed inside. The timer showed 1:00—one minute, zero seconds.

The room became animated as the eyes of men too afraid to change the world grew wider, filling with panic, which forced a laugh out of the Russian colonel. Next to him, Sergei merely smiled, his hands crossed in front of him.

"What?" asked Gerasimov. "Is it me you don't trust, or Russian technology? Our cyber warfare engineers from the SVR are the finest in the world at invading hostile computer systems. They locked this bomb out of American hands, reprogrammed its control software, and programmed this interface for our mission. I trust it with my life. And yours."

While the men looked on, he tapped on the interface again. The timer turned red and began counting down.

"Colonel . . . ," someone said, their eyes grown wide.

*56, 55, 54 . . .*

The men were not nearly as amused as the colonel.

*49, 48, 47 . . .*

They started to back away. "Please, Colonel," begged one of them.

Gerasimov looked at him. "I have been informed," he said, "that someone has been speaking out of turn with our Turkish allies. They were advised of the scope of our operation before I had the chance to tell them myself. This has cost the operation and Mother Russia a considerable sum."

*34, 33, 32 . . .*

Sergei's smile faded along with the other men's. "Now, who would do such a thing?"

*27, 26, 25 . . .*

"Who?" he repeated more forcefully.

One of the men piped up. "It was Vladimir," he said, pointing to a man standing next to Sergei.

The colonel turned to him. "Is this so?"

Vladimir was about to wet himself, judging by how tightly he squeezed his legs together.

*18, 17, 16 . . .*

Sergei's forehead broke out in a sweat.

Gerasimov asked again. "Well?"

"Yes, Colonel, I'm sorry!" whispered Vladimir, sounding like his throat was filled with sand from the dusty plains nearby.

*9, 8, 7 . . .*

Gerasimov tapped the screen a few times, and the countdown timer on the B61's display held at *3.*

He nodded to Sergei, who scooped the boning knife off the table and, with one deft swipe, sliced open the man's throat above his Adam's apple. The cartilage of his larynx glistened bright white even as the blood gushed from the jugular veins on either side of his neck. He collapsed to the ground and clutched at his throat. The air rushing past his vocal cords made a high-pitched whistling and wheezing sound, a bloody mist filling the air. Then the wheezing turned to a coarse gurgle. Gerasimov watched with curiosity as the vocal cords vibrated without purpose, a massive pool of blood spreading out around him.

Sergei tossed the knife down onto the processing table as the five remaining men stared on in terrified silence. Gerasimov gave him that *come hither* wiggle of his fingers. When Sergei showed no sign of comprehending, Gerasimov pointed to his waistband. Finally, Sergei understood and drew his gun, handing it to Gerasimov. The colonel took it and raised it, shooting the man who had snitched on his comrade in the forehead.

Message sent.

*Loose lips, et cetera.*

He handed the gun back to Sergei, who tucked it back into his holster and scooped up the empty casing that had been ejected onto the concrete floor.

"Now," said Gerasimov, the sweet smell of cordite hanging fresh in the air. "I trust the rest of the operation will proceed as planned, yes?"

Four men nodded enthusiastically. One stepped forward, pointing his chin at the nuke.

"It will be wrapped in a lead blanket," he said, "to shield it from detection by radiation portal monitors. Then it will be placed into a fish freezer before being loaded onto one of two Turkish-flagged trawlers. One trawler will act as a decoy and steam west, rendezvousing with a freighter that will transport a freezer full of fresh fish to the Port of Durrës in Albania. But the real cargo will be on the second boat and will be offloaded twenty kilometers from here. From there, it will be flown to its final destination, Colonel. All arrangements have been confirmed. It will be in position as scheduled, sir."

"Excellent." Gerasimov turned and walked outside to the Merc G-Wagen, folding the magnetic cover over the tablet to put it to sleep and tucking it under his arm as he climbed into the passenger seat. Sergei followed, and as they drove along the pier, he spoke at last.

"You had me worried, Colonel. I wasn't sure you would be able to disarm the bomb in time. But then I knew you must have some kind of immobilizing device or a mock version of the software running, yes?"

"Hmmm?" said Gerasimov, hardly paying him any attention. "No, Sergei. No immobilizer. I was only glad I remembered my passcode." He smiled broadly. "But now we are certain the tablet works."

# CHAPTER 46

Admittedly, they hadn't made as dignified an exit as Alex had planned. After Caleb's tirade and her hockey analogy, they'd found themselves alone in the hallway outside Colonel Mendez's office.

But neither the colonel nor Major Douglas had taken offense to what was said—or, if they had, they hadn't let on. In fact, the major had offered to drive them into the city himself. At first, Caleb had declined, but when they'd presented themselves downstairs to turn in their visitor badges, a Security Forces technical sergeant had been dropping off a Humvee for the major.

Alex, Caleb, and Major Douglas stepped outside of the squared-off, vanilla-painted Wing Building, and ran straight into Colonel Greeley. Despite the circumstances, the base commander appeared energized and wore a broad smile. His gray-blond hair, professionally coiffed and parted to the side, fluttered like a windsock in the evening breeze as he crossed the driveway toward them.

"All good?" he asked, pointing an almost accusing finger in their direction, a cadre of OSI investigators and Security Forces squadron members at his heels.

"Great, sir," Alex replied.

*As great as could be expected with a thermonuclear bomb missing.*

"Excellent!" he replied. "The Titans are counting on you." Ever the optimist, it seemed, he pumped a fist in the air as he wished them well. "The world is watching. Find our nuke!" he concluded, disappearing into the building.

*Words to live by.*

Major Douglas herded them into the Humvee. "Let me be your Uber driver tonight," he insisted.

He navigated off the base, past a phalanx of security as tight as any Alex had ever come across. The Security Forces squadron was out in full force, its members searching every vehicle coming or going, including theirs.

"Lots of activity for a base on lockdown," she said.

"An army marches on its stomach, Alex. Or in this case, an air force flies on it."

"Quoting Napoleon?"

"Like him, we recognize that thousands of airmen and civilians depend on the regular flow of provisions onto the base. No way around it."

Soon they were heading into the city of Adana, driving through a muggy late afternoon.

As they rolled along Girne Boulevard toward the Seyhan River, the six minarets of the Sabanci Merkez Mosque came into view, jutting skyward in a manner that reminded Alex of ICBMs being launched. The mental image was disconcerting given the unresolved sitstat.

She picked up on the smell of spices, coffee, and dust billowing in through the windows. Above it all, she recognized the aroma of the city's most famous dish, the Adana kebab or *kıyma kebabı*: a long, minced-meat kebab grilled on flat metal skewers over red-hot charcoal. Smoke hovered over Merkez Park, the site of a local food festival across the Seyhan. The park was nestled between the Central Mosque on its south end and the Galleria Shopping Mall to the north in the city's center.

Major Douglas and Caleb sat up front comparing notes on fishing hotspots back home and around the world. They wondered aloud what they might catch in the Seyhan River or in the lake above the dam that fed into it.

"Hey, Major, I'm kind of hungry," she called from the backseat.

He glanced at her in the rearview mirror. "We're almost at your hotel. Don't you want to grab a bite there?"

She pointed across the river. He nodded his head, and instead of turning right toward the Sheraton Grand Adana Hotel, he carried on over the bridge, turning up Fuzuli Street to take them into Merkez Park.

A text from Jonathan Burgess, her newest best friend at Interpol, appeared on her phone when they were halfway across the bridge.

> JB: New info on Krysten's email
> AM: Call you later?
> JB: Sooner is better
> AM: 5 minutes?
> JB: Roger

*Roger? JB was clearly enjoying his new connection with Ops. Maybe a little too much.*

As Major Douglas searched for a parking space, crowds of people streamed past the Humvee. Most were oblivious to its presence, while others peered inside through the open windows, hoping to catch a glimpse of an American. Americans in Turkey were like osprey on the lake above the Seyhan Dam— everyone knew they were around, but it was rare to catch a glimpse of one in the wild.

The crowd around them was dressed in a Westernized style. Turkey was a secular country, with the Turkish Constitution providing for freedom of religion and conscience. And while 90 percent of Turkey's eighty-three million citizens practiced the Islamic faith, there was a noticeable absence of the more austere clothing that women in Islamic countries around the globe were frequently required to wear. Men and women dressed in smart casual attire: trousers and short-sleeve shirts or golf shirts for the men; sleeved tops or summer dresses for the women. More conservative attire was reserved for religious events, inside mosques during a service, or even sightseeing. The crowd tonight would have been at home strolling the streets of New York, LA, or Washington in the summer.

"You coming?" she asked the major.

Douglas looked down at his OCP camos.

"Sure, why not." He removed his holster and stowed it in the center console. "Can't go wandering around among the citizenry wearing my SIG," he said with a smirk. "It'll offend the country's sense of peace and sovereignty."

Alex discreetly tapped the pistol concealed under her untucked shirt.

*Not giving mine up,* she thought. *In Glock we trust.*

They had only taken a few steps into the park when Alex glanced at her phone and pretended to read a text.

"Shit," she muttered.

"Everything okay?" asked Caleb.

"Maybe. You go ahead," she said. "I have to call my landlady—something about a burst pipe."

"That can't be good," said Major Douglas.

Although the smell of food was making her stomach rumble, she thought it best to step away from the men to talk to Jonathan. She watched as they disappeared into a throng of people among the food stalls, then she dialed Jonathan.

"What's going on?" she asked.

"I'm still trying to recover the rest of the data from Krysten's email," he said. "But it's corrupt. I can tell you that, among other things still in there, there was probably a map with notations."

"Of where?"

"Don't know."

The men already had their kebabs and were walking away from the food stall as she arrived. She opted for a *cag* instead of the Adana kebab as she continued her conversation with Jonathan.

"Also," he said, "I know who Cronus and Rhea are."

"You might have led with that."

"They're two of the twelve Titans from Greek mythology."

"Titans?" *Really?*

"The Titans were the children of Gaea and Uranus—Mother Earth and Father Heaven, respectively. They were the elder gods before the Olympians became gods."

"*Shit,*" she muttered.

"Cronus," he went on, "was the leader of the Titans, and for a time, he was the ruler of all gods and men. Rhea was his sister-queen. Cronus and Rhea married and had several children. Their children became the Olympians. Among them was Zeus, who eventually dethroned his father."

*Was Krysten pointing the finger at Colonel Greeley, Titan 1? And Colonel Mendez, Titan 2?*

She explained to Jonathan the relevance of that little tidbit of information.

"That could well be," he said. "One last thing: Do the words *lectures, wagers,* or *cherry* mean anything to you?"

"No," she replied, running the words around in her head. "Why?"

"They occur frequently throughout the code inside the message, like they were actually part of the message and not the code, if you know what I mean."

"Not really."

"Inside any program or app, there are lines of code and lines of commentary. The former are instructions that the computer carries out. The latter is more like a narrative for anybody viewing the code—comments, explanatory notes, that sort of thing. In this file, the words *lectures, wagers,* and *cherry* appear within quotation marks in the commentary sections. It seems those three words are a message in and of themselves."

She ran them around in her head to see if anything triggered.

*Lectures, wagers, cherry.*

The white-haired proprietor standing in front of the charcoal pit grabbed a wooden stick and pierced slivers of juicy, dripping lamb meat off the huge *döner,* the rotisserie spit piled thick with seasoned chunks of meat mounted over the charcoal pit. He placed it on a bed of flatbread and grilled green peppers.

*Lectures, wagers, cherry.*

"*Lectures.* Could it have something to do with the university in Paris, the Sorbonne?" she asked.

She took the plate of food and stepped out of line.

Caleb and the major walked toward her with their half-finished kebabs.

"Maybe. I'll email you a report," he said. "Better yet, I'll drop it into your secure vault on the server. You can access it later. Where you off to now, then?"

"Paris has to be our next stop."

"Why Paris?" he asked.

"Nothing concrete, but Krysten's message referenced our first meeting in Paris. And the Peace Summit is happening at the Sorbonne. And the note seems more literal than symbolic by the minute. And now you're telling me about three words that might say something about a lecture. So, Paris seems as good a place as any to start."

She rejoined the men in time to hear Caleb asking the major if he had any theories about who stole the B61.

"Twenty-two years in the Air Force and nothing like this has ever happened on my watch—obviously. We're interrogating our own people, but the Turks are another matter. They are responsible for joint NATO weapons security operations with my team."

"By that, you mean the nukes," said Alex, careful to check that no one was within earshot.

"Affirmative. But I'm not allowed to go near Turkish forces members myself. AFOSI is handling that through the Turkish Air Force leadership structure. Meanwhile, two Turks are unaccounted for, and the Turkish commander isn't being particularly helpful. He was the one who dispatched my security squadron members to the southeast part of the base to check on a perimeter alert, while his guards—the two who are missing—remained at the maintenance shed."

"Why is this the first we're hearing about this?" asked Alex.

"It was all in my report. I thought you would have received that package by now."

The hair on the back of Alex's neck bristled like the hackles of a wolf. She was sure she hadn't seen that reported anywhere.

"Colonel Greeley can't even leave the base until Turkish intelligence interviews *him*. Can you believe that? We shouldn't even have our nukes in this godforsaken country. Bloody ingrates. Pardon my French, ma'am," he said to Alex.

She thought about Jonathan's report on Cronus and Rhea. *Maybe the Turks know something the major doesn't.*

"You're not a fan of them being here?" she asked, uncomfortable to find herself walking two paces behind the men along the narrow path.

"Not a fan?" he repeated. "That's putting it mildly. The Turks attempted a coup a few years ago that failed. Back then, some of the Turkish Air Force jets at Incirlik were used to attack their own people. The Turkish base commander at the time sought asylum with the United States for his role, but it was denied. He was arrested and executed. Again, they tried to implicate the 39th Air Base Wing commander in their failed little revolution, but Uncle Sam wasn't having any of that bullshit—" He looked over his shoulder at Alex again by way of apology.

She raced ahead, turning around to walk backward in front of the men. "Major, I don't care if you use your big-boy words around me."

"Right. Anyway, they talk about the Balkans being a powder keg, which it is, of course, but this place has got to be a close second. Plus, they have nukes via Uncle Sam. It was only a matter of time before the Turks managed to steal one."

"That's what you think happened?"

"Of course. Everything okay back home?"

"What?"

"Your landlady—burst pipes or whatever."

"Oh, yeah," she said, almost tripping. "All's good. I told her she could enter my apartment to check it out and let me know."

The major's phone chirped. He stuffed what was left of his kebab into his mouth and answered it, signaling to Alex and Caleb that he had to take the call. They watched as he walked off along the path beside the river.

"What are you thinking?" Caleb asked as she fell in step beside him.

She filled him in on her conversation with Burgess; that, based on what he told her about Titans, Cronus, and Rhea, it was possible the two colonels were involved, at least from the perspective of Krysten's email. The status of Major Douglas wasn't entirely clear yet.

"I get the feeling, though," she said, "that Colonel Greeley is probably all he appears to be—a hard-nosed Mr. Rogers type and a legitimate people-person kind of boss. I don't see him being involved, but I could be convinced otherwise."

"I'm with you. I mean, whenever an armored car gets jacked, who is almost always behind it?"

"Right," she replied. "The ones guarding the goods in the first place."

"I think it's got to be the same here," he said. "Even if the Turks *are* involved, they would be hard-pressed to steal a nuke from an American airbase without help from someone high up the food chain."

"So that leaves us with Titan 2 or the Security Forces commander."

"Or both. Or neither."

She looked out across the river to the eastern portion of the park on the other side. It was more tranquil and placid there, with palm and lemon trees planted along its banks. Major Douglas walked toward them, sweat built up on his forehead, despite the cool breeze from the river. He tucked his phone into his pocket.

"Agreed," she said to Caleb, dropping her paper plate into a garbage can as the major rejoined them.

"Great news," he said. "We got a tip on the location of our stolen nuke."

"What? So what are we waiting for?" asked Alex. "Let's go!"

# CHAPTER 47

ADANA, TURKEY

The roads leading out of Adana toward their rendez-vous with Major Douglas's tipster wouldn't have held up to any serious scrutiny against US highway engineering and construction standards. They were narrow—especially for a Humvee—and casually marked with mere suggestions of where vehicles should travel instead of actual demarcated lanes. The buildings along the route were at times indistinguishable from the road itself, and while not scenic, it was at least green with vegetation. The major seemed to know where he was going.

Twenty minutes into their journey, they were approaching what would have amounted to a beachfront vacation area back home in the States. Nightclubs, restaurants, and cafés sprang up and Alex could make out a large body of water through the trees and foliage to their right. The lake created by the Seyhan Dam had an irregular shoreline with countless coves and bays formed by landmasses that jutted out from the downslopes of the surrounding hills. She glanced down at a map of the area on her phone, the land's contours reminding her of Chesapeake Bay's northern reaches from Annapolis on upward.

Major Douglas turned onto the Çatalan Bridge,

which connected Adana to the villages and vacation properties on the north side of the lake.

"How much farther?" she asked, like many a child on a road trip.

"My contact is meeting us at the Miami Café, just on the other side. Five minutes."

"Is anyone from your team joining us?"

"Not yet. I don't want to scare him away. Have you seen some of my guys?"

*Good point.*

She hadn't had time to strategize this meeting with Caleb. The major hadn't said much along the way, only that he had contacts in key government positions who kept him apprised of anything that might constitute a threat to the airbase. While she wasn't overly concerned with the potential of a setup or ambush, her spidey senses were getting a little tingly.

A minute or so later, Alex spotted the vertical MI-AMI CAFÉ sign at the side of the road. Major Douglas turned into an entrance between a pair of palm trees, the driveway sloping down toward a covered patio with the waters of the lake just beyond.

"What's the plan?" asked Caleb.

Douglas nodded toward the edge of the water on the other side of the café.

"We're to meet along the shore between here and the next café up the beach."

"Then I guess we should go."

The three of them climbed out of the Humvee. Alex stretched her arms and shoulders behind her to get some flexibility and movement back after the rough ride in the austere truck. She watched the major tuck the keys to the Humvee up under the front bumper, an old Army trick.

The café was empty, save for one lone couple off in a corner. The man and woman appeared to be in their late twenties or early thirties. Both wore dark denim jeans and white sneakers. The woman sat facing in Alex's direction and made eye contact briefly. She was olive-skinned with dark eyes and long, straight brown hair that hung forward over her shoulders. She wore a light-colored, loose-fitting button-up blouse. Her companion sat with his back to them and wore a familiar-looking lightweight royal-blue-and-white windbreaker.

They looked for all the world like they belonged here, just two people enjoying a snack and a beverage, far from the madding crowd. She made a mental note to keep an eye on them.

Their trio cut across the patio and out the other side. Alex glanced over at the couple's table. They were still leaning in toward each other, holding hands, not paying any attention to who passed through the café.

A comfortable onshore breeze wafted toward them as Alex scanned the area. It was deserted, not that she expected to see many people here. There was no beach to speak of nearby. Small fishing boats bobbed in the lake, but most were hundreds of meters away. Sandy beaches were located farther up the coastline, away from the muddy shoreline in front of them.

Along the slope and near the edge of the lake, low bushes and trees clung to the loamy soil. It reminded her of the foothills in Afghanistan, terrain that presaged the treacherous mountain ranges to come. There were far too many places for someone intent on an ambush to hide and not enough cover or concealment for her comfort. If circumstances dictated, it would be challenging for her, Caleb, and the major to avail themselves of any protection afforded by the land.

"Major, is your contact really going to be out this far?" she asked. "There's nothing here."

"Turkey is a tricky country, Special Agent Martel. Full of all kinds of deception and betrayal. My contacts are all pretty wary. They like to conduct business away from prying eyes."

Alex glanced back up to the patio behind them and noted that the couple seated in the corner were gone.

*They could have just finished their drinks and left,* she told herself. But her spidey senses now tingled even more.

They were approaching a rise that obscured the view of the other side. Alex brushed her elbow against her Glock for reassurance.

*If we're being watched, there's no point telegraphing where my weapon is.*

Either something was going to happen once they crested the sandy rise, or not at all. She hoped Caleb was making similar calculations.

"Just over this hill," said Douglas.

They came over the top of the hill, and Alex could see another building and patio like the Miami Café fifty meters ahead. She relaxed and took in a deep breath of the cool, fishy-smelling air, in part because the exertion mixed with her growing apprehension had left her somewhat winded.

"Almost there," he assured them.

Alex scanned left, right, front, and rear. She didn't like that there was still ample opportunity for someone to hide behind the flora surrounding them. But as they descended the slope toward the other café, she began to consider that this might not be a trap after all. Maybe they really *were* about to meet one of his contacts who would hand over information about the missing nuclear bomb, just like the major said.

"That's far enough," called a heavily accented voice from a stand of short palms behind them.

Or maybe they weren't.

Alex turned to face the voice. A chill ran down her spine, and it wasn't the breeze off the lake. A man stood in front of her holding a GSh-18, just like her assailant in London.

*Coincidence? Pffft.*

The Russian pistol was pointed directly at her chest, something she was rather fond of keeping just the way it was. That is, without holes.

"I see you've finished your drinks," she said, harnessing courage. "How were they?"

The man was the one who had been sitting in the café. His female companion now stepped out from behind him, holding an MP-443 Grach.

"That's cute, *Boris,*" Alex said to him. "You get the lighter pistol, and *Natasha* gets the heavier Grach. What's that say about you?"

"Be quiet, Agent Martel," he said through a thick Russian accent.

"Uh, *Special* Agent Martel," Caleb corrected.

Alex could make Caleb out slightly behind her on her left. He had instinctively drifted away from her gun side. She kept her posture slightly bladed with her left shoulder presented ahead of her. Her stance, coupled with Caleb's location on her off-hand side, would help conceal her right hand moving to draw her Glock, if necessary, although it would leave her in a less advantageous shooting position.

To her right, Major Douglas had his hands raised slightly as well.

She eyed Boris up and down the way men had done to her time and again. "Your outfit is a little too on the nose, though," she said, continuing to distract him with conversation while she—and she hoped Caleb—could hatch an action plan.

"Stop talking." He raised his gun until it was pointing at her face.

"I thought I recognized the jacket when I was

walking across the patio," she replied. She pointed to the logo embroidered on its chest. "Chelsea Football Club, yeah? The English Premier League team formerly owned by Russian billionaire Roman Abramovich? I mean, come on, if you had worn a Man-U jacket, I might never have figured out you were Russian."

"Shut up."

"And the pistols, that GSh-18 and Natasha's Grach. Standard equipment for pretty much every Russian law enforcement, military, and government agency. Not being very stealthy here, kids."

The woman must have been getting tired of watching her male counterpart get verbally abused by another woman. Clearly, that was *her* role in the relationship. "Stop talking already," she said to him. Then, addressing Alex, "And what's with *Boris* and *Natasha*? This is not our names. You Americans always think you're smarter than everybody else."

Caleb chimed in. "Fair point, Alex."

Alex shrugged. Before she set off a gunfight, she hoped to find out what was going on.

*No point killing anyone before I'm able to extract the necessary intel. Are they in on the theft? Do they know where the bomb is? Or are they just here to clean up someone else's mess?*

She turned to Major Douglas. "Is this what you call your *Turkish government contact,* Major?"

He stepped toward the Russian couple, pulling his SIG from his pants.

"I guess the jig is up," he said. "You got me, Alex. But the plan is evolving."

"I was going to ask you if that was a gun in your pocket," she said. "I knew you couldn't be *that* happy to see me. Frankly, I'm disappointed."

"A little sleight of hand, I'm afraid, as we were exiting

the Humvee. I thought we were getting along famously, right up until that phony phone call from your *landlady*."

"The phone call was real. It just wasn't who I said it was. Let me guess. The call *you* received right after mine was from your Russian handlers."

"Very good," he said, standing next to Boris now. "The colonel was terribly dismayed to hear the content of your call with Interpol."

"Colonel Gerasimov, I presume. How predictable. How is Viktor?"

She was kicking herself for being so careless. She should have used one of the burner phones to talk to Jonathan but instead had used her Interpol work phone.

"So, what's the plan now? You just going to kill us right here?" she asked, gesturing around her.

The major shrugged. "Sounds about right. It's as good a place as any," he said. "But first, hand over your gun. Slowly."

She hesitated. The major raised his SIG.

"Sorry, Alex, but even that compact Glock you're carrying adds bulk to your impeccable figure. Hand it over."

Using her thumb and two fingers, she removed it from her holster and gently tossed it a few feet in front of her.

"Now you," he ordered Caleb, swinging the SIG in his direction.

Caleb unholstered his own SIG Sauer, a P320 RXP XCompact.

"Finally, I get to see it," said Alex, "and you're handing it to another man."

"You saw it in London."

"I was still woozy. It looks so much smaller now than it did then."

"Give me a break. There's a chilly breeze off the

lake," Caleb said, tossing his pistol onto the ground next to hers.

Only a couple of meters separated the two groups. Not quite enough for her to launch at any of them without taking a bullet, given that she and Caleb were outnumbered three to two.

"Enough," Natasha scowled, waving her Grach at them.

"You at least going to do us the professional courtesy of telling us what's going on?"

Major Douglas shook his head.

"Sorry, Alex. This isn't some cheesy movie where the villain spills his guts with the master plan just before the hero finds his way out of his apparently futile predicament—"

"—uh, *her* predicament," she corrected.

"Again, apologies," he replied. "I've been told I need to become more inclusive to keep up with the new, improved Air Force."

"A girl can dream."

She caught Natasha stifling a grin. She may have been irked with the repartee, but she seemed to share the sentiment.

"Technically, it's *their* predicament. Hello?" said Caleb.

"Well," added the major, "I hate to cut this little pronoun powwow short, but I gotta run. I actually do have to meet someone about the disposition of a nuke. Besides," he said, looking down at his clothes, "I can't exactly get these nice cammies covered in blood. One of the Titan colonels would ask uncomfortable questions. And that Titan 2 can be a real hard-ass."

"Go, Major," said Natasha. "We will take care of these complications for you."

This was a good development, but not a great one. On the one hand, it evened up the odds. Two on two was a much fairer fight than three on two, even if the other two held them at gunpoint.

On the downside, the major was walking away. It was possible that she and Caleb would be killed and the B61 lost forever. Or it would be detonated or used to extort somebody somewhere.

The major tucked his gun back into his pocket. "Sorry, kids. Caleb, Alex, it was nice meeting you. See you on the other side."

Alex considered offering a smart-ass rebuttal but decided not to inflame their current circumstances. Two on two were indeed healthier odds. There was no point giving the major a reason to linger.

The four of them watched him scramble back over the rise and disappear on the other side. Boris waved his GSh-18 at them.

"Walk this way, please," he said, directing them away from the lake and into the grove of palm trees and shrubs to his rear.

The vegetation might not muffle the sound of the gunshots, but it would make it more difficult for anyone to see what was happening in this already secluded spot. And the good people of Turkey weren't necessarily going to be keen to investigate the sound of gunfire or telephone the authorities.

Alex and Caleb both had their hands raised as they walked between Boris and Natasha. If she was going to make a move, this was the time. She was four feet ahead of Caleb. But before she could do anything, a commotion arose behind her. *What the . . . ?*

She turned and saw Caleb diving headlong at Boris, tackling him around the waist. They crashed to the ground as a giant lizard skittered out of the way. She didn't wait for Natasha's response. Instead, she turned toward her to engage. Natasha had anticipated the move and punched her in the side of the head, knocking her off balance and into the dirt.

As Alex fell to the ground, Natasha raised her Grach. Caleb dove on her, grabbing her arm. She still managed to squeeze off a shot that impacted the dirt to Alex's left. While Caleb fought with Natasha, Boris had recovered his footing and was reaching for his GSh-18 lying beside him. As he snatched it up, Alex threw herself into him, seizing the gun by the barrel from underneath. He punched her with his free hand repeatedly as they wrestled for control. He squeezed off a round. Searing pain shot through her left hand as the barrel and slide, heated by the smokeless powder exploding from the confines of the cartridge, burned her fingers and palm. But the bullet missed her. Now she was holding on to the gun for dear life. He pulled the trigger over and over, but her hand, wrapped tightly around the barrel, had kept the slide from being forced backward by the exploding gasses. This prevented the spent shell from being ejected and a fresh round being chambered from the magazine. As long as he couldn't free the gun from her grip and manually rack the slide to chamber another round, the gun with all its remaining steel-core rounds was useless.

He hit her again and again, trying to make her let go of the pistol. Several strikes connected with her face, the side of her head, and her upper body, but she held the barrel tightly. She smelled as much as tasted the coppery notes of blood in her mouth and nose.

She pivoted and rotated in, turning her back toward him, both now teetering off-balance. The move brought her left arm over her head, her hand still gripping the barrel of the gun. She pushed back against him and drove her right elbow into his solar plexus, felt the air escape his lungs against the back of her neck. As fast as the strike of a snake, he wrapped his free arm around her throat, and she felt the pressure of the stranglehold building, compressing her carotid arteries, threatening to cut off the blood supply to her brain. Off-balance, they fell to the ground with her between his legs. She whipped her head back in an effort to smash his face with her skull, but he was far enough off to the side that she connected only slightly with his shoulder. She clutched at his arm, instinctively trying to pry it away from her throat, her other hand still in a death grip around the barrel of the semiautomatic weapon. Then he released his grip on the gun and flexed his right arm, bringing it up to complete the rear-naked choke.

Her vision went dark, filled with flashes of light and distant stars. Awareness dawned on her that she would be unconscious within seconds. She didn't know where Caleb was anymore; she had lost track of him as he battled the woman. She brought the gun, still held by the barrel in her left hand, above her head, trying repeatedly to hammer her assailant with it. But all she succeeded in doing was to land glancing blows with no effect. She felt the darkness descending on her, felt consciousness slipping away. She let go of his forearm and placed the butt of the gun into her newly freed hand. She racked the slide, the rounds stacked inside the magazine pushing up, casting out the spent casing, the tension of the recoil spring slinging a fresh round into the chamber. She dropped her hand and felt the tip of the barrel stop against something. She hoped it wasn't the ground; hoped even more that it wasn't her own leg. She squeezed the trigger, heard the explosion of gasses, felt a jolt. She pressed the trigger again. Same noise. Same jolt. The grip around her neck loosened but didn't release. She felt an exhilarating rush of circulation and of returning consciousness. Knowing she wouldn't pass out now, she raised her arm bent at the elbow, the tip of the barrel against something behind her, and pulled the trigger.

The sound was deafening. She instantly descended into near-deafness, almost a sensory-deprived state. She felt a gush of warm, sticky fluid against the back of her head that ran down her spine. The man's chokehold around her throat faltered. His grip released, and he fell backward as she fell to the side. She rolled away and came up into a low crouch, ears ringing, pointing the gun with trembling arms at the limp body lying supine on the ground, three-quarters of its head blown away, the rest a pulpy, hollow, bloody mass.

She spat on the ground and wiped her mouth with the back of her hand. It came away bloody. Her face throbbed where her would-be executioner had repeatedly struck her. Her chest and back ached. She felt like she'd been hit by a truck.

She swung around and saw the woman straddling Caleb, dropping elbow blows to his head. Alex shouted for her to stop, aimed the gun at her back, and called again. The woman's attack was relentless; Caleb was using his arms to block the blows from landing on his face, already bloodied. He bucked and tried to get her off but couldn't. Her legs were hooked around his hips and upper legs, pinning him to the ground.

"Stop!" Alex shouted again, but the woman didn't even turn to look at her. Her hair flew wildly as she pounded on Caleb. She reached down and grabbed a rock lying on the ground close by, raising it over her head.

The gun in Alex's hand bucked three times, and the woman collapsed onto Caleb's chest. Two crimson holes appeared in her back between her shoulders. The third round had entered through the back of her head and exited the front.

"You okay?"

Caleb didn't answer. He just lay there gasping for air, trapped, trying to push the woman off his body. Alex moved in to help him.

"No!" he yelled, twisting under the woman's weight to roll her body off him. "Go after the major. We need to find that bomb!"

When she hesitated, he shouted again.

"Alex! Go!"

Her mind was still in a fog, but his voice cut through. She ran stumbling toward the Miami Café, then doubled back.

"What are you doing?" he shouted.

She searched the ground and came up with each of their guns.

"Here," she said, tossing him his SIG Sauer before breaking into a run. "And I was right about the damned Russians!"

# CHAPTER 48

MIAMI CAFÉ, ADANA, TURKEY

The café seemed farther away than Alex remembered. Her legs felt more like logs, and she grimaced from the pain in her face and upper body. It hurt to swallow. It hurt to breathe. She stopped to catch her breath and to see if she could spot the major. Her mouth felt full of steel wool, dry and stinging.

No doubt he had heard the unsuppressed gunshots. They wouldn't have fit the sound pattern he was expecting from a double execution, so maybe he had become wary and held back to see if he'd been followed. Had he made it to the parking lot and driven away, or was he hiding somewhere, intent on ambushing anyone who came after him?

She pressed on. Before reaching the café, she paused and stepped behind a wall to check her gun. Satisfied it would still function properly, she gripped it with both hands as she rounded the corner and cleared the patio. No sign of the major.

She came out of the restaurant and took a few tenuous steps toward the parking lot. The major's Humvee was still there. As she got closer, she was startled by a sound behind her and dove for cover behind the big vehicle just as gunshots rang out.

Alex peered through the windows of the Humvee and spotted the major running toward the only other car in the lot. It was the vehicle she had noticed earlier when she had assumed it belonged to the couple dining on the deck—the erstwhile Boris and Natasha. She ran to the Humvee's rear and fired two shots, but each missed their mark as he bobbed and weaved in anticipation of her return fire. He fired more rounds at her, taking cover behind a tree, then sprinted to the green Dacia Duster sport utility vehicle and slid in behind the wheel.

She ran toward him, her gun leveled. Alex really wanted to take him alive, but that might be more his choice than hers.

"Out of the car, Major!" she shouted, planting her feet in front of the SUV and pointing her Glock at his face. She wasn't back to 100 percent after her struggle with Boris, but she didn't think she could miss from this range.

The Dacia's engine came to life, and he drove straight at her, forcing her to dive out of the way. She rolled on the ground, flashes of pain jolting through her like heat lightning in an August sky, and fired several shots, shattering the SUV's rear window. But the major wheeled the little green sport utility onto the roadway and took off, tires squealing up the road.

She ran to the Humvee and jumped in, feeling for the keys in the ignition. Nothing. She looked down at the floor and felt around under the driver's seat. Still nothing. Then she remembered. She jumped out of the vehicle, ran to the front, and slid her hand under the front bumper, coming away with the keys clenched in her fist. She fired up the Humvee and looked around to see if she could spot Caleb. There was no sign of him.

*Come on, come on! Where are you?*

She honked the horn as if that might help and

frantically searched the other side of the patio for him, but he wasn't there.

She couldn't let Major Douglas get away, so she dropped the truck in gear and took off after him. Fifty meters up the road, a figure leaped from the shrubbery into the middle of her lane. She swerved and hit the brakes to avoid running him over, then glanced in her rearview mirror.

*Caleb!*

She threw the truck into reverse and stopped beside him. He yanked open the passenger door and jumped in.

"You look like shit," she said.

"Ditto."

"Buckle up," she said, flooring it.

* * *

The Humvee bumped and lurched along the secondary highway north of the Miami Café. It was vastly underpowered and more at home off-road, in the desert and dirt, or on ultra-smooth blacktop at sub-highway speeds. The narrow, rutted, cracked, and broken pavement of the backroads of Turkey wasn't the most well-suited terrain for this truck and seriously impeded their progress in the ad hoc high-speed chase.

"Can't you go any faster?" asked Caleb. "We need to get to the major and find that nuke before someone blows up an American city."

"I think you mean *any* city."

"My oath—like yours—is to America. So, with respect, Alex, anywhere but the homeland."

"Great campaign slogan."

"Well, it's not official."

Alex kept her left hand off the steering wheel as much as possible, periodically, glancing at the tender flesh on her palm. It stung from the burns she'd taken holding the barrel of the Russian pistol. The pain and redness reached the pads of her fingers. So far, though, it appeared she had suffered only first-degree burns for her efforts. There was no blistering. Yet.

Soon they came to a three-way intersection and were faced with a choice: left, right, or straight. Alex slowed.

"Which way?" Caleb asked.

To the left, a narrower, twisty road led up the hillside past a restaurant with a large covered patio. To the right, the road curved around a bend along the curving shoreline of Seyhan Dam Lake. She drove straight.

"Why straight?" he asked.

Since she had no answer, she ignored the question. She stomped on the gas, accelerating beyond what she thought was wise for the rigid Humvee. She was doing seventy-five, weaving around bends in the road that gradually took them higher up a hillside. Coming out of a corner, they met a man on a moped loping along in the same direction, and Alex blew past him in the oncoming lane, narrowly missing him and a minivan coming the other way.

"Holy shit, Alex! Be careful!"

"You can have it fast, or you can have it safe. But you can't have it fast and safe. Which'll it be? This isn't a Toyota Camry."

He showed good judgment by not answering, although she caught him snugging up his seatbelt out of the corner of her eye.

Tall cliffs of dried clay towered over the road. Scrubby vegetation limited their visibility around corners as they bumped their way ever higher into the countryside. Soon they came to another decision point, but this time Alex didn't hesitate, opting to stick with the road they were on versus making a left turn.

Caleb glanced over at her but kept quiet.

They came around another bend as they approached what seemed like the plateau of the roadway. Cresting a hill, Alex saw a vehicle about five hundred meters off in the distance.

"What color is that?" she asked.

Caleb squinted into the distance.

"Not sure," he said. "Something darkish. Maybe gray, maybe green?"

"Damn right it's green," she replied and floored it.

Thirty seconds later, they had covered half the distance to the green Dacia Duster ahead of them.

"Got you now, you bastard."

Major Douglas must have known they were on his six and increased his speed. They stopped gaining ground on him with the laboring Humvee. The major passed a truck on the road ahead. Alex caught up to it and tried to go around, but as she did, she came nose to nose with a diesel-fuel truck coming in the opposite direction.

"Don't say it," she warned Caleb, swerving back into her lane.

The truck went past, and she tried again, this time squeaking by. The major had managed to put some distance back between them. She knew it was only a matter of time before they caught him. She didn't know when that would be, but she was confident she could keep up with him until they did. She looked down at the fuel gauge, the needle hovering below a quarter tank. Hopefully, they wouldn't run out of gas first.

The road got twisty. Major Douglas's Dacia Duster proved much more nimble than their Humvee, and Alex found herself losing a bit of ground to him again. Small farms, roadside fruit and vegetable stands, and the occasional home lined the route as they descended into a valley. Then something else caught her eye. She glanced down into her side-view mirror and saw the unmistakable shape of a plane coming up behind them at low altitude.

"What the hell is that?"

"What's *what*?" asked Caleb. He scrunched down lower in his seat for a good look into the passenger-side mirror.

Alex could clearly make out a toothy grin painted on the nose of the approaching aircraft.

"Holy shit!" she said.

Caleb saw it, too. "I think it's a—"

He hadn't managed to get the words out before the unmistakable note of the Warthog's jet engines screamed over them. They crouched lower and looked up at the beast through the windshield as it flew straight on, then banked left to come around.

"What's it doing out here?" he asked.

"I've got a bad feeling about this," she replied.

Although the road was winding left and right, Alex occasionally caught a glimpse of the major's SUV ahead of them. They weren't gaining on him, but they weren't losing any ground either.

"Do you think they found out about the major, and are here to keep tabs on him until the troops get here?" Caleb asked.

"Or—" Alex said, watching in the mirror as the Warthog approached fast from their rear again. She saw a pulse of smoke from the front of the plane. She was already veering hard right into an open field when a burst of 30mm cannon fire from the seven-barreled Gatling gun mounted on the plane's nose impacted the road behind them. One of the one-and-a-half-pound projectiles struck the back of the Humvee, causing it to bounce wildly in the dirt.

"Fuck!" she said. "Call someone!"

"Who am I going to call?" he asked. "Nine-one-one?"

"I don't know . . . Someone at the base. CIA. Anybody, but get this plane off us before we're pulverized!"

Caleb had his cell phone in his hands.

"No service," he said.

Alex peered over her shoulder and saw a three-inch-wide hole through their roof and down through the rear seat where she had been sitting earlier. She steered back onto the highway and hit the gas.

"This isn't good," she said.

"No shit, Sherlock," was Caleb's succinct response.

She had the Humvee back up to sixty or so. The sides of the roadway had encroached on them again as they passed through a narrow canyon, giving her hope for the time being. She followed the curves while glancing into her mirrors periodically for any sign of the A-10. The road straightened out, and up ahead about a quarter mile, she could see the green Dacia entering another bend. To their right, a dirt field slid off toward the Seyhan River. A boulder-strewn cliff face rose from the road to their left and ran along for a few hundred meters.

In her mirror, Alex saw the A-10 rising up behind her.

"Hold on," she said. "Here it comes again."

She hit the gas to build up speed, which she knew was dumb, considering she was racing an A-10 Warthog.

"Get ready," she said. "When I think it's going to fire at us, I'm veering into the field on our right."

"Alex, if you take it too fast, we will roll."

"Other options?"

No reply.

She watched as the looming shape of the aircraft swelled in the mirror. The visored head of the pilot was visible inside the domed cockpit. If only she could signal them to let them know she and Caleb were the cavalry, not the escaping bandits.

When she thought she saw the nose of the plane dip, she took it as her signal to get out of Dodge. She cranked the wheel hard to the right just as the *brrrrrrt!* sound of the aircraft's guns split the evening air.

The Humvee turned sideways and hit the shoulder as a burst of cannon fire tore into the asphalt and their vehicle. It jolted them hard and twisted them 180 degrees, so they were facing the rocky hillside instead of the open field, skipping sideways down the road.

Alex tried to regain control, but the Humvee was barely touching the ground. The impact of the rounds had destroyed the vehicle's drivetrain. They hit the cliff at an angle, ran up its side, and then struck a rock that flipped them. They barrel-rolled down the side of the hill, tumbling over and over until they came to rest on the Humvee's roof in the middle of the road.

Alex hung suspended upside down in her seat. Her head, already aching from before, was full-on pounding now. The air surrounding them was filled with dust and dirt. The smell made by the depleted uranium rounds punching through cold-rolled American steel was otherworldly. And there was something else, too.

*What's that?*

Her brain finally computed what she was smelling: *smoke*.

"Caleb!" She looked over at the passenger side of the Humvee and saw him dangling by his seatbelt, his arms hanging down. *Or up?* She wasn't sure.

"Caleb!" She slapped the back of her hand against his shoulder, but there was no response.

*I have to get out of here. I have to get us out of here!*

She managed to depress the seatbelt release and fell onto her head on the ceiling of the inverted vehicle. The bulletproof windshield was shattered. The driver's window was simply missing. Every window was gone. She twisted onto her belly and began to crawl out. She was halfway clear of the vehicle when a pair of coyote-brown combat boots appeared in her peripheral vision. Bloused OCP trouser cuffs disappeared inside them.

"Hello, Alex."

Before she could return the greeting, the boot kicked out at her face. She wiggled sideways, and it caught her in the shoulder instead. The force of the blow rolled her onto her back, and her eyes met the grinning face of Major Douglas.

She caught his next kick with both hands and twisted him off-balance. As he stumbled, she drew her Glock and swung it in his direction, but he had regained his footing and threw a front kick that knocked it out of her hands.

She scrambled the rest of the way out of the Humvee and dove at him, propelled by adrenaline and rage, ensnaring both his legs in her arms. He bent over and enveloped her waist, lifting her off the ground. There were no rules in a street fight except to survive, so she punched with as much force as she could muster up into his groin and felt her fist connect with her target. He released her and doubled over as she scrambled away from the smoldering Humvee and stood up.

"Caleb!" she shouted again, hoping he wasn't dead and he'd be able to extricate himself from the vehicle before it burst into flames.

The sound of the Warthog came back into focus as it swooped back around in the distance and headed straight for them. She dove again at the major, but he scrambled out of the way. She regained her footing and landed a spinning back kick at the back of his legs, felling him to his knees. She pounced and landed with an elbow strike to his shoulder. Her aim was off, and it missed breaking his collar bone, but he screamed out in pain regardless.

Next, she delivered a forearm strike to his face and

went in for a follow-up punch, but he parried it with his arm and jumped back up to his feet. He stared at the incoming A-10 and froze.

"Where's the nuke, Major?" No answer. "Major, the bomb—where is it? It's over."

"It's not over, Alex. Not by a long shot."

He lunged at her, and she grabbed him in an armlock. The A-10 was approaching at high speed. She let go of him and tried to wave the pilot off, fearing what would happen to Caleb if they completed their strafing run. At the last second, she dove for cover against the side of the hill as the Warthog fired a burst of cannon fire.

*Brrrrrrt!*

Several rounds hit the Humvee again, but most impacted the green SUV the major had been driving. The Dacia Duster bounced into the air and landed hard on the road again, looking like a green brick of Swiss cheese, then teetered over onto its side, black smoke streaming from it before it burst into flames.

Alex tackled the major and knocked him to the ground, but she was too weak from her previous engagement with Boris and now her battle with Major Douglas to have much of an effect.

"Major, whatever your reasons are, they can't be worth the consequences of a nuclear bomb getting into the wrong hands."

He quickly wrestled her off him and threw her onto her back.

"It's not in the *wrong hands,* Alex," he said, standing over her, emphasizing *wrong hands* as if she were a misguided child.

"What's the target? Just tell me that."

The Warthog was coming around again.

The major looked down the road as the aircraft lined up its run. He scooped his pistol up from the ground and pointed it at Alex. She leaped to her feet and threw herself behind the Humvee as he released a barrage of gunfire from his SIG.

The Warthog was getting closer—fast.

"Don't worry your pretty little head about it, Special Agent. You'll be dead in a minute anyway!" he yelled as he ran for the open field.

"Major!"

She would have gone after him, but Caleb was still in the Humvee. She didn't know if he was alive or dead, but she needed to get him out. *Now!*

# CHAPTER 49

Caleb was still suspended upside down in the Humvee. Alex saw that he was still breathing as she reached in to check his pulse.

"Caleb!" she shouted. "Caleb, we gotta get you out of here."

She tried to release his seatbelt but couldn't depress the mechanism. She snatched her Kit Carson–designed CRKT M16 tactical knife from her pocket and sliced through the webbing with the integrated seatbelt cutter. Caleb dropped ungracefully to the roof of the upside-down vehicle. Grabbing an arm, she dug her heels in against the asphalt, then dragged him so that his upper body was partially outside the passenger window of the smoldering wreck. The burns on her left hand were excruciating, but she repositioned herself to grasp him under his shoulders, and, pulling with all her might, little by little, he came away from the Humvee until his waist was clear.

He was still unconscious. Crouching behind him, she sat him up and wrapped her arms around his broad chest, interlocking her hands in front. With her last reserves of energy, she drove her legs backward, pulling him completely free of the inside of the vehicle. She dragged him another thirty feet and lowered him behind a boulder partway up the slope beside them.

Someone had taken it upon themselves to call in an airstrike against Alex and Caleb within the borders of a US ally. That someone was most likely Major Douglas, commander of the 39th Air Base Wing Security Forces squadron at Incirlik—the man currently running across an open field toward the Seyhan River.

Out of breath and completely spent, Alex raised her head and saw the major was now a hundred meters out in the field. The Warthog was almost on top of their position, seventy-five feet off the deck. She glanced back at the Humvee and saw the stock of the M24 rifle she had noticed earlier when the major drove them all to the weapons maintenance shed. It was protruding from what was left of the vehicle. She ran toward the Humvee and snatched up the gun. Looking up, she saw the smiling, toothy grin painted on the nose of the Warthog dip toward her, the sound of its jet engines a full-on scream. She ran back and threw her body over Caleb's as the massive supersonic rounds impacted the Humvee, followed by the *brrrrrrt!* of the Gatling gun, the sound waves from the gun traveling much more slowly than the 30mm, one-and-a-half-pound projectiles that traveled at 3,300 feet per second.

Alex shielded her ears with her hands. Even so, the noise was deafening. Firing seventy rounds a second, the Hawg laid down over a hundred rounds that impacted around her, pulverizing the asphalt roadway like the giant spiked fist of a furious god. The Humvee and what was left of the green Dacia were shredded.

"What the hell—?" Caleb was jarred back to

consciousness with the concussive impacts of the rounds landing nearby and the cacophony of noise around them.

Alex leaned forward to complete a quick trauma survey and secondary assessment of his injuries. There was bruising and some minor bleeding on his face and upper body from the crash and the fight earlier, but there were no additional holes from Warthog rounds or shrapnel and no broken bones.

"How you feeling?" she asked, suppressing her own pain.

"What'd I miss?" he asked, blinking his eyes into focus.

"Everything."

She scooped up the rifle to inspect it more closely. It miraculously appeared undamaged. The M24A2 was chambered for the 7.62×51mm NATO cartridge. This variant of the M24 usually came with a removable five-round magazine, but it was missing. Likely, that was still inside the Humvee, so it was as good as gone.

She retracted the bolt and saw there was a round in the chamber. She removed it and inspected it closely. Looking at the tip of the bullet and then checking the headstamp confirmed it was a match-grade 7.62×51mm, 175-grain M118LR hollow-point boattail cartridge. She touched it gently to her lips before putting it back into the chamber, then closed the action.

The Air Force countersniper to whom this rifle belonged had taken good care of it. The attached scope was a fixed-magnification Leupold 10×40. She peered through it, panning left and right.

"What are you doing?" asked Caleb, still lying flat on his back.

Smoke hung low, suspended in the dense, cooling air, but was otherwise still.

*No wind.*

Major Douglas appeared with the mil-dot reticle superimposed over his back as he crossed the grass-and-dirt plain to the river. She was familiar with the Leupold scope, had deployed with it and with this weapon many times before. She knew the reticle's markings, its subtensions.

"Alex?"

The rifle felt comfortable and familiar gripped in her hand as she crossed the road. She reached the other side and flipped down the legs of the bipod, setting it gently onto the gravel. She lay down, spreading her feet shoulder-width apart, heels down, toes pointing outward. She lined the rifle up with Major Douglas, who was now a good couple hundred meters out in the field. She aligned her body behind the gun, tucked the butt into her shoulder, the weight of her head resting on her cheek, which in turn rested on the stock of the rifle.

The rifle and her body were one. She had become the final element in this sniper weapon system.

His back was still to her. The image in the scope was wandering, undulating throughout the reticle. Her muscles were fatigued, her heart rate too fast, her breaths too short and quick.

"Alex!" Caleb called to her from where she had left him behind. "Alex, let the base cops take him in. How far's he going to get?"

She cleared her mind, zoned out the drone of Caleb's voice.

*Trust your instincts. Trust your training and experience.*

She could hear her late husband Kyle's voice talking to her.

*Alex, focus on the reticle. Just breathe.*

The image in her scope settled. She placed the

crosshairs at the base of the major's neck and drew an imaginary line across his shoulders. Counting upward in her scope, the distance from the top of his shoulders to the top of his head measured 1.2 mils on the reticle's scale. Major Douglas had said this rifle had been at the range just yesterday. She hoped it was zeroed to a hundred meters. She had one bullet. All her calculations would be based on that assumption. It had to be right.

Caleb was by her side now. He shouted to the major. "Give it up, Major. Come back!"

It was thirty centimeters—twelve inches—from the top of the shoulders to the top of the head on the average man. She ran a calculation through her mind she'd run a thousand times before. She knew the ballistics for the M118LR cartridge loaded in the rifle. It had been her bread-and-butter cartridge in Iraq, Afghanistan, and Syria. She knew the bullet's weight, muzzle velocity, and ballistic coefficient. More important, she knew its trajectory and the bullet drop over the distance to her target. She was striving for a good shot, not a perfect shot.

From her mental calculus, she determined the range to target: 250 meters. There was a negligible breeze coming off the river at twelve o'clock.

Satisfied she had all the needed data, she dialed in the elevation for her estimated distance. Her burned hand throbbed, but she pushed the pain aside.

"Alex, don't kill him. We need him alive to find the bomb."

The major turned to face them. He was shouting something at them from more than two and a half football fields away that she was unable to make out. His gun was in his hand, and he was waving it at them. He pointed it in their direction, and she saw the barrel spit flame in the diminishing light around them, followed by the subdued pop of the gunshot in the distance. The round he fired landed nowhere near them.

"Alex, look—the cavalry is coming. You don't have to kill him." He was worried she was losing her shit. She wasn't, and she tuned him out.

She took her eyes off the scope and looked down the road toward a column of approaching Humvees and police cars, maybe half a klick away.

"Let them take him in, Alex. You have rules you live by. Interpol has rules. The FBI has rules. Hell, even *I* have rules. We don't need to kill him."

She cast her eyes downrange again and resettled her breathing. She saw two Humvees drive off the road in her peripheral vision, directed by Caleb's intense waving in the major's direction. Major Douglas turned and started shooting at the Humvees, to no effect.

Alex reconfirmed the firing solution in her mind, flicked off the safety, and brought her finger inside the trigger guard. The bipod braced the front of the rifle. Her support hand was tucked under the rear of the buttstock, curled around a fistful of dirt.

A voice in her head said:

*Send it!*

She slowly pulled the trigger rearward as she exhaled. The slack in the trigger had been taken up.

The Security Forces squadron Humvees pulled within ten meters of the major. He was shouting something at them, gesturing with his gun. Suddenly, he raised the gun to his head.

*BOOM!*

A split second later, the SIG Sauer flew out of his hand, shattered into pieces by the impact of her bullet. The major grabbed his bleeding hand as he was tackled by members of his Security Forces squadron, who secured him with flex cuffs and perp-walked him back to one of the Humvees.

"Holy shit!" said Caleb. "That was the most incredible shot I've ever seen. You shot the gun right out of his hand!"

"I missed," she said, thumbing the safety on and standing up. She handed him the rifle as she brushed past. "I wasn't aiming for his gun."

# CHAPTER 50

A moonless night had arrived along the Seyhan River. Warning systems from police and other emergency vehicles illuminated the site of the incident with pulses of red and blue light. It struck Alex as surreal that wide-open landscapes could transform into claustrophobic spaces in the absence of daylight. As darkness enveloped her, her world closed in. Not always, but now.

The medic had patched a laceration under her eye with butterfly closures. It was the same laceration she'd received in London during the shootout, grown bigger after the fight with Major Douglas. He'd irrigated the burns to her hand with saline solution, then placed nonstick gauze pads between her fingers to keep the skin from fusing together before wrapping it in a roller bandage.

Now she sat on the rear step of a Ford high-top ambulance and stared into the blackness toward the river. Tonight, she had almost done the unthinkable and killed Major Douglas in cold blood. At the last instant, she'd shifted her aim by no more than a hairsbreadth in her reticle. While he didn't deserve to wear the same uniform for which others had laid down their lives, it wasn't for her to decide whether he lived or died.

Caleb was right. She lived by a set of rules. Chief

among them was service before self. Nothing in her rulebook, her code, justified taking a life in the absence of an imminent threat to herself or others, or a lawful order by a commanding officer. As loathsome as the major was for his complicity in a crime that might yet result in the loss of hundreds of thousands of innocent lives, Major Douglas hadn't met that standard. Arguably, he was more valuable alive than dead, in the faint hope he would provide intel on the nuke's location or destination.

Colonel Mendez approached from the back of a Security Forces squadron Humvee, where she had been interrogating Major Douglas since her arrival on the scene.

"Quite an eventful end to the day," she said.

"So, this isn't your average weeknight then?"

Alex had to tread carefully. Given the information Jonathan had deciphered from Krysten's email, Mendez—Titan 2—was still a person of interest in the case of the missing nuke.

"Hardly." The colonel took a seat next to Alex. "My God, what a twenty-four hours it's been," she said. She reached into her pocket and pulled out a pack of Marlboros, removing one for herself. She was about to put it away but then held the pack out to Alex, who declined. "Didn't figure you for a smoker, but thought I'd offer."

Alex looked over at another ambulance parked on the road opposite to where she sat with the colonel. Caleb was shirtless on the stretcher, sitting upright as an EMT took his blood pressure and ran an electrocardiogram.

"How is he?" the colonel asked her.

"Him? He'll be fine. I get the feeling he's been through worse."

Mendez considered Alex's bandaged hand and face. "And you?"

She shook her head, dismissing the colonel's concerns. "I'm good."

"It's not always the wounds we see that do the most damage," she said.

Alex said nothing. Mendez had a keen appreciation of the warrior psyche. Or for clichés.

A silence fell between them, allowing each a moment to catch their breath.

"Can I ask a personal question?" asked Mendez.

"Shoot."

Mendez gestured around them at the smoldering debris of cars, the damage to the road caused by the Gatling gun of the A-10 Warthog, the police and military vehicles and personnel, the ambulances. "This ever get to you?"

"How do you mean?"

"I mean, I know you have extensive experience in combat, but—"

"But what? It was my job. Just like catching bad guys now is my job."

"How do you stay centered? How do you not go completely mad?"

"Who says I don't? Look, taking a life is never easy. Adjusting to violence isn't easy. Being attacked and almost killed is definitely not easy."

"So how do you keep doing it?"

"I like to shoot."

"I can see that," Mendez replied.

"No, I mean the discipline of shooting, the math, the art. The *zen* of it. It's what works for me. It's my meditation." Mendez's face scrunched up in confusion. Alex continued. "Some people go to church. Some do yoga. When I get stateside, I go see my shooting sensei—my mentor—and we plink steel plates at a thousand yards for an afternoon. It cleanses me."

Mendez smiled and shook her head. "I'm more the

yoga type," she confided. Then, changing the subject, she said, "Major Douglas isn't saying much. Once he gets his hand sewn up at the base medical center, OSI will interrogate him, as will several other alphabet-soup agencies, I'm sure." She took another drag and exhaled. "He called the base and reported that, after he dropped you and Caleb off at your hotel, he'd gotten a tip about the location of the missing nuke and went to recover it on his own. When that got reported up to Titan 1 and me, it all sounded too good to be true, but there wasn't time to question him about it. He immediately called back and said he'd been attacked and that the perpetrators had stolen his Humvee at gunpoint with the recovered warhead inside. He asked for an A-10 in the hopes of disabling the nuke to keep it from falling into the wrong hands."

"How could he have thought he'd get away with that?"

Mendez shook her head. "As I said, Colonel Greeley and I had no time to second-guess or countermand his order. Major Douglas is our force protection and base security squadron leader. The colonel and I were satisfied he was taking steps under extreme circumstances to recover the nuke or keep it from being used against an unknown target."

Mendez sounded as though she was trying out her own defense strategy in anticipation of a court martial.

"But wouldn't a direct hit from the Warthog's munitions rupture the nuclear weapon's shielding and cause a radiation leak?"

"Most likely, but better a leak of radiation we can contain than the detonation of a thermonuclear device on someone else's order. Plus, she chose not to use her AGM-65 Maverick missiles. KC—our fighter pilot—had real concerns about the possibility of collateral damage and the veracity of the intel."

"*KC?*" asked Alex.

"Major Kim Campbell, but *KC* stands for Killer Chick—just don't tell her I said so."

"No, ma'am. I guess we're lucky she didn't blow us to bits then."

"Major Campbell's Warthog was loaded up with armor-piercing incendiary rounds—depleted uranium kinetic energy penetrators. They'd go all the way through your up-armored Humvee, you, the B61, and then halfway to hell, but they have no explosive properties."

"Well, I feel better."

"She's a professional, Alex, like you. She did what she had to do. And you're not dead."

"There's that."

Alex understood the two colonels' response to the situation. Events were unfolding quickly in real time, and Mendez and Greeley had Major Douglas—an experienced and trusted officer—making tactical decisions in the battle space. They'd chosen to support him, no matter how radical his solution seemed. Critical decisions made in the heat of battle were easy to second-guess after the fact, but it took real leadership to recognize and support field-expedient solutions. Analysis would come when the situation was resolved. That's what after-action reviews were for—to analyze actions taken and to adopt and apply lessons learned.

"Where'd it go off the rails for the major?" she asked.

"That will be part of our inquiry," replied Mendez. "We've had some issues, for sure, with active and retired military taking on extreme views and then acting on them. It's not something we're proud of, and it's definitely something we need to fix."

Alex was beginning to eliminate Colonel Mendez from her list of suspects. The passion and conviction with which she spoke led Alex to believe she really hadn't known what was going on. But while that might free her from culpability in the theft of the bomb, some would look at her inability to see what was happening or to prevent it as a stain on her military record. It was probable she would lose her post, even if she wasn't court-martialed. There would be senior military leaders, especially those with ambitions and aspirations that exceeded their current billets or natural abilities, who would not let the colonels off the hook on an incident of this magnitude.

"By the way, when he was sure Caleb and I would be killed by his accomplices, he confirmed the name of a Russian player we are acquainted with. Keep that to yourself," she said, lightly body-checking the colonel with her shoulder.

"I take it that's your next stop?"

"Hope so. If we can find him."

"The police found the two bodies you left for them near the Miami Café. I think they're going to want to talk to you."

"You might need to run a little interference for us on that. I, for one, have no desire to be questioned by Turkish investigators. Not with a missing nuke and the head of a Russian special operations unit implicated by name."

Colonel Mendez nodded.

Alex looked up at the other ambulance, where Caleb was wrestling with the wires attached to his chest. It seemed he and the medics were having a disagreement concerning the proposed treatment and discharge plan as he disconnected himself from the heart monitor. Finally, he jumped out the back doors of their rig and strode toward them.

Still shirtless, he joined Alex and Colonel Mendez, ripping sticky ECG dots off his chest and tossing them to the side of the road. She couldn't help but notice his physique—broad, well-muscled shoulders and arms, a V-shaped torso, and more than a suggestion of a six-pack. That combination made up the sum total of her favorite things about her days on her college swim team. She also noted a prominent scar over his sternum extending out along the ribs on his left side that reminded her of her own scar, the one running across her back.

It was helpful to be reminded occasionally that he was a warrior and a veteran of many battles, like her.

"What was all that about?" she asked.

He pulled his black golf shirt back on. "You know medics," he said, hooking his chin toward the ambulance he had just exited. "Always trying to get you to go to the hospital."

"I think it might be in their job description," said Mendez.

"Yeah, well, I ain't going. How you doing?" he asked, looking at the bandages on Alex's face and hand.

"I've had worse days."

He nodded knowingly. Then he turned to Colonel Mendez. "Any word?"

"The major isn't saying anything right now. We've taken his phone, but it's unlikely we'll be able to access it. He wasn't using his Air Force–issued device."

"So, we're not going to get any info from him. Where's that leave us?"

"Air Force OSI is interviewing everyone who even remotely might have worked with the B61s. And all of Major Douglas's Security Forces team will be put under a microscope as well. What's next for you guys?"

"We have some leads to follow up on," said Alex.

"Oh?" said Caleb.

"I'll fill you in later."

"What about your Russian friend?" asked Mendez.

Caleb replied, "My people pinged him right here in

Adana earlier today. But as of late this afternoon, CIA tracked him on his way to a conference in Paris."

"Oh?" said Alex.

"I'll fill you in later."

"All roads lead to Paris," she said.

# CHAPTER 51

S taff Sergeant Davis welcomed them aboard the US Air Force C-37B.

"Nice to see you again, Special Agent," she said. "You must have some real clout. Someone lifted the lockdown on the base just so we could land here to fetch you and your friend." She smiled at Caleb. "I'm Imani."

It was her slightly-more-than-standard smile.

"Caleb," he said, eyes bright, a wolf assessing a lamb.

Alex rolled her eyes.

"You guys take up mixed martial arts while you were here?"

It took Alex a moment to realize she was referring to their injuries.

"Long story. Let's just say some people weren't happy to see us."

Alex was relieved CIA and Interpol had arrived at the same conclusion that their next stop should be Paris. With few other leads, it seemed the best option. Gerasimov had gone there from Turkey already, and while not exactly a smoking gun, where the man in charge of Directorate 13 went, trouble seemed to follow.

Once the plane was aloft, Alex accessed the secure network onboard and finally submitted her completed after-action and use-of-force reports detailing the events in Arnhem two days ago. Or was it three? Both Interpol and her FBI masters would be pleased to get them, but the outcome of their internal inquiries was less certain, especially considering more recent events here in Turkey. With that done, she kicked off her shoes, put her feet up on the leather sofa, and fell fast asleep.

* * *

### VÉLIZY-VILLACOUBLAY AIR BASE, FRANCE

The flight from Incirlik Air Base to a military airport eight miles southwest of Paris took three hours. As they approached Vélizy-Villacoublay Air Base from the east, Alex spied the Eiffel Tower jutting from the landscape along the Seine through a starboard-side cabin window. Just as the iconic iron structure drew people in from all around France's capital, so were Krysten's clues pulling Alex to the conclusion that Paris was at the center of this mystery.

The jet taxied to a spruce-green aluminum-clad terminal and parked on the apron next to a French Air Force Eurocopter Super Puma. As they came to a stop, Imani appeared and addressed Caleb.

"Mr. Copeland, we're going to take on fuel, and then we'll be ready to go, sir. You'll have to wait in the executive lounge inside the terminal for about twenty minutes while we refuel."

"Thanks."

"What's that about?" asked Alex.

"We're being recalled to Washington," he replied, wiggling his phone at her.

She presumed by *we,* he didn't mean him and Staff Sergeant Davis.

"What are you talking about?"

"Check your email. You're coming, too," he said as

they made their way along the aisle to the steps at the front of the aircraft. "The Agency picked up chatter suggesting a credible threat to the homeland relating to the missing B61. British intelligence picked up the same intel." Caleb knocked on the doorframe twice as he stepped off.

"By *British intelligence,* you mean Kane?" she asked, starting down the stairs ahead of him.

"I didn't ask, and the deputy director didn't feel it necessary to share the source of her intel with me in a text message, secure or not. But I assume Kane is involved." There was just enough of an edge to his voice to let her know he was irritated. "Why do you have such a hard-on for the guy?"

They reached the tarmac and crossed the breezy apron's expanse toward the terminal. A member of the ground crew wearing a reflective vest over his French military BDUs eyed them up and down, no doubt wondering what the American couple was bickering about.

"I don't trust him," she said, stopping outside the glassed-in entryway.

"Cut him some slack, Alex. Maybe he's messed up because his partner was just killed. Oh, and by the way, she was a Russian spy."

"That's not it," she replied, the wind blowing her hair across her face. "He makes me uneasy."

Caleb shrugged. "He's English. They make all Americans uneasy. Give it a rest. More important, Interpol has cut you loose. CIA and the FBI have ordered us both to DC." He adopted a more conciliatory tone. "We can review the new intel together when we get airborne again. Then we can draw up a battle plan and do whatever Uncle Sam needs us to do to keep the homeland safe. If it turns out we're needed here in Paris, we'll come back."

She couldn't let it go. The Russians had a hand in stealing the bomb. She knew it, Caleb knew it. It's unlikely they were keeping it for their own purposes—they indeed had enough of their own—but maybe they were. But what purpose would that serve exactly? Maybe their intention was to hand it off to another group to have them do their bidding in whatever nefarious way they had concocted, the way Iran used Hezbollah and Hamas and others as their proxy militias. She didn't think Russia was cozying up to Iran, but she wouldn't put it past Directorate 13 to raise the stakes in a game of brinksmanship in order to bump America off its lofty perch as the dominant global superpower. Maintaining alliances required a delicate balance and competent diplomacy. After years of open dissent and turmoil, it wouldn't take much to upend the NATO alliance.

Alex turned and walked into the building. She didn't want to go to Washington. She needed to stay here and do what her gut was telling her to do. Krysten had broken her cover as a British MI5 officer and exposed herself as a Russian intelligence officer to reveal critical information. Alex chose to interpret this act as a genuine gesture to come clean and prevent a global crisis with potentially catastrophic consequences.

*Am I being naïve?*

"Nothing we have seen so far points to any kind of attack back home," she whispered to Caleb as they walked through an open reception area. "In fact, everything we've seen and heard would imply the Paris Peace Summit is a potential target."

Caleb touched her arm. "This way," he said, pointing to an overhead sign directing them to the executive lounge.

"What you mean is Krysten implied it. But you're ignoring that, more accurately, Anna Baronova supplied you with that information. Obviously, there's new intel," he said. "Our analysts have looked at it. Among other arguments, the Russian president and a full diplomatic delegation are already attending the Sorbonne conference. His wife is probably out sightseeing and buying up everything along the Champs-Élysées, along with all the other wives and husbands with kids in tow. Why would the Russians do that if they were about to nuke Paris?"

"I haven't figured that part out yet," she admitted.

"Well, they wouldn't," he said. "It would be helpful if you looked at the big picture once in a while, Alex. Admit it, all your suspicions about Paris being a target come from the information you got from Krysten, a Russian agent—an illegal working as a British intelligence officer."

He had described Krysten using the term *illegal,* referring to an intelligence operative who had infiltrated a target country without the protection of diplomatic immunity. It was true. She had. And by assuming a new identity and even a new ethnicity, Krysten was, in essence, like a trapeze artist performing without a net. It was the ultimate in black ops, and the most dangerous kind, as it gave her zero protection in the event of capture while providing her masters with much more than simple plausible deniability. Their freedom from implication would be unequivocal.

They found the lounge and stepped inside. Lucky for them, it was devoid of other travelers.

"It's not out of some false allegiance, Caleb," she said. "I know now what Krysten was. But why would she have taken such risks, such extraordinary steps, to show me—to show *us*—clues pointing to Paris? Everything suggests that those actions, her sending me the email, her pointing me to the safe-deposit box,

her letter to me confessing who she was, got her killed.
Those are not the actions of someone trying to lead me
away from the truth."

"I gotta say, Alex," he continued, "that's more than
a little naïve on your part. And it's frankly the kind of
blind loyalty that doesn't look good on you."

"*Look good* on me? I don't give a shit how it looks,
Caleb—"

"Maybe you should," he blurted.

"What does that mean?"

"It means people are watching and taking notice.
It means she was a Russian spy. You know, the people
we're trying to prevent doing bad things to the US
of A. The ones you're supposed to be stopping, as a
special agent in the National Security Branch of the
FBI. It means your friendship with Krysten shows a
particularly critical misjudgment on your part."

"In hindsight, sure. But she duped a lot of people."

"Well, she duped the Brits. And she duped you."

She could have punched him in the face. Her fists
were clenched so tightly by her side that she could feel
her nails carving holes in her palms. She was sure her
face was a beacon of rage.

"To hell with you, Caleb!"

His face lit up like he was going to fire back. But
just as quickly, his anger seemed to dissolve. "Look,"
he said, his voice quiet, "she was compromised, one
way or another. Whoever was on to her and killed her
might have known about her treachery for a long time
and set her up. Forced her to appear remorseful and
contrite. Maybe they were threatening her family back
home. Who knows? She might have been coerced into
feeding you fake intel to put you on the wrong trail."

Alex remained silent. She had already thought of
that.

"Look, I hope you're right," he said. "I hope that's

not how it went down. I hope, in the end, she chose the righteous path for righteous reasons. I hope the bomb is not on its way to the States *or* anywhere else. But you and I have to be realists, and hope is not a strategy. Director Thomas was emphatic. Chatter coming from various intelligence agencies indicates the target might be New York. I'm to continue on back to Langley to regroup with my team and work the leads there, and you're to join me."

"I'm not part of your team."

"Resistance is futile. You know that. Whether you like it or not, we serve the same master. And right now, the master is sending us both to Washington."

"You said the target is New York."

"*Might be* New York."

She wasn't totally convinced, but she conceded she didn't have all the pieces of the puzzle yet. Hopefully, those would fall into place when she reviewed the dossier on the secure server aboard the Air Force jet on the flight across the Atlantic. She was beginning to resign herself to the possibility that Krysten's email, the key, the safe-deposit box, and the note had all been somehow revealed to her through a scheme to throw her off the trail of the actual plot: a 9/11-level attack on the homeland. She had no idea whether that was by Krysten herself or by a Russian team making it look like Krysten. And, in the end, it didn't really matter. She may have been duped, but if so, there was still time to recover. If not for her ego, then for her country.

Alex left the lounge to visit the ladies' room, leaving Caleb in the corner wrestling with a Nespresso machine. Looking in the mirror, she realized she had been wearing the same clothes since she'd awoken in the Radisson Blu Hotel in London's Leicester Square.

*Was that yesterday?*

She undressed and stepped into a shower stall and

braced herself against the wall, resting her forehead against her folded arms. The hot water cascading down her head, back, and legs found its way into her cuts and abrasions and stung as it cleansed them. The bandages on her hand and face fell away. Despite the discomfort, she dialed up the heat and stood there absorbing the torment for a full three minutes before turning to the task of washing her hair and ridding herself of the dirt, debris, and dried blood she had accumulated over the past twenty-four hours.

The hot water running down her body had the added effect of accentuating her exhaustion, making her legs wobbly. She turned down the temperature to something more bracing, the goosebumps rising over her, awakening her to the task ahead.

Alex dried off and pulled on a pair of stone-green stretchy cargo pants and a light-colored polo, leaving it untucked, then dried her hair with the provided hairdryer. Reluctantly, she put her Glock into her backpack, making her feel more vulnerable and exposed than she would have if she had showered naked on the tarmac.

On her way back to the executive lounge, she bumped into Staff Sergeant Davis.

"Special Agent Martel," she said. "We're ready for you and Mr. Copeland. You can board now. Wheels up in ten minutes."

She thanked her and went to fetch Caleb, who was shooting an espresso when she entered the room. They moved together through the departure lounge, where an armed military sentry checked their passports before allowing them to continue airside. His partner looked on, holding her Heckler & Koch assault rifle across her chest and eyeing them dispassionately.

Once they were through the checkpoint, Alex spoke. "Guess the French have upped their threat status."

"As should everyone. But we're still flying to DC."

"I didn't say anything. You convinced me already."

"I spoke with the deputy director while you were gone. She's eager to meet you; said the International Operations Division at FBI has cleared you to work with my team on this."

"It would be nice if someone would tell me these things occasionally."

"Don't be so sensitive." He scanned the tarmac. "You know how bureaucracies work. I'm sure there's a slew of emails flying back and forth between The Hague and DC requesting signatures on transfer notices. It's only a matter of time before one of them reaches you."

He was right, of course. The wheels at the Department of Justice turned at a snail's pace. She imagined it was the same over at Central Intelligence.

She climbed aboard the aircraft and found what was becoming her usual seat toward the rear. Once again, no one else boarded with them. This was a form of travel she could get used to.

She plopped herself down into the plush leather cushions of the Air Force Gulfstream's sofa and tossed her backpack next to her. Then she checked her iPhone for messages. Sure enough, an email from Bressard had come in forty minutes ago. It was pretty straightforward—she was being released from Interpol by the secretary general in Lyon to return to the FBI's National Security Branch, International Operations Division, in Washington, DC. There, she would continue the investigation with her colleagues in the Weapons of Mass Destruction Directorate and liaise with Caleb's team at CIA. She had been officially relieved of her legat duties in the Netherlands to return to the DOJ fold stateside.

She was beginning to understand how pro athletes felt.

The Gulfstream aircraft's two Rolls-Royce turbo-fan engines began to spool up. Imani entered the cabin looking magnificent, her smoky quartz skin glowing in Paris's warm light.

"Buckle up," she announced. "We'll be taking off shortly." She lifted Alex's backpack into an overhead bin. "I'll secure this for takeoff."

Caleb sat across the aisle, buckled into his seat. At the sound of the twin engines revving up, Alex felt the anticipation that came before every takeoff—a combination of trepidation and excitement. She psyched herself up for the transatlantic flight and cinched up her seatbelt.

Caleb was right. The best thing they could do now was to regroup in the States. Whether it was at CIA in Langley or at FBI headquarters in DC didn't matter. What mattered was that they pooled every available resource to identify the target of the threat. There might still be time before the bomb got into the country. Despite the technical challenges of doing so, Alex was guardedly optimistic that it would be possible to detect the B61 thermonuclear bomb being smuggled into America.

As the aircraft rolled along the taxiway, she was glad Caleb had helped turn her thinking around. Loyalty had always been her strong suit, never her burden. It had never led her to have faith in people who didn't merit her trust. Her intrinsic bullshit detector had kept her clean—until Krysten. Now it seemed everything about their friendship had been a lie. Had Krysten used Alex for her malign purpose when they'd met in Paris? She realized she might never know, but it was a safe bet.

In the meantime, Jonathan would keep working to reveal any other secrets Krysten's email might hold. Interpol would continue the investigation into her espionage activities, along with MI5 and other organs of British intelligence. They would have to sort out how a Russian agent had penetrated their network so deeply.

The US Air Force C-37B lined up perpendicular to the runway, its jet engines spinning up intermittently as it crept forward behind a pair of French Mirage fighter jets. As Alex gazed out the window at them, her phone rang.

# CHAPTER 52

"Are you in Paris yet?" Jonathan Burgess was calling from Interpol headquarters in Lyon.

"Just leaving," she replied.

"What do you mean *just leaving*?"

"I mean that as we speak, we're getting ready to roll down the runway. They're sending me to Washington. Technically, I'm no longer with Interpol."

"What?"

"An hour ago, Secretary General Clicquot released me back to the Department of Justice. I'm on my way to FBI headquarters in DC to continue the investigation there. Why are you calling me on this phone? Is it clean?"

"I ran another sweep. It's clean. But you can't leave Paris."

"What are you talking about?"

"I mean your gut telling you there's going to be an attack in Paris . . . I think you're right."

"Jonathan, you only have a few seconds to get to the point before we go airborne."

Caleb glanced across the aisle at her with a quizzical look.

Jonathan continued. "I decrypted some of the

messages hidden in the photo files, the steganography I told you about?"

"The point, Burgess."

"There's more than a few files embedded inside the JPEG files Krysten sent."

Her dogged curiosity had been getting her into hot water recently. No more. "I'm not involved with that anymore. Anything to do with Krysten is now an Interpol and British intelligence matter. I'll be working on the theft of the thermonuclear gravity bomb—"

"That *is* my point—they're connected. Krysten was supplying you with information to prove the Russians plotted to steal the bomb."

Alex watched the pair of French fighter jets surge down the runway. Their nose gear lifted off the tarmac. Within seconds, they were streaking vertically into the sky. Their jetwash and wake turbulence would dissipate in seconds, and air traffic control would clear the Gulfstream for takeoff.

"How do you know they're connected?"

Caleb, still strapped into his seat, sat taller and leaned in to listen to her conversation. The aircraft's engines wound up again as the pilot lined the Gulfstream up with the far end of the runway.

"The photos contain maps and drawings of Paris and the Sorbonne University, as well as travel itineraries and fake documents for known Russian operatives into and out of Paris."

"Jonathan, as suspicious as that seems, it's how they operate. Heck, it's even how we operate."

"There are also itineraries and travel documents for some of these same people for Turkey, along with detailed plans of Incirlik Air Base with maps and charts."

The back of her neck tingled.

"And," he continued, "I found blueprints for a weapons maintenance facility."

"Stop the plane!"

"What?" said Caleb. "No, we're not stopping the plane, Alex!"

The engines revved and the aircraft began to shake in anticipation of the pilot releasing the brakes to allow them to hurtle down the runway. Alex leaped out of her seat and grabbed her backpack from the overhead storage.

"Alex, what are you doing?"

"I'm getting off."

The plane lurched ahead and began to accelerate. Alex ran forward, fighting the mounting g-forces trying to push her back to the rear of the aircraft.

"Imani, tell the pilots to stop the plane!" she shouted, running toward the cockpit.

Staff Sergeant Imani Davis was strapped into her seat next to the door. A shocked expression spread across her face as Alex raced past and started pounding on the cockpit door.

"Stop the plane! Abort takeoff!" she yelled.

The plane continued to accelerate, nearing takeoff speed. Beside the door was a telephone handset. She grabbed it and began shouting into it, struggling to keep her balance.

"This is FBI Special Agent Martel. I am ordering you to stop this aircraft. Now!"

She realized at that moment how ridiculous she sounded and had no idea if anyone inside the cockpit could even hear her over the roar of the twin engines. But then she was violently thrown to the floor by the sudden application of brakes and reverse thrust. The aircraft trembled and shuddered along the runway as the pilot fought to peel off the jet's forward momentum. In mere seconds it came to a stop within an aircraft's length of the end of the runway. A few seconds more, and the cockpit door burst open. Standing in the doorway was one pissed-off Air Force pilot.

"What the hell is going on back here?" He first looked at the flight attendant, Staff Sergeant Davis, still strapped into her seat. Then his eyes turned to shoot daggers at Alex, who lay curled up on the floor beside the cockpit where she had fallen. "Are you the one responsible for this rejected takeoff?"

He stood six-foot-four in a six-foot-two-tall cabin, filling the doorway leading into the cockpit of the C-37B. Alex picked herself up off the floor and stood in front of him, considerably smaller in stature.

"I just received information relating to a major incident that's unfolding, and I couldn't let this plane get off the ground."

"You're an FBI agent?"

"Special agent, yes." She wasn't sure she should be splitting hairs just now, but whatever.

"Well, Special Agent . . . ?" He was grasping for her name.

"Martel. Captain . . . ?"

"Lieutenant Colonel, since titles seem to be so important to you."

She checked his nametag. *Jack Stewart*. "Colonel Stewart, I'm Special Agent Martel."

"Yes, I believe we've established that."

By now, Caleb had appeared behind her. The lieutenant colonel eyed him up and down, but Caleb raised his hands in surrender and backed a few feet down the aisle.

"Like I was saying, Martel, I don't care who you are. You put my aircraft, crew, and passengers in jeopardy." His voice was as rough as sandpaper and ripe with a Texas twang. "You have no authority here unless I say you do."

She straightened up. "Yes, sir."

"I was told we were on a priority mission to get you two stateside."

"Things have changed," she said.

"No, they haven't," Caleb piped up.

"Yes, they have."

"Well, which is it?" asked Stewart. "I don't have time for bullshit."

"No, sir, nothing has changed," Caleb said more forcefully. "We're still going to Washington. I'm sorry for—"

"No, we're not!" said Alex.

Stewart crossed his arms over his formidable chest and stared from one to the other.

"We can't ignore this latest information," she said.

"We sure as hell can," Caleb replied. "It doesn't change a thing. There is still an imminent threat to the homeland. It has the same relevance as all the info we received before. Consider the source, Alex. You can't trust her."

Colonel Stewart watched with curiosity as they continued to argue.

Alex turned to him. "Do you mind?" she said. "This discussion is highly classified."

It was his turn to raise his hands in surrender. "Go ahead," he said. "I'll just pedal us off the runway while you two chat it out. That okay with you, *Special Agent* Martel?"

\* \* \*

CHARLES DE GAULLE AIRPORT, PARIS, FRANCE

The containers marked QUAI DES BELGES from the Vieux Port Fish Market in Marseille, France, arrived aboard a commercial flight. Inside the 750-acre cargo facility at Charles de Gaulle Airport, the crates themselves—from the smallest to the largest—were kept cold with dry ice inside the air-conditioned plant as they were processed.

Ripe with the fragrance of the ocean, the containers were deemed a priority shipment. Inspectors checked shipping labels and ensured manifests were in concordance with their listed contents. But in a country whose annual appetite for fresh fish and sea-food exceeded eighty pounds per capita—more than anywhere else on the continent—the focus was on speed, not thoroughness, especially on a hot day. The markets and restaurants of Paris demanded that their fish, oysters, mussels, octopus, and other goods harvested from the oceans arrive without delay. From sea to table in eight hours or less. And anyway, this domestic shipment from Marseille didn't warrant the same scrutiny that a foreign shipment might be subject to.

A forklift loaded the pallets into the delivery truck, and the driver was sent on his way. He drove along the airport's northern perimeter road, blending in among the other cargo trucks fanning across the country. Twenty minutes later, he circled a roundabout in a quaint little village outside the capital and pulled into a parking lot, a forest of weeds pushing up through fractured asphalt adjacent to a deserted tobacco processing factory.

Two men, made stocky from a life of physical labor in the Ural Mountains, emerged from an older-model Renault Clio and approached the small diesel-engine truck. A man of North African heritage stepped out, a smoldering hand-rolled cigarette dangling from his lower lip.

They walked together to the back of the truck and rolled up the door. Sergei Malkin climbed in and pried the lid off a container. After a quick inspection, he nodded to his colleague.

"Everything in order?" asked the truck driver in broken English.

"I'm not sure," said Malkin, pointing into the crate. "What is this?"

"What?" the man spat.

"This," Malkin said, pointing more emphatically.

The man climbed into the back of the truck, and Malkin stepped back to give him room to inspect the precious cargo. The tall, thin man bent down for a closer look inside the crate.

"I see nothing," he pronounced, turning to face Malkin.

"My mistake," said Malkin, plunging a seven-inch Damascus steel blade into the man's abdomen just below his rib cage. He held the man by the back of the neck and aimed the knife upward. Once it was buried to the hilt, he thrust it deeper, twisting the ebony handle and skewering the man's heart and lung.

Malkin's partner backed the truck up to the edge of the adjoining field, and Malkin rolled the corpse out into the tall grass.

Traffic was predictably heavy as the two men drove into the heart of Paris. Arriving at the Seine thirty minutes later, they crossed the Pont d'Austerlitz into the Latin Quarter that straddled Paris's fifth and sixth arrondissements. They drove along Rue Buffon, the southeast boundary of the Jardin des Plantes. On the opposite side lay the Sorbonne University International Conference Center, where the Paris Peace Summit was already underway. Their route circumvented the security perimeter in place for the world leaders' conference. The truck weaved through side streets until it arrived at its destination: an alley next to a small but popular American-style burger joint frequented by students and locals, a short distance south of the conference site.

The driver backed the truck between the buildings, guided by another man and his compatriot at the rear. Together, they off-loaded the nine-hundred-pound cargo onto a lithium battery–powered rough-terrain pallet truck. Their next task would prove even more arduous.

The four men delivered the shipment to its final destination in an unmapped subterranean vault deep within the Paris catacombs. They weaved through ancient passageways and hidden tunnels, in some places finding themselves knee-deep in water, until they reached the designated underground chamber. Here it would remain hidden beneath the Sorbonne, away from the scrutiny of an international security force and out of the reach of the catacomb tunnel rats known as the cataphiles.

No one would know it was there until it was too late, and Paris had been transformed into a slurry of destruction in a fiery nanosecond of infamy that would live on from that moment forward and forever.

\*\*\*

VÉLIZY-VILLACOUBLAY AIR BASE, FRANCE

"You're flushing your reputation down the toilet, Alex. It's career suicide."

"I don't care about my reputation. I have to do what's right, not what *seems* right."

The two sat in the forward cabin of the G-37B discussing the merits of her plan. Despite the national security concerns surrounding their next steps, Staff Sergeant Davis had made them put their seatbelts back on as the pilot taxied the aircraft back to the terminal.

*Safety first,* she had said, and neither was keen to argue the matter with the Air Force NCO.

"Interpol has already fired you—"

"They didn't *fire* me—"

"—and both Central Intelligence and the Bureau assume you're coming back to Washington to help track down a rogue nuke that the Russians or their proxy want to use to turn New York City into a charred pizza."

She gave him a look.

"I'm at a loss for metaphors, okay, Alex? I said this before, your oath is to America, not to the people of Paris or France or any other part of Europe or the world."

"My oath, Caleb, is *to support and defend the Constitution of the United States against all enemies, foreign and domestic; to bear true faith and allegiance to the same, and to well and faithfully discharge my duties as an FBI special agent. So help me God.* That was my oath, same as yours, give or take. That is my commitment to my country, and that is what I'm going to do."

"By running around some foreign capital looking for a nuke when it could be arriving on America's shores imminently?"

"I will remind you that the president of the United States and a shitload of other American diplomats and dignitaries are here in Paris right now. They are at a conference whose sole objective is the pursuit of world peace. But that same undertaking could become the backdrop for the murder of tens or even hundreds of thousands of innocent people. And for what? To disrupt a relatively stable and harmonious world order? No one else is paying attention, Caleb. I have to do something."

Imani slipped past them to open the door of the aircraft.

"What if you're wrong?" he asked.

"I'm not."

"But what if you are?"

"I trust you, Caleb. You're on the case." She

lowered her voice. "Hopefully, if the nuke isn't here, there will still be enough time to track down the bomb before anything happens at home."

She felt his eyes boring into her, full of pity. Or disdain.

"If you do this, I can't help you. You'll be on your own. You know that, right? You'll likely be fired and brought up on disciplinary charges for professional misconduct; maybe even go to prison. You'll be untouchable, Alex. Probably forever."

"The attack on New York City, if there's going to be one, is supposedly weeks away. Maybe months, according to what our scant intelligence is saying. I get it. I was born and raised in the Empire State. That makes it personal. But *I'm* talking about an attack that could happen in days, maybe hours, the outcome of which would rival the darkest days in history. Right here, right now. The clock is ticking, Caleb. I trust my gut. I wish you would trust me a little as well. If that's what someone is trying to make happen, I'm going to stop it if it's the last thing I do."

# CHAPTER 53

A local taxi picked Alex up outside the terminal. When she told the cabby she was headed into the heart of the city, he emitted a perceptible groan and muttered in French, complaining that much of the autoroute leading into central Paris was under construction. The security zone around the university, he said, would make it virtually impossible to get her close to where she wanted to go.

"Just get us there quickly," she told him.

"*Oui, bien sûr*," he groaned. *Yes, of course.*

His griping was misplaced—Alex didn't care.

She had to call Bressard, but she wasn't sure what she would say to him. Point of fact, he wasn't her boss anymore, Alex having been released from her duties by the secretary general of Interpol and ordered back to Washington by the DOJ. But he was all she had: the only person she felt she could talk to right now. She braced herself and dialed. No answer. She tried a couple more times with the same result.

*Damn.*

She thought about what Caleb had said to her in Turkey. *Stewed on* was actually more accurate. He had accused her of being prideful, suggesting that she was being blinded by it. It wasn't much different than what Kyle used to tell her.

*Was it true? Am I too proud to admit when I'm wrong? Should I have seen the truth about Krysten sooner? Am I wrong now?*

Self-doubt wasn't her style, or hadn't been. But self-reflection had always been a part of her professional practice as a soldier and special agent, so maybe there was room for improvement. Today, though, she needed to follow her gut.

Forty minutes later, the cabby crossed the Seine and then crossed back again to the Left Bank at the Pont d'Austerlitz.

"I won't be able to take you any closer," he announced in French. "I will have to let you out next to the Jardins des Plantes."

He took the traffic circle at Boulevard de l'Hôpital, and as they crossed Quai Saint-Bernard, she saw the twelve-foot-high security fencing to her right blocking the roadway to all but accredited vehicles.

"Let me out here."

He pulled over and she bailed out of the cab to the sound of horns blasting. As good as any New York cabby, he swore and flipped off everyone out his window.

Google Maps promptly displayed her location with a pulsing blue dot. She oriented herself facing southwest into the botanical gardens and started to walk.

\* \* \*

SORBONNE UNIVERSITY INTERNATIONAL
CONFERENCE CENTER, PARIS, FRANCE

On the Pierre and Marie Curie campus in the fifth arrondissement of Paris, the Sorbonne University International Conference Center sat nestled back from the street among a series of interconnected multistory square buildings with shared courtyards. An industrial Lego-block design that looked plain and boring from an aerial perspective, the university was nevertheless one of the greatest centers of higher learning in the world.

It wasn't lost on Alex that the Paris Peace Summit was held annually on a university campus named after the woman who had co-discovered the elements polonium and radium. In fact, it was Marie Curie who'd coined the term *radioactivity*. She was the first person and the only woman to win the Nobel Prize twice. She was also the only person to win the Nobel Prize in two different scientific fields of endeavor for her discoveries.

Madame Marie Curie had been one of those fiery, independent, brilliant titans of knowledge and scholastic achievement to whom Alex owed so much for having kicked open doors held closed to women for so long.

After crossing the Jardin des Plantes, Alex arrived at the outer security cordon. It was as heavy a police presence as she had anticipated. Only, with the presidents of France and the United States in attendance along with another dozen or so world leaders, the phalanx of riot police was exponentially stronger. A good thing for the summit, but not particularly auspicious for her.

Protesters' chants filled the air, denouncing everything from G20 fiscal policy to the perils of flatulent cattle. Security Forces and French police were holding the line at intersections around the perimeter. As Alex walked through the crowd, she overheard protesters reveling in the news that unrest in the capital was spreading, and demonstrations had grown to encompass all manner of grievances against the French government with segments of the nation's yellow vest movement joining in.

She passed through the first checkpoints by waving her FBI credentials and intimating that she had a meeting at the conference center. A police official with his hands full managing the unrest before him reluctantly permitted her to pass, no doubt confident that the inner cordon of security would weed her out if she, in fact, didn't belong.

As she approached the checkpoint leading into the forecourt of the conference center, her eyes were getting misty. The semisweet smell of tear gas was carried on the breeze funneling toward the Seine. Alex ordinarily would have found its effect merely nostalgic, but she had worked up a sweat on her walk from the taxi from the day's high heat and humidity, and some of the CS particulate had found its way into the cut under her eye. She dabbed at it with a tissue, gently brushing away any residue, the chemical stinging her wound as she approached the checkpoint.

Alex was stopped at the gate by a humorless sentry who was neither impressed nor swayed by her shiny gold FBI shield and identification card.

"*Non, madame, vous ne pouvez pas entrer,*" he told her, consulting his laptop. *No, ma'am, you may not enter.*

She debated with him in fluent French but found she had reached her limit in civil discourse when she failed to provide him with a valid reason for her to enter, or even a contact person on-site. She hadn't fully considered her game plan on the way from the airfield in Vélizy-Villacoublay where she'd left Caleb, and now found herself winging it in the hopes that an idea would form on the fly. So far, that hadn't happened.

She needed to reach Bressard. He could get her inside. Once beyond the fences and gates, she could figure out what to do. She redialed his phone.

"Alexandra, miss me already? How is your flight?"

Bressard was in a good mood, his typically baritone voice airy and upbeat.

"I'm still in Paris."

"Oh? I thought your flight would have been airborne by now."

"It is."

"Then I don't understand."

"I got off the plane."

If ever there was a pregnant pause, this one was having twins.

"Chief?"

"I heard you." His voice had plummeted an octave below its normal range.

"Did you see the report from Burgess yet? He decrypted the hidden messages in Krysten's message."

"Alexandra, you no longer work for Interpol. You're an FBI special agent."

"I always was."

"An FBI special agent who is supposed to be on her way to Washington."

"Jonathan found more evidence. Evidence that Paris will be the target of a possible nuclear attack. I know it sounds crazy, Chief, but let me run it by you. Then I'll need you to get me into the Paris Peace Summit. There's somebody there I need to speak to."

"Where are you now?"

"Outside the IPP access gate."

She was hovering outside the gate through which internationally protected persons and their entourages passed, the sentry keeping a wary eye on her.

There was another brief pause before Bressard's voice breathed into her ear, his tone shifting to near normal. "Step back."

"What?"

"Take two steps back and look directly into the security camera mounted above the guard booth," he said.

She did as she was told. A moment later, the phone rang inside the sentry station. The guard who had refused her access answered it.

"*Madame,*" he said a moment later, waving her forward. "*Vous pouvez passer maintenant.*" *You may pass now.*

"How'd you do that?" she asked into the phone, but Bressard had already hung up.

As she walked through the gate, the guard reached out his hand.

"But first I must search your backpack," he said in English.

He wasn't going to be happy when he discovered her loaded Glock.

\*\*\*

BAR VENDÔME, RITZ PARIS HOTEL

Gerasimov sat under the arched Belle Époque glass roof of the Bar Vendôme, contemplating the current situation. In the main bar, a pianist filled the room with soothing music, while on the patio, the linden trees provided cooling shade beneath the gentle rustling of their leaves. His iPad sat on the table before him, an on-screen timer set to three hours not yet counting down. That would provide ample time for the president to attend this afternoon's meetings and prepare for the reception gala in the evening. Only, by then, the colonel and his crew would have created a ruse to force the evacuation of several—but not all—of the Russian diplomats from Paris before the B61 thermonuclear gravity bomb exploded, swallowing most of Paris, along with the Russian president, in the ensuing conflagration.

The chic brasserie was nestled in the Ritz Hotel in the first arrondissement within the Paris district known as *le premier.* The Louvre Museum and the Tuileries

Garden nearby were two of Gerasimov's favorite places in the City of Light, equally for their attestation to the marvels of human achievement in the arts and their capacity to soothe his unsettled spirit.

It was almost a shame they would soon be wiped off the map.

It was possible that some of the treasures within the historic museum would survive the nuclear blast—perhaps some of the art and antiquities within the deepest of the belowground exhibit halls and vaults—but if they did not, that would merely be the price exacted by his greatest achievement: the elevation of Russia to supremacy over America and the Western alliance known as NATO. He was convinced Paris would recover within the span of a generation or two, as had both Hiroshima and Nagasaki after America destroyed them at the end of the Second World War. And during the time it would take for that to happen, Russia would grow in geopolitical influence while continuing to sow discord through the ongoing dissemination of misinformation that Americans and their allies were so keen to lap up.

In the meantime, with an American thermonuclear bomb exploding in the belly of the French capital, the cacophony of voices from angry nations would all but quash the last remnants of the belief in America's moral superiority. The alliances forged by the nations of the West over nearly a century would be torn asunder.

The fact that the Russian president had not discovered Directorate 13's true intentions was fortuitous. Meanwhile, Gerasimov's underlings were assured that the highest level of Russian leadership was sanctioning their mission. They believed their actions to be righteous if President Sergachev declared them so. But a regime change was necessary. Gerasimov wasn't entirely sure that he would survive the fallout—literally and metaphorically speaking—but his country would come to recognize him and General Tikhonov as extraordinary patriots. At last, Russia would be free of its vain president's greed and evil, and could plot a bolder course under the leadership of General Tikhonov, whom Gerasimov believed would be its next president.

Gerasimov regarded his tumbler of bourbon, a double shot of Pappy Van Winkle's fifteen-year-old Family Reserve. The waiter had brought it with a side of chilled distilled water, but he drank it neat. To do otherwise was blasphemy. Served in an exquisite diamond-cut crystal tumbler, the whiskey glowed a luminous amber in the sunlight streaming through the glass roof. He swirled the bourbon around the glass, the lightly viscous liquid caressing the crystal, then brought it to his nose and inhaled deeply; a slow draw of breath that conveyed the essences of vanilla, honey, cherries, oak, tobacco, and a hint of dark chocolate. If this were the last glass of bourbon he would ever drink, he was going to savor it.

He glanced up to see General Tikhonov walking toward him wearing a freshly pressed Casual Uniform Option One of the Russian Army. A light green shirt fixed with a black tie was worn under an olive-green jacket and matching trousers with azure piping—azure being the color denoting Spetsnaz GRU officers. An azure band encircled his peaked cap, which he removed and placed on an empty chair next to him.

Gerasimov punched the start button on his iPad to begin the three-hour countdown, then closed its cover. He pushed his chair out from the table and stood, buttoning his Savile Row jacket to greet his boss.

"Sit, Viktor, sit," Tikhonov said. "Rémy Martin XO," he called over his shoulder to the approaching waiter, who left as quickly and quietly as he had arrived. "I see you are always working," he continued, indicating toward the computer tablet on the table. "I am pleased with the progress you have made on our project. Are we on schedule?"

"Exactly as planned, sir."

Tikhonov nodded approvingly. "Any complications?"

No point elaborating on the Interpol woman and her friend from the CIA. "None that I cannot manage, General."

"Fantastic, Viktor." The waiter returned and placed a snifter of cognac in front of the general. "He has requested that you join us at the meeting this afternoon."

Gerasimov understood the *he* in this context meant President Sergachev. "Thank you, General. I am honored."

"I am glad you are getting the recognition you deserve from our supreme commander-in-chief for whatever time he has left." He cupped the glass of Rémy in his hand and swung it in wide circles, warming the liquid to release its bouquet. Then he raised it in a toast and downed it in one shot. "Our motorcade will leave in ten minutes," he said, pushing out his chair. "You will join us at this afternoon's meeting so as not to raise any suspicion."

It wasn't a question. "Of course, General."

# CHAPTER 54

The guard, a uniformed lieutenant of the French National Police, rifled through Alex's backpack, peering inside as he shuffled items around. His eyes widened, and his hands ceased their movement. Then he pulled her FBI-issued Glock 19M out from the bottom of the bag, along with her three spare mags.

"*Qu'est-ce que c'est?*" *What is this?* he asked, holding the gun in the air between his thumb and forefinger like an oozing wedge of Époisses de Bourgogne. He switched to passable English. "Why are you carrying a pistol in France?"

*Fair question.* "I can explain," she said, holding her FBI creds aloft.

Several more officers gathered around.

"This is not permitted," he said, with even less humor than before.

"I am here on official business."

"Perhaps it is so, but American police cannot carry weapons in France—"

She wasn't sure how to justify her illegal possession of a firearm in his country. "Ordinarily, I would agree with you, but I'm here—"

A voice came from behind them. "*Tout va bien, monsieur l'agent.*" A very senior-looking official in uniform walked toward them. *Everything is fine, Officer.* "I will take care of the matter from here," he said, his voice as rough as unhewn wood.

The man was fifty-ish, tall, and fit. He walked with a dignified bearing and erect posture and wore a double-breasted navy-blue police uniform adorned with rows of service decorations. A red braided cord was threaded under the epaulet on his left shoulder, and intricate embroidered gold brocade covered his policeman's cap. The crowd of officers parted before him. He bore a curt smile as he approached. The sentry held Alex's Glock toward him and raised his shoulders in the form of a question.

"Yes, it is alright," said the uniformed police official. "Mademoiselle Martel is a guest of the Republic, here at my request. As my guest, she may keep it. I will see to her."

*"Oui, Monsieur le Préfet. Bien entendu, monsieur."* *Yes, Prefect. Understood, sir.*

The prefect of police provided command and oversight of the National Police and other emergency services operating within Paris and three surrounding municipalities.

The lieutenant handed her pistol and magazines back to her. Alex assumed if he approved of her *having* it, he wouldn't mind her *wearing* it, so she slid it into her holster, which she then clipped over her belt, securing two magazines in place as well.

"Follow me," said the prefect.

She followed him into the lobby of the building, where he led her into a security office off the atrium. A man stood in front of a bank of security monitors displaying images from around the conference center, both inside and out. Outside along the perimeter of the security zone, the size of the crowds had grown even larger since she had passed through only a short while ago. The prefect cleared his throat, and the man turned around.

"Hello, Alexandra."

"Chief Bressard?"

He took a step toward her to examine the cut under her eye, her fat lip, and the hand she was favoring. "Are you alright?"

"I'm fine, Chief." She dabbed at a bit of fluid leaking from the cut with a tissue. It still stung from the CS gas outside. "I had no idea you were going to be at the summit."

"I could say the same for you. I see you've met Prefect Deschamps."

She turned toward him and extended her hand. "Thank you for interceding out there."

"*Enchanté,* mademoiselle," he said, taking her hand and bowing his head. "My men are not accustomed to foreign police carrying firearms in France."

"Of course, sir. Forgive me."

"Your chief—" he began.

"Former chief," Bressard corrected.

"Monsieur Bressard was providing me with an update when you arrived fortuitously at the checkpoint." He smiled broadly. "But I am afraid I am not convinced there is a stolen nuclear bomb in Paris, Special Agent Martel."

"I understand, sir. May I share with you what we know?"

"I am a very busy man," he said. "As you no doubt observed on your way in and can see on these monitors, the natives of Paris are restless. Our city's reputation for large demonstrations and unrest is, I'm afraid, well-deserved. I must proceed to our command post in the integrated security center to meet with my senior officers."

"Is it far?" she asked.

"As a matter of fact, it is just one floor below us."

"Excellent, Prefect! Can we walk and talk?"

\* \* \*

By the time they arrived at the integrated security center—a pair of adjoining conference rooms with the center divider panels retracted into the walls—Alex had given Chief Bressard and Prefect Deschamps the CliffsNotes version of what she knew: Krysten's note, the contents of her safe-deposit box, the photographs, and the information digitally buried within them.

"I'm afraid I don't see it, Special Agent Martel," the prefect said. "Taken from a credible source, I might have to agree with your assessment, as preposterous a notion as it is. But I am told by Chief Bressard that this woman, this intelligence officer, was, in fact, a Russian mole."

"Yes, but—"

"I'm sorry, mademoiselle. As you can see, I am extremely busy." He waved a hand toward the hive of activity. They were surrounded by dozens of agents and officers at work coordinating the efforts of a joint task force of French military and police resources.

The prefect continued, "Now, if you will excuse me—"

But Alex was convinced Paris was the target, and a thought came to her having to do with Krysten's note. There was a line in it that was eating away at her. *What did it say again?* She pulled out her phone and scrolled through her email until she found it.

"The catacombs!"

"*Pardon,* mademoiselle?"

"The Paris Catacombs," she repeated.

Now Bressard was looking on anxiously.

"What about them?" asked Prefect Deschamps.

She turned to Bressard. "Chief, Krysten's note mentioned Paris, as well as alluding to Titans, as in the military personnel at Incirlik."

"Yes, and we have already discounted her note as disinformation, Alexandra. Surely you can see that?"

She ignored him. "One line in the note said . . . hang on, it's here—"

"Ms. Martel," interrupted the prefect. "I really don't have time—"

She read from Krysten's note: "*Everyone has skeletons they'd rather keep hidden in their closet.*" When the men continued to stare blankly at her, she filled in her thoughts. "When I first read that, I thought it was an explanation or an apology for her deceit. I mean, we all have secrets we'd rather the world didn't discover, don't we? But now I think she was talking about the catacombs, where the skeletons of six million Parisians are resting. Right beneath our feet, in one big proverbial closet."

Bressard had been studying her intently and now turned to the prefect.

"Monsieur Deschamps, could this even be possible?"

"That is your theory, Ms. Martel?" asked the prefect. "That the bomb is hidden in the catacombs?"

"I think so, yes."

"You think so. A hunch then."

"On its own, it may not seem like much. But together with the rest of the note, the other evidence, and the clues where she mentions Paris and hints at the airbase and thermonuclear weapons in Turkey—these things together reflect a significant volume of circumstantial evidence that we can't ignore."

"Why the catacombs?" asked the prefect. "I mean, you are talking about a nuclear bomb that, if detonated anywhere within Paris, could conceivably level the entire city. It could more easily be concealed in a rented truck or a delivery van, *non*? Why drag it through *les catacombes de Paris*."

"They would do it because they are spiteful. The vice commander of the airbase explained that the bomb had been redesigned to incorporate significant bunker-busting capabilities, to defeat the bunkers the Russians had built for President Sergachev and his government. Planting it inside the catacombs would be a way of sticking it to America and the West for what they may perceive as our arrogance, perhaps for flagrantly threatening the self-absorbed Russian president this way."

"It is an interesting theory, I must admit," said Deschamps. "A little weak, but interesting. The Police Nationale have been scouring the tunnels that make up the catacombs for weeks leading up to this summit to secure them. It is simply not conceivable that this could be done as you describe. Besides, I quite agree with the assessment of your CIA and British intelligence that the planned target of the attack is New York City." *Again with British intelligence.* "Now, if you will please excuse me."

She was disappointed but undaunted. "*Monsieur le Préfet*," she said to him as he began to turn away. "If I could borrow some of your valuable resources—just one or two officers—I think I can prove my hypothesis, sir, and track down that nuke in the catacombs."

"Special Agent Martel, you are most persistent." He thought for a moment. "The French have a saying: *Prouver que j'ai raison serait accorder que je puis avoir tort.* Do you understand what this means?" He didn't wait for a response. "It means, *To prove that I am right would be to admit I could be wrong.* Do you understand?"

It was a little pompous. She saw his point but didn't believe for a second she could be wrong.

He went on. "As it seems unlikely I'll be able to

get rid of you, you are welcome to remain in Paris to conduct limited inquiries under the direction of Chief Bressard. I will instruct the sentry whom you met at the gate to keep an eye on you. If there is a bomb, find it," he said. "But keep out of trouble. And please do not kill any citizens of France while on French soil. Lieutenant Blanc will come to find you presently. Please wait for him in the security office upstairs. *Au revoir,* mademoiselle."

With that, he turned and disappeared into the hive.

Bressard wore a broad smile, his dimples peeking out above his finely groomed beard.

"What?" she said. "Thanks for being so supportive."

"I've learned from experience, Alexandra, that sometimes the best way to help you is to keep out of your way."

# CHAPTER 55

Alex and Bressard reached the top of the stairs and crossed the atrium to the security office. A woman, elegant in a navy-blue off-center blazer over a white blouse, skirt, and heels, marched toward them, a silk scarf gently luffing behind her like a nautical flag on a luxury vessel at sea.

"Chief Bressard," she called.

"Secretary General. I wasn't expecting you until tomorrow."

Interpol's top official turned to Alex. "Special Agent Martel. I recognize you from your photographs."

"It is . . . I am," replied Alex. The woman looked younger in person than she did on video calls. Her blond hair was pulled back in a tight bun. In her heels, she stood over six feet. "So nice to finally meet you, Madame Clicquot."

The secretary general of Interpol was both its chief and chief executive officer. Madame Clicquot was responsible for conducting the organization's day-to-day activities as well as the business functions that supported the investigative work.

"I am a little surprised to find you here, Alex," she said, gazing at Bressard. "I seem to recall signing your transfer documents handing you back to the FBI less than an hour ago."

Bressard piped up. "I can explain."

"I trust you can," she said.

But before he could, a commotion outside the glass doors of the conference hall caught their attention. A fleet of vehicles led by a contingent of motorcycle officers pulled into the courtyard. Led by an armored SUV, each bore the tricolored white, blue, and red flag of the Russian Federation. The group disembarked and strode into the building.

A man of medium stature with thinning fawn-colored hair and a perpetual willowy grin led the way, appearing for all the world like he owned the place, as a phalanx of others trailed behind. He walked robustly, with a slightly awkward gunslinger's gait, his right arm unmoving with each stride.

*President Sergachev.*

His deportment seemed an odd carry-over from his days as a KGB foreign intelligence officer, where he'd risen to the rank of lieutenant colonel. Or maybe he wore a bulky weapon beneath his immaculate suit and was trying not to bump it with each pass of his forearm. Either way, the Russian president and his entourage were on a collision course with Alex, Bressard, and the secretary general of Interpol.

"Who's that with him?" asked Alex.

"Major General Pavel Tikhonov, the head of Directorate 13," said Madame Clicquot.

*Of course,* she thought.

"And behind them," said Bressard, "is his heir apparent and commander of operations—"

"Colonel Viktor Gerasimov." She knew him straight away.

Before Bressard could stop her, Alex was off

marching toward the Russian delegation. He and Madame Clicquot hurried to keep up.

"Alexandra!" called Bressard in a whispered shout. But she didn't hear him or chose not to respond to his call.

She headed straight for Gerasimov, which took her right into the Presidential Security Service detail's path. President Sergachev stopped, his permanent smile growing more expansive at the sight of this woman brushing past his bodyguards. The SBP agents ventured to block her, but Sergachev issued a command in Russian, and they opened a path instead. The lead agent stepped in front of her and pointed toward her sidearm, but she dodged past him like he wasn't even there. Sergachev continued to watch, waiting along with everyone else to see what would happen next.

The close-protection agents had formed a tight circle surrounding their president and his men, with Alex now in the inner sanctum. Bressard and Madame Clicquot stood on the outside looking in.

"Mr. President," she said, greeting him as she breezed past, stopping in front of Gerasimov.

"Special Agent Martel." The colonel stood before her in a business suit, smiling down from his six-foot, two-inch frame. "Your reputation precedes you. And I must confess to being somewhat of an admirer. As you demonstrate even now, your methods are quite direct. One might say brash."

"Speaking of *brash,* do you think I don't know it was you who stole the bomb from the American air base in Turkey?"

He laughed. "Not even a little foreplay first?" He glanced at the men around them. "I like this woman," he said. Even President Sergachev chuckled.

"You were in Adana yesterday and arrived in Paris today," she said coolly. "We have Major Douglas in custody. It's only a matter of time before he implicates you and Directorate 13."

Gerasimov's smile faded, replaced by a steely gaze.

A voice came from behind her. "Special Agent Martel." She spun around. President Sergachev was addressing her.

"Mr. President."

He searched beyond his phalanx of men, catching sight of Bressard and Madame Clicquot beyond. Alex followed his gaze and noted that Lieutenant Blanc, the French policeman from the gate whom Prefect Deschamps had assigned as her minder in Paris, had walked up as well.

"You are an agent of Interpol, yes?"

"It's complicated."

"Tell me, Agent Martel. Why aren't you in America trying to find this bomb you accuse one of my men of stealing? This accusation is absurd, of course."

His eyes left hers and bored into Madame Clicquot's. But if his intention was to intimidate her, she wasn't fazed in the least. She returned his gaze with a bright smile, a kindergarten teacher humoring a petulant child.

"Wake up and smell the sunflowers, Mr. President," said Alex. "I thought I would stay in Paris for a while and take in the sights. In fact, I understand the catacombs are a fascinating place to visit." She searched Gerasimov's face for a tell of any kind but saw nothing but a dispassionate gaze, which in itself was telling.

"You shouldn't waste your time, Sasha," the president said, calling her by the Russian diminutive form of her name. "It would be a shame if while you were chasing phantoms around Paris, a bomb was to explode in Times Square and—how should I say it in English— fry the Big Apple." His ridiculous smile grew even more prominent.

She stepped into his personal space, ignoring any

notion of physical distancing. His protection detail bristled and moved toward her, but they backed off with a slight raise of his hand. She looked him up and down. She had a good two inches on him.

"You are much smaller in person than I imagined, Mr. President. But you are living up to your reputation as a man without a soul."

He moved even closer until she could feel his stale breath on her and smell his musky cologne.

His grin evaporated. "In that case, Sasha, I am delighted we understand each other."

"It won't work, Dima." It was her turn to use the diminutive of Dmitry, which she'd recalled from a magazine article. "I will find the bomb. And I will find anyone who conspired to be part of the plot. And I will take down anyone responsible for whatever happens next, no matter who they are. There will be no hiding, Dima, not even for you in your nuclear-bomb-proof bunker at Kosvinsky Mountain."

"Such an ambitious objective. However, Alexandra, as the man who must approve such grand plans, I can assure you *Rossiya* had nothing to do with the theft of this thermonuclear bomb. Perhaps America should take better care of its toys, yes? Good day, Sasha."

President Sergachev turned and walked away. Gerasimov brushed past her, smiling.

Blood pounded inside her ears as other delegations—Canada, the United Kingdom, Japan—arrived and marched toward the amphitheater. Others would arrive shortly, too, including the United States.

Madame Clicquot appeared at her side. "I suggest we retire to the security office to discuss your future," she said, turning to lead them across the atrium. Bressard looked somber, gently shaking his head as if to warn her, *Don't even think of replying.*

Inside the office, Madame Clicquot commandeered

a corner cubicle. She turned to Alex, and she wasn't smiling.

"That was reckless, Special Agent Martel. Tell me why I shouldn't slap you with charges of professional misconduct and insubordination and put you on a plane to America right now."

"Because I don't work for Interpol anymore," she said. "And because you know I'm right, Madame Secretary General. And because we gained additional intel from that little tête-à-tête."

There was a beat before she replied. "Indeed," she said. "President Sergachev mentioned New York. And he did it in the hopes you would regard it as confirmation of what Western intelligence has been telling us. He might have done this to shift Interpol's efforts away from Paris, which is, of course, what the FBI has asked us to do. Tell me, Special Agent Martel, if Paris were the target, as you contend, then why are the Russian president and a rather large delegation of diplomats still here?"

Alex had no answer. Madame Clicquot continued.

"I am not convinced there is a nuclear bomb here—" Alex was about to jump in, but Madame Clicquot silenced her with a raised hand. "But I would be a fool to risk so many lives because of my pride. The FBI is expecting you back in Washington immediately. Tell me, Alex, are you willing to stake your career and your personal reputation on this hunch? Because if you are wrong, neither Chief Bressard nor I will be able to save you from the excoriation you will most assuredly face at the hands of the Department of Justice."

"Madame Clicquot, Chief Bressard," she said, addressing them both. "I have never been more convinced of anything in my life than I am of this."

There was a pause before Clicquot answered. "I will buy you time until the end of the day to find that bomb or evidence of its existence. And I will see about getting you additional manpower. But, as you have seen, the Paris prefect is extremely busy, and everyone, including the Americans, believes the bomb is on its way to New York City. If you are not successful, you'll be on a red-eye flight for Washington before the night is done. Understood?"

She was about to respond when her phone rang. It was Jonathan.

"I know where the bomb is," he said.

# CHAPTER 56

SORBONNE UNIVERSITY INTERNATIONAL
CONFERENCE CENTER, PARIS, FRANCE

What do you mean you know where the bomb is?"
Alex asked.

Madame Clicquot and Chief Bressard looked on
eagerly. Alex tapped the screen to activate her speakerphone.

"Jonathan, you're on speaker with Chief Bressard
and Secretary General Clicquot."

"What? Oh, hello." Jonathan's voice bordered on
shrill, half an octave higher than usual. "Okay, well,
maybe *know* is too strong a word, or if there's actually
a bomb anywhere—"

"Get to the point."

"I identified a location you need to check out," he
said.

"How? Where?"

"It's been bothering me for a while now, but as I decrypted Krysten's email, three words kept repeating
throughout the code: *Lectures. Wagers. Cherry.*"

"I remember you telling me," replied Alex.

"I was able to decipher much of the data embedded
in her email. As you know, it turned out to be maps
and schematic drawings pointing to Incirlik, along with
other details."

Madame Clicquot chimed in. "But we have already

established that this might all have been a ruse; disinformation to point us in the wrong direction." She caressed the silk scarf around her neck like it was a pet.

"By pointing us in the *right* direction?" he asked.

"It's happened before. Provide just enough truth to hide the bigger lies."

"Yes, Secretary General, but I discovered a repetitive string of three words that kept cropping up without any context. *Lectures. Wagers. Cherry.* The string is always buried in data I can't fully decrypt, but it always appears the same. The words are always in lowercase, preceded by three forward slashes, and separated by a period with no spaces."

Chief Bressard asked, "And what do they mean?"

"The string of text is a geographical reference. It points us to an address."

"What are you talking about?" Alex asked.

"I'm going to send you a link to an app called what3words. It's a geocoding system that breaks the planet down into three-meter squares—roughly ten feet by ten feet—and assigns each square a three-word string unique to that location. So instead of long strings of numbers like UTM or other mapping systems, you only have to know three words to pinpoint any location on the globe."

"And where does that string point us?"

"To an alley beside a restaurant in the Latin Quarter. As the crow flies, you're less than three football fields away. When you get the link, download the app, then enter the string of words into the address search bar."

She did as he instructed and entered ///lectures .wagers.cherry into the search bar. Up came an address for an American-style burger joint a few blocks away in the Latin Quarter.

"What now?" she asked.

"Well, if I were you, I'd go check it out."

"Not so fast." Secretary General Clicquot stopped Alex as she turned to exit the security room. Her expression was grave. "I will advise the Bureau that you have been delayed in France to pursue leads on behalf of Interpol; that additional relevant information has come to light."

"Thank you, Madame Clicquot," said Alex.

"I still do not believe the bomb is here, but I will allow you leeway to investigate. And, Alex, rest assured this *is* the final course of action you will take on the matter here in Paris. If your efforts prove fruitless, you will be on a plane tonight for Washington."

"Yes, ma'am."

Clicquot turned to the French police lieutenant. "Go with her. If she finds nothing, bring her back here so we can ensure she gets on a plane."

"*Oui, madame.*"

Chief Martin Bressard chimed in. "And promise me, Alexandra, if you find anything, you will call for backup."

\*\*\*

PARIS CATACOMBS, PARIS

With violent protests spreading all across the French capital, Alex knew better than to hope that Bressard would be able to muster any help if she got into trouble. She and the prefect's designee were on their own.

Lieutenant Hugo Blanc was a career policeman assigned to the public order unit of the French National Police force. He had secured for them an unmarked Renault to drive to 20 Rue des Boulangers, just south of their location within the fifth arrondissement.

"How far we going?" she asked.

"Assuming we can get through the crowds at the first

ring of defense, it should take no more than five minutes."

He circumnavigated the university campus within
the security zone. As they approached the barricades,
the riot squad platoon opened the gates and let them
pass. The crowd was remarkably compliant, merely yell-
ing at them as they beat their fists against the Renault.

"See?" he said. "*Pas de problème.*" *No problem.*

No sooner had the words passed his lips than a series of projectiles struck their car—eggs, tomatoes, and
water balloons filled with yellow liquid. She didn't ask
as he shrugged and flicked on the windshield wipers.

He turned right on Rue des Boulangers and followed
it around a bend to a little hole-in-the-wall eatery called
the Mobster Diner at number 20. There was a line out
the door. Beside the restaurant was a narrow dead-end
alley.

"What do you think?" she asked.

"The food must be good. So many people."

"Not what I meant."

"It seems not to matter then what do I think," he said.
"What do *you* think is of greater importance."

She directed him to back down the alley and park.
She confirmed with the what3words app that this was
the location—*///lectures.wagers.cherry.*

Her heart was pounding.

"This is it," she said.

"Now what?" he asked.

She exited the small, unmarked police car. The alley was dark, perennially in the shadow cast by the five-
story buildings that surrounded it on three sides. Along
the walls were several service doors. She tried opening them. Surprisingly, all of them yielded when pulled,
but they seemed to go where one might expect. That
is, into unremarkable entrances and hallways within
the buildings. Not sure what she was looking for, she

tried the last door. This one was shorter than the others and shaped more like an ancient gate into a cemetery. Its wood was grayed from the ravages of time, and the hinges were antique and made of steel or iron. And it didn't open.

Nothing quite piques the interest of an urban explorer like a locked door.

It moved enough that it banged against the deadbolt with each pull, but there was no way to unlock it that she could see.

"What is it?" asked Hugo, arriving by her side.

"It's locked."

He walked back to the car and popped the trunk. He returned carrying a Halligan bar, a multipurpose breaching tool favored by fire departments and law enforcement worldwide.

"Here," he said, presenting it to her.

"It's your bar—you give it a try."

"I am here to facilitate, not to break and enter."

She rolled her eyes. She had used versions of the Halligan downrange when she was with ISA and again while doing breaching training with the FBI. She inserted the claw end into the gap, placing the tips of the fork above and below the bolt holding the door closed. She began to pry, and when that alone didn't work, she began to rock the long handle backward and forward, the tips of the claw sliding deeper with each pass, digging into the doorway's soft wooden frame.

"Help me," she said.

"We do not have a warrant. I cannot assist you breaking into these premises. The prefect has not authorized this."

"Are you kidding me? There's probably a nuclear bomb somewhere inside, and you're worried about forcibly entering without a warrant?"

"*Ah, putain!*" he said, using the French equivalent

of an f-bomb, only slightly softer and more socially acceptable. "What do you mean a *nuclear bomb*? No one told me this. I only overheard you speaking of a *bomb*. Not a *nuclear bomb*. I am supposed to help you with getting information, not with a scene from *Mission: Impossible*."

"Are you going to help or not? I need you because you're stronger and taller than I am. I don't have the leverage."

"You are a terrible liar. But, okay," he said, taking control of the tool.

Alex was a strong woman by any measure, but Hugo Blanc outweighed her by a good forty pounds. He started rocking the Halligan bar, and within seconds the door popped open.

"Great work!" she said.

They stepped inside the dark passage and pulled the door closed behind them. Blanc leaned the tool against the wall and withdrew a small LED flashlight from his duty belt. He turned it on and twisted the head of the light to spread the beam, lighting up a sloping passage that disappeared into the darkness somewhere ahead. The passage seemed quite ordinary, lined in concrete of a seemingly recent vintage.

"Yes, wonderful," he said. "We are in a dark tunnel that leads deeper into other dark tunnels in the bowels of Paris looking for a nuclear bomb. Splendid work, Hugo."

"Look." She pointed to scuff marks on the ground where wheel marks, perhaps from a heavy cart, had been made in the dust and dirt. "Let's go."

"Excellent. I think we should report where we are."

"Not until we find something worth reporting."

"So, are we going to wander aimlessly through these tunnels? Until what?"

"We'll know when we know."

"American optimism," he quipped.

The passage descended the equivalent of several stories below ground level, the temperature dropping perceptibly as they walked. The walls and ceiling were lined with large-diameter pipes and heavy-duty wire conduit. Old or not, it appeared to be little more than a utility service tunnel. There were no skeletons anywhere to be seen. If these were the catacombs, Alex was disappointed.

They moved quickly until they arrived at a fork in the passage. A wooden sign affixed to the wall offered two handwritten choices: to the left, the Panthéon. To the right, Jardins des Plantes.

"Which way?" Hugo asked.

She glanced at the ground but didn't see any scrapings. "I don't know. This is your city."

"Le Panthéon is west of where we started," he said.

"And the Jardins des Plantes is close to the conference center where the summit is being held, right?"

"Yes."

"Then we should go right."

They turned toward the new passage, which was much darker and noticeably cooler. She shivered.

"Are you cold?" he asked.

"I'll live," she said, rubbing her arms.

He stopped her and shone his flashlight along the wall until he came across a makeshift electrical panel. It was just a crude wooden box with wires coming out.

"What is it?" Alex asked.

He opened the box and flipped a switch inside. Alex watched, stunned, as small bulbs strung the length of the tunnel lit up and gave off dim light in the passageway. She looked back at Hugo.

"The cataphiles do this," he said. "They clip into existing electrical services above or inside the tunnels so they can explore and do the things they like to do down here, whatever that is."

Looking around, it was apparent the character of the tunnel had changed to something hewn from the stone.

"We are inside the ancient tunnels now," he said.

They quickly came upon more wheel tracks. As they followed them, her phone rang. She answered. It was Chief Bressard.

"I've tried you twice already."

Alex peered at the display on her phone.

"I only have one bar. We're underground, so I don't expect I'll have a signal much longer."

"Alexandra, the demonstrations have turned violent and dynamic. The resources of the French police are stretched thin. We won't be able to send you any help if you need it."

She could barely make out his words.

"What?" she said, but the signal was lost. She got the gist of his message.

*Shit was happening topside, and help was far, far away.*

She had heard that before.

The walls of the tunnel were no longer lined in concrete. The whole passage they walked was carved out of the earth, which appeared to be made of limestone.

"I thought six million Parisians were buried down here," she said.

"This is true, but it is not the whole story. *Les Catacombes de Paris* is a bit of a misnaming. The section of the tunnels that became the ossuary comprises only a small portion of the underground *carrières de Paris*—the quarries of Paris," he explained. "There are hundreds of kilometers of tunnels running parallel as well as above and below each other all over the city."

"But why did they build such an extensive network of tunnels?"

The low-wattage incandescent bulbs were strung at roughly fifty-foot intervals and gave off a gloomy haze at best as they walked.

"A lot of limestone was needed to build the modern city you see aboveground. But when Paris's overflowing cemeteries started to collapse into the basements of homes in the eighteenth century, Parisians grew understandably upset at the mess and, of course, the reek from the dead bodies. They moved six million dead Parisians from all the cemeteries into the abandoned quarries below the city. The ossuary occupies only a few kilometers of tunnels, but most Parisians still refer to the entire complex as *les catacombes*. The French believe it is romantic. And perhaps in a horrible way it is."

As they rounded a bend, the passageway continued, but Alex noted that the tracks had disappeared again. She backtracked a hundred feet and realized whatever was being pushed had turned off the main passage. She followed the marks on the ground into a smaller passage that opened into another chamber, twenty feet by fifty feet. The chamber was empty, but as Hugo shone his flashlight around, it lit up the opening of a large hole in the floor.

"Pass me your flashlight," she said.

Hugo handed it over. Alex approached the hole, wondering how stable the ground beneath her was. Sprawling out on her belly, she shone the light into the void, wondering which would scare her more: a hole full of skeletons or a void containing a thermonuclear bomb set to go off.

"*Fais attention.*" *Be careful,* said Hugo.

An electrical cord descended through the center of the hole. The flashlight's beam caught a platform some twenty feet below where the line ended. It was attached to an articulating boom, which in turn was attached to a mechanized lift system.

"My stars," Hugo said. "How did they get that machine in there?"

"What do you think?" she asked him.

"I think I have a long life to live if I don't follow you into this hole."

"Where's your sense of adventure?"

"At home with my wife and children, who I would very much like to see again at the end of this day."

Above her dangled a remote control to operate the boom. She grabbed it and shone the light on it. It seemed straightforward enough. She brought the platform up and, after a couple of tries, lined it up with the hole in the floor. Moments later, they were balanced together in the center of the platform, Alex using the onboard controls to lower them into the darkness as Hugo reminded her he didn't want to become the newest permanent resident of the Paris Catacombs.

# CHAPTER 57

Viktor Gerasimov stared out a panoramic window in the reception hall on the twenty-fourth floor of Zamansky Tower. More frequently referred to as just *the Tower* by users on campus, the building seemed incongruously placed in the middle of one of the university quadrangles on the Sorbonne campus, its purpose a mystery to outsiders.

A short distance away, the spire of Notre-Dame de Paris again reached for the heavens. The medieval Catholic cathedral on Île de la Cité, whose construction began in 1163 CE, had survived the ravages of conflict and fire for nearly a millennium. It had flourished in much the same way as a forest is rejuvenated after the detritus of centuries is purged in flames.

This, he realized now, was an analogy for his plan. Paris was the metaphorical forest in the path of the wildfire. It needed to be razed to halt the cancer of America's self-righteous ideology of exceptionalism in order to allow the beautiful flower that was Russia to blossom in a new global order.

A knock at the door took him out of his spell. Behind him, Sergei Malkin went to open it.

"I don't know why I have been summoned, Viktor, but this is highly unusual."

"Everything about what we are doing is highly unusual, Mr. Kane."

Daniel Kane stepped inside past Malkin. "Well, it's perilous. I don't like it."

"Tell me, Kane. Why is the Interpol woman here in Paris?"

"I have no idea. I was as surprised as you are to hear it. She was directed to Washington but chose to remain here."

Gerasimov assessed Kane's body language and decided he was telling the truth. "She found a key in Anna's—sorry, *Krysten's*—apartment that led her to a safe-deposit box in London. From there, she learned much about our beloved Anna's past. This has left us exposed," he said.

"I was not aware until Tatiana called me after their confrontation outside the bank."

"It should not have been Agent Martel who discovered this key."

"No, Viktor. Both MI5 and Scotland Yard missed it."

"Yes, and this allowed Special Agent Martel to make her way to Turkey, and now to Paris. She knows too much. We cannot afford any more interference."

"Perhaps Major Douglas betrayed you. Or perhaps the CIA tracked your movements from there to here."

"Nonsense."

Gerasimov could see the tension building in Kane's shoulders. He might have been a fool, but he wasn't a complete idiot. He was apparently still able to intuit the presence of personal jeopardy. But then, even a rat could sense the presence of a bigger predator.

"We are in the final few hours of our mission, Mr. Kane. The bomb will detonate at nineteen hundred hours. That's seven P.M."

"I am aware what nineteen hundred hours means."

"That should give you enough time to evacuate your

prime minister and the rest of the British delegation. Unless you choose not to, of course."

He checked his watch. "Yes, well, we shall see."

"Even as we stand here, our little lady friend is searching for the bomb. You will go with Sergei to ensure it is safe and that she hasn't found it."

Kane turned nervously to Malkin, who was smiling. "Me? Why me? The tunnels are filled with skeletons—I don't like it."

"Sometimes you have to step over the bodies, Mr. Kane."

"But I know nothing about bombs or explosives."

"We need manpower, not technical experts," he said. "And we need a face Special Agent Martel will trust, should you encounter her in the catacombs. We cannot afford for anyone to tamper with the weapon." He pointed to his iPad. "I have the remote control in my possession, but there is no telling what could happen if someone attempts to disarm it. Understand?"

"I understand, Colonel."

"If you want to be paid the fortune you demanded from the Russian government for your services, this is the final act I expect of you on this mission."

Like a cat realizing it was about to be given its fix of catnip, Kane agreed.

"I will text you soon with our rendezvous point. Keep your phone on," said Malkin.

With that, Kane left.

"Colonel," Malkin said. "I can handle the bomb and this Interpol woman. I do not need this weasel with me."

"I think there is no need for Mr. Kane to exit the catacombs once you have secured the device, Sergei. Perhaps he can join the other residents there."

Malkin smiled. "Yes, Colonel."

\* \* \*

PARIS CATACOMBS, PARIS

Alex and Hugo walked along the limestone tunnels one level below where they had previously been—tunnels that had been carved out centuries before by men toiling beneath the city with picks and axes under conditions she couldn't fathom. The tunnels were nearly four or five feet wide and six feet tall. As their journey continued, they came across a flooded section and pushed through the knee-deep water for a couple hundred feet.

*Great. It's not enough to be worried about a nuclear bomb and skeletons. Now I'm thinking about what might be swimming in here . . . snakes, rats . . . ugh.*

Alex stumbled on submerged rocks once or twice—at least she hoped they were rocks—but on each occasion was able to recover her footing before going for a swim. She turned on her phone's flashlight. Coming out of the water, they entered a dry section of tunnel strewn with the femurs and skulls of long-dead Parisians.

She stopped in her tracks.

Coming up behind her, Hugo said, "I have visited the tourist area of these tunnels and have seen the skeletons stacked neatly and with deference. And I have raided sections where illegal gatherings were going on. But to see the bones of my ancestors scattered haphazardly like twigs or the scraps from a scavenged feast seems an unholy sight." He crossed himself, and they moved on.

Alex tried to avoid stepping on any of the human remains. They were violating sacred ground, but she convinced herself it was for the greater good as she made several apologies under her breath. She bent over a few times to gently move a bone or a piece of skull so she could place a foot down without stepping on anything.

Eventually, the scattering of bones petered out, and the passage was clear again.

She checked her watch.

"It's five fifty-five," she said. "What time is the gala?"

"Cocktails are at six. Dinner at seven," replied Hugo.

"And to think we're going to miss it."

"I left my tuxedo at home anyway."

A hundred feet farther along, they came upon what appeared to be a newly excavated opening in the wall. The air here was thick, heavy with moisture and centuries of stale air. The hairs on the back of her neck were raised like the hackles of a predator sensing a threat.

"Do you know where we are?" she asked Hugo.

"I am not an expert," he said, sniffing the air. "But I believe this network of tunnels should have ended one hundred meters back. When we dropped down a level, I think we entered a section closer to the River Seine that should have been sealed off, even from the cataphiles."

"How do you know?"

"The rockface changes as we approach the river. Look, the color is even different," he said, shining his light on the wall. It was true. It seemed paler in color. Dustier. "I am not a geologist, but this might be a deposit of gypsum, which is much softer than the Lutetian limestone used for making buildings. It is more prone to cracking, and cracks in the wall bring flooding from the river. I'm sure we are near or even under the Sorbonne, in the prohibited activities zone, almost at the Jardins des Plantes next to the university." He sniffed the air again, like a bloodhound on a scent trail. "Can you smell that?"

She nodded. The air was dank, but she could smell the pungent fragrance of a lush forest as if it were emanating from the walls themselves, delivered from the surface sixty-five feet above them.

She signaled Hugo to stay quiet, then cautiously moved through the gap. A passage led straight on for another fifty feet before taking a sharp turn. She stopped.

"What is it?" he whispered.

"I thought I heard something," she said, listening intently. Then, "Nothing."

As they moved on, Hugo asked, "If we encounter someone alone, a guard or a lookout perhaps, should we arrest them?"

She shook her head. "I can tell you only work the riot squad."

"I don't understand."

"I mean, that's not a very tactically sound idea. If there's one, there's more."

"What does that mean?"

"It's something a deputy US marshal drilled into me after I messed up at Hogan's Alley," she said, referring to the tactical training facility at the FBI Academy. "Marshal Cameron always told me, *See one, think two.* I modified it a bit."

"I like his better."

"Me too."

At the junction, Alex crouched and peered around the corner into a circular vault thirty feet in diameter and twenty feet high, lit by two racks of LED utility work lights. On the far end of the chamber, another tunnel led off into the darkness. Against the wall across from her sat what appeared to be a wheeled equipment trolley. Atop the rack lay a pointy cylindrical device measuring eleven feet long by a foot in diameter. Attached to it was a bright orange tail assembly kit.

# CHAPTER 58

H oly shit!"

Somehow it came out as a whisper.

"What?" whispered Hugo from behind her.

Alex turned to him. "We found the bomb."

She looked down at her cell phone, hoping to be able to call Chief Bressard—still no service. She opened the camera app and snapped pictures for scale and perspective, making sure both the sound and the flash were off. Then she laughed at herself—always planning for the after-action report, even in the face of a nuclear bomb that would leave no trace of her or her phone should it go off. It was the ultimate act of wishful thinking.

She crept out of the passage and stepped down into the chamber. It sat two feet below the level of the tunnel from which she emerged.

"What are you doing?" asked Hugo.

"What's it look like I'm doing? I'm going to get a closer look."

"Why would you do that? We need to go back and tell everyone what we've found so they can send in the Army."

"Two problems with your idea: one, we don't know if it's set to detonate. And if it is, it would be nice to know how much time is left before it goes off. And two, what if we don't make it out?"

"Why wouldn't we make it out?"

"We might not be the only ones down here, Hugo." He quickly glanced into the tunnel behind him.

"Okay, then. *On y va*," he whispered. *Let's go.*

Her first objective was to clear the tunnel on the opposite side of the room. She exchanged her phone for her Glock, and out of necessity, cut directly across to the space. When she got near the tunnel entrance, she pressed herself against the wall and carefully stuck her head around the corner. This passage, too, was lit by widely spaced low-wattage bulbs. In the dim light, she could see for fifty, maybe seventy-five feet before the tunnel rounded a bend.

She called to Hugo. "Clear," she said.

He emerged from the tunnel to join her as she walked over to the B61-12 thermonuclear bomb. She involuntarily shivered as a chill ran up her spine.

"I cannot believe this is a nuclear bomb," said Hugo. "Do you know anything about it? Can you defuse one?"

She didn't answer. Instead, she looked at the bomb, identical to the one Colonel Mendez had shown her and Caleb at Incirlik Air Base. The flap over the ten-by-three-inch control panel was unscrewed. She took a deep breath and lifted the cover, letting it rest on the hinge.

"*Ah, putain!*" she exclaimed.

Unlike the unit they had seen at Incirlik, there was a red LED clock below the permissive action link panel, the nuclear bomb's system interface. The display showed 00:52:35 and counting down. The PAL was composed of twelve switches, just like on the bomb at Incirlik. There was zero chance she'd be able to guess the alphanumeric code.

She checked the dial-a-yield setting. It was pointing to the B61-12's maximum output of fifty kilotons. Less than an hour remained until time ran out and the nuclear bomb exploded, vaporizing half of Paris in a nanosecond and turning the other half into a zone of destruction that would kill, maim, or displace millions. Not to mention that the explosion would turn the city into a radioactive lake when the boundaries of the Seine disappeared from the blast. The underground structure of the catacombs would reflect and magnify the shockwave throughout its entire network, collapsing the city into the limestone void. The waters of the Seine would flood the space left by the hollowed-out earth, spelling Armageddon for Paris and the surrounding regions.

The trickle-down effects were too numerous to comprehend. Again, Alex shuddered at the thought.

She studied the controls and tried to recall what Colonel Mendez had told them. All the while, the clock ticked down. She reached for the yield control.

"What are you doing?" Hugo exclaimed.

"I'm going to see if I can turn the yield down."

"What will that do?"

"Hopefully, not set it off."

"What?"

"Well, actually, I'm hoping it will make a smaller bang if it does go off."

"That's not much of a consolation."

She thought about what Colonel Mendez said, about the bomb having an anti-tamper mechanism. Even if the settings she dialed in didn't take effect, maybe she could cause it to register that the system was being tampered with. This in turn could make the bomb mis-detonate and become inert. Of course, according to Mendez, to *mis-detonate* meant to fire off the equivalent of a pipe bomb, the explosive equivalent of four or five pounds of TNT, to deform the plutonium core. She was no explosives expert, but she was sure that to accomplish that end goal required a significant explosion—one that would likely kill both her and Inspector Clouseau if they were close enough when it exploded.

She placed her hand on the control, turning it four clicks counterclockwise into the off position. A red light flashed and a buzzer sounded twice. It didn't sound promising, but she had no way to know. Next, she tried turning the environment setting from the GND setting, which she assumed meant *ground*—the bomb's laydown or subterranean detonation mode—and dialed it back to the off position as well.

Another red flash and double buzzer. At least there wasn't a loud bang.

"Did it work? Is it off?" asked Hugo.

"I don't think so," she answered.

"What now?"

She peered into the side of the device, hoping to find a way to trigger the self-destruct sequence. Obviously, playing with the switches wasn't going to be enough. She would have to try something more invasive. She debated ripping the control module off completely, but the uncertainty of what that might do gave her pause.

*What if that sped up the countdown? Or triggered the nuclear blast?*

She recalled seeing a poster-size schematic drawing on the wall of the weapons maintenance building in Turkey. It included a simplified illustration of the bomb in a disassembled state. While she couldn't remember many of the details of the drawing, she recalled that most of the unit's sensitive systems—radar, guidance, and trigger—were contained behind the nose cone. Perhaps if she removed it, a solution would reveal itself to her.

She moved to the tip of the nuke. The cone was fastened to the fuselage by a dozen Torx screws, the same type as on the cover of the control panel.

"I don't suppose you have a set of Torx screwdrivers on you, do you?" she asked Hugo. He gave her a blank stare and shook his head.

She pulled out her folding knife and pressed the tip of the blade into the top of one of the screws, but there was nothing there for it to bite on.

A sound coming from the tunnel from which they had emerged caught her attention. Before Hugo could even turn his head in that direction, Alex had dropped her knife and brought her gun up. A figure emerged from the darkness holding a gun.

"Don't shoot!" the figure said.

The man was holding a SIG Sauer in his right hand that Alex recognized instantly.

"Caleb?"

"I come in peace," he said.

"Maybe, but you almost got blown to bits."

"That's what I hope to avoid."

"Who is this?" asked Hugo. "And why is every American in my country carrying a gun?"

Alex lowered her weapon. "Hugo, this is Caleb. He's—"

Caleb filled in the blank. "I'm her partner."

Alex jumped back in. "I was going to say, he's with CIA. We're not partners."

"We work together."

"Not the same."

"Can we please focus on the bomb?" pleaded Hugo.

Alex picked her knife up off the ground. "You don't happen to have a Torx key set on you, do you?"

"As a matter of fact . . ."

Caleb holstered his gun and reached under his shirt, removing a multitool from his belt. "I ride a Harley.

Some of the screws on it are Torx." Among the various paraphernalia on the multitool were different-sized Torx-head screwdrivers. "Try one of these."

She took it from him and, on the second try, struck pay dirt.

"There's a bit of luck," she said.

"Some of us like to call that *preparedness,*" he shot back.

In under a minute, the nose cone of the B61 was off. Alex set it on the ground, and the three of them peered into the business end of the bomb. They could see the GPS satellite and laser guidance systems, as well as the radar airburst fuse and impact fuses.

Caleb was breathing down her neck. "Right behind the guidance system and fuses should be the physics package of this beast," he whispered. "The warhead."

The gravity of the situation weighed heavy on her. It wasn't hard to be both in awe and terror while beholding this weapon.

"Isn't it radioactive?" asked Hugo. Alex and Caleb both turned to him. "I mean, it *is* a nuclear bomb. Doesn't it contain, you know, radioactive material?"

"It would be nice to have a dosimeter or radiation monitor," said Alex. "But we don't have one. Let's assume the bigger threat would be not being able to stop this bomb from going off."

"Any bright ideas?" asked Caleb.

"Yup."

She reached inside the fuselage with both hands, behind the electronics, and started pulling. The bomb rocked back and forth on the wheeled rack, but it was held in place securely with tie-down straps. She felt the components bend but not break.

"This is your plan?" asked Hugo, backing away.

"Some help would be nice."

Caleb came up alongside her and stuck his big hand

into the gap Alex had made. Soon, electronic components and wires were being tugged from their fittings until, at last, with one mighty pull together, the entire assembly came out in their hands as they fell backward.

Alex dusted herself off and checked the LED clock display: T minus 00:41:16 and still counting.

"Okay, options," she said. "Nothing we've tried so far seems to have worked. We can sit here and continue to mess around with a live nuke in full countdown mode with forty minutes left, and maybe we'll disarm it—"

"Or maybe you will accidentally detonate it," Hugo warned, having backed away to the entrance of the tunnel.

"Right," Caleb said. "One of us could run back topside for help."

"Yes, but there is just over half an hour left until that thing explodes," Hugo said. "We would never make it out and back in time. It is not possible."

"He's right," Alex said. She could think of only one other way to deactivate the bomb. She made her decision. She stood up and pulled out her Glock.

"What are you doing?" cried Hugo.

"The only way to render this bomb safe is to make it think it's being tampered with. I was hoping that removing those components would do the trick, but it didn't."

"So now you're going to shoot it?" he asked. "*Merde!* That's crazy, even for an American. You cannot shoot this nuclear bomb. We will all die!"

"I would listen to him, Special Agent Martel."

Alex turned in the direction of the other tunnel. The voice, with its heavy Russian accent, came from the mouth of a big man pointing a gun at her head.

# CHAPTER 59

Who the hell are you?" asked Alex.

"I am the man who is going to make certain Colonel Gerasimov's plan is executed without disruption," said Malkin. "With what little time you have left, you may call me Sergei. Drop your weapon, please."

She considered shooting him, but he kept himself partially concealed behind the tunnel wall. Conversely, she presented an easy target for him and his Beretta. Given the rapidity with which the other Russians she had encountered these last few days escalated to violence, she had no doubt he would shoot her if the moment seemed right. So, she did as instructed, dropping her gun into the dirt at her feet.

"Kick it toward me."

She did, and it slid five feet ahead of her.

"Now you," Malkin said to Caleb. "Lift your shirt slowly and throw your weapon down."

He pulled his SIG and tossed it next to Alex's Glock.

Malkin stepped forward into the light. "You can come out now," he called.

Alex peered over her shoulder to where Hugo had been, thinking Malkin meant him. But Hugo had disappeared into the darkness somewhere behind her. Then a man emerged from the tunnel where Malkin had appeared and stepped into the light next to him.

*Kane.*

"You son of a bitch," said Alex.

"What kind of way is that to greet an old friend, Special Agent Martel?" he asked, as pompous as ever. "Especially a kindred intelligence officer like yourself."

"I'm not an intelligence officer."

Caleb looked at her, hurt. "I thought we were partners."

"Well, we're not," she said, shrugging her shoulders.

"Not yet," he added.

"How optimistic," said Malkin. "And touching. You have caused us much trouble, Agent Martel."

"I'm only just getting started."

"You Americans. Always possessed of such optimism. This is not a trait that many of my countrymen share with you."

"For good reason," she replied. "Your president is an asshole."

"He would be disappointed to hear you say such things. I heard he enjoyed meeting you earlier. He said you have bigger balls than most of the men who serve under him."

"I'll work even harder to earn his admiration once I'm finished here."

"Such bravado," said Kane. "Krysten was a lot like you. Perhaps more than you realize. In fact, it's what attracted me to her in the first place."

"I'm sure she was just reeling you into her trap."

"As it turns out, that's exactly what she was doing."

"So, how exactly did it go down, Kane?"

"I'm embarrassed to say it's the age-old story—boy

meets girl, boy falls in love, girl turns out to be a Russian spy."

"Almost biblical," quipped Caleb.

"I caught Krysten accessing sensitive, compartmentalized information she had no reason to be reviewing, and when I confronted her, she turned on her feminine charms. Before I knew it, I was providing highly classified intel for love and money. I had betrayed my marriage and my country. And in the end, when I learned she had grown a conscience and wanted to back out of the Paris plot, I sold her out to Directorate 13 for an awfully large sum."

Alex shook her head. "Congratulations, Kane. You managed to complete the asshole trifecta."

"Must be nice to be so smug, Ms. Martel."

"If by *smug* you mean I have never betrayed my country, then I'm guilty as charged."

"Never say never, Alex. It happened in the blink of an eye. One day I was a detective inspector with Scotland Yard being overlooked for promotions, the next I was a mid-level intelligence officer watching other, less worthy individuals climb the ranks. When a beautiful woman with a bucketload of money happened by, well, let's just say the moment to finally reap the rewards for my public service suddenly fell into my lap."

"How was Krysten killed?"

"Are you sure you want to know?"

"Humor me."

"Ask him," said Kane, pointing to Malkin. "He was there."

Malkin gave a tight-lipped grin.

She wasn't prepared for her reaction to Malkin's callous display. A rush of heat rose up her neck and into her cheeks. It didn't go unnoticed.

"Oh, Alexandra," said Kane. "I think you really do want to kill someone right now."

"I can think of a couple of good candidates." Her hands were itching, and her fingers involuntarily balled up into fists.

Kane walked over to the B61 and checked the time remaining. "Well, I for one don't see much point in harboring grudges. Let bygones be bygones, I say."

"What's the plan then, Kane?" asked Caleb.

"Well, many of the Russian delegation have been safely flown out. Shame the Americans and my fellow Brits are still here, though, along with President Sergachev."

"You're just going to let this happen and let them die, along with hundreds of thousands of others?" asked Alex.

"In a word, yes. I was dead-set against it in the beginning, but it's amazing what a bunch of zeroes after a number can do to give you a whole new outlook."

"You're a psychopath, Kane."

"More sociopath, I think. But don't worry. You won't have to put up with me much longer. What should we do, Sergei?"

Malkin raised his gun.

"That's what I thought. With only half an hour left until this little beastie blows up, we don't have any time to waste. A helicopter is waiting for us after all."

Malkin cocked the hammer of his Beretta.

Just then, a shot rang out from the tunnel behind her. Malkin cried out in pain and dropped to a knee as his own gun spit fire, blood flowing freely from his right bicep. Alex heard the bullet from his gun zip past her ear.

She somersaulted forward and retrieved her Glock from the ground. By the time she brought it to bear where Kane and Malkin had been, they had both disappeared back into the tunnel. She fired two shots after them, the sound of gunfire ear-splitting in the confined space.

*The bomb. I have to disable the bomb.*

"Cover me," she called to Caleb, but he was already diving for cover as more shots emanated from the tunnel.

Hugo screamed out in pain. "*Je suis touché!*" he called. *I'm hit!*

Alex turned to see him crumple to the ground. Caleb raced over and dragged him deeper into the tunnel. Alex fired a half-dozen shots into the other tunnel to suppress any return fire. Then she emptied the rest of her Glock's magazine into the front of the B61-12.

Sparks flew, and smoke curled out from the tip of the bomb. Five short beeps emanated from the bomb in rapid succession, followed by a loud buzz. Alex looked at the display on the B61's control panel as Caleb fired more shots toward the tunnel in which Malkin and Kane had taken cover. It flashed 00:00:10 and began counting down.

"Shit!" she yelled. "Caleb, run! We're out of time!"

She bolted for the tunnel where Caleb had dragged Hugo. She grabbed him by the belt, and together they backpedaled as fast as they could as far into the tunnel as they could get.

"Cover!" she yelled, and they both dropped down on top of Hugo, pressing themselves as flat and as close to the ground as possible.

Alex had felt the concussive force of blast waves many times before. She prepared for this one as best she could—she pressed her body onto Hugo's, low to the ground, in line with the expected shock wave, facing away: mouth open, eyes closed, arms above her head, hands covering her neck. But when the explosion came, it was like nothing she had ever seen, heard, or felt before. While the power of the blast was exponentially less than almost any she had been exposed to downrange, the difference was they were in a confined space and within fifty or sixty feet of the explosion.

The ceiling, walls, and tunnel reflected the blast wave, magnifying it as it traveled away from the site of the explosion. Fortunately, the angle at the entrance to the tunnel shielded them from most of the shrapnel, but not all. They were enveloped by a tornado-force gust of wind lasting just a few seconds that lifted them momentarily off the ground before dropping them back to earth again several meters down the tunnel.

After it had passed, Alex felt her lungs fighting against her efforts to breathe, spasming inside her chest like an empty water balloon whose sides were stuck together. She tried to inhale, but there was just no air. Her clothes were torn and she was covered in cuts and abrasions.

The loudest sound she could hear, in fact the only sound, was the ringing in her ears. She opened and closed her mouth like a guppy, rolled off whomever she was laying on, and prayed that soon some air would find its way into her lungs.

*Please, God, let me breathe.*

The tunnel was filled with smoke and dust and the acrid post-blast smell of a polymer-bonded high explosive. On top of the smoke and the haze, her brain was in a fog, and she had the worst case of hypoxia-induced bed-spins imaginable. Finally, a second gust brought with it cool, breathable air. She sucked it in, gasping, hungry, swallowing big gulps of it. The oxygen it carried fed her starving brain, and slowly her focus returned.

*Caleb. Hugo. The bomb.*

She got to her knees and crawled through her pain to the first body she found. It was facedown. She rocked its shoulder. "Hey! Hey, can you hear me?"

A groan, and then a face turned up toward her. It was Hugo. Alive. He had taken a bullet in his ballistic vest, but he was alive. He was conscious and breathing and could focus on her. All were good signs. She propped him up against the wall and moved on.

Another body. Caleb. He was supine, eyes closed, head lolled to the side. Only a few of the lights in the tunnel had survived the blast, and she had a tough time seeing him clearly, but his chest was rising and falling in a regular pattern, albeit too quickly. Her medic brain kicked in and she detected the coppery, sweet scent of blood in the air. She ran her hands over him and stopped when they got warm and sticky over his abdomen. She searched for her phone and turned the light on. Lifting his shirt, she found a shrapnel injury to his lower abdomen with a partial evisceration. An eight-inch section of bowel protruded through his skin. She had no dressings, no abdominal pads, so she pulled his shirt back down and placed his hands over the area, but they slid off.

"Caleb! Can you hear me?"

He wasn't responding. His pulse was thready. He was bleeding internally and was going into hypovolemic shock. He needed surgery—if he survived that long.

*The bomb.*

She somehow found her gun lying next to Hugo and exchanged its empty magazine for a fresh one. She listened for any sounds that might suggest either Kane or Malkin was waiting for her in the carved-out chamber. She poked her head around the side of the wall into the main chamber. One LED utility light remained functional and still cast a faint glow across the space. There was no sign of anyone else there with her, so she holstered her pistol.

A low rumble shook the floor beneath her feet like distant thunder.

She crept silently on her hands and knees over rubble to where the bomb had been. Some of the ceiling above had collapsed. Next to the trolley, a four-foot-wide hole had opened in the ground, but Alex couldn't tell how deep it was, just that it was filled with blackness. Avoiding it, she lifted chunks of rock and stone until she could see what was left of the bomb.

The explosion had ripped it apart, leaving a jagged hole where the nose cone and warhead had been. Now, it was just an empty shell, a barely recognizable chunk of scrap metal. Alex shone her phone's light around in search of the warhead.

She came across a milk-can-shaped metal drum two-and-a-half feet long by a foot in diameter. The top and side were dented like someone had taken a sledgehammer to it. She had no doubt she was looking at the results of the mis-detonation. Not having a radiation survey meter on hand, she chose not to linger near the damaged warhead for long. Even intact, it would be emitting gamma and neutron radiation. Damaged as it was, its contents of plutonium, uranium, deuterium, tritium, beryllium, and whatever else was in there could additionally be leaking alpha and beta radiation particles in sufficient concentrations to make her sick—now or years from now—if she breathed it in or left it to coat her cut and abraded skin; if it didn't kill her outright.

More rumbling. A stream of water entered the chamber where she stood. It washed over her feet and found a path into the newly formed hole in the floor of the cavern. What had Hugo said about gypsum and the cave wall this far in? *It is more prone to cracking, and cracks in the wall bring flooding from the river.* Had the explosion she triggered to neutralize the bomb created a breach in the wall somewhere? Water filled the chamber quickly. Secure in the knowledge that the bomb had been deactivated, she needed to get back to Caleb and Hugo and get them out of here.

From behind her, she heard a man's gravelly voice. "You bitch!"

# CHAPTER 60

She turned to see Sergei standing there, his clothes in tatters, like her own. Blood streamed from a cut on his forehead as well as from his ears and nose. His face was plastered with a wet mask of chalky dust. His gun was pointed at her. He pulled the trigger, but the hammer fell with a click.

She had no time to draw her own weapon before he lunged at her. They went to the ground hard with Alex on the bottom. He straddled her hips and laid his thick hands around her throat.

"You have ruined everything! I am going to kill you like I killed that traitor bitch Anna!"

Anna. *Krysten.*

She couldn't speak. She couldn't breathe. But she was filled with rage: mind, body, and soul. Her windpipe and carotid arteries were clamped off in his vise-like grip. She struggled hard beneath him, trying to lift her hips off the ground. She reached for her knife, but his position blocked it from her grasp. The depth of the water around her was rising. It lapped against her cheeks and poured into her mouth. She didn't know if Sergei would strangle her first or if she would drown. With a few more pelvic thrusts, she was able to shift his weight up to her waist. She pulled her legs up and, with great difficulty, hooked her left leg under his right arm. Blood oozed from his bicep where Hugo had grazed him with a bullet earlier. She trapped it in the crook of her knee and squeezed with all her might. He cried out in pain, and his grip fell slack around her throat. She wiggled an arm free and picked up a rock, swinging it hard into the side of his head.

Dazed, he fell off her. She pounced on top of him, punching him repeatedly in the face. He rolled her off him like a toy, and she was thrown backward, landing with a splash in a deep pool of water. She struggled against buoyancy momentarily before regaining her footing. Sergei stood and lunged for her again. If he got hold of her one more time, she was dead. She drew her Glock and fired two rounds into his chest, sending him staggering backward, then one into his forehead to finish him.

*Hearts and minds.*

He crashed forward into the knee-deep water at her feet. She shoved him away and watched as he floated in the stream of rushing water toward what was now a vortex around the chasm in the floor. His body got caught up in the whirlpool, circled around twice, and then disappeared.

Exhausted, she dropped to her knees in the water. "For you, Krysten," she whispered.

\*\*\*

Soon after she had found her way back to Caleb's side, the catacombs filled with the sound of running feet and anxious shouted voices. The water had begun to rise above the level of the passageway's entrance from the chamber. She raised Caleb's head onto her lap and spoke softly, caressing his face as she shivered from the cold and the rush of adrenaline. She checked his abdominal wound. It was bad, but hadn't gotten worse, which was a good sign.

"The bomb is defused. It's safe now," she told him. "Caleb, stay with me."

Hugo still sat with his back against the wall, sore but alive. "Will he live?"

She ignored his question. Too often, she had been asked that same thing as a medic, and after, when she was no longer engaged in the art of saving lives. It was never something she cared to answer. Invariably, whatever she said was a lie.

"Caleb," she whispered. "Please don't die on me."

She felt a dampness on her cheeks but couldn't be sure if it was water from the Seine or her own tears. She brushed at it with the back of her hand.

Soldiers and policemen arrived. Medics in hazmat suits immediately began to treat Caleb. One medic hooked him up to a cardiac monitor, administered oxygen, and placed sterile dressings soaked in saline solution on top of his abdominal wound. Another started a large-bore intravenous line. She looked at Alex briefly before averting her eyes.

Medics came for her as well and, against her objections, gently placed her into a litter to be carried outside. As she was being loaded into an ambulance, she heard a familiar voice.

"Alexandra!" She turned at the sound of her name. It was Bressard. "Are you alright?" he asked. But it was a rhetorical question, and he seized her in an embrace with the strength and love of a father.

Along with Caleb and Hugo, she was CASEVACed away from the Paris Catacombs.

# CHAPTER 61

The conference room on the sixth floor had no windows. Instead, the walls were covered with FBI paraphernalia and a rogue's gallery of Bureau directors, past and present. The current director stared out at Alex from his framed image on the wall between the flags at the front of the room, and she felt an uneasiness about his gaze.

The tribunal reentered the room, led by the assistant director of the FBI's Office of Professional Responsibility. He sat opposite her and opened his brief while two others took their seats on either side. She felt miles away from the world, alone and isolated.

Alex wore a dark navy cotton pantsuit with a white blouse, her hair swept back in a ponytail. For the occasion, she carried a purse just large enough for her badge, gun, and spare mags. It was the only time in memory she had come to the office armed with a handbag.

"Special Agent Martel," began the AD. "We have reviewed your testimony before this tribunal, together with your after-action report from Paris and accompanying affidavits from several other individuals. As you are aware, Chief Martin Bressard of Interpol as well as Secretary General—" here he paused to consult his notes from earlier "—Secretary General Celeste Clicquot have each submitted statements offering evidence of mitigating factors with pronounced exigent circumstances at the time of the events in question. These have been entered into the record."

Alex adjusted in her chair.

"Notwithstanding that the actions performed by you resulted in the deactivation of an American thermonuclear device in Paris, this tribunal has determined that your actions, though timely and even valiant, occurred subsequent to ignoring a direct order reassigning you to the Bureau's headquarters in Washington, DC, where your duties were to continue tracking down the perpetrators of the crime—*to wit* the theft of the thermonuclear gravity bomb from Incirlik Air Base in Adana, Turkey—while continuing to liaise with other federal agencies.

"Having failed to comply with this duly authorized order, we the tribunal find you guilty of one count each of insubordination and dereliction of duty. You are hereby discharged from the employ of the Federal Bureau of Investigation effective immediately. Please surrender your credentials and service weapon before you leave this room. You have sixty days to appeal this finding." He kept his eyes focused on his notes.

Alex's jaw dropped.

"That is all, Miss Martel. You are dismissed."

*Miss Martel.*

She rose from her seat and removed her Glock 19M and three spare magazines from her purse, along with her gold FBI badge and identification card, and placed them in front of her on the long walnut conference table. She wanted to say something, to fight their decision, but it was no use. She didn't understand it, but she knew she couldn't change it.

Silently, she turned and left the room.

\* \* \*

The two additional members of the tribunal exited the boardroom shortly behind Alex, leaving Assistant Director Alan Vankin to ruminate on his thoughts. The career G-man and attorney at the Bureau had led the Office of Professional Responsibility for going on six years. This particular finding and dismissal weren't the first to disturb him, but it was the first dismissal he had been pressured into making by the FBI director himself.

*The Bureau could use an overhaul.*

The door opened, and an African American woman entered, dressed in a smart-casual outfit of dark slacks and a cream-colored blouse. The only visible jewelry she wore was a gold-colored watch and a simple wedding band.

"Deputy Director Thomas, come in," said Vankin. He was polite because he knew he didn't have a choice. And because, as an assistant director of the FBI, he understood the game of politics better than most. "Please, take a seat."

She remained standing. "This won't take long."

"I take it you saw?"

"Yes, I watched the proceedings on the monitor in your office." She smiled soothingly. A practiced smile. "I wanted to thank you personally for your dedication and public service, Mr. Vankin. I know you expressed your desire for a different outcome to the FBI director."

"Yes, well, we can't always get what we want, can we, Ms. Thomas."

She placed her hands on the back of a chair, still warm from where Alex had been seated moments before.

"Not true, Assistant Director Vankin. The CIA never forgets a favor. And now we owe you one."

# EPILOGUE

### NEAR THE BORDER BETWEEN UKRAINE
### AND ROMANIA

The lush vegetation of the Eastern Carpathian Mountains provided good cover. Alex had set up in her hide shortly before dawn, her layered clothing insulating her from the damp and the chill that crept down through the hills during the late summer months at this altitude. She was grateful to be facing east, the rising sun warming her until she was perfectly cozy next to her Barrett MRAD MK22 sniper rifle, chambered in .300 Norma Magnum.

Paris had been saved from a conflagration of biblical proportions, but the events continued to haunt her dreams. It would take time to compartmentalize those memories.

The president of France was going to present Alex with the Legion of Honor, the country's highest order of merit, for her actions. She had tried to decline, but he would not hear of it during the phone call he'd placed personally and insisted it be done at the earliest opportunity. Lieutenant Hugo Blanc of the French National Police would also receive the honor.

Russian president Sergachev and Major General Tikhonov denied any knowledge of the theft of the bomb from Incirlik or subsequent plans, despite mountains of evidence to the contrary. But even as they continued to refute that they or a rogue colonel had been involved, the GRU leaked Colonel Gerasimov's coordinates to the CIA through back channels.

Shortly after, it was said that Tikhonov ran afoul of the president, who was rumored to have personally put a bullet in his head in the basement of the yellow brick building in central Moscow known as Lubyanka.

As for Kane, no one knew for sure. He might have survived the events in the Paris Catacombs or been lost forever, swept away in the waters that filled the lower chambers after the explosion caused a breach in the walls and the River Seine poured in. What was one more skeleton among millions?

An international consortium led by French engineers was able to mitigate the damage beneath the city, and rehabilitation work was underway to shore up any structurally weakened sections of the catacombs. The Inspection Générale des Carrières—the organization that administered, controlled, and maintained the catacombs and former quarries of Paris—planned to increase the frequency of inspections of the entire network, but it was generally assessed that the city was safe and would be good as new in due course.

Her earpiece woke up. "Sierra One, delivery vehicle en route. How copy?"

"Good copy," she replied. "Our helicopter is inbound."

The airfield and designated landing zone were six hundred meters away. She was expecting the Russian troop transport helo to approach from the south. If all went well, she would be able to execute her mission and exfil to the rear before additional resources were brought in to capture or eliminate her.

She had confirmed the settings for her scope multiple times. She had worked through the data and rehearsed the engagement in similar terrain and under similar environmental conditions in the weeks leading up to this deployment. She'd made copious notes for the variables at play in the event that the helicopter came in on a different path, or the wind kicked up, or the temperature rose or dropped, or it began to rain. All these factors and alternate scope settings were recorded on her DOPE card, written in her notebook, and taped into the cover of her lens cap. And they were in her head.

She was ready.

She removed the box magazine from where she had been warming it under her shirt and slapped it into the mag well. Ten rounds of the finest match-grade ammunition were loaded, chosen specifically for this target package and scenario. The .300 Norma Mag bullet could stay supersonic out to more than double the expected distance of this engagement, ensuring stability throughout its flight path. And it would fly flatter, produce less recoil, and be subject to less wind drift than its closest counterparts in similar calibers.

She racked the bolt and fed a round into the chamber.

Her comms lit up again. "Target is confirmed portside front seat. Green light, Shooter."

"Stop calling me *Shooter*."

Twenty seconds later, she heard the bassy *whoop-whoop-whoop* of the helicopter coming up through the low valley. She turned her head to the right and caught sight of the camouflage-patterned Russian Mi-171Sh-VN, sometimes known as the Storm.

Apropos of the moment, she quoted an unknown author and whispered aloud, "Fate whispers to the warrior, *You cannot withstand the storm.* The warrior whispers back, *I am the storm.*"

She flicked off the safety.

The helo was coming in fast and followed the conventional approach path the recce team had plotted. As it got nearer, it slowed in preparation for landing. She searched for the target through her scope. Colonel Viktor Gerasimov sat where the spotters had placed him—portside forward seat in the Storm.

As the helo banked toward her on final approach, it hit the marks she had ranged with her laser rangefinder. Gerasimov loomed large in her Nightforce scope, coming straight on. She held the crosshairs over his forehead and moved her finger inside the trigger guard, then began the slow exhale of breath while applying firm rearward pressure on the trigger.

*In, out, rest, two, three.*

She released the shot. The bullet left the rifle with a firm buck against her shoulder. She watched its contrail split the dense, humid air, and in under half a second, the bullet pierced both the helicopter's polycarbonate windshield and Gerasimov's skull, still traveling at two thousand feet per second. The terminal ballistics were clearly evident by the splatter of brains and blood throughout the aircraft's cockpit.

"Target down."

"Copy, Sierra One."

With the inside of the windshield coated with the contents of the former colonel's skull, the helicopter wobbled until the pilot could adjust. There would be no threat from this aircraft as it pursued a safe landing to preserve the lives of the remaining souls on board.

"We've confirmed remotely from the TOC as well," Caleb said. "Proceed to exfil, Sierra One. A QRF is standing by if needed."

"Copy. Bugging out now."

"And welcome to the team, Shooter."

Alex allowed herself a smile.

"See you back at base," she replied. "Shooter out."

# ACKNOWLEDGMENTS

Inescapably, any attempt to acknowledge the kindness and generosity of those who helped me on my writing journey is doomed to fail. After all, how could I catalog all those who have shaped me, reined in my exuberance, encouraged me to manage my expectations, or taught me to be better at this craft? And seeing as this is my debut novel, a lifetime of gratitude begs to be expressed—a Herculean task, to be sure.

Be that as it may, here is my attempt to recognize as many of these people as possible. To anyone I forget to mention (and there will be many), my oversight reflects my memory and not my estimation of your contribution.

To those who encouraged me early on by telling me, "If you want to write, then just write," know that no truer words have ever been spoken, no better advice given. So, thank you to writers and showrunners **Adam Barken, Mark Ellis, Stephanie Morgenstern,** and **Jeffrey Alan Schechter.**

Writing is a solitary business, but those who do it find ways to connect virtually and in person to network, learn, share knowledge, and generally cavort. I joined the **International Thriller Writers (ITW)** in 2017 and attended **ThrillerFest** in New York City the following summer, which set me on an irreversible trajectory toward acquiring an agent and getting a publishing deal. Many people took me under their wing on that first outing: **Kim "KJ" Howe, Simon Gervais, Samuel Octavius, Anthony Franze, Heather Graham, Kathie Antrim, Brian Andrews, Jeffrey Wilson, James Grady, David Morrell,** and **Lee Child,** to name a few. Each is a writing luminary, yet they took the time to talk shop with "the new guy" and share some of their wisdom.

Additionally, **Simon Gervais** became my good friend, confidant, advisor, and fellow appreciator of good food and fine wine!

As a former long-serving paramedic and police tactical medic, I have first-hand experience in multiple facets of tactical operations. But I still relied on many experts in their respective fields for additional insights and details when writing this story. Some must remain nameless, while others I'm going to acknowledge explicitly. So, special thanks to: **Colonel Kim "KC" Campbell,** US Air Force, Retired, A-10 Warthog pilot extraordinaire, who provided a deeper glimpse into that aircraft's capabilities; **Perry Gammon,** a former Canadian Special Operations Forces Command (CANSOFCOM) sniper and cofounder of Open Air Accuracy Inc., for his hands-on mentoring in the art, science, and discipline of long-range precision shooting; **Joshua Long** for providing insights into the US Air Force Security Forces Squadron; **Don Bentley** for sharing some of his knowledge of helicopters and generally being a nice guy; **Joshua Hood** for helping me revise Alex's backstory; my good buddy **Jack Stewart** for all our chats about everything, for answering questions about aviation, and for putting me in touch with others who did the same; **Paul McKinley** for conversations about Huey helicopters and all that can go wrong in flight; **Ed Miller,** my friend and former tactical medic teammate, who introduced me to Paul; and to **Staff Sergeant Alan Penrose** and members of the Ontario Provincial Police Tactics and Rescue Unit (TRU), alongside whom I had the privilege of serving for many years. To all of you, I absorbed more from you than you will ever know. Any errors or omissions are mine and may reflect a need for brevity, artistic license, or respect for security issues.

A special shout-out to friends and mentors who have read, reviewed, offered constructive feedback, or otherwise answered my questions and queries: **Robert Dugoni, Marc Cameron, Mark Greaney, Jack Carr, Peter James, Brad Taylor,** and **Hannah Mary McKinnon,** all of whom helped spur on my desire to persevere on this journey that is, at times, fraught with challenges and disappointments. And thank you to **Ryan "The Real Book Spy" Steck,** who worked with me to edit my first completed manuscript. His support, encouragement, and teaching helped me become a better writer.

In the world of protective intelligence, two acquaintances are notable for their bodies of work and their generosity of spirit: **Fred Burton** inspired and informed some of Caleb's character, and **Mike Trott** helped make connections. Thank you, sirs, for all you have done and continue to do.

To my good friend and author **Drew Murray,** I appreciate that you're always there to take a text, answer a call, offer advice, commiserate about politics, or share a good meme. I value our friendship.

Other friends and fellow authors who have helped and inspired me are **Taylor Moore**, **Chris Albanese**, **Sean Cameron, Michael Houtz, Samantha Bailey,**

**Linwood Barclay, J.T. Patten, Lawrence Colby, Jason Allison,** and **Don Winslow.** Your friendship and kindness sustain me. Thank you!

Thanks to my literary agent, **John Talbot,** for believing in me and taking a chance. May this novel be merely the first waypoint down a long and fruitful road.

To the good folks at **Minotaur Books,** thanks for seeing the promise in Alex and me. **Joseph Brosnan,** you were the first to read the manuscript and take a gamble on me. To my editor, **Sarah Grill,** it is a pleasure working with you. You have a keen eye and a great sense of this story. Your deep appreciation for Alex may match even my own. **Sara Thwaite,** thank you for your copyediting brilliance. And to the many people at **Minotaur** and **St. Martin's Press** who toil away behind the scenes, including **Stephen Erickson** and **Hector DeJean,** I'm writing these acknowledgments before I have had the privilege of meeting most of you, but I know this ride is going to be a blast!

I didn't deliberately set out to write a novel with a female protagonist. Special Agent Alexandra (Alex) Martel came into being via the inspiration I found through women I have worked with throughout my career. In many ways, Alex is an amalgam of several actual soldiers, paramedics, police officers, and other leaders in their respective fields. Among those who unwittingly helped breathe life into this character: professor/paramedic **Lynne Urszenyi,** police sergeant **Kathy Vellend-Taylor,** registered nurse and emergency preparedness expert **Claudia Cocco,** and emergency management senior administrator and thought leader **Justine Hartley,** to name a few. Still others I haven't and will likely never meet but whose lives and accomplishments inspired and informed Alex's character: US Silver Star recipients **Sergeant Leigh Ann Hester** and

**Specialist Monica Lin Brown;** and British Military Cross recipient **Sergeant Michelle Norris.** I hope my words in this paragraph and throughout *Perfect Shot* illuminate the contributions and valor of these women and all those who answer the call to serve and put themselves in harm's way.

I also wish to express my gratitude to **Andrew and Shirin Preston, Christina Preston, Heather Harrison, Martin Kenneally, Cynthia Martel, Trevor Lang, Glenn Gosling-Cannell,** and others who read early drafts of my writing, supported and encouraged my earliest efforts, or lent something of themselves to the story. Thank you.

Extra-special mention to **Jonathan Burgess,** who embodies the spirit of his namesake in the story—intelligent, industrious, good-humored, an IT and logistics wizard, an all-around nice guy, and a great person to work with. Thanks, JB!

And a very special thank-you to **the readers** who have picked up this book. I am immensely grateful that you have chosen to spend your valuable time reading its pages. I hope you were rewarded with a story that entertained you and that you'll keep fondly in your hearts like a new friend.

To my wife, **Lynne Urszenyi,** thank you for believing in me and supporting my dream. Your enthusiasm for my writing has been a pleasant surprise. I love the time we spend talking about story and plot and what Alex would or wouldn't do or say. You are my first reader, editor, and critic, and I am grateful for you every day. Your love means the world to me.

To our children, **Michael** and **Meghan,** who were raised not to complain unless they were bleeding from a non-compressible artery (paramedic humor), thank you for tolerating me as your father—it couldn't have been easy. I am so proud of the strong, resilient, and compassionate people you have become. The world needs more like you.

And finally, to **Mom,** who encouraged me to read and asked me to read aloud to her, demonstrating to a young child that storytelling was another way to love and be loved. I'm forever grateful.

Read on for an excerpt from

*Out in the Cold—*

the next novel from Steve Urszenyi, available
soon from Minotaur Books!

# CHAPTER 1

Alexandra Martel turned, spotting her approaching quarry weaving through the crowd.

*Got you now.*

All around her was the smell of the sea, the briny scent cutting through the cologne and perfume of the well-heeled guests aboard the luxury megayacht *Aurora* as if to remind them that, for all their wealth and refinement, the sea was more formidable. *Aurora* and all she represented were merely transitory things bobbing on its undulating and unforgiving surface.

As her target breezed past, Alex exchanged her empty glass with a new flute of champagne from atop his tray. *Mission accomplished.* She sipped as the tuxedoed waiter smiled and moved on. Her mood was light, buoyed by the atmosphere of celebration and, perhaps, the champagne.

The spacious enclosed salon pulsed with music as multicolored lasers slashed through the darkness. Fog machines belched mist from an elevated stage. An ornate starfish mosaic encrusted with thousands of LED fibers seemed to scuttle across the dance floor as she strode through a pair of sliding glass pocket doors into a much quieter corridor.

The guests had boarded the ship at its home port

in Antibes, France, the coastal town situated on the Mediterranean Sea between Cannes and Nice. At 148 meters—more than 485 feet—*Aurora* wasn't short on private spaces. Somewhere in one of the many salons on this deck, Alex would find the person she was actually looking for.

Madame Celeste Clicquot, secretary general of Interpol, had excused herself twenty minutes ago, telling Alex she had to meet with someone. But she had been evasive when Alex inquired further. That was out of character for Clicquot, who, since the events in Paris in the early summer, had been more open and forthright with Alex about her work affairs.

Alex opened a door into a lavish sitting room filled with plush velour settees, Persian rugs, vases, and sculptures from the Far East. Across from her, a man emerged from a doorway to what appeared to be a small private salon. He was older and unfamiliar to her, wearing a business suit that gave him the air of an outsider on this boatful of merrymakers. Stepping out from behind him was Celeste. Alex thought better of calling out to her and instead receded into the darkness. She watched as the man turned and shook Clicquot's hand, then hurried down a hallway toward the vessel's bow.

When Clicquot had taken a few steps in her direction, Alex stepped out of the shadows into the salon, taking a long sip of champagne for effect.

Clicquot spotted her and called across the room. "There you are!"

"Oh, hey! I thought I'd never see you again," said Alex.

"It is this boat, my dear. It's so massive."

She took Alex by the hand and led her back toward the dance hall. They emerged into the crowd of guests showing off their moves on the dance floor, where Clicquot found another waiter and relieved him of two fresh glasses of bubbly.

"I'm still working on this one," Alex protested, shouting to be heard above the din.

"Who said either of these is for you, my dear?" Clicquot replied, draining one in a single gulp.

*Oh, what the hell. Live a little,* Alex thought.

She polished off her own glass and seized another from the waiter's tray.

"You are a devil," Clicquot said conspiratorially. "Come. Follow me."

She led Alex up a highly polished chromium spiral staircase, her midnight-blue silk dress billowing in the breeze like the spinnaker of a grand sailing vessel as they climbed the stairs.

The deck they entered was open to the sea and as dark as its murky depths. A warm breeze wafted over the ship's gunwales as it steamed ahead. Clicquot guided them to a terrace overlooking the vessel's stern and dropped into a cushioned rattan deck chair. A glass-bottom swimming pool two decks below in the ship's beach club shimmered like sky-blue plasma. Behind them, a ribbon of luminous white foam split the sea, illuminated by a waxing gibbous moon hovering over La Baie des Anges—the Bay of Angels.

Clicquot continued to sip her champagne, staring ahead blankly, looking pensive. Maybe it was the champagne, but tonight she seemed troubled by some unspoken angst—one moment, she was a lively flame; the next, a smoldering candle doused by some foreboding from within.

"Madame—"

"*Madame?*"

Oops. Not a flame—a flame*thrower*.

"I'm not your boss anymore, Alex. And outside of office hours, I cease being the secretary general of Interpol. Well, mostly. So tonight, here on this boat, I am simply *Celeste*."

Alex waited a beat before speaking. "Celeste, is everything okay?"

Clicquot leaned back in her chair and stared out to sea, taking another sip of champagne. Finally, the edges of her mouth curled up slightly.

"You are an impressive woman, Alex. Before Interpol snapped you up—*borrowed* you from the FBI—you had already established yourself as a formidable investigator. And, of course, your military accomplishments are legendary. But we still had no idea what we were getting into when you signed on to your secondment."

Alex leaned back against the pillowy seat cushion and kicked off her boat shoes.

"Despite your actions being what your former FBI handlers called *insubordinate,* what you did in Paris helped establish Interpol as a preeminent policing organization, not merely one that acts as an administrative liaison among its member agencies. You single-handedly advanced global policing by a decade. We're going to miss you, Alex. In fact, I already do."

For what the FBI had labeled *insubordination,* Alex's employment was terminated, and, with it, her secondment to Interpol had ended. The Department of Justice didn't subscribe to her *exigent circumstances* defense or appreciate the Machiavellian methods she had employed in Paris. For Alex, though, a morally imperative goal justified any means to achieve it. And a soon-to-explode nuclear warhead fit within that definition.

Alex wanted to ask her friend what was going on, but sensing the looming question, Clicquot silenced the thought with a gently waved hand.

"Chief Bressard lobbied hard to bring you into the organization," Clicquot continued. "I am indebted to him for his foresight. From the outset, I had reservations about your hard-charging methods. But despite my more conservative inclinations, Martin convinced me you would be a strong asset to Interpol. You have proved him most perceptive."

"Well, I'm glad. Chief Bressard became like a second father to me. I never wanted to leave Interpol, but my actions had consequences."

"Who knows? Maybe you'll be back one day."

Madame Clicquot's mood was lifting, so Alex quelled the urge to ask about it further. And though she was curious, now wasn't the time to ask about her downstairs secret rendezvous with the stranger.

All in good time.

The lights from shore off their port side shone in the distance. Higher above, the shape of a rocky peak capped in shimmering lights stood backlit against a star-filled sky.

Clicquot followed her gaze. "Everything is more beautiful when seen from the deck of this incredible yacht. My dear friend Valtteri, her owner, asked that I invite you and Caleb aboard for this little party following your investiture into France's Legion of Honor."

"I've yet to meet the elusive Valtteri."

"Tonight, you will. I promise." Her face lit up in a devious smile. "He's quite something. And as you can see, he is very successful."

Looking around them, that might have been the understatement of the evening.

As if on cue, a man's voice drifted in out of the darkness. "There you are. I thought I'd never find you again."

"Valtteri! Finally," Celeste replied. "I thought you might never break free."

"I'm sorry," he said, stepping from the shadows. "Investors."

"Ah, yes. The important people," she teased.

"None more so than you." Valtteri bent and kissed her on the cheek. He perched on the arm of Clicquot's chair and took her hand in his. This wasn't the same man Alex had seen her friend with moments ago.

*So, if this is Valtteri, who was the other guy?*

\* \* \*

Caleb Copeland leaned over the ship's railing, looking on as the trio below sipped champagne and chatted under a string of lights that offered scant illumination. Alex was half turned away from him, looking remarkable in a summer dress, her tanned, bare shoulders drawing him in like a moth to a flame. The allure was intoxicating and impossible to ignore. Her pull on him was undeniable, whether she wore a ghillie suit, tactical gear, or a bare-shouldered dress.

They first met on a mission in the Netherlands involving a high-octane helicopter chase where he witnessed firsthand her world-renowned sniper skills. He was there in his capacity as a CIA paramilitary operations officer and branch chief, offering tactical support on a matter of national security deemed to be of the highest priority to the United States. To that end, he was there to enlist Alex into the Central Intelligence Agency and onto his team. She was an FBI special agent on loan to Interpol and a decorated soldier. He needed her unique skill set, so was determined to alter that arrangement. But Alex being Alex, she had rebuffed his recruitment efforts.

At the time, no one could have predicted that Alex would become the central figure and hero in a story fit for Hollywood. Most of the details of that operation would remain classified for decades to come, but the hunt for a stolen thermonuclear bomb had almost ended with the destruction of one of the world's greatest cities. Paris was still recovering from its near miss with catastrophe. If not for Alex's stubbornness and disregard for her personal safety, the powerful nuke would have detonated below the City of Light. Not only would Paris have been obliterated, but the global order would have been forever altered.

Alex, he learned, was a force of nature greater even than the nuclear weapon she had saved Paris from. Following the incident, his recruitment of her to his team within Ground Branch had been a success, even if it had taken some secret backroom brokering from CIA deputy director Kadeisha Thomas to finish the deal.

Alex was now a CIA contractor, a paramilitary operations officer on Caleb's elite team inside Ground Branch. And yet there she sat—her inner warrior concealed beneath the camouflage of a floral dress.

Reality is merely an illusion.

Madame Clicquot sat to Alex's right: the shepherd dog next to the lamb. Who was who depended on the circumstances. The man with them was Clicquot's boyfriend and the multibillionaire owner of *Aurora*. Caleb had yet to make his acquaintance but recognized Valtteri from his file.

As he watched the threesome chatting below, he heard someone approaching from behind.

"Are you ready, Mr. Copeland?" a man said. Caleb nodded. "I'll give you that tour now, starting with the security office and armory. My boss tells me that's what you were hoping to see first."

"It is," Caleb replied.

"I'm Jocko. Mr. Street mentioned you're Special Forces."

"Ex, but that was a long time ago."

"And now?"

"And now I'd be very interested in looking around this amazing vessel."

The security officer nodded. Caleb acknowledged his discretion with a smile and a clap on the back. "Lead on, Jocko."

\* \* \*

"Alex," said Celeste. "I'd like to introduce you to Valtteri."

His bearing was bold, confident. A breeze tousled his wavy blond hair, and his smile revealed shallow dimples and laugh lines that gave him an amiable appearance. As he leaned forward, the patio lights illuminated his fiery eyes.

"It is great to finally meet you, Alex. Celeste has told me so much about you."

"I'm afraid she has kept you a secret until now."

"Not a secret," Celeste corrected. "We're just being discreet."

"Celeste detests the mere whiff of a scandal," said Valtteri.

"And would this be one?"

"Not in the least," said Celeste. "But one's personal life should be just that—personal."

Alex couldn't have agreed more.

"Shall I refresh our drinks?" Valtteri asked, raising a bottle he held at his side. But before he could refill their glasses—

*BOOM! BOOM! BOOM!*

The ship rocked as a series of concussive blasts echoed across the sea.